Also by Margo Candela

Underneath It All

Life Over Easy

More Than This

a novel

margo candela

 Touchstone
A Division of Simon & Schuster, Inc.
1230 Avenue of the Americas
New York, NY 10020

First Touchstone trade paperback edition August 2008

TOUCHSTONE and colophon are registered trademarks of Simon
& Schuster, Inc.

For information about special discounts for bulk purchases, please contact
Simon & Schuster Special Sales at 1-800-456-6798 or
business@simonandschuster.com.

Designed by Mary Austin Speaker

Manufactured in the United States of America

10 9 8 7 6 5 4 3 2 1

Library of Congress Cataloging-in-Publication Data
    Candela, Margo.
        More than this: a novel / Margo Candela.
            p.   cm.
        "A Touchstone book."
    1. Hispanic American men—Fiction. 2. Working class men—Fiction.
    3. WASPs (Persons)—Fiction. 4. Upper class women—Fiction. I. Title.
    PS3603.A5357 M67   2008
    813'.6—dc22   2007047427

ISBN-13: 978-1-4165-7134-6
ISBN-10:   1-4165-7134-5

For Elias

Acknowledgments

I'd especially like to thank my sister Monica for listening to me ramble on about ideas and reading my manuscripts in various states of disarray; my friends Laura, Heather, Anne, and Paula, for their words of encouragement; John, for inspiration; and my editor, Sulay, for seeing me through this whole crazy process with unflagging kindness and enthusiasm.

saturday . . .

chapter one
Reasons for Leaving

Evelyn

I adjust the mirror to the side of the easel so I can see my naked back reflected in the one behind me. When I get the angles just right, I try to see myself objectively and fail do so, as usual. I can't ignore the roll of pudge around my middle. At the same time, I admire the muscle definition in my shoulders—a testament to being able to do fifty straight-leg push-ups before my arms start to shake. I can't help but smile.

I pick up my Gauloises Blonde cigarette and take a puff, smoking being one of the few nasty habits I've picked up after almost a year living and re-creating myself in Paris. I tap the ashes into the chipped teacup I found on my first excursion to the Porte de Clignancourt flea market so many months ago. When I'm ready, I shift a little so my spine curves to the right and the subtle shadows of my rib cage press against my skin. I can see the back of my head with my long dark hair in a messy bun held in place with a pair of small ivory knitting needles I found in Prague, my naked back, shoulders, and a healthy portion of rump, but not my face.

With the lit cigarette between the fingers of my right hand, I pick up the brush with my left and start painting.

Alexander

My mouth feels dry. I'm having a little trouble swallowing, but my heart rate is steady. I could be at home watching TV and thirsty, but too lazy to get up and grab a beer, not about to make one of the most important purchases of my life. I try to work some spit into my mouth. The only thing that'll help is getting this over with. It's moments like these when I realize nothing in life has taught me one useful thing about being a man—not my parents, all the women and girls I've dated, not my law degree or a year in Manhattan. I'm still as clueless about what I should do with my life as I ever was.

I take the ring between my fingers, hold it up to the light, pretending to admire it for what it means, not for what it costs. It's a princess cut on a platinum band. Important to get it right because that's what she wants. The saleslady, with her heavy perfume, assures me it is a near-flawless two-carat diamond. Also important, because the whole point is to get her the best, for people to be able to see how much she's worth from across the room.

All I have to do is reach into my wallet, pull out my credit card, and it's mine. I mean hers.

Evelyn

I hear the yelling in the courtyard before I actually register it has anything to do with me. I pull on my silk robe and walk to the window, massaging the cramp out of my lower back. I've been working in front of the canvas for a couple hours straight, putting the final touches on my version of a self-portrait.

I stick my head out the window to see the old woman who lives in the lower flat physically barring a chic, middle-aged Parisian wearing a structured black suit, towering high-heeled boots, and a red bag on her arm, from storming the doorway that leads up to my apartment.

"Madam Moreau? *Va-tout très bien?*" I call down to the old

lady, hoping everything is okay, evidence to the contrary notwithstanding.

The two women (and all the neighbors watching from their windows) look up. The woman in the black suit points at me.

"There she is! Evelyn Morgan, the whore who is fucking my husband," she says by way of a how do you do. "I am the wife of Laurent Baschet, you American alley cat!"

Except she screams in it French so all my neighbors can hear and understand, because she, of course, is French and, it seems, married to the man I've been involved with, who is also French and evidently very married.

"Evelyn. Perhaps it would be best to invite your guest inside," Madam Moreau calmly suggests, as if a deliveryperson has knocked on the wrong door.

I slam the window shutters closed and for a moment want nothing more than to give in to the urge to melt into a puddle on the floor with a plate of dark chocolate–dipped madeleine cookies washed down with a glass of whole milk from the toothless dairy farmer who comes in once a week from the country to sell his wares at the market down the street. But even if I wanted to, there's no way I could indulge. My body just won't let me eat like I used to.

"Open up this door, slut!" She pounds on the door. For a moment I wonder how she could have sprinted up the stairs in those heels. "Husband thief! Show your face!"

I push myself away from the wall, cinch the sash on my robe a little tighter, and scamper barefoot to the door, desperate for her to just stop yelling. I rip it open, momentarily stunning her into blessed silence. She looks me up and down, then pushes past me and plants herself in the middle of my studio, daring me to do something other than stand there meekly. She's already won, she knows it, but she's not satisfied yet.

"I'm sorry." It's all I can think to say in my clipped, prep school French.

"Sorry! You're sorry," she spits, her face as red as her fingernails. "I'm disappointed in Laurent. The stupid *chiennes* he fucks usually have a little more spirit."

"I didn't know he was married," I gasp. "He never . . ."

He. Laurent Baschet. My painting teacher, my mentor, my everything for most of the past year. We met at a reception given to introduce the new crop of students at the Parsons Paris art school to one another and the esteemed faculty who would be molding us into the artists of tomorrow, even if we were just expats with time and money to spare.

He kissed me on each cheek, held my hand, looked into my eyes, and said, "Evelyn Morgan. A beautiful name for such a beautiful girl, who has the hands of a true artist."

Up until Laurent, I hadn't considered myself anything but an overeducated, directionless former fat girl with a multidisciplinary degree from Brown, which I then supplemented with another B.A. in design and technology from Art Academy in San Francisco after I realized there wasn't much I was qualified to do besides read eighteenth-century novels in French.

The plan was to develop my doodles into something that could be considered art while living in my much divorced aunt's Left Bank apartment and posing as a struggling art student. It seemed romantic and, at times, even real to me.

At least it did up to just about now.

"Are you simpleminded, as well as a slut?" she rasps out in her husky smoker's voice. I bet her brand is also Gauloises Blonde, the cigarette Laurent introduced me to.

"I swear to you, madam, he never told me he was married," I say truthfully.

Of course, there were clues, but I chose not to see them. And I chose not to ask him. Why would I? I was in love with him, and the idea of the new reinvented me. Why ruin it with reality?

"What did he tell you? That he loved you? He's never met anyone like you." She laughs. "That's what he tells all of them. You're just another piece of ass to him, you stupid girl. Like all the others. But he always comes back to my bed. I'm his wife and the mother of his children!"

"I didn't know! I swear . . . I didn't. I never would have . . . I'm not that kind of person . . ." I trail off, unable to form the words through my sobs.

"My God. Laurent is getting complacent in his old age," she says calmly with almost a tinge of pity in her voice. "I would have thought this husband of mine would like more of a challenge and a girl with spirit."

"It's over," I cry, and wish she'd do the same or go back to screaming at me. I could stand either, but not her contempt. "It's over."

"Of course it is, my dear. When you see my husband, tell him his wife and children will be in the country for the rest of the week." With one last withering look, she turns on her heel and walks out.

I let myself feel pathetic and betrayed for a minute, and then I make a dash for my phone, tripping over the rug and sprawling onto the floor. My robe is wrapped around my head, leaving me naked as the day I was born. Instead of getting up or even covering myself, I curl into a little ball and cry.

Alexander

I walk up and down the sidewalk in front of her favorite brunch place, ignoring the couples who look so in love or are hiding behind their early Sunday editions of *The New York Times*. I keep moving and try to work up the nerve to walk in, drop to one knee, and offer her the proposal she's expecting.

Sigrid has a girls' get-together every other Saturday because, as she says, "I hate women who get a boyfriend and then drop their friends just to hang on his every word. Don't you hate women like that? Don't you, Alexander? You don't think I'm one of those women who plan their lives around their man? Do you, Alexander?"

I've learned to neither agree nor disagree with what Sigrid says. It makes life easier for the both of us. To make sure she doesn't notice my lack of commitment, I distract her with gifts. Spur-of-the-moment trips to fancy spas and expensive bottles of rare wine to eat with Ritz crackers and peanut butter (her favorite snack). Money flows through my fingers like the imported vodka she likes mixed in novelty martini drinks that are ten dollars a pop.

With Sigrid, it's one endless party, being seen in the right places with the right people, being the couple all our friends say they wish they could be. In private, we fight about something stupid and then make up just as loudly within a day or so.

I rub my hands over my head, feeling the short hair under my palms. Nowadays my haircuts set me back $160. I used to get the same short buzz at my neighborhood barbershop in San Francisco for $20, including tip. Aside from the nice head massage with a quarter cup of fancy shampoo and free glass of wine, I can't tell much of a difference between the two buzz cuts except the price. But it makes Sigrid happy for me to go to the same person who cuts her hair. She likes to joke to her friends that we share everything, including a hairstylist.

With Sigrid, I can pretend to be a whole different person, one who doesn't have to care that the busboy clearing tables or the guy washing the martini glasses in the kitchen is an undocumented Guatemalan living in a two-room apartment with ten other people who have to sleep in shifts. I've spent the past year pissing away whatever I've earned as an associate lawyer at the firm of Crook, Asshole, and Jerk on clothes I can't afford (for the both of us), weekend trips to the Hamptons to get drunk with people I'd never call friends while sober, and loving every minute of it.

I've told Sigrid I love her even though I can go hours, days, without thinking about her. Why ask her to marry me? Simple. I've royally fucked up my career as a sharp Manhattan lawyer by asking too many questions about doing some pro bono work for those exploited Guatemalan bus boys, and pretty much signed my walking papers by talking to the cleaning staff about unionizing. On Friday, I was escorted out of the office and told not to show my face until I got my priories straight. Sigrid is all I have left.

One of the waiters comes outside to smoke a cigarette. He gestures with his lighter. "The place is full of estrogen; I don't think you want to go in there without reinforcements."

"My girlfriend likes to eat here," I say stupidly, the small velvet box feeling like an anchor in my hip pocket.

"Everybody's girlfriend likes to eat here, dude." He flicks cigarette ashes onto the sidewalk. "What gets me is they order all this food and they don't eat any of it. Why go out to a restaurant if you aren't going to eat?"

"They eat it later, at home. Alone." I lean up against the wall next to him. "I caught my girl doing that more than once. She told me she can't eat in front of her friends because they spend most of their time talking."

"Whacked." He blows smoke rings and offers his pack of cigarettes at the same time. "I've said it once and I'll say it until I die—chicks are whacked. Wickety whacked."

"Thanks. I don't smoke." My parents schooled me all too well in the evils of Big Tobacco for me to consider ever taking it up as a hobby.

"Smart," he says as he lights a new cigarette with the stub of the one he just finished. "So when's your girl showing up? Better be soon. The kitchen's running low on nonfat, no-cal pretend pancakes."

"She's already inside. The blonde."

"Which one?" he asks as he flicks the still-smoking butt onto the sidewalk.

I take a look through the window and realize most of the women in there are various shades of blond. "She's sitting under the painting with the circles in the bright colors."

"Table six. They've ordered a pot of coffee but are holding off on ordering brunch." He crushes the butt of his cigarette with the heel of his scuffed waiter shoes. "They have a bottle of champagne on ice but haven't touched it. I guess they're going to be celebrating something."

Everything goes wavy, and I feel myself sway on my feet. I reach up and yank down on the collar of my shirt so I can get some air into my lungs before I pass out.

"Hey? You okay?" He takes a step forward and puts a hand on my shoulder.

"I'm fine." I breathe in and out.

"I gotta get back in." He claps me on the shoulder, a worried look on his face. "If you want, I can talk to the hostess. She can squeeze you in if you're dying for low-fat whole-wheat pancakes."

"Thanks, but I think I'm already being squeezed."

Evelyn

It's dark outside when I finally convince myself I have no choice but to open my eyes. I shift around on the floor, trying to ease the pain in my hip and shoulder from lying on my side. Funny, it's time likes these when I almost miss my old padding.

"Evelyn? *Ouvre la porte, chérie.*" Laurent has made an appearance. I sit up, closing my robe, as the noise that woke me gets louder. "Evelyn?"

"Go away, you lying bastard," I mumble just loud enough for him to hear.

"Don't be that way, *chérie.* Open the door." He jiggles the knob. "This isn't dignified."

"Dignified!" That's all it takes to snap me out of my stupor. I get up and stalk to the door, practically ripping it off its hinges. "Your wife—*wife*—calling me a whore—a *whore*—in front of my neighbors? *That's* not dignified, Laurent."

"*Chérie,* you're overreacting." Laurent tries to take me into his arms, but I sidestep him. "I see you are going to make this difficult." He holds up his hands when he sees I'm about to launch myself at him. "As you should be! This unpleasantness could have been avoided, and I blame myself for it, Evelyn."

"How big of you, Laurent, to take responsibility for being an adulterer and making one of me, too." I turn my back to him, searching for my shoes.

"I will take care of this. It's how it is." Laurent wanders over to the window, leans a hip on the sill, and lights up a cigarette. He waves the smoke away like he does my concerns. "It is expected for the wife to make a stand, *chérie*. Nothing but theatrics."

"So I'm supposed to be okay with being your official mistress and get over being your clueless girlfriend?" I give up on the shoes and look for something heavy, settling on the flea market vase I purchased earlier this week.

"Well, yes." He blows a steady stream of smoke out of his nose and smiles at me.

I light my own Gauloises, and flick my bangs out of my eyes so that he can see I'm serious. I recently let my hairdresser talk me into bangs. Yet, I have to admit, I like them. Since I can't wear sunglasses indoors, it's the next best thing to having something to hide behind.

"Well, yes?" I snap the fingers of my free hand. "Just like that?"

"Of course, things will have to change now that my wife is aware of our arrangement." Laurent shrugs his shoulders under his perfectly cut blazer. "We will have to make some concessions."

"What arrangement? What concessions? Do you mean we'll have to sneak around more? Less? Forget it, Laurent. We're over." I brandish the vase at him, spilling water and flowers onto the floor. "Beyond over! Finished! Done!"

"Evelyn. You're not one of those hopeless puritanical Americans with their empty moral crusades?" Laurent comes toward me, keeping his eyes on mine. "We can make this work. I want to make this work, *chérie*."

"You lied to me." I let him take the vase out of my hand as I crumple into him, hunching down, since at five ten I'm just as tall as he is.

"Not lied. I was, perhaps, less than forthcoming with some

details about my life, *chérie*," he murmurs into my hair. "You can understand why."

I smile into his neck. If Laurent is guilty of editing details about himself, so am I. Maybe more so. He doesn't even know my real name.

"Haven't I always said I'd take care of you?" His hand wanders lower, down my spine to my hip, where it stays as he presses me closer to him.

"I don't need you to take care of me, Laurent."

"A feminist!" He laughs, pushing his pelvis into mine. "It's time you leave this dreary studio. I can help you find a real apartment, *chérie*."

"The thing is, Laurent, this isn't where I live." I gesture around me to the small room I've been using as my studio and supposed humble living quarters.

"I am not criticizing your choice in lodging, Evelyn." From his tone and past reluctance to stay longer than a few minutes, we both know this makes him a liar as well as an adulterer. He reaches for me, and I take a step back. I want to see his face when I tell him.

"You did well finding a room on the Left Bank, Evelyn, but there is no need to be a martyr. I can offer you some financial assistance now that our situation has changed."

"You're not listening to me, Laurent." I grab his hand and lead him downstairs, taking the key out of my robe pocket, and unlock the floor-to-ceiling double doors that lead into the apartment I've been sneaking into after he drops me off in front of the converted maid's room upstairs. "This is where I live."

Laurent steps into my aunt's three-bedroom apartment, pausing by the StairMaster that sits impudently on the gleaming parquet floors by one of the windows with its breathtaking view of the Eiffel Tower. He makes his way into the American-style kitchen, weaving through the tastefully appointed furniture, all done in shades of ivory and chocolate.

"I don't understand." Laurent turns around and finally stops to face me. "You are watching this place for the owners?"

"No. It's mine. Well, my aunt's." I twist the sash of my robe into a knot, trying to see past Laurent's stunned expression to read what he really thinks. "She owns it, but she's in New York with her current husband and . . . so it's where I live. . . . Where I've been living all this time."

Laurent is a moderately successful painter, augmenting his income with teaching and occasional art director work in movies. Though his family has a house in the country, so does every other Parisian. For all I know, it might be no more than a shabby cottage on a patch of land outside the city limits. I've never been invited, and now I know why.

"I don't understand, Evelyn." He sounds annoyed.

I walk into the kitchen and grab a box of tea sent to me by my mother in a care package every first day of the month. I hand it to Laurent and stand back.

"Tea?" He turns the box around in his hands, as if looking for some clue.

"You see the name there?" I point to the label. "Reed. I'm a Reed on my mother's side."

"Like the kiosks?" Laurent points toward the window, where we can see the glowing lights of one of the phone-booth-size contraptions.

Reed Coffees and Fine Teas have carefully populated three continents with more than ten thousand automatic coffee and tea kiosks. Choices are limited, quality assured, and the price is less than one would pay at, say, Starbucks. I've seen people wait in lines, in the rain, for their morning coffee or tea. Even here in Paris, where waiting in line is considered undignified.

"Do you see what's next to it?" I grab his hand, maneuver him to the front window, and point down to the ATM, known as *un guichet automatique de banque* or GAB, tucked into the same vestibule between doorways.

"The GAB?" Laurent asks.

"Sinclair Partners. I'm a Sinclair, too. On my father's side."

"I don't understand, Evelyn." Laurent shakes his head. "You're speaking in riddles."

I take a deep breath. "My real name is Evelyn Morgan Reed-Sinclair. Morgan is my middle name, not my last. I'm not a struggling art student, I don't work as a nanny and English tutor. I left home a year ago because . . . I needed time for the inside me to catch up with the outside me. Or maybe it's been the other way around. Either way . . . The new me."

"The new you?" Laurent asks, taking an abrupt seat on the couch behind him. He has that familiar sardonic look he gets when he finds my attitudes of the *l'Américain typique* variety.

"This"—I sweep my hand down my body—"is only half of what I used to be."

"You are not making sense, Evelyn." Laurent pats his pocket for cigarettes, ready to dismiss my confession. "Frankly, you sound insane."

I walk over to my purse and reach inside. "You know those fat tourists you make fun of? I used to be one of those fat American dairy cows, as you call them." I hand him a fresh pack of Gauloises and a laminated picture I always keep with me.

Laurent looks from me to the snapshot taken just eighteen months ago, right after the surgery in which I had a lap band put in to shrink my stomach and, therefore, how much I could eat. Somewhere buried in all that flesh, 250 pounds of it when the picture was taken, is me. Still me, despite the fact that I weigh 100 pounds less and moved thousands of miles away from home to try to escape myself. In some ways, I'm still the fat girl willing to make do with what life offers her because fat girls can't be picky.

"This is not funny, Evelyn." He shoves the cigarettes and picture at me. "And that? That is disgusting."

Or maybe not.

"Out." I point to the door. "You need to leave now."

"I was indiscreet with my choice of words, Evelyn." He's trying to apologize but looks annoyed with me for having to do it. He moves toward the door. "I am willing to overlook your revelations. I should now go to my wife. She's very upset. I will call you when you are more rational, Evelyn."

"Don't bother, Laurent. I never want to see you again."

"Chérie," he begins, sensing he's pushed me a tad too far.

I pick up an ashtray and hurl it against the door so it disintegrates with a satisfying crash just behind him. "I swear, Laurent, if you say one more word, I'll smash your fucking face in."

After a few moments, I realize he's walked out with my cigarettes. It doesn't matter—I've just quit.

Alexander

From the velocity with which Sigrid tosses her purse (a tan leather sixteen-hundred-dollar Chloé I gave her to make amends after my stupid but truthful admission that I prefer brunettes) onto the table by the door, I can tell she's annoyed. And when Sigrid is annoyed, the whole world can do no right by her.

"Hey, baby!" I wave the remote at her, taking my eyes off the program I'm halfway watching about the frozen tundra and the people who manage to scratch out a pretty happy living there. "What's shaking?"

Sigrid stomps past me and slams the door to the bathroom without looking in my direction.

I grab hold of one of the stiff cushions she likes to keep on the couch and toss it up into the air, letting it spin, catch it, and then toss it up again. I listen as Sigrid runs the water in the sink, opens and closes the squeaky medicine cabinet door, and I wait for her to come out, not moving from the safety of the couch.

A little more than three months ago, I agreed with Sigrid's suggestion that it would be best to move out of my West Harlem studio apartment into her more spacious Upper West Side one-bedroom for the sake of our relationship. Since then we've had less sex than we did when we lived apart, but shared a significant moment when we agreed that zebra-striped towels from Pottery Barn were a wise joint purchase.

I crack the tension in my neck by snapping my head a couple of times to each side, a habit I developed from years of swimming. My parents figured out it was the only sport that would shut me up, because I couldn't talk without drowning myself. I swam through high school, into college, and came as close as anyone can to almost making the Olympic team. I had the speed, the build, and just enough height at six three to be a real contender, but in the end I came up just short, like I always have. Like I just have with my girlfriend.

Sigrid stomps out of the bathroom and turns off the TV. She turns around to face me, her arms crossed over her chest and a scowl on her face that would freeze an Eskimo—sorry, Inuit—in his tracks.

"Hi, honey!" I pat the space next to me, making sure to set the pillow back in the precise spot where she likes to see it. "How was brunch? You bring back anything good?"

"No, Alexander"—she holds out her empty hands and bare fingers for me to inspect—"I didn't come back with *anything* from brunch."

An opening as wide as the Lincoln Tunnel, but I choose to take a side street down Bonehead Way. "You want to order something from the Chinese place down the street?"

"I'm not hungry," Sigrid snaps. She's still standing in front of the TV, so even if I was stupid enough to try to turn it back on, I couldn't. "We need to talk."

No guy likes to hear a woman say these words, even when he knows he deserves them.

"Okay. Let's talk."

I fix my face into an attentively blank but sincere look. One I perfected in the office of my high school guidance counselor when discussing my talent for fucking up. I'm sure he, Mr. Figgis, would have taken me out back and beaten the crap out of me if he could have. The only thing that kept him from doing it was the threat to his pension. We both knew I'd end up doing okay. I was a golden-brown boy, like my friends used to say. I got the grades, the girls, and the get-out-of-juvie-free card, and he hated me for it. Like Mr. Figgis always said, "You were born lucky, Mr. Velazquez. And the sad thing is your kind of luck will get you as far as you want to go. Now get the hell out of my office, and if I catch you under the bleachers again, I'm suspending your ass."

I'm getting the feeling Sigrid is about to complete Mr. Figgis's unfinished business.

"I can't fucking believe you, Alexander."

"Baby, what is it? Tell me what's wrong and I'll fix it." I'm an asshole. There's no way Sigrid can tell me I was supposed to propose to her without looking like the most needy and pathetic woman in Manhattan.

The phone rings. I look at it but don't make a move until I'm confident my irate girlfriend won't lob the TV at my head.

"Velazquez Bern residence. Alexander speaking." I smile at Sigrid. She doesn't smile back. The next moment a high-pitched squeak pierces my eardrum and I almost drop the phone. I hold it out to Sigrid, but I'm able to make out "Ecstatic! Part of the family! Summer wedding!"

"Siggy, I think it's your mom."

She snatches the phone out of my hand. "Not now, Mother."

She tosses it, hard, and I have to duck out of the way so it doesn't bean me. "You're upset; I can see that, Sigrid. And all I can say is I'm sorry."

"Sorry doesn't make it okay, Alexander." She perches on the armchair, suddenly calm. "It doesn't even begin to make it okay."

I clear my throat, the primitive part of my brain kicking into high gear. She's backing me into a corner, forcing me to make a decision we both thought was a foregone conclusion. I'm the one who dropped the ball. Didn't come through for the team. Choked. With no other avenue of escape, I go on the offensive.

"The firm let me go on Friday."

"What does that mean?" Even with the distance between us, I can see her pupils dilate with shock. "You got *fired*?"

"Yeah." If she wants me to be her husband, there's really no reason for me to sugarcoat the reality of it all. "They weren't too happy with me doing that pro bono work on the side with the janitors."

"The fucking janitors again? Why do you do this to me? To us?" She gets up, wringing her hands as she paces back and forth. "Never mind, I don't want to hear it. We can fix this. I'll call Patrick. He can get you an interview with his firm. Monday. I'll have to call in a favor, but I'm sure he can find you a place there."

"I don't want your ex-boyfriend to get me a job, Siggy." I stand up and take her by the shoulders. "Your ex-boyfriend isn't much different than the assholes who fired me."

"Who the fuck cares, Alexander? They're janitors for a fucking reason. You have other responsibilities to me. To us. Not to some fucking no-English-speaking illegal immigrants."

I blink a couple of times and then reach into my pocket and pull out the velvet box. She sucks in her breath at the sight of it.

She looks at it but doesn't take it. She steps away, crossing her arms again. "I can't marry you, Alexander. Not until you get your shit together."

I smile at her, looking straight into her narrowed green eyes. "I don't recall asking you to marry me, Sigrid."

sunday . . .

chapter two
Missed Connections

Evelyn

"Miss Sinclair?" The flight attendant pauses to wait for some reaction from me. Her perfume, something floral, is carefully discreet. "We're approaching JFK. You'll need to put your seat up in a few minutes."

I feel a gentle hand on my shoulder but don't make a move to sit up or take off the eyeshade that's hiding my red and swollen eyes. I relax as she moves off to another passenger. I know she won't do much more than ask me to put my seat up, and if I don't, I don't. It's one of the benefits of flying first class; you can be a major bitch or bastard (within reason) because the ticket price covers a certain amount of self-centeredness.

I showed up at Orly airport this morning with only a suitcase and a desperate need to leave Paris as quickly as possible. I took the first flight I could get, grateful for a ticket, even with a layover. And since there was no one to pretend for anymore, I booked myself a first-class ticket for both flights, spending more money in one swipe of my American Express card than I had all year living in my aunt's apartment. It was worth it. At least in first class I had the relative privacy to cry in my fully reclining seat not squashed between tourists in coach, who surely would have wondered what the hell was wrong with me. Here, in first class, I could be left alone as long as I behaved myself.

I reach over and press the button to bring the seat back upright as the plane comes in for a smooth landing.

Instead of taking advantage of being let off first, I wait until everyone has filed out. I look around, noticing the emptiness of the plane. Even the pilots have deplaned. The flight attendants, on the other hand, are standing in a cluster of navy blue polyester a few rows away, whispering to one another other and gesturing toward me.

I stand up, keeping my eyes on the floor, and quickly dash past them before subjecting them (and myself) to any further embarrassment. From the terminal, I make my way to customs and go through the motions of pretending I'm a functioning adult.

The agent glances at my passport and ticket before he hands them back. "You're almost home, Miss Sinclair. You'll want to go on to the next terminal for your flight to San Francisco."

"Thank you," I answer automatically before walking over to the shuttle train.

I snake my way through security (even a first-class ticket doesn't buy an exception for certain FAA rules and regulations), and once through, I ignore the path that'll lead me to the safety of the first-class lounge, where I could wait out the two hours until my next flight in pampered comfort.

I stop by a bank of pay phones and consider calling James, my best friend and the only person who knows I'm on my way back to San Francisco and under what circumstances. I pick up the receiver and then put it down. Right now I just want to be anonymous, no backstory or drama.

I let myself be swallowed up among my fellow travelers and wander the terminal feeling the resigned excitement of those around me that comes with air travel these days, gradually letting my mind and body acclimate to being back in the States. It all seems so familiar but foreign to me at the same time. I veer toward a Starbucks, a little embarrassed at how quickly I'm willing to shed my carefully studied European sensibilities, and let the process of my re-Americanization begin.

"Can I start your order?" a guy behind the counter asks me as I edge up closer to the cash register.

"Yeah . . . I'll have . . ." I stop and think. It's been over a year since I've had anything remotely like the beverage I'm about to drink. A couple of years ago I'd have asked for something big, blended with nothing but empty calories, topped with whipped cream, and promising a few moments of pleasure. "A nonfat latte, tall. Please."

I pay, stand off to the side waiting for my drink, smile at the person when he hands it to me, and then drop it into the nearest trash can.

I need something stronger than a latte.

Alexander

I pay the cabbie, adding a few extra bucks for the use of his cell phone to call my best friend, Pete, to tell him I'm on my way back to San Francisco. My own phone, along with the rest of all the nice crap I've accumulated, is at my ex-apartment with my ex-girlfriend.

I'm wearing yesterday's khakis and button-down shirt, a couple days' worth of stubble and have a hell of a headache from spending the night in the hallway, hoping Sigrid would soften her block-of-ice heart and let me in to get my toothbrush. When she didn't and I wouldn't leave, she called the cops, who bought me a cup of Reed coffee from the corner kiosk and advised me to come back later, with flowers, after she'd had a chance to cool down. Instead, I counted out the cash in my pocket, hailed a cab, and asked to be taken to JFK.

I get in line and make my way up to the ticket agent of the first airline I see. Once there, I hand over my credit card and ID. "Hi, I need to get to San Francisco as soon as possible. One way."

"Any baggage to check?" she asks, using an unsharpened pencil to type instead of her fingers.

"I've got plenty, but today I'm traveling light. It's just me and my wallet."

She gives me a wide smile. It's called charisma, and I have it in spades, or so I've been told.

"I have one seat left in first class, a few in coach for a flight that leaves in an hour and a half." She looks from the monitor to me, waiting for my answer.

"Let's do first." I might as well fly home with my tail between my legs in style. "Why not?"

"First class it is." She swipes my card, frowns, swipes it again, and then gives me an embarrassed look. "I'm sorry, Mr. Velazquez, but this card had been declined."

"Okay." I take the card back and hand her another. "Try this one."

"Sure thing." She swipes it and waits. "One more try . . ." Swipes again and waits some more before leaning forward and lowering her voice. "Um . . . There seems to be a bit of an issue with this card, too. Maybe you'd like to talk to your credit card's customer service rep, Mr. Velazquez, and clear this up with them?"

"Okay." I don't have enough cash to get back into Manhattan anyway. She dials the number, speaks in low tones, then hands me the phone and lowers her eyes discreetly. "Hi, there's a problem with my card?"

"Good day, Mr. Velazquez, my name is Rebecca and it is my

pleasure to help you out today," says Rebecca by way of some customer service call center deep in the heart of India.

"Thanks." I wait and hear some typing and more Indian-inflected English in the background.

"Mr. Velazquez, it seems you are over your credit limit but can purchase a lesser priced coach ticket with no problem. Will that be satisfactory with you, sir? If so, please hand the phone back to the agent and we will conclude the transaction."

"Yeah, thanks, Rebecca." Now it's my turn to lower my eyes in embarrassment. "She wants to talk to you."

A few pokes with the pencil later, my coach ticket is spit out by the printer.

"Have a pleasant flight, Mr. Velazquez," the ticket agent says as she waves the next person up to the counter.

I'm not surprised when I'm pulled aside at security. A single guy, kind of dark, with the makings of a beard, no luggage, and a one-way ticket would make me nervous. I'm thoroughly scanned, my shoes examined, and asked to wait for a supervisor.

"Hello, Mr. Velazquez." A guy in a rent-a-cop uniform steps into the open holding pen where maybe dangerous people like me are kept until we can prove we have no intention of doing anything but going home or starting a vacation. "Can you answer a few questions for me about your travel plans?"

"I know how this looks, and I won't even harp on the racial profiling or the sheer ineffectiveness of the whole process." I hold my hand up to keep him from telling me I'm an asshole and in no position to criticize his job choice. "I'll give it to you straight, sir. I haven't brushed my teeth or changed my clothes since yesterday, so excuse me if I smell. I lost my job on Friday because I asked too many ques-

tions about why we weren't doing more work for the common people who have plenty of legal problems and no access to lawyers. On
top of that, I failed to ask my scary ex-girlfriend to marry me, and
she kicked me out of our—really her—apartment. I barely was able
to buy that ticket, and since I have no job, I have no idea how I'm
going to pay the bill because I'm broke. Unless you know someone
in the market for a $17,000 engagement ring? And even if I wanted
to go back to the city and beg her to take me back, I can't because I
just used most of my cash to overtip a cabbie for letting me use his
cell phone to call my best friend back in San Francisco, who tells me
his wife just walked out on him for another man. All I could say was
I was sorry, even though I knew all along he shouldn't have married
her but I didn't have the balls to tell him when I should have. And if
you let me get on the plane, sir, I'll have to face my family, who think
I'm a royal fuckup. The last thing on my mind is doing anything else
stupid. I just want to go home, take a shower, and forget I ever set
foot in Manhattan."

He looks me up and down, reaches into his pocket for a packet
of sugarless gum and a ten-dollar bill, and hands them to me along
with my ID and ticket.

"No joke?"

"Have a nice flight home, Mr. Velazquez."

I walk through the terminal and look for a bar where I can get
something to drink while I wait for my flight.

Evelyn

I take a seat on one side of a mirrored pillar that bisects the horseshoe-
shaped bar so I have something to lean my head against.

"What can I get you?" The bartender slides a cardboard drink
coaster and a bowl of mixed nuts in front of me.

Tears well up in my eyes at this small act of kindness. "A glass of white wine, please."

"You okay, miss?" he asks, adding a small pile of cocktail napkins.

"I'm fine, thank you, just a bit under the weather."

I grab one of the napkins and blow my nose as discreetly as possible. When he steps away to pour the wine, my hand automatically reaches for the nuts before I remember I shouldn't. To distract myself, I dig through my purse, pull out a fountain pen, and begin to doodle on the coaster to keep my hands busy.

I was always what our family doctor referred to as "stout," his kind word for chubby. My mother, of course, wouldn't hear of it, so I started my first diet before I could even spell the word. One of the tricks I picked up from the countless doctors, nutritionists, hypnotherapists, and quacks Mother dragged me to was to keep my hands busy, by either drawing or knitting.

I'm not surprised to find myself sketching the familiar sight of my own hands with knitting needles.

"That's pretty good," the bartender says as he sets the glass of wine on another coaster in front of me. "You an artist or something?"

"I like to think of myself as one." I hiccup behind a napkin. I always get the hiccups when I'm upset. I hand him my credit card to pay for the drink, being devoid of U.S. currency at the moment. I look around as if I'm expecting to see someone I recognize.

"Are you waiting for someone?" he asks. "You can page them at the check-in counter."

"There's no one to page," I say. Then the tears really start flowing.

"Hey, you okay?"

"I'm fine, really. I just need to . . ." I nod and try to smile.

"Are you sure?" he asks, but is already turning away to tend to a new customer, who's taken a seat on the other side of the pillar.

I get up, forcing myself to walk calmly to the bathroom, where I can cry in the privacy of a toilet stall.

Alexander

I take a seat at the bar, reaching across the mirrored pillar for a bowl of nuts, realizing not only do I want to get drunk but I'm starving.

"Hey! Miss!" the bartender calls out. "Your credit card?"

"You want me to go after her?" I offer, already standing up.

"Nah, she'll be back. If not, I'll have her paged. What can I get you, guy?" The bartender distractedly slides a cardboard coaster in front of me and wipes down the counter at the same time, working the rag around the bowls, watching for customers over my head.

"A beer, anything but domestic. In the bottle." I may be broke, but there's no way in hell I'm going to swill a Budweiser during my last minutes in New York. I can barely afford my coach ticket home, but I won't compromise on the beer. "And a shot of tequila. Keep the change."

I lay the ten-dollar bill on the counter so he knows to pick appropriately.

"Coming right up."

While I'm waiting, I reach over and grab a few cocktail straws, twisting and knotting them so they look like a dog. It's a habit that's turned into something of a party trick. I can take anything from paper clips to restaurant receipts and fold them into just about anything. Flowers mostly. Girls love them.

The bartender sets a bottle of Dos Equis in front of me, pours a generous shot of decent tequila, and moves off as a group of people crowd around the other end of the bar.

I down the shot, grunting as it hits my empty stomach. I reach for a handful of nuts and chew while keeping my eyes on the bar. I sip at my beer, determined to make it last. To distract myself, I set the coaster on its side and spin it, watching it go round until it lands on its backside. Instead of being blank, someone has sketched on it a pair of hands, women's hands from the look of the delicate fingers, that are knitting. I pick up the coaster to look at the drawing more carefully and am embarrassed to feel tears well up in my eyes.

All the women I've ever loved—my mother, my sister, my aunts, my grandmothers—have been knitters.

Sigrid wasn't a knitter, and I didn't love her any more than she loved me.

"Alexander Velazquez, please report to the check-in counter at gate sixteen. Alexander Velazquez, please report to the check-in counter at gate sixteen."

I chug back most of my beer, sliding the coaster into my hip pocket. When I stand up, I feel a little woozy and can't help wondering how much worse my weekend can get.

"Hi, you paged me?" I ask the motherly looking woman behind the counter at the gate. Her name tag reads PEGGY. The security guard to whom I told my life story is standing next to her. I tip my head toward him and try to look nonthreatening and sober. "I'm Alexander Velazquez."

"We have you booked on our next flight to San Francisco, with no bags. I was talking to Ed here, and we have a seat open in first class if you don't mind leaving right now, Mr. Velazquez."

"You're serious?"

"Not everyone from New York is a jerk, Mr. Velazquez," Ed says.

I walk around the counter and hug Ed and then Peggy. "Thanks. Really."

Peggy gives me a squeeze and pats my back. "You can go ahead and board now, sweetie."

I take one last look around and then turn my back on New York.

Evelyn

Once in the stall, I can't cry no matter how hard I try. I feel like too much of a fool. A giggle escapes me, and I try to cover it by coughing behind a wad of one-ply toilet paper.

Laurent isn't going to come after me. He's married, and his wife, no more than twenty-four hours ago, asked me to stop fucking her husband. She didn't even bother to use the French term (*baiser*), although I'm fluent in the language and, obviously, the act. I double over laughing as quietly as I can. The other women around me must think there's a nutcase loose in the terminal bathroom.

I get myself together, wash my face at the sink, and go through my purse for some lip balm, instead coming up with my "fat photo." Laurent's big thumbprint is smudged over my face. I wet a paper towel and rub it off. As I tuck it back into my wallet, I realize I've left my AmEx at the bar.

For a moment I consider ducking into the first-class lounge, using one of the phones to cancel it, and thus avoiding the embarrassment of having to show my blotchy face at the bar again. Instead, I smooth down my hair, square my shoulders, and head back.

It's gotten a lot busier since I slunk off to the bathroom, and the bartender is at the other end trying to decipher the orders from a group of Japanese tourists. I spot my glass of wine, still sitting there waiting for me, but instead I stand by the spot next to it, right where an almost empty beer bottle and shot glass are sitting, but that's not what catches my eye.

I pick up the little figure and hold it in the palm of my hand. It's a dog. When I push the tail down with my finger, the head bobs.

"You're looking better," the bartender says and slides my card and bill toward me. He reaches over and sets the glass of wine in front of me.

"Thank you," I say, realizing I'm smiling. "I do feel better."

I take a few courtesy sips and then walk to the first-class lounge, slipping the little figure into my purse as I go.

monday . . .

chapter three
Domestic Relations

Alexander

I stare up at the ceiling of my bedroom, listening to Pete moving around in the kitchen, brewing coffee and getting ready to leave for the office.

I roll over toward the window, expecting the comforting scent of warm dryer sheets coming up from the Laundromat downstairs. Nothing. I sit up and take a deep breath, getting a nose full of cold San Francisco morning air.

"What the fuck?" I hop out of bed, pulling on a pair of shorts I dug out of the hamper. Even though I haven't been in my apartment for a year, there's still dirty laundry I forgot to do before I left.

"What's that?" Pete calls from the kitchen. He's staying with me while Melissa, his soon-to-be ex-wife, moves her stuff out of their Nob Hill condo. "You say something, Alexander?"

I tear past him, barefoot and shirtless, down the stairs and stand in front of the locked gate of the Wish 'n' Wash, which is supposed to be open at 6:00 A.M. according to the sign posted behind the grubby window.

"I hope you didn't leave your stuff in there last night," a woman walking by says. "The guy who runs it never opens up before noon, and then he closes whenever he wants to."

"How long has this been going on?" I ask.

"God, I'd say for about a year now. I'd never set foot in that craphole, but wouldn't you know, there isn't anywhere else to do laundry around here. The guy who owns it is a real jerk, a rich yuppie who lives in Marin or something. He's totally making all this money but can't be bothered to even make sure the dryers work. What does he care, right?"

"Right," I mutter. That rich yuppie would be me, and I don't live in Marin. I live, as of last night, right above this craphole.

"Try again later," she says, and waves as she walks on. "You might get lucky."

A year before I left for New York, I landed a job as the in-house lawyer for a combo porn, sports, and stock website, and watched my personal net worth exceed my wildest dreams after some family-friendly media conglomerate bought us out. I had more money than I'd ever dreamed of. I flirted with the idea of either climbing Everest or getting really fat on some unnamed beach in Fiji for a couple of years.

Instead, I invested in a run-down two-story building ("Noe Valley adjacent!" my real estate agent exclaimed) with most of the bottom floor consisting of the only place to do laundry in a six-block area in either direction. When I was touring it, she raved about the proximity to the J-Church light-rail line, the great coffee shops to the left, and the taquerias to the right. She knew I was a man who could appreciate a four-dollar latte prepared by a tattooed and pierced bisexual just as much as a three-dollar shrimp taco made by an undocumented mother of three.

I put a fresh coat of paint on the walls, got all the machines up and running, changed the name from EZ Clean Laundreria to the Wish 'n' Wash, and reopened for business. With that taken care of, I gutted the entire top floor, tearing out the rabbit-warren rooms, and turned it into an open-floor-plan, loftlike pad.

That I revitalized a former site of a crumbling, rat-infested home to drug dealers, users, and brave squatters didn't buy me any goodwill with my new neighbors. Instead, I became a symbol of all that was wrong with San Francisco. I was an elitist, pushing the artsy and working-class folk out of an already overpriced housing market with a casual phone call to my money manager.

Right before I left for New York, I turned the Wish 'n' Wash keys over to Reggie, the guy I'd hired to run the place for me. Now I find out people can't even wash their clothes, and if I'd ever bothered to check in with Reggie besides just checking the bank account where he made the modest weekly deposits, I may have wondered why business was flat at best.

No wonder they hate me and think I live in Marin.

"What's up, buddy?" Pete steps out of the doorway that leads up to my place. He's holding two cups of hot coffee and my keys. I seem to have interrupted him in the middle of getting dressed, as he's wearing dress socks and his black Wallabees with the cutoff sweatpants and faded FBI T-shirt he slept in, whose small print reads FEMALE BODY INSPECTOR. "Isn't the Wish 'n' Wash supposed to be open by now?"

"Yeah. It is."

I push the grate open with a loud screech after jimmying the key in the rusted lock, push open the inner door, and step inside what was supposed to be a cash cow. The place is a mess. Most of the machines have hand-lettered out-of-service signs taped to them, where the floor isn't chipped, it's just plain grubby, and almost every surface is covered in graffiti.

"Jesus, Alexander, if people lived here, you'd be a slumlord," Pete says.

"Thanks, man. Don't you have to get to work?" I scratch my bare belly with the keys.

"So what are you going to do?" Pete asks, shoving one of the cups at me.

"Fire Reggie for one." I take a sip. It's hot, dark, and strong, just the way Pete likes it. I grimace at the bitter taste, having gotten used to the milder cup of Reed coffee I'd pick up from the kiosk on the way to work in New York.

"And then?" Pete knocks his back like it's mother's milk.

I look over at him. "I have no idea, my friend."

Evelyn

I tiptoe across the floor into the bathroom, realizing I won't be able to flush until my younger sister, Tannin, either falls asleep or leaves her flat below mine. We've shared the two-unit building in the Cole Valley part of the city since our late teens, when our parents reasoned it was time we lived on our own and provided us with a place, thrice-weekly maid service, and a credit card just for ordering in food.

I hear Tannin stumble around her place and realize she's probably trying to fix herself some coffee. Envisioning yet another visit from the fire department, I slip on my sneakers and favorite ratty sweater and head downstairs using the staircase that connects our flats by way of the kitchens.

"What the fuck!" Tannin shrieks, dropping a metal mixing bowl to the floor with an awful clatter. She's wearing a silver wrap dress, sky-high heels, and enough makeup to make a drag queen take a second look. "Evelyn! Is that you or a ghost?"

"It's me." I bend over to pick up the mess, trying to delay her getting a good look at me.

"You look . . . different." Her eyes are as wide as saucers, and not just because she's still a little high from her night out. "Love, love, love the bangs."

"Thanks." I reach up and smooth them, cringing at her words, not wanting her to notice that I do look a lot different and it's not because of the bangs. "I got them cut by a hairstylist who claimed he used to trim Jane Birkin's bangs."

"Birkin? Like the purse?"

"Exactly." I rinse out the teakettle and fill it with fresh water before setting it on the stove.

"Oh, my God! Do our parents know you're back? Why are you back?" she asks as she throws her size-zero body against mine.

She's about five inches shorter than I am, with long blond hair I envied as a girl. Whereas both our parents and Tannin are small in stature, fair-haired with perpetual golden tans, I'm tall (topping out at five ten when I was a painful fifteen), pale skinned, dark haired.

She settles her butt down on the counter. "Mother told me you were in Saint-Tropez with your mystery boyfriend."

"No boyfriend. Not Saint-Tropez. Just me in Paris with my paintbrushes and knitting needles." I walk to the fridge to see if she has any food in there but find a wall of Diet Coke. "New diet, Tannin?"

"It's great! I just drink a can when I'm hungry and"—she snaps the fingers on both her hands—"just like that I'm not hungry anymore. I can go days, *days,* without eating real food. You should try it. But you don't have to. You're *so* skinny, Evelyn."

"No, I'm not. I mean thanks." I reach for a couple of mugs and go to sit at the small café table she keeps in the corner by the back window.

"Mother will spring such a boner when she hears you're back." Tannin takes a seat opposite me, a jangle of silver bracelets punctuating her every move. "She can throw together one of her famous dinner parties for your birthday on Wednesday."

"I'd rather just lay low for a few days," I say, knowing that if I wanted to keep my being back in town quiet, I should have checked into some tourist hotel downtown. I've never been inclined toward any of the family-sanctioned activities of dressing for dinner, mastering the art of polite but substance-free conversation, and continuing the tradition of marrying well.

"You can't!" Tannin throws her skinny arms up into the air. On the inside of her left wrist are the various stamps from the nightclubs she visited last night. "You know how Mother gets off on these things. She lives to entertain, Evelyn. And you being back will take the heat off of me."

"What'd you do?"

Tannin is always doing something to irk our mother, and until I left, it was my job to patch things up between them.

"I slipped some ecstasy into James's crepe on Saturday at the House, and somehow the mayor's wife, the cow, ended up eating it instead of him."

"No, Tannin." I drop my head into my hands, mostly to cover my smile.

"Well, yeah, I did it as a joke."

"This is almost as bad as the cake covered in chocolate Ex-Lax shavings you brought to the Junior League recruitment brunch. Worse. Starting with possession of an illegal controlled substance."

"It was only a *little* ecstasy. Either way, the mayor didn't seem too upset about it." Tannin shrugs so the shoulder of her dress slips off, something I'm sure it's been doing all night. "If you ask me, I did them a favor. Put a little spice into their Saturday night tumble. Because in their prenup, according to that gossip cow Sissy, *she* had to get the lawyers to make him give her a good boning at least once a week."

I look at Tannin for a moment, trying to digest what she just said. "Wouldn't it have then been better for the mayor to get the ecstasy?"

"Not my problem." Tannin crosses her eyes, annoyed with me for bringing up the small details. "I did my part, the rest is up to them."

I reach over and pat her hand. "I'm sure they'll be sending over flowers and a thank-you note any time now, along with the cops."

"So . . . what happened, Evelyn? Is it that guy you were seeing?" Tannin's voice is serious but tinged with curiosity.

My sister is the queen of spectacular relationship flameouts and a tad competitive in that department. She likes to date big and break up even bigger. I think being called a whore in Paris by my lover's wife would rate pretty high up on her scale, but I'm not ready to go into specifics, since I know what I say to her will go straight to our mother. No one except James knows about Laurent. The few times Tannin or Mother came to Paris, I managed to be out of town to avoid the messy questions they were bound to ask about what was going on in my life and how I'd managed to lose a hundred pounds in the process. Questions that I can expect to be asked now and most likely will have to answer.

"Sorry?" I say, playing dumb.

"Well, whatever"—Tannin jumps into my lap, losing one of her stilettos—"you look great!"

"And"—I kiss the top of her expensively blonded hair—"isn't that what really matters?"

Alexander

I pocket the new keys from the locksmith and put up a sign in the window that reads CLOSED FOR REMODELING, then add one that reads UNDER NEW MANAGEMENT. I hope the two pieces of paper will stave off the angry mob with pitchforks and burning torches.

"Hey? You there?" The woman's raspy voice emits from my cell phone after having told me to hold ten minutes ago. I've had to call four different numbers to track down Reggie so I can fire him.

"Yeah, still here." I try to crunch the phone between my ear and shoulder as I sweep all manner of lint, pieces of trash, and dust into a pile in the middle of the floor. "I'm holding for Reggie."

"He's asleep, and I'm not going to be the one to wake him up." She turns up the sound on the TV so it's all that much more pleasant to be on the phone with her. "Okay?"

"Yeah, don't bother, *ma'am*." She sounds like she's younger than a ma'am, but I'm annoyed and there's nothing a woman under sixty-five hates more than being called "ma'am." "Tell Reggie he's fired and he shouldn't bother showing up whenever it was he was going to bother to show up for work. Okay?"

I hang up, shove the phone in my waistband, and resume sweeping, even though I know nothing short of a blowtorch will make a difference in how this place looks.

"I'm off to the office, honey pie!" Pete brandishes his travel mug full of commuting coffee at me. He's wearing his Monday suit, a drab gray, with a white shirt and a blue tie that makes him look like a security guard at a law firm, not a lawyer. "You try and stay out of trouble, young man. No more alienating your neighbors."

He's trying to seem chipper, but from the dark circles under his eyes and the extra droop to his shoulders, I know he's still reeling from Melissa walking out on him and then walking back in to ask him to clear out while she packs up her stuff to move to her _friend's_ flat in North Beach.

"I'll have dinner waiting, sweetie!" I wave after him before I think twice and take off after him. "Hey, Pete!"

"Yeah?" Pete is strapping down his backpack to his ancient Honda scooter.

"How about if I take you out for a beer or three? Later?" Pete's going home tonight, and I don't think he should have to face his empty apartment sober. "I need to go downtown anyway, buy myself something decent to wear."

I won't get very far in my new life in a wardrobe of basketball shorts and ratty T-shirts, and I doubt Sigrid will lovingly pack and mail me the suits I abandoned, along with her, in Manhattan.

"Sure. Hey. I can put in a word for you at the firm. Rodney, my boss, is looking for pretty boys like you. And it helps that you haven't been disbarred or anything." Pete looks at me closely. "You haven't been disbarred? Have you?"

"No, Pete. Thanks, man."

"You'd do the same for me." Pete gives me a labored smile before his head disappears inside his helmet.

I twirl the broom around like a light saber and wind up smacking myself on the side of the head. Disgusted with the lack of progress I've made both here and with my life, I toss it inside, lock up, and head upstairs to go back to sleep.

Evelyn

With little hope of staving off the inevitable dinner party my mother will want to throw once she finds out I'm in town, I go through my closet in search of something appropriate to wear. I pull out my go-to black suit. Slipping the skirt over my clothes, I fasten the clasp, let go to face the mirror, and watch as it falls to pool around my ankles.

"Well, that's a pleasant surprise." I grab an armful of clothes and dump them onto my bed, not bothering to try anything on.

"What are you doing?" Tannin asks. She's in her pajamas but still has a face full of smeared makeup. She climbs into my bed, kicking the heaps of clothes onto the floor. "None of that's going to fit. Thank God. You can finally give all of it away to the fifty-year-old midlevel executive lady-man who it belongs to. You've really lost a lot of weight, Evelyn."

"I'll have to go . . . shopping."

I dread shopping. I hate the whole process of stripping down, trying things on with the end result being that nothing looks or feels right.

"I'll go with you to make sure there aren't any further fashion lapses. And invite what's his face," she says, snuggling into my pillows.

"James?"

Tannin and James, my two most favorite people in the world, have a love-hate relationship. They love me but hate each other. Or at least act as if they can't stand each other. Deep down we all know they'd be perfectly happy if they found themselves stranded on a deserted island together as long as they got regular care packages of *W* magazine and obscure Bulgarian mineral water. I've learned to step aside and let them bicker—it's their way of communicating.

"Yes, him. Have him meet us at Neiman's. Or we can go to Crocker's." She yawns. The Crocker Galleria downtown, with its collection of high-end shops, is Tannin's Mall of America. "Between the two of us, we can get you out of the sack you're wearing."

I'm wearing my dark eggplant, knee-length, and yes, I admit it, rather shapeless cotton smock dress, on top of a long-sleeved black turtleneck, knit black tights, and my favorite boots I got on a trip to Prague. The suitcase I packed in Paris is full of smock dresses and swingy jumpers in wool and silk. I had them made by a Vietnamese seamstress based on a sketch I drew after watching *Funny Face* one too many times in the early days, when I was too intimidated to leave the flat and wander the streets of Paris on my own.

After the surgery, the doctor advised me to wear a full-body compression garment for as long as I could to help my skin "snap back" as the weight started to come off. After a few months, I got so used to the snug feel of it, though I didn't need it anymore, that I compromised on tights and a turtleneck under a dress.

"It's not a sack," I say but can't help looking down at myself.

"Sorry, sacklike dress." Tannin tosses a pillow at me, her skinny arms barely able to launch it a few feet from the bed.

"They're all the rage in Paris." I can't help but feel a bit defensive. I rather like my uniform and am in no mood for a makeover, especially if it involves shopping. I spent a whole month weighing the pros and cons of bangs.

"That's so funny, Evelyn, because rage is exactly what your outfit makes me feel when I look at it."

Tannin, with her tiny body, perky boobs, and lifelong pursuit of minimal body fat, has never let anything remotely resembling a sack, even one with a designer label, anywhere near her body. For the last couple of years, she's been on an 1980s Ungaro dress kick and somehow makes the big flower prints, bold shoulders, and daring V-necks look quintessentially Tannin.

"Whatever. You need a gown for tomorrow night. Unless you have one of those sacks in chiffon."

Gown. Is there a more horrifying word?

"What's tomorrow night?" I ask.

"Evelyn. I'm truly shocked!" Tannin sits up, pinching her face so she looks like our mother. "The Something Something to Save, Heal, or Bring Attention to Some Obscure but Media-Friendly Cause Gala Benefit Hullaba-*fucking*-loo, which you cannot attend dressed like Sister Agnes of the Perpetual Blue Balls. How could you ever forget?"

"Pretty easily, actually."

I climb into bed with her. I'll bag up the clothes to donate later. Right now, I think it's smarter for me to conserve my energy.

Evelyn

I hold Tannin's large triple nonfat latte while she digs through her purse for money to give to a panhandler. So far she's stopped to give handouts and spritzes of perfume to five different people on our way to meet James.

"Tannin," I say quietly, not wanting to seem rude in front of the guy who's holding out a tattered soda cup. "We're going to be late. James is on his lunch hour and has to get back to work in less than an hour."

"Don't be so elitist, Evelyn. We all have to do our part," she says as she dumps a couple of bills and some change into the cup, careful not to touch the guy.

"I'm not being elitist, Tannin," I say, falling quickly back into a familiar scolding tone. "What I'm trying to be is punctual."

"Fine. I'll put on my blinders to the crushing and pungent issue of homelessness in the city, Evelyn, if that will make you happy." She entwines her arm in mine, and we start back on our way. "Anyway, I only have twenties left. I want to see some dancing or open sores for anything more than a couple of bucks."

"You truly are a more fashion-conscious Mother Teresa, Tannin."

"Thank you," Tannin says primly, adjusting her sunglasses before taking hold of her drink.

My sister has never had a problem with the way things are. The Reeds and Sinclairs are rich, always have been, and always will be.

As a Reed-Sinclair, Tannin has never known another life or even questioned the one she has. My sister loves being rich and has never seen the point in pretending otherwise.

Unlike me. The failed pretender of the family. In Paris I was finally living my own life, by my own rules, at my own pace, and making my own decisions. Up until Laurent's wife ruined my little fantasy, I think I was doing okay on my own.

"What are you frowning about?" Tannin says, giving me a nudge in the ribs with her sharp elbow.

"Nothing." I force myself to smooth out my face, knowing Tannin will put Botox injections on the agenda with little more thought than it takes for her to scroll down her phone book and land on her plastic surgeon's number. "James!"

James is leaning against the wall of Neiman Marcus smoking a cigarette. I break into a run, dragging Tannin along with me.

"You're back and you look great!" James says as he hugs me. He checks me out. "I see you've been watching *Funny Face* again."

"I told you." Tannin smirks.

James throws an arm around my shoulders and guides me inside. I reach back and grab Tannin's hand so we form a little scrum through the doors.

"I had them pull some stuff," James says as we head up to the second floor. He knows my dislike of shopping runs as deep as his and Tannin's fascination for it goes the other way. "Just to make things slightly less painful for all of us."

We follow a saleswoman who shows us into a private dressing room with a settee, champagne, and a fruit tray. She stands off to the side, already knowing she's just here to make things easier for James.

"It doesn't matter what I wear. No one will notice." I usually stay well out of the limelight at events. These things are my mother's and Tannin's territory, not mine. I just have to look decent enough, be polite, and keep an eye on my sister. "Maybe I can wear something I already have?"

"No, you can't," Tannin says, pulling out a slinky halter gown that would look great on her. "Nothing in your closet fits you anymore."

"Even that flower print dress?" James asks. "The one you wore when we went on that Barry Ellison guy's boat."

"It was a yacht, and it was Larry Ellison's," Tannin says. "You barfed on it. Remember?"

"I did? Good for me. It was hideous." James shudders and turns to face the rack of gowns again.

"My mother gave me that dress. Vintage Lilly Pulitzer," I offer as a lame defense of it.

"Next time I'll barf on your mother." James quickly rejects four gowns and hands them over to the saleswoman. "It was WASP child abuse, Evelyn."

"You should bring it up when _Vanity Fair_ does an exposé on the family," Tannin joins in, having slipped into the halter-neck dress.

"I will, of course, provide juicy nuggets credited as 'a close family friend who doesn't wish to be named for fear of not being allowed to sponge off the family.'" James looks Tannin up and down, and with a small shake of his head nixes the halter gown for her and me. "See? It all works out for everyone. You get revenge on your mother, and I still get invited over for brunch and tennis."

"I'm not sure I'm ready to go out just yet. Jet lag." I sit down, cross my legs, and commence jiggling my foot to work out some of my growing nervousness. There's no point in rushing James or

Tannin. He won't let me walk out the door until he's completely happy with the way I look, and Tannin can shop for hours without a break.

"Nice try, Evelyn," my sister says with a cruel laugh. "If I have to go, you have to go, and you so owe me for having to stand in for the both of us for the last year and a half. Oh, this one!"

"God, are you blind, woman?" James says with enough disgust in his voice to make me look up at the dress Tannin is holding against herself.

"What's wrong with it?" she asks. The gown has a vivid floral print that actually makes my eyes hurt.

"It looks like some Florida floozy threw up all over it, but it's perfect for you, Tannin."

"Exactly the look I'm going for." Tannin slips out of the black halter and into the flower dress, not bothering to duck behind the screen.

"Now this one will make your tits look fabulous, Evelyn," James says, not sparing my sister's thong-clad ass a second look.

It's a proper silk gown, long, and pools at my feet, with so much boning it almost stands up on its own. The fitted top will keep everything up there locked and loaded. I can just shimmy into it, zip up the back, and won't have to worry about straps or bulges with the aid of a trusty body shaper underneath. It's sexy without being obvious, classic, and made with a woman with curves in mind.

"Thank God." I jump up from the settee, ready to pay for it then and there.

"This dress makes a statement." He holds it up to me.

"Yeah: I haven't had sex in five years and my thighs rub together." Tannin immediately claps her hand over her mouth. "I'm so sorry, Evelyn! I didn't mean that you haven't . . . or your . . ."

"Shut up, Tannin." James walks over to me, bumping her out of the way. "Trust me, once you have it on, you won't want to take it off."

"I doubt that, but I'm willing to give it a try," I say before ducking behind the screen to take off my clothes; the tights I leave on.

A half hour later I have on a pair of black, three-inch Christian Louboutin satin pumps with almond-shaped toes and slight platforms so I can tower over everyone another few inches. A gold metallic clutch that barely fits my cell phone and keys along with some complementary jewelry round out the look.

Even Tannin looks impressed. "Your waist is so tiny now, Evelyn."

"Good. Let's go and get you back to work before you get fired, James," I say, ducking back behind the screen.

"How is that working thing working out for you, James?" Tannin asks.

"It sucks, Tannin. I won't even pretend it's worth my time, but a boy has to do what a boy has to do before he lands his sugar daddy. For now I am the unhappy and bitter receptionist for UGot It.com."

"I thought you liked your job?" I ask, pulling on my turtleneck and stepping back into my dress.

"One doesn't like one's job, Evelyn. One endures it until one lands a sugar daddy who will allow one a lifestyle of working out and laser hair removal."

"Sounds like a pretty good life to me," Tannin says, not realizing that it's pretty much the life she has now.

"How is everything going?" the saleswoman asks, surveying the mess we've made.

"Great, thank you," I call out before Tannin and James can suggest alternatives and keep me here any longer. "Can you have everything delivered by this afternoon?"

Alexander

I have a choice to make here. I stand across the street exactly where the Macy's men's store meets with Neiman Marcus. I need to figure out if I should be an impractical ass and go buy a new suit at Neiman Marcus or be a practical jerk and head into the Macy's men's store.

I cross the street, veering to the left to avoid a panhandler who smells like expensive perfume with an undercurrent of homelessness, and walk into Macy's.

I'm not surprised when the sales staff give me the once-over and then go back to folding sweaters. I can't pass for a tourist, and I'm too clean to be a vagrant. I make a first pass through the suit department to see what my options are. And they're limited on my budget.

"Can I help you?" The obviously most junior salesperson has been sent forth to deal with me.

"I'm looking for a suit. Couple of suits, shirts, ties, and shoes."

"Really?" she asks.

"Really."

If I stop to think about it, I don't really need a suit. I *want* a suit. My dad never was one of those clothes-make-the-man kinds of guys, but he did teach me about keeping my shoes shined, my hair neat, and never growing a mustache before fifty. The one suit he owns comes out only for weddings, funerals, and the occasional court appearance. He's a sleeves-rolled-up-and-Dickies-work-pants kind of man. When he wants to step it up, he wears a pair of gray slacks and a crisp, light-colored guayabera.

I made my mother iron my jeans on my first day of kindergarten, and instead of sneaking *Playboys*, I hid *GQ*s under my mattress when I was a teenager. By the time I was in junior high, I was well versed in Windsor knots and the wrongness of double-breasted suits. Wisely, I choose to keep these opinions to myself until I had something to back them up with.

For me, pursuing a career as a lawyer wasn't just about love of the law (which is in my blood); it was about the suits. Suits are power, they mean you have a damn good reason to get dressed in the morning. From the time I put on my First Communion suit when I was eight, I knew I'd be spending my life in them—they're like my second skin. I could practice law in khakis and a Gap button-down like the idealistic Stanford prelaw grads in my mom's small pro bono law office; but what's the point? Sure, I'd be a lawyer, but I wouldn't look like a lawyer.

"You're a forty long?" She pulls out two suits, a navy blue and a dark gray, nothing fancy but serviceable. "These are slim cuts. A little more modern and would look less boxy on your frame than our traditional suits. What do you think?"

"Looks good," I say, not bothering to check the label, instead focusing on the price tag.

"And they're both thirty percent off today," she adds hopefully.

"Even better."

We make a quick lap of the shirt and tie section, then shoes, square-toed lace-ups, and socks and underwear, where she discreetly steps off to the side to let me pick out my own.

"Do you need a briefcase?" she asks.

"I have something at home I can use for now." I retreat to the dressing room, and even though everything is straight off the rack, the fit is pretty decent. I step outside wearing the navy blue.

"Oh my," she breathes.

"Thanks. Is it okay if I wear it out?" See what I mean? It's all about the suit, even a moderately priced one bought on sale.

"Sure, yes. I'll just snip off those tags."

I stand still while she buzzes around me with a small pair of scissors and then hand over my credit card with a lump in my throat. I wait while she rings everything up, trying to figure out how much I've put on that card, and am relieved when she comes back, the rest of the stuff in bags with a smile on her face and a receipt for me to sign.

"It was so nice to help you today, Mr. Velazquez. Here's my card. If you ever need anything, just give me a call."

"Will do." I look down at the card. "Judy."

I walk out, the long way, through the main sales floor, and pause by the watches, just for shits and giggles.

"Hello, sir, is there anything I can help you with today?" asks a sales guy who had ignored me earlier.

"Nope." I walk out and head toward Pete's office.

chapter five
Career Opportunities

Evelyn

"Are you sure you're okay if I don't go with you, Tannin?" I ask outside Neiman Marcus. "I can be back here in twenty minutes tops. Or you can walk down with us?"

"I'm going to get my massage at Maiden Lane and then head back home to recuperate." She's bummed a cigarette off of James and is making an effort not to blow smoke in my face. "That's about all I can handle for the day. You two go on."

"I'll see you later at home, then." I give her a kiss, as does James. "So where are you working now?" I ask as we set off to walk the ten blocks or so to his office. "You got what?"

"Some lame-o Web company. The place is such a joke. The dick in charge, Ted"—James takes my arm and veers to the left to avoid a homeless guy peeing in an alleyway—"is such a tool. He's trying to make me be his executive assistant *and* the receptionist. I told him I'd hire him somebody, but I haven't gotten around to it yet."

"Won't you get in trouble?" I pick up the pace, not wanting to make him any later than he already is.

"Slow down!" James pants.

"I don't want you to get in trouble because you and Tannin couldn't decide which purse went with a gown I don't even want." I keep up a brisk walk even though James has begun to lag behind. "We can catch a cab if you want."

"I smoke, am a bottom, and have the bone density of an eighty-year-old woman, Evelyn. Walking is the only healthy thing I do."

"Well, when you put it that way." I slow down in consideration of my best friend's sole healthy lifestyle choice.

"So what happened?" James asks as he flicks his butt into the street. "With Laurent?"

"It ran its course. I'm okay," I lie. I can't tell James about the look on Laurent's face when he saw that picture of me. It made me more ashamed than angry at him. Ashamed that I was once that girl, that I still am despite what I might look like to the outside world.

"So just like that? You're back?" He puts an arm out to keep me from crossing into oncoming traffic.

I nod and look away, suddenly feeling tired. I made a huge mess of things, I know it, then walked away and left it all behind in Paris. Now all I want is to forget and focus on getting James back to his desk so his boss doesn't yell at him.

"It's complicated," I say. "Not really, I just happened to fuck the wrong guy, who was wrong for so many reasons."

"Don't worry about it, Evelyn. You've done everything right until now. You deserve to fuck up once in a while." James pats my shoulder. "Remind them that Tannin isn't their only problem child."

"Thank you. I'll make sure to mention that to my mother when I see her tonight."

"Don't go. What's the big deal?" This advice comes from the person who once sat out almost a week's worth of classes at Pearson Prep because PBS was running a *Brideshead Revisited* marathon. James managed to convince the headmaster to let him write up a detailed report, including acting out a few of the scenes, so he wouldn't lose his scholarship. "Say you have jet lag, cramps, gonorrhea."

"And since I forgot to buy those little Eiffel Tower souvenirs, I won't be showing up empty-handed." I smile at my own joke. "Gonorrhea is the gift that keeps on giving, after all."

"Stay home, have a good cry"—James ignores me—"make an appointment with a shrink and have the shrink write you a note that says you can't be around your family because they get on your nerves. Or, here's an idea! Pretend you are a temp and say you have to work late because your fake boss is an asshole."

"If only it were that easy, James." I sigh. "I have a lot of explaining to do about . . . stuff."

"So you lost a hundred pounds while in France, where you ate cheese and duck fat and drank wine for breakfast. It makes sense to me," he scoffs. "You had an affair with your art teacher, who happened to be married to a very loud wife. Big deal, Evelyn. You're human, face it."

"I'll have to tell them the truth sometime." They're bound to notice the weight loss, and I doubt the bangs will distract them as easily as they did Tannin.

"Pfft. The truth is overrated," James says, pausing outside 115 Sansome Street for one last smoke before he has to go in. "Hey, you want to come up and check out where I leave a little piece of my soul each day?"

"Sure." I look up at the building, wondering what it would be like to have to spend most of the day working a real job. "It might be interesting."

Alexander

I'm too early to even consider talking Pete into ducking out of work, so I walk down to where the bike messengers hang out between calls and read over today's issue of the *San Francisco Express* that someone left on a bench. The cover is splashed with the picture of a busty but expensive-looking blonde, holding her hand out to ward off the camera under the headline CANDY TELLS WORKERS TO SUCK IT.

"You got any change?"

I look up into the face of a strung-out-looking kid. "Sorry, man. All tapped out for the day."

"Don't be an asshole, man." He scratches at the nasty looking scabs on his arm. "Just a buck or a quarter so I can get something to eat."

"Sorry, not today." I fold the paper and set it down.

"Fucking yuppie," he says loud enough for the bike messengers to look our way. "Fucking yuppies are running this fucking city. Forcing the real people out. Gentrification and all that shit."

"I'm not . . ."

That I, a kid who grew up brown and in the Mission, can be considered a foot soldier of gentrification, is both absurd and a backhanded compliment. It means I've made something of myself. It means I look good enough in my midpriced suit to give a strung-out kid the impression that I'm a full-on sellout. I stand up and head toward Pete's office, equally pissed off and feeling guilty I couldn't and didn't want to help him out.

I take the elevator up to the fifth floor of 114 Sansome and step into a scene out of *Logan's Run,* a movie I watched compulsively as a kid. Everything is shades of black, gray, or blinding white, and the air itself feels antiseptic, exactly the way TV and movie lawyer offices look.

"May I help you?" a woman asks from behind a low, sharp-edged reception desk. She looks like one of those expressionless fembots from that Robert Palmer video where he wore that sharp suit.

"I'm here for Pete McCray. Alexander Velazquez." The less I say, the less she'll have to pick apart and the more she'll assume I have legitimate business with Pete at this hour of the day.

She raises one penciled-in eyebrow, then, without taking her eyes off me, speaks into the tiny microphone that curves around from the back of her head. "Mr. McCray? You have a guest . . . a Mr. Velazquez. . . . Of course. . . . Mr. Velazquez, if you would follow me."

I smooth down the lapels of my new suit, stow my shopping bags behind her desk, and hotfoot it to catch up to her. Her heels may be high, but she has no problem walking in them. She stops by a door, opens it, and steps aside, leaving behind a pocket of air that is noticeably chilly.

"Alexander!" Pete stands up and gives me a quick man hug and affectionate blow on the back. "I was just talking to Rodney about you."

"Pleased to meet you, Rodney." I turn to a guy with a receding hairline in a Brooks Brothers suit.

"Rodney Heller, one of the founding partners here at Williams, Heller, Lincoln." He pumps my hand up and down a few times, making up in his grip what he lacks in height. "Alexander, great to meet you. Pete says you're on the market and looking for a gig? Wallace, hold all my calls."

"Of course, Mr. Heller." She steps out and closes the door behind her.

I flex my hand when he finally releases it to get the blood flow going again. "I was recently with the firm of—"

"Not to worry, Alex. Who here hasn't been fired at least once or twice in his life?" Rodney laughs.

"I haven't," Pete offers up.

"Petey here tells me you're a Berkeley grad? Bezerkly." Rodney, in his crisp suit and shiny tie, leans back in his chair. "We're Harvard men around here, but we'll try not to hold it against you."

"I went to Berkeley, too," Pete says.

"I met Pete on my first day of rush," I add.

"Did you pledge?" Rodney perks up. I may have just met Rodney Heller, but I'm sure he has Greek letters tattooed somewhere on his body. I'd bet my closed-down Laundromat on it.

"No. Never got around to it. I was hitting the books pretty hard," I lie. I didn't pledge because I thought frat boys were all assholes, and I still do.

"Neither did I," Pete adds. "I mean pledge."

Rodney gives him a quick look and continues, "Listen, Alex, we run—"

"Alexander," Pete interjects.

"You couldn't have shown up at a better time," Rodney goes on, ignoring him. "We're in a bind here. I'm this close to reeling in a major, *major,* new client, and we're going to need some fresh blood."

"I got back into town last night, but if you want to set up an interview for next week—"

"Alex, I'm talking like now—today, tomorrow, Wednesday at the latest. I want you on board ASAP." Rodney sits down and starts pulling papers together. "Take this home, read it, get back to me. Get a feel for the client base we're aiming for. I'm in a bind. You got me bent over. I'll do anything short of murder to make sure you're part of the Williams, Heller, Lincoln team."

"That's a lot to think about, Rodney—"

"Hey, man, I know where you're coming from. Take the rest of the day. Get back to me tomorrow morning. But before you leave, let me show you your office." Rodney hops up and starts for the door. Pete and I have no choice but to follow. "Primo spot. My other guys have been chomping at the bit for it, but man, I'm willing to take the heat."

As we make our way down the dark, gray-carpeted hallway, I can't help but notice all the vacuum marks are perfectly parallel to one another.

"You ready for this?" Rodney stops at a closed door and gives me a look like he's about to open a passageway to my fantasies.

I look over at Pete. His eyes are as big as saucers. "I'm not sure," I answer.

"Whaddaya think?" Rodney steps aside, looking like a desperate real estate agent showing off a model unit. He starts to breathe out of his mouth to avoid sucking in the obvious fumes of freshly dried paint. "Fan-fucking-tastic. I had it in mind for myself, but for you, Alex, I'm willing to give it up."

The office is big, bigger than the one I had in New York, with three big windows that face the building across the street. It looks like a Design Within Reach catalog threw up in here. There's a de rigueur black leather couch tucked under the window with a sculptural coffee table sitting in front of it.

"I thought this was your new office, Rodney." Pete wanders in, looking like a bride touring a potential newlywed love nest. He takes a seat on the couch, running his hands over the tufted leather. The two just don't go together. He's more of a glen-plaid-La-Z-Boy-complete-with-a-cup-holder-on-each-arm kind of guy.

"Aeron chair, top of the line, hand-knotted silk rug, from Nepal or Tibet or some such place like that, Dordoni desk, but if you prefer something more traditional, we have an antique mahogany desk in storage," Rodney says, steering me to the wall opposite the desk, where the art is.

"I think that's the desk I'm using, Rodney," Pete says from where he's now inspecting a stone Buddha head sculpture next to the stack of law review magazines.

"Robert Longo lithographs. Men in the City series." Rodney points to each one, and we pause to admire them in turn. "These three are my own personal collection. From home."

"I don't know what to say, Rodney." Being that I'm in no position to turn down a job, I should say yes and leave it at that.

"Call me tomorrow." Rodney throws his arm around my shoulders like he's my new best friend. "Better yet, give me your number and I'll call you."

I pat my suit pocket before I remember that my cell is three time zones away. "I don't have a local cell."

"Doesn't matter. Wallace can set you up with one." His arm still around me, he steers me over to the office chair and sets the folder in front of me. "Give those clips a read-through. Pete and I just have to wrap a few things up, and then you guys can be on your way. Welcome aboard, Alex."

He holds out his hand, and I hold out mine, and we shake. I look over at Pete, who has a confused expression on his face that I'm sure mirrors mine.

Evelyn

I sit on the standard-issue office couch a few feet away from the circular reception desk. Instead of manning his post, James is wandering around the office in search of two sticks of sugarless gum, one mint, the other bubble gum flavor. I don't chew gum. A nasty habit Mother could and would never abide, even though the Reed family also happens to be the world's fourth largest manufacturer of chewing gum and mints.

The phone gives another series of rings, cuts off just before the fifth, and kicks over to voice mail. And then it rings again. I can't stand it. I step behind the desk and snatch up the handset.

"Hello? Um . . . You've reached the offices of . . . You got it." I scramble around for a pen and sheet of paper, thinking I can at least take a message and pass it on to James when he gets back. "Can I help you? . . . I'm sorry, she, uh, is not available and, uh, voice mail is down, but I'd be happy to take a message and make sure she gets it. . . . Thank you. Have a nice day."

I sit down, so my eyes are level with the counter, and adding the time and date when a blue coffee mug enters my field of vision.

I look up and into a face that is so familiar I feel like I already know its owner. He has the well-scrubbed, bland good looks of all the prep school boys I grew up with, complete with the carefully trimmed light brown hair, parted to the right, blue eyes, straight teeth, and a chin that's a tad on the weak side. Exactly the type of person Mother wants me to bring home, down to the golden yellow and light blue striped tie he's wearing.

"Hi." He turns the cup so the logo faces me. The cup matches the colors of his tie and reads UCLA ALUMNI in hard-to-miss lettering.

The phone rings, and I automatically answer it. "You got it. Please hold." I look down in search of the hold button and, not finding it, lay the handset on the desktop. "Hi. Can I help you?"

"Is James around?" he asks in his nicely rounded vowels. He fiddles with the cup, drumming his fingers on the rim.

"You went to UCLA?" I ask, to be polite and stall for time.

"Got my MBA there. Anderson." He blinks his watery blue eyes and then puts his cap back on. "So you the temp I asked James to rustle up for us?"

"Yes. I am here only temporarily." I chance a quick look around me in the hope that James will appear. "Evelyn Morgan from the, uh, temp agency."

He nods. I nod. We nod at each other.

"Great," he finally says. "Welcome to the family."

I stand up and shake his hand. "Thank you."

I manage to not let my knees give out until he's well away from the psychedelic custom-made glass-and-concrete partition that separates James's desk from the guts of the office.

Alexander

I sit with Pete, nursing a beer in the first bar we came to. I take the piece of paper someone left taped to the grate of the Wish 'n' Wash to express their own sentiments about the coming renovations ("About time, asshole!") and fold it into a dragonfly.

"So." I hand it over to Pete, who stares at it before giving it a halfhearted trip through the air and setting it down on the scuffed bar top. "Hey, dude, what's the deal with Wallace? Is that her whole name? Like Madonna or Cher?"

"I don't know," Pete mumbles into his beer, "no one has ever called her anything but Wallace, so that's what I call her."

"Ah." I nod. Pete is afraid of her. Which makes me feel slightly less lame, since I'm afraid of her too.

"From what I've heard from those assholes Bryan and Brian, she's sleeping with either Rodney or some Russian mobster. They're full of shit, so I don't know. And she never eats. Ever," Pete says, warming up to the mystery that is Wallace. "She just drinks Diet Coke. I offered her gum once, and she said she doesn't snack between meals. So not only does she consider Diet Coke food but she thinks gum is a snack."

"Sounds like you've given this Wallace thing a lot of thought."

Pete shrugs. "So you going to take the job? I would if I were you. It's a real nice office. And I know you didn't come back to become a Laundromat tycoon."

"Not sure, Pete." We both know I've as good as signed on to join the stud stable of Williams, Heller, Lincoln—the same kind of aggressive and media-savvy law firm that fired me in Manhattan, and as much as I like to think I left with some principles, I still have something to prove to New York, myself, and Sigrid. Not necessarily in that order. "Really not sure at the moment what I'm going to do with myself."

"What was in that file he had you read?" Pete's been waiting to ask, and from the hitch in his voice, I can tell he's on the verge of being offended that I haven't shared this info with him sooner.

"Just some news clippings." Said like a true lawyer. Do not complicate the truth with details.

The clips Rodney handed me chronicled the sordid and highly readable saga of Candace Hall.

A year ago, Candace slept her way into fame and fortune by convincing Redford Maxwell Hall, sixty-eight, confirmed bachelor and San Francisco real estate mogul, to marry her during a weekend trip to Napa. They blew back into town, had a lavish party at Red's, now Candace and Red's, Pacific Heights mansion complete with fire-eaters, acrobats, and $1,000 bottles of champagne and a

$12,000 wedding cake. The new Mrs. Hall wore a half million dollars in diamonds and a $55,000 dress that was notable more for its color (pure white) than for what it cost.

Some people said it wouldn't last, while others countered it would as long as Redford didn't run out of money to feed his new wife's insatiable appetite for the finest things in life. It wasn't too long before stories on the less than happy marriage of Candace and Redford started making the gossip column rounds. Then the story really got good.

Red conveniently dropped dead the night before he was to meet with his lawyer to draw up divorce papers and end his tumultuous twelve-month marriage to his less than blushing bride. She had been rumored, among other things, to be stepping out on her fat, rich fuck of a husband with her personal trainer while denying her husband entry into her bedroom.

Red, it turns out, wasn't a complete cuckold, though that was going to be his divorce defense. He had been paying a visit to the studio apartment where he had installed his twenty-three-year-old mistress, Honey Palmer, a dancer at the Lusty Lady, when he suffered a massive heart attack. On top of her. According to the many interviews Honey Palmer gave, she was to be the second Mrs. Hall. Red was in love with her, as she was with him.

Candace, so the story goes, was in the tub when she learned of her husband's passing, and before she bent over to dry her toes, she'd inherited her husband's money and properties, and had Honey Palmer evicted from the studio apartment she now owned.

The funeral she and her professional event planner arranged was fit for a head of state, complete with the coffin delivered to the church in a horse-drawn glass carriage, her following behind under a hat and black veil, while bagpipers playing "Amazing Grace" and "My Heart Will Go On" set the mood.

The eulogist, a retired U.S. senator who had benefited greatly from Red's largesse, made no mention of the fact that Candace and Redford had been separated, or the pending divorce (confirmed by Red's longtime lawyer, who was not invited to the funeral), or the hysterical stripper girlfriend across the street, who'd also been barred from attending the service by a security team hired by the grieving widow.

Since her husband's death, Candace has been on a quest to polish up her image and buy her way into good standing with San Francisco's elite and influential society set. Not helping her campaign at redemption is the lawsuit brought by former employees of her short-lived dog clothing manufacturing business, a little something Redford agreed to bankroll to keep his new wife busy. The former employees of Canine Couture by Candace are suing her for failure to pay overtime wages or, if you believe the other side's lawyer, pesky wages in general.

Money, power, sex, the scandalous death of an eccentric San Francisco character, a hot rich widow, and let's not forget the stripper girlfriend, who claims her dead lover had promised to pay her way through acupuncture school. You can't make shit like this up, and you don't have to. All you have to do is pick up an issue of the *S.F. Express* and read about it.

Rodney, it seems, has a hard-on for this case, and as per my reading, Candace has been making her way through San Francisco law firms at a pretty good clip, so it was only a matter of time before we, I mean they, got a whiff of her perfume at Williams, Heller, Lincoln. And for some reason Rodney thinks I can see the benefits of providing a client like Candace Hall legal services.

"You should take the job, Alexander," Pete says gamely. Williams, Heller, Lincoln put him through two months of interviews, and from what I know they're still hazing him after two years on the job.

"I'm not sure I'm his man." I gesture to the bartender to bring us another couple of beers.

"It doesn't matter, *Alex*." Pete fishes through the peanut bowl. "You're his."

I knock back the rest of my beer, belch, and say, "Story of my fucking life, Petey."

Evelyn

"Where are you and why are you still there?" Tannin asks, her voice coming through with an echo. She has me on speakerphone as she drives from our place to the offices of UGotIt, not You Got It, as I initially thought. "I thought you were upstairs asleep."

"I'm—" I look around to make sure no one, least of all my new boss, is around. "I'm at 114 Sansome Street. Just double-park outside and we'll hop in. I need to finish up some work, but I should be done by the time you get here."

"What work?" There's a symphony of car horns in the background, but Tannin keeps talking. "You've never had a job a day in your life, Evelyn. Why start now?"

True enough.

"It's complicated. I'll explain when you get here." I hang up on Tannin and resume feeding business cards into the scanner, making sure each one pops up on the screen before moving on to the next one.

"Evelyn?" James skids to a stop in front of the cubicle where

I've been collating papers, assembling press kits, and sort of hiding out from him. "Evelyn?"

"Hi, James." I feed another card into the scanner. "I'm almost done here. Tannin is on her way, so we can catch a ride with her to my parents'."

"What are you doing here?"

"Working." I make sure the cards are alphabetized and stack them into a neat pile before securing them with a rubber band.

"But you don't work here," says James, thoroughly and justifiably confused.

"You were looking for gum and Ted assumed I was from the temp agency so I've been sort of going along with it," I say in a rush, hoping a rapid delivery of the facts will lessen their insanity. "So I thought I'd just, you know, pitch in for the rest of the day. Then one thing led to another, and tomorrow I have to come in early because it's bagel day. Ted said I could get the name of the place from you, so if you could write it down here or e-mail it to me at Evelyn dot Morgan at UGotIt dot com, that would be great. And did I mention Tannin will be here in about five minutes?"

"I'll go get my coat."

I shut down the computer and make sure everything is pretty much where I found it for its owner, who is on vacation. I walk into Ted's office, hoping to just put the cards on the table and leave, but he's in there. "Hi, um, Ted? Here are your business cards. Everything is scanned in."

"Great," Ted says without taking his eyes off his monitor. "See you tomorrow."

"Okay. Good night then."

Ted doesn't answer; he's gone back to whatever he was doing.

Downstairs I watch James struggle to light a cigarette in wind that seems to be coming from every direction, trying to formulate how on earth I'm going to explain all of this to him, Tannin, and my parents, who'll surely have questions.

"James!" Ted steps out into the wind and claps James on his shoulder, sending his finally lit cigarette flying out of his hand. He's wearing a blue cap with a UCLA Anderson School of Management logo on it. "Great job, my main man, on finally finding someone who knows her stuff."

"Her name is Evelyn." James doesn't bother to hide his disgust for his real boss and my faux boss as he smashes the cigarette under the heel of his boot.

"Yeah, of course it is. See you two tomorrow, and don't forget to order me a multigrain bagel, Evelyn." Ted gives me a toothy smile.

"Of course." I pull out the spiral pad I've been taking notes in. "It's on my list."

"Hey, little boy, you want some candy?" Tannin calls out as she pulls up to the curb. I do a spastic jig to try to wave her off. "What the fuck is wrong with you, Evelyn? Do you have to pee-pee?"

"This a Mercedes S63 AMG," Ted says, pushing ahead of James, who was about to climb into the passenger seat.

"I guess so." Tannin giggles. The girl really can't help it. Our mother claims Tannin winked at the doctor who delivered her. Having stood by for most of my life while she's flirted with all manner of males, I believe it. "It's my errand car. Evelyn, are you going to introduce us?"

"Ted, this is . . . This is my friend . . . Tannin." As far as everyone at UGotIt.com is concerned, my name is Evelyn Morgan, and since I can't very well let them go without bagels just because I'm impersonating a temp, it seems easier to use the name I put on my time sheet. "Tannin, this is Ted. He is . . . the . . ."

"CEO of UGotIt.com," Ted answers for himself, his eyes firmly on the dashboard.

Tannin assumes he's checking out her legs and angles them toward him. "Tannin Reed-Sinclair, so pleased to meet my _friend's_ boss."

"Reed-Sinclair?" Ted sounds like a starving man who's suddenly been presented with a juicy steak served by a naked woman balancing a stein of cold beer on her head. _"Reed? Sinclair?"_

"I'm off the clock, Ted"—James reaches for me and stuffs me into the backseat—"and unless you're going to authorize overtime pay for the temp here, we gotta get going."

I duck down so I'm hidden in the shadows and wait for the inevitable.

"What the fuck, Evelyn?" they both ask at the same time.

"Je n'ai aucune idée de ce que vous parlez, mes chéris," I say, knowing they both failed French at Pearson.

Alexander

"You lousy fartknocker!" my sister, Nayelli, says upon pulling open the front door of our parents' house. "Did you get that suit at the Goodwill?"

"Shut up, Nayelli." I smooth out my lapels with a momentary pang for the suits I left behind in New York. "What's that you're wearing? Pajamas and a robe?"

"These are *scrubs,* Alexander." She points to the name tag on her white coat. "See here where it says Dr. Nayelli Velazquez-Connors? That means I'm a *doctor* and *married.*" She always was an overachiever and not very gracious about it. "And I hear"—she steps aside so I can close the front door—"that you are neither married *nor* employed."

"That's where you are so wrong, Nayelli." I give her an awkward hug, trying not to crush my future niece or nephew, who is almost eight months along in his or her gestation in my sister's belly. For my consideration, she punches me on the arm. Hard. "Just today I got offered a job at Williams, Heller, Lincoln."

"Oh, fuck, you did not," she says, rubbing her hands together. "They are just going to piss themselves when they hear it, Alexander. Way to go, really."

I smile and nod at an intimidated-looking couple, most likely fighting an illegal eviction, something Mom specializes in. They're standing in the living room with an earnest-looking law student who is trying to communicate with them in his choppy high school

Spanish. Our mom runs her one-woman law office, along with a rotating cast of volunteers and interns, out of the house.

I move past Nayelli down the hallway that runs the length of my parents' house and opens up into the kitchen in back, where everyone can usually be found.

"Dead man walking. This is going to be good," Nayelli whispers in my ear and then yells without bothering to move away, "Lloyd, pop me some popcorn!"

"Alexander!" My mom envelops me in her layers of earth mother clothes, and I'm careful not to step on her toes. Since she's the boss, she sets the rules, and shoes are optional. "I'm just finishing up in here," she says, pointing toward the living room, which she's turned into a waiting room for clients. "Please, Alexander, try not to say anything to upset your father."

"I'll try, Mom." Behind me, Nayelli lets out a loud snort.

"No. Alexander." She takes my face between her hands. "Not try. Do."

"Okay, Mom."

"Where do you think you're going?" She hooks a finger into the waistband of my sister's scrub pants. "Go help your husband set the table, Nayelli."

I take my time walking down the hallway, making sure to avoid the creaky floor planks even though my dad has Pacifica Radio blaring and is having a loud conversation on the phone while cooking dinner.

"Listen to me, Julio. We won't let them get away with this *chingadera, vato*." Dad waves me over with a soup ladle. He holds his arms out for a hug and doesn't let me go once I step into them. "Let me *chequear* with *el* Tony, and we'll get all the *chamacos* out there tomorrow night. Make some signs, 'The Roosevelt has a heart of stone,' something like that. I can't be there, I'm taking my lady dancing tomorrow night, Julio. I'll call you back, my son is home."

"Hi, Dad." I peek around him to see what smells so good.

"I hope you're hungry, Son. My famous *carne con chile verde,* homemade flour tortillas—better than your grandmother's, God rest her soul—Mexican rice, otherwise known as just rice and an *olla* of beans."

My father's parents may not have taught him how to speak Spanish, thinking it would spare him and my aunts and uncles the struggles they faced, but they did teach him how to cook all the Mexican dishes they brought with them from Zacatecas. The Spanglish and curse words he picked up from friends and around the school yard.

"I am hungry, Dad. Lemme give you a hand."

I make my way to the crowded island in the middle of the kitchen and start rolling out the golf-ball-size dough balls and hand the tortilla to my dad, who sets it in the middle of the cast-iron *placa* we've been using since before I was born.

He takes a deep breath, inhaling the scent of singed white flour. "Nothing better than sharing good *comida* with the ones you love, Son."

"Guess what, Dad? I have some news of my own to share."

Evelyn

Tannin parks in the green zone our parents made a sizable donation to have painted on the curb in front of the eight-bedroom, four-story, Georgian-style mansion that's been in the Sinclair family for five generations. I've learned not to bother trying to make excuses for it and everything it stands for, which doesn't explain why I tell people my name is Evelyn Morgan.

"Your parents live in such a dump," James says, lighting a cigarette as soon as he gets the door open and then shivering as he steps into the fog that blankets Sea Cliff where my parents live.

I stand there for a moment, looking up at the place where I was raised, and sigh.

"Hmmm." Tannin takes a few drags off of James's cigarette, looking over her shoulder to make sure Mother, a board member of the California Lung Society, isn't watching. "Maybe I should have told *les parents* you were coming to dinner, Evelyn. But it just slipped my mind."

"It's so unlike you to be such an airhead, Tannin. I'm truly surprised!" James hands her a breath mint.

"No." I step back and bump into the fender. "I'm not going in there, and you can't make me."

"You can tell everyone about your new fake job where you're impersonating a temp." James takes my hand and pulls me onto the sidewalk.

"You just have so much news, Evelyn." Tannin takes my other hand, and they pull me up the stairs.

"So this is how it's going to be, huh?" I shake them loose, smooth my hair, and flick my bangs out of my eyes. "Well, fuck the both of you."

"Oohh," they say at the same time. I ignore them and sprint up the steps and inside the door, which is being held open by one of the live-in housekeepers.

As soon as my black suede flats hit the parquet floor, I realize I've walked into a vipers' nest. My mother, Lila Josephine Reed

Sinclair, is almost forehead to forehead with her best friend and constant enemy, Sissy Ross. Both are dressed almost exactly alike, in jewel-toned cashmere twinsets, Ralph Lauren stretch jodhpurs, and Chanel ballet flats.

"I hear she's ordered a dress, black I hope, which she plans to wear to the benefit on Friday." Sissy's voice is full of salacious enthusiasm for her favorite topic of conversation—gossip. "If she were to ask me, which she hasn't, I'd tell her it's much too early to be seen around town again."

"I'll have to make some excuse, I suppose." Mother sighs. "Under the circumstances."

"Of course, Lila," Sissy readily agrees. "Who could blame you?"

My father, Gerald Maynard Sinclair IV, still in his bespoke English suit, is nursing a tumbler of whiskey on the couch and wisely staying out of the way.

"Evelyn?" Mother stands up, sending the linen napkin she'd laid on her lap to catch crumbs from the cheese and crackers she probably took an hour to pick out but won't touch, floating to the floor. "Evelyn!"

"I'm back." I walk in and give her a kiss on the cheek. She lets me go, a look of utter surprise on her face.

"Evelyn." My father steps in for a quick hug and kiss before sitting back down with a bemused smile. My father has looked six-tyish ever since I can remember. Not movie star sixty but slightly stodgy sixty-plus with a dignified air. I once got him a pipe for Christmas, even though I'd never seen him smoke. I was eight.

"My goodness, Evelyn." Sissy takes me by the upper arms, squeezing a tad too hard as she inspects me from head to foot. "You look so *French*. I just love what you've done to your hair, but then you've always had good hair. So thick and full of body. If it wasn't for your hair, I'd hardly recognize you. It's darling."

"Thank you, Sissy." I give her a tight smile. I can practically see her calculating how many pounds I've lost and who she's going to call first with the news.

"Did you tell Mother and Daddy about your new job, Evelyn?"

Tannin glides in and takes a seat next to our father, pulling James down with her for a ringside seat. She ignores Sissy, something she's been doing since she was fourteen and Sissy made the mistake of sharing her concerns that Tannin was developing a tad too fast with Mother, who then seriously considered sending her to an all-girls' finishing school in Switzerland.

"Job?" Mother looks confused and annoyed. We're springing too much information on her when she was expecting a quiet night in. "What job?"

Aside from a brief stint as "a girl about town," Mother has never held a real job. After she graduated from Bryn Mawr, it was understood she and Daddy would marry, as they had been dating since their Pearson Prep days. She spent a brief period in New York smoking cigarettes in white wrist-length gloves and taking cabs to and from work as a junior editor at *Vogue*, the fare coming to more than she earned in a day.

"Tannin is confused, Mother." I keep my voice level. "What's for dinner?"

"And what about Paris and art school?" My mother is not one to be so easily deterred. "Did you tell your aunt Jane you were leaving the apartment? Or am I going to get another one of her hysterical phone calls because of this?"

"Oh, that's over and done with," I say with cheeriness that borders on open hostility. "And all taken care of."

No one says anything, and the tension level rises with each passing second. It's like I never left.

"My goodness, Lila, I just can't get over how *French* Evelyn looks," Sissy finally says after having her fill of silent drama. "Maybe I should go to Paris and come back a whole new woman."

Alexander

We eat in silence; even Lloyd, who can usually be counted on to chatter about his day at work, has picked up on the tense vibe around the kitchen table.

"I haven't actually accepted any offer," I finally say. "In fact, no official offer has even been made, so this disapproval is premature."

"Alexander"—my mom speaks up before my dad can start yelling again—"it's not that we disapprove."

"Yeah, but you're not too happy about it either," I mumble, deciding to keep the news of my fucked-up almost engagement to myself.

"Another fancy-pants law firm, Son?" my dad asks. "Why? You can work with your mother—"

"Sergio"—she puts a hand on my dad's arm—"we just want you to be happy. And if you think taking a job at this firm is the right thing for you, we support you."

"Is this about the fancy-pants school we wouldn't let you go to?" my dad asks.

"No, Dad. Even though my shrink is of the opinion that it is."

In the ninth grade I was offered a scholarship to Pearson Preparatory. It was way the hell on the other side of town, I'd have to take two buses to get there, but it may as well have been on the other side of the planet. Pearson was where senators sent their kids, where they called Easter break "ski week," and it was where I desperately wanted to be when I found out how different it was from the life I felt my parents were forcing on me.

My mom, who'd gone to school on scholarships and grants herself, agreed Pearson would give me a top-notch education but wasn't sure it was the right environment for me. My father, a labor activist, turned it down on pure ideology—the maintenance and cafeteria staff weren't unionized. So instead of attending Pearson in a blue blazer, white oxford shirt, and tie, I found myself protesting outside of it for a week in jeans and one of my many union T-shirts. Or at least my teenage version of protesting—I spent most of the time ducking behind my old man, cap pulled low over my face, and mouthing union chants that were as familiar to me as the *Brady Bunch* theme.

They never unionized, my dad was arrested for obstructing the sidewalk (my mom got the charges dropped), and I went back to Dolores Park High School, where I hung out with my loudmouth friends, ditched, pretended to smoke, drank a little, dated a lot, and did everything short of getting arrested to torture my parents for not letting me go to Pearson.

"Your patients do anything supercute today, Lloyd?" Nayelli asks her husband, a pediatric surgeon, in a panicky voice. Even she doesn't like where the conversation is headed.

"As a matter of fact, I had one today ask me if he could get the heart of a lion," Lloyd starts.

I resume eating, knowing this conversation isn't anywhere near over.

Evelyn

Mother corners me outside the downstairs powder room, where I retreated just before dessert was served. As soon as I did, I realized I'd reinforced suspicions that I'm bulimic.

"Is this about Thad?" she asks, bringing up my last (and only serious) boyfriend, Thaddeus Preston Merrick IV, who after we broke up I used as a reason for wanting to move to Paris.

We had been dating for ages, and our inevitable nuptials were the buzz as the San Francisco society wedding of the near future. It was just a matter of me accepting his great-great-grandmother's diamond-and-sapphire platinum ring, which he'd already sent to the jeweler to be sized (my mother helpfully providing my ring size), and agreeing to a time for our lawyers to meet to draw up the prenuptial agreement. We were a sickeningly perfect match—our families ran in the same circles, we had comparable levels of wealth and education, we worshipped infrequently at the same church—but he didn't make my heart beat faster.

If I were to ask my mother and maybe even my father about love and marriage, I'm afraid they'd answer that how one's heart reacts when the other person enters a room is a silly and inconsequential thing when considering a proper mate.

"No, Mother. This has nothing to do with Thad." Who I haven't thought of for more than a year, by the way, I'm tempted to add.

"He's married now," she adds. "He ended up eloping in Fiji or some such irrational place with that girl he started seeing after you decided to spend some time in Paris."

"Yes, I know, Mother," I answer her. "You faxed me the announcement."

I knew Thad wasn't the one when he surprised me with a complete tea service for my birthday. Not lingerie, a first edition of a favorite novel, or even an innocuous gift card, but a twenty-four-piece tea service. As soon as I opened the box, I knew I couldn't marry him. What kind of man gives a woman he's supposed to be passionately in love with a tea service? Even an antique French one rumored to have belonged to Marie Antoinette? As I looked at each cup, so thin and fine I could almost see through it, I saw us a few years from then, having stilted dinner conversations, retreating to separate rooms as soon as we could while our picture-perfect progeny took it all in for their future therapy sessions. Thad, of course, thought I was joking when I told him about my concerns. He'd already picked out the antique sideboard to display the service on, and we were to use it at our engagement party for our parents' friends before hitting a rented club to celebrate with our friends. I realized Thad was more like a brother to me and couldn't be further from being the love of my life . . . or rather a *step*brother since I'd had sex with him and it would mean I'd been having sex with my brother. Anyway, all Thad cared about was that his tea set trumped any tea-related gift I'd ever gotten from anyone else. For Thad the thrill was in coming out on top and it didn't really matter if I came with him.

"In fact"—Mother lowers her voice—"I ran into him just the other day and he asked about you."

"Mother. And I'm not interested even if he wasn't married. Plus, the sex wasn't so great," I blurt out.

Tannin once broke up with a perfectly decent guy after he gave her a drugstore Chia Pet for her birthday. He thought it was funny, she didn't. He soon found himself with a Chia Pet lodged in the window of his Mercedes, and no Tannin. She was practically engaged to another guy by the next week who she ended up breaking up with due to his lack of sense of humor. Thad would never have given me a Chia Pet. To be perfectly crude, Thad barely went down on me.

"Evelyn, what on earth does good sex have to do with marriage?" Mother's cheeks turn pink, like mine do, with exasperation.

"A lot?"

I've had plenty of good sex in my life, even a few near great experiences, and yes, it should matter. It's not on the top of my list, but it's pretty high up there—somewhere between being a good dancer and not clipping his toenails in the living room.

"Such a silly girl." Mother sighs and gives me a stiff hug. "Have you seen Ying? We need to go over your menu for Wednesday. I'm thinking soups."

tuesday . . .

chapter seven
All in a Day's Work

Alexander

I take my time, nursing a cup of coffee from the Reed kiosk down the street while standing in front of the Wish 'n' Wash trying to delay opening the grate as long as possible. My goal is to spend the day working my ass off while searching my soul.

"I hate that place. I'd rather burn my clothes than use those machines." A guy walking his dog pauses to let his mutt lift its leg and piss on the grate and he shares his thoughts with me at the same time. "The guy who owns it wants to knock it down and build lofts. He's an asshole."

"So I hear." I watch the little river of yellow make its way to the curb. "And that about sums it up."

"Someone should firebomb that place," he adds as he begins to walk away.

"Hold on now," I call after him, but he keeps walking.

With no reason to delay any longer, I open the grate and head into the storeroom in search of tools and cleaning supplies. I throw everything into a bucket and dig out a shovel, since I have a feeling I'm going to need it.

I drop everything onto the middle of the floor and almost keep walking upstairs to put on my suit. I can't. I owe it to myself, Pete, and my parents to at least pretend to wrestle with my decision to either fight the good fight with my mother or go for the glamour and glory as a lawyer for Williams, Heller, Lincoln.

My dad always said to start from the bottom and work my way

up, so I begin with pulling up loose linoleum tiles and tossing them into the beat-up trash can, which is filled with single socks, T-shirts that have seen better days, and old dryer sheets and newspapers.

After the fourth trip to the Dumpster out back, I've tossed aside my T-shirt and start demolishing the pathetic counters by the dryers. I duck underneath to try to wedge the blade of the shovel between the counter and the wall, and discover there's even graffiti down here. This place really is a pit.

"Alexander?"

At the sound of Sigrid's voice, my head meets the underside of plywood, and then everything goes black.

Evelyn

It's early, before seven, so I take a cab to UGotIt and have the driver leave me off a couple blocks away just in case anyone else is also getting to the office early. As I round the corner and look up to the fifth floor, the lights are off and the place looks deserted.

I let out a breath of relief until I realize I have no way of getting inside. I check my watch; the bagel guy is supposed to be here in ten minutes. I square my shoulders and approach the security desk, determined to convince the sleepy-looking guard behind it that I have legitimate business here.

"Hi?" I wait for him to look up from the copy of *The Wall Street Journal* he's reading. "Hi. I work up on the fifth floor. At UGotIt?"

"Uh-huh." He yawns.

"I'm supposed to set up the conference room before everyone gets here and I don't have a key." I shift from foot to foot.

"Uh-huh." He gives me a why-should-I-give-a-shit? blink.

"I'm a temp," I offer unnecessarily.

"Nester"—this from a fellow at the newsstand that is tucked into an alcove by the security desk—"get up, go let her in so she can do her job, and then you can go back to sleep."

"Shut up, Hilmi," the security guard snaps. He makes me wait for a few more seconds before he pushes himself away from the desk and gets up. "You have to wait until I help out this guy here."

This guy turns out to be from the bagel place. "Delivery for UGotIt and Evelyn Morgan up on the fifth floor."

"That would be me! I'm Evelyn Morgan," I say, with such false enthusiasm I expect even the bagel guy to ask to see some ID. Instead he sets the bags on the counter and waits. "Oh! Can I pay with a credit card?"

"Sure. I just need to call it in." He reaches for his cell phone just as I realize that Evelyn Morgan doesn't have a credit card.

"I'll just pay cash if that's okay."

"Works for me." The guy shrugs. He couldn't care less.

I hand over four twenty-dollar bills, and grab the bags. "So, can you let me go up now?"

Alexander

When I was five, my *tía* Lupita pinched my cheek as she told my mother I would grow up to be "a real lady-killer." They both laughed in a throaty way that scared me and then sent me off to play with my cousins. Instead of joining in on chasing the neighbor's cat, I climbed a tree and refused to come down until well after dark.

After a soggy nightmare that night, I confessed to my father I was a killer in the making. He didn't laugh but stopped changing the sheets on my twin-size bed and carefully explained what she meant by "lady-killer." He did this even though he had to be up in a couple of hours for work and had only gotten home a few hours before from his other job. The way my dad explained it, being a lady-killer sounded interesting—way more interesting than being a fireman, some superhero's sidekick, or even the superhero himself. I was a lady-killer.

I had my first girlfriend, a first grader, by the end of the week. And according to that one session with the New York shrink Sigrid made me go to, my attitude on women, romance, and relationships has pretty much remained the same since then. I'm what women's magazines call "a player" but with the possibility of being rehabilitated. At least this is what the shrink told Sigrid.

Sigrid.

I open my eyes and stare up at the ceiling. There's even graffiti up there. I turn my head slightly, and the tip of Sigrid's pointy shoe is just an inch from my eye. "Hey. You're here."

"Is this what you left me for, Alexander?" She stares down at me. "What you left your job for? To do manual labor in a fucking Laundromat?" She looks around, clearly disgusted and not the least bit impressed.

I sit up, rubbing the top of my head, not surprised she didn't ask me if I was okay. "I got fired from my job, and I own this fucking Laundromat. I'm in the process of renovating it," I retort.

"I can see that, Alexander. We need to talk." She walks out and stands on the sidewalk.

"We could have talked over the phone," I say to myself.

"Alexander?" There's an edge to her voice, she's close to cracking.

"Coming, Siggy." I might be a jerk, but I'm not an asshole. "You want some coffee or something?"

It took a lot for her to get on a plane and fly out here, and I feel bad about that; if she'd called me first, I could have told her not to bother. I take my time pulling on my T-shirt and locking up. When I'm done, I have no choice but to face her. I look at her, in her black trousers, black sweater, black shawl perfectly draped over her shoulders, with her black stilettos firmly planted on the sidewalk. People walking up the street to catch the train over on Church Street slow down to look at her. She looks good, she always does, but she looks so out of place here.

"Coffee would be a start," she says in a tone of voice that's as cold as the morning air.

I walk a little ahead of her to the café across the street, nixing the idea of a cup of Reed's since we'd have to take it back to my place. I order us a couple of cups, and when I reach into my back pocket, I find the coaster from the bar at JFK.

"Alexander!" Sigrid snaps. "Coffee?"

I pick up both cups and carry them to the table but don't sit down. I lean over, kiss Sigrid on her smooth forehead. "I'm sorry, Sigrid."

"What do you mean, you're fucking sorry?" People look up from their lattes and half-pound muffins. "Sorry, Alexander? You're sorry?"

"Come on." I grab her hand and lead her back to my place.

Evelyn

I make a slow turn around the conference room table where I've set up the buffet, separating the varieties of bagels into pyramids. I nudge the two stacks of paper cups for coffee I brewed in the kitchenette and orange juice I ran out to buy at the Walgreens when I realized there weren't any knives for the cream cheese and lox. So far my day's work has cost me a hundred dollars, and it's not even 9:00 A.M. yet.

I fan out the paper napkins next to the plates and stand aside as the employees of UGotIt start to trickle in.

"Good morning." I help out as needed, circulate, introduce myself as the temp when asked, and put hostessing skills I had no idea I possessed to good use. Mother would be proud if she never discovered the specifics.

"Evelyn." The crowd parts and a few people scamper out of the way as Ted comes into the conference room.

"Good morning, Ted." I hand him his bagel.

"Thanks." He doesn't even glance at it before setting it on the table with the rest of the bagels. "I need to talk to you in my office."

"All right." My heart starts thumping like a bunny rabbit in a pillowcase. "Is there some sort of problem?"

"I'd prefer if we discussed this in my office." He scoops up his bagel and a whole container of fat-free cream cheese.

"I understand." I pick up my cup of tea and follow him out.

I'm a tea person, big surprise. Loose tea, bigger surprise. At home, on windowsills and tucked in between the art books on my bookshelves is my rapidly growing collection of teapots and related accessories. And when I say "growing," I mean out of control growth. Like an untreated melanoma of sorts, but rendered in porcelain, sterling silver, and bone china.

I have no idea how this started, besides preferring tea to coffee and having stated such when asked which I cared for. After the first few teacups and pots, I was slightly bemused, but appreciative all the same. Now all I can do is smile, send a prompt thank-you note, and make space where there is none to display it. James has bucked the trend by giving me an assortment of enormous lifelike and sculptural dildos from Good Vibrations, but I can't very well display those. And Tannin likes to arrange surprise trips to Fiji or Helsinki and, once, a spa that specializes in nothing but colonics and near starvation cuisine.

I take a seat in front of Ted's desk, noticing that the business cards I labored over are still sitting in the middle of his desk, where I left them last night.

Ted begins to dismantle his bagel. First cutting it in half with a plastic knife, then scooping out the inside with a spoon. He sets the hollowed-out bagel shell to one side and starts to eat the bread part, dabbing each clump with cream cheese while he clicks through his e-mail.

I shift in my chair, wondering if I should just confess and let security escort me out before more people arrive. If I go quietly, which I plan to do, it shouldn't make it to the papers. The last thing I want is my name and picture in the *S.F. Express* for everyone to gloat over. And they'd probably use an old picture from when I was fat, so I wouldn't even get the satisfaction of seeing my new bangs rendered in newsprint.

"So how do you like working here, Evelyn?" There is a glob of cream cheese in the corner of his mouth.

"Very well, thank you." I focus on his forehead, unsure if I should tell him.

"Give me a little background."

"Background? Oh! My background. My family is from here, San Francisco." I swallow, trying to mentally edit my education to what is most applicable. "School-wise, I, uh, took some classes at the Art Institute in, uh, computer design and technology."

"So you know your way around computers and have an art background." Ted nods as if he already knew this somehow. "Exactly what I need, Evelyn. Exactly. Talk to Paul from HR. Tell him to call the temp agency and take care of all the details for transferring you over full-time."

"I'm sorry?" Did he just offer me a job?

"So how do you know Tannin Reed-Sinclair?" Ted now begins to fill the bagel shell with cream cheese.

"We went to school together." Which is true.

"So you've known her and her family for a while," Ted says, more for his own benefit than for mine.

"Um. I guess you could say that. I'm not close or anything, to her family. I mean, she's a good friend but, you know, very different from me." I'm saying too much. I take a gulp of tea and wind up scalding the roof of my mouth.

"Ted." A woman, obviously very annoyed, marches up to his desk and plants herself between me and Ted.

"I'm in a meeting, *Jessica*." Now Ted looks annoyed.

"Like I really give a shit, *Ted*." Her voice is raspy, as if it were coming out of a sixty-year-old lounge singer who's seen much better days. "Someone sat at my desk. I told you I didn't want anyone sitting at my desk while I was gone."

"I'll go." I stand up. I shouldn't be here. I don't even officially work at UGotIt, and from the way they're spitting out each other's names, I can tell there's more than a desk that's come between these two.

"No, Evelyn, you stay. *Jessica,* this is my new executive assistant." Ted points at me, and my gulp feels like it echoes in the silence that follows. I give Jessica a lame wave, and Ted continues. "My liaison. You can tell her what your problem is and she'll take care of it."

"I'll take care of it?" I look back and forth between them. Now would be the time to make my permanent exit. Forget this ever happened and let James explain who the crazy woman was who pretended to work at UGotIt for a day.

"Right. She'll take care of it, *Ted*. Is it her job to make sure you wipe your mouth too, *Ted*? Because if it is, *she* isn't doing a very good job of assisting you."

"Knock, knock!" We all turn to look at a woman standing in the doorway of Ted's office with a coffee carafe in her hand. "There you are, Evelyn. We're out of coffee in the conference room?"

"I'll take care of it." I stand up, nod to Ted and Jessica, and make my way to the kitchenette to brew more coffee.

Alexander

"I'm here because of work, Alexander." Her voice is in rhythm with the click of her heels as she climbs the stairs behind me. "So don't get any ideas."

"Okay." I'm willing to let her have the upper hand since I don't want any more drama and I'm pretty certain I don't want to have sex with her. Almost positive. Pretty sure. We'll see how it goes once we're inside. I unlock the door and step aside, holding it open for her. "I won't."

She breezes past me, leaving a trail of her perfume, Shalimar. "My office is working on a project, and they sent me here to check up on it." She's holding her purse as if it's a shield instead of embossed crocodile. "I have to attend an event tonight or else I wouldn't have bothered."

"I understand, Sigrid." I nod twice. A third nod might be construed by her hypervigilant state as insincere. "This is purely business."

"Fuck you, Alexander." She starts to cry.

I take her hand, lead her to the couch, and sit her down. I beeline for the bathroom, bring out a roll of toilet paper, and hand it to her. She looks at it and cries harder.

"I have to go to this fucking party," she says between sniffles. "And there was no way for me to tell my cunt boss I couldn't go because my asshole boyfriend walked out on me. I had to fly all the way here, pretending you were with me."

"Sigrid?" I take a deep breath, God help me. "Do you want me to go with you to the event tonight?"

"It's the least you could fucking do for me, Alexander." She blows her nose, getting it together surprisingly fast. "I'll tell everyone at the office you had to stay behind, some family thing, and I'll go on vacation and then let the word out that we've decided to go our separate ways."

"Sounds like a plan." I sit down, feeling the coaster in my pocket. I pull it out and look at it.

"What's that?" she asks, momentarily distracted from her agenda.

"I found it at the airport." I set it down on the coffee table between us, propping it against the cell phone Rodney had the scary receptionist at Williams, Heller, Lincoln give me yesterday. The cell phone chirps to life, and Rodney Heller's name pops up on the screen.

"Whatever. I have your black suit at the hotel." Sigrid stands up after seeing who's calling. "Be there at five-thirty, and please shower before. Under the circumstances, I don't want you in my shower. And then that's it. I never want to see you or hear from you again after tonight. Understand?"

"Completely." I stand up and guide her to the door. "Do you need me to call you a cab, Sigrid?"

Evelyn

I stand by the windows as two guys from tech maneuver in a couple of filing cabinets and an unpainted slab door that, when put together, will function as a desk. For me. As Ted's new executive assistant, it has been deemed necessary for me to have an office. Since space is tight, this new office is in the room that houses the Foosball table, dartboard, and beanbags circled around the big-screen TV that's hooked up to at least three different video game consoles.

"So it's true." James wanders in, still in his coat and scarf from one of his smokes. "You really are a freak, Evelyn. And coming from me, that means a lot."

"Thank you." I busy myself trying to untangle cords and plugs for my computer.

"For God's sake, let the nerds do that."

"I don't want to bother them." I shrug, putting the wires down. When Ted marched me over and told them to set me up in there, I got a decidedly hostile feeling from them. "I can do it myself."

"If they're giving you a hard time, I'll forward my phone to them and let them deal with it." James may not do a lot of work, but he's incredibly busy. "That'll teach them to fuck with a friend of mine."

"Speaking of which. Ted and Jessica?" I ask, knowing James will take the bait. James loves to gossip; it's something he has in common with Mother and Tannin. "Is there something I should know as Ted's executive assistant and liaison?"

"Old news, girl. They used to bone but broke up. She went on three-week paid vacation, got her title bumped to Art Director, but no office. From what I hear, she's pretty pissed Ted has given you the rumpus room."

"I didn't ask him to give me this office or any office. He just did. It seemed easier to go along with it." I wander around with a wastepaper basket, clearing away the half-full cans of soda and beef jerky wrappers, and straighten the plastic video game cases that are stacked in an unstable tower on the floor.

"Please, Evelyn. Ted's not smart enough to use you as a tool for emotional revenge." James plops down on one of the beanbags, grimaces, and stands back up again. "He's using you as his fall girl."

I go back to the mess of wires, willing James with every cell of my body to just stop talking. He doesn't.

"UCLA MBA Ted—has he told you he got his MBA at UCLA yet?—found out how much time people were spending in here farting into the carpet and drinking free soda, and he was not happy. So if you're here, Ted's executive assistant, his eyes and ears, they'll have no choice but to keep their slacking asses at their desks."

I stand there between the makeshift desk and beanbags, and realize I again have a choice to make. I take a deep breath and ask, "So do you think you can get the tech guys in here to help me hook up the computer?"

chapter eight

Fun and Head Games

Evelyn

"There's no time, James." I bat away his hand and the curling iron he's holding. "Just put in a ponytail and be done with it."

"A ponytail?" Disgust drips from every word.

"You ready to go?" Tannin calls from downstairs. "The car's here and we're going to be late."

"A nice ponytail. Please, James," I plead with him. I'm fully trussed up, made up, and the only thing left to put up is my hair.

"I don't care if we're late." Tannin's voice gets louder as she starts up the stairs. "We could just skip the whole thing and order pizza."

"Just because you insisted we take the train here doesn't mean I should have to sacrifice my vision, Evelyn," James says.

"And Chinese food," Tannin continues, her high heels clicking across the wood floor of my hall. "I have plenty of Diet Coke, so we're all set on drinks."

"Do what you want. Just please, hurry." I look at the clock on the wall. It's ten after seven, and it'll take at least half an hour to get to where the benefit, gala, or whatever it is, is being held.

"Fine." James picks up a paddle brush and starts to comb my hair back into a high ponytail.

"Are you guys coming?" Tannin stands in the doorway, illuminated from behind by the hallway sconces.

I gasp. Even James gasps.

"Thanks!" She gives us a huge grin. She turns a slow circle so we can see her from all angles. The top of her dress is low-cut, in the back and front, but made of, thank God, black satin, the skirt made up of delicate white lace, and that's about it.

"Tannin, you can't go outside like that." I stand up and grab my robe and throw it over her. "I can see your *religion*."

"So?" She walks over to the mirror and checks her makeup. "It'll give those bitches something to chatter about."

"They'll chatter, all right." James snorts. "You'll be the talk of the night."

I shoot James a look. If he's not going to help, he should at least not encourage her. "Have you considered, Tannin, that this is an American Heart Association benefit and, perhaps, some of these people actually have bad hearts?"

Tannin shrugs. "I doubt that any of them have a pulse, Evelyn."

Both of our doorbells ring simultaneously. Mother has sent around a car to make sure we get there on time, on time being twenty minutes ago.

"I'll go see about the car," James says, and disappears. He's wearing his deep purple velvet suit with matching suede platform boots.

I look down at my black, very opaque dress and decide, once again, it's up to me to be the voice of reason and the provider of panties. I reach under my skirt and start tugging.

"What are you doing?"

"Saving your bare ass." I hand over my extra-control high-waisted brief. "Put it on."

"You've got to be kidding." She backs away, shaking her head.

I hold my hand up to stop her. "Put it on, Tannin, or I'll tell Mother about your little ecstasy prank."

"Fine, but if I get some French STD, *I'm* telling Mother I got it from your granny panties." She slips it on, and through the miracle of spandex, something I can get on my size-twelve body contracts enough to fit her size-zero frame. "Happy?"

"Ecstatic."

Alexander

Sigrid may never want to see me again, but she wants to be seen with me looking my best, down to a new pair of $2^{(x)}$ist trunks.

When I got to the Park Hyatt, after demolishing most of the Wish 'n' Wash and filling the Dumpster to the top, I was showered and shaved with a couple of Band-Aids on my fingers. Without so much as a hello or what happened to your fingers, Sigrid shoved a garment bag at me and told me to get dressed. I almost cried when I unzipped the bag.

Inside was my black Armani Collezioni three-button, notched-collar suit with flat-front, straight-leg trousers. It was the suit we'd picked out together a few weeks ago with the unspoken understanding I'd wear it on the night we celebrated at our engagement dinner with friends and family.

I look down at my watch, the David Yurman with a black alligator strap I kept on the dresser and one of the few pricey gifts Sigrid ever gave me. "Siggy?"

I get up to straighten my tie, Hermès dark blue and black basket weave, presented to me by Sigrid in bed the night before the almost, not quite, and never to happen pretend surprise proposal.

She's been holed up in the bathroom since I came out of the closet, so to speak, and I'm starting to wonder if this whole thing about her having to attend an event for work wasn't some kind of trap to get me to come over and put on a nice suit so she could kill me.

She opens the door and stands there, looking like she's stepped out of one of the oversize pages of *W* magazine, her personal Bible. The dress she's wearing is an intense shade of red, like highly oxygenated blood, strapless, and comes up high on her trim thighs. The front is folded into origamilike, undulating fabric waves that frame her tanned torso. Her very blond hair, touched up so regularly that I have no idea of the true color, is scraped back in front and so tight I'm wondering how she manages to blink. The rest is hanging down in a long ponytail.

"I was wondering if you could help me with my hair," she says in a soft voice. "I just can't seem to manage to do anything with it."

"Sure." I circle to stand behind her, noticing that the dress is cut low in the back and the skirt is gathered so it reminds me of red theater curtains going up right before a show. "What do you want me to do?"

"Whatever you want."

What I want to do is go to the hardware store to buy a gallon of Spackle. On the bed, my phone rings. Sigrid walks over and picks it up, looks at the name, and then tosses it back on the bed.

"What's this thing we're going to, by the way?" I ask, desperate to make some conversation that has nothing to do with me staring at her naked back or the person who's called me four times today.

"It's for the American Heart Association. My company"—Sigrid is one of those sharp-edged PR girls TV networks create shows about—"is partnering with the West Coast branch on a few things this year, and I'm here to make nice with the natives.

"Who's Rodney Heller?" she asks, going to stand in front of

the dresser, where she's laid out her Mason Pearson brush, ties, pins, and bottle of holding spray. It's funny to see all of it here, as if she's transported her vanity table from her apartment to some business-class hotel room in downtown San Francisco.

"Just some guy. He works with Pete. You remember Pete?" I've been avoiding taking his call, but I know I'll have to give Rodney an answer soon.

I reach for her ponytail, braid it quickly, and then wait for her to hand me something to pin it up and back with. "That's the best I can do."

"It's perfect." She looks at herself in the mirror. "You look great, Alexander."

"Thanks." I give her a smile. "You look stunning, Sigrid."

I walk over to the door and watch as she gathers her purse and shawl and realize how easy it would be to just say yes to Sigrid, yes to Rodney, and yes to not having to think for myself while wearing a nice suit.

Evelyn

The new, lighter me is flattered while the old, fatter me is hurt that people I've known for years through my parents have no idea who I am.

"Evelyn? My goodness, dear, isn't it remarkable what a little change in hairstyle can do to a person" more than one person exclaims after introducing herself to me only to be informed by Tannin that I'm not some visiting East Coast cousin.

I walk over to the buffet table, ask a waiter for a glass of water, and watch as James and Tannin expertly waltz around the dance floor. Even with my return from Paris with my new haircut, Tannin's almost naked lower body is still the buzz of the ball. On our way in, I had to walk quickly to avoid getting my picture taken when she stopped in front of the photographers. The last thing I need is to see my face and real name in the papers.

What would my boss say? I'm supposed to be at work right now arranging his Netflix queue so he doesn't go a day without a movie, making sure his Goodreads.com profile page is updated with the right books, cleaning up the spelling and grammar on both his MySpace and Facebook pages, and working out a color-coded calendar that includes all manner of UCLA alumni association events and mixers.

"So what's this about a job?" My father comes up to stand next to me and takes my arm, and we start walking around in a slow semicircle so Mother doesn't catch us not contributing to the success of the event by standing in one spot and having an actual conversation.

"Oh, it's nothing." I smile placidly as we pass people we know.

"Nothing?" he asks.

When it comes to money and business, I can say anything to my father. It's all the other stuff he gets uncomfortable hearing about. My father has worked only for the family business, the last twenty-five years as its president, and he'll stay there until the very end. Sinclairs never retire; they die in their executive leather chairs. For him a job is not "nothing," it's a way of life.

"It's just something for now. Until I figure things out, Daddy."

So far I've figured out being Ted's executive assistant has meant following him around the office while taking down random notes as thoughts occur to him and, most important, acting as an intermediary between him and the rest of the company.

Ted does not want to deal with anyone one-on-one. As his

"gatekeeper," I have to figure who and what to bother him with. Right after I cleared away the last of the bagels and set up the computer (on my own), people began to e-mail me and line up at the Foosball table to request an audience with MBA Ted, as he's known, or more accurately, to have me deal with Ted so they didn't have to. When I'd gathered a half dozen names and issues I could not in good conscience as an interloper handle, I reserved the conference room, where Ted worked his way around the table, issued edicts, and sent everyone back to their cubicles. I sat to the side, taking more notes, and made sure one of his many UCLA Anderson School of Management mugs was always filled with coffee, black, two Equals.

As soon as the meeting was over and after I was dismissed from Ted's office, where he recapped the whole thing, I found a line of the same people in front of my desk asking for clarification and permission to go ahead and implement a course of action Ted hadn't gotten around to addressing.

"There is always a place for you at the firm, Evelyn."

"I know, Daddy."

I could take a job at the firm and coast along on his generous coattails complete with a corner office and an assistant for my assistant and not be expected to do much more than show up every so often for a job especially created for me, interoffice stationery designer, where I wouldn't cause much trouble and could make use of my half-million-dollar education. Wealth and privilege are part of my parents' (and my) DNA, and they just can't understand why I haven't grown into my sense of entitlement. I'm almost thirty, after all, and my idealistic years should be well behind me.

"It wouldn't be so bad, working for your old man."

I pat his hand and we keep walking.

We, me, Tannin, the people we grew up with, were never expected to earn an actual living while stretching our wings, but we were expected to do something. As our parents have the business and philanthropic world covered, we, their progeny, were forced into uncharted territory. At least this was the idea. While my peers from Pearson Prep, a lot of whom are here mixing seamlessly with their parents, have tried to make it as writers, filmmakers, or founders of innovative, if unprofitable, companies, I became a struggling art student and Tannin a party girl simply because we could afford to.

"Thanks, Daddy, but I think what I'm doing right now could really be something." Something most likely illegal and definitely insane. "I'm not feeling too well, jet lag. Would you tell Mother for me?"

"Of course, Evelyn." He gives me a concerned look, and I half expect him to press the back of his hand to my forehead to see if I have a temperature. "Have Ike run you home. I'm sure the situation outside the hotel has cleared up by now."

"Daddy, I'll be fine." I make my way onto the dance floor, where James and Tannin are now doing the hustle. "Guys?"

"Evelyn, come dance with us!" Tannin shimmies, raising her skinny arms over her head.

"I'm going home. I'll catch a cab. Don't worry about me."

"You sure?" James asks, but he doesn't stop dancing.

I watch them dance for a few more seconds before I make my way out of the ballroom, my relief growing with every step that takes me farther away.

I can get a cab to UGotIt, have one of the security guards let me into the offices so I can catch up on the work I didn't get to do while sitting in on Ted's meetings, and no one ever needs to know.

Alexander

I take hold of Sigrid's elbow between my thumb and forefinger in the elevator and figure it's a good sign that she doesn't jerk away.

Wait, that's a bad sign. We're broken up. We're over. I'm just here to complete the picture, like a very big purse.

"So where to?" I ask when we step outside the lobby. "Do we need to get a cab, or can you walk in those shoes?"

"We can walk from here, I think." Sigrid, as a rule, does not walk anywhere. This immediately makes me suspicious.

"Are you sure?" The bell captain makes the universal can-I-get-you-a-cab? motion, and I wave him off. "I guess we're walking."

"Alexander?" The way Sigrid says it makes my hair stand on end. "Do you love me? At all? Did you ever?"

I keep walking, passing a steady stream of tourists in their fleece pullovers with embroidered Golden Gate Bridges on the front.

"Alexander?"

There is no right answer to this question, and that's the exact reason why Sigrid has asked it. In public.

"Sigrid, baby, what we had was great." I decide to be honest, because it's easier than telling her what I really feel. "With you I was a whole different person, the person I thought I wanted to be."

Sigrid smiles at me and moves in closer, snuggling up to my side like she used to do when she was happy or had spotted friends.

"That's exactly what I told Dr. Ferber." Dr. Ferber is Sigrid's shrink, the one she made me see and who she runs everything by. "Dr. Ferber said you just needed time to get comfortable with this new phase in your life. Our life."

"Yeah." Dr. Ferber is an ass who charges $175 for a fifty-minute hour to tell Sigrid what she wants to hear. "I guess Dr. Ferber is right. I need more time."

"Exactly!" I feel the jolt of energy snap through her body. "Exactly! So here's my thought . . ." Sigrid has always presented her thoughts as spontaneous bursts of inspiration when really what she'll say next was always a foregone conclusion. "You stay out here for a while, I'll go back to New York, work my connections, and land a PR job here in the city, and you can start at another firm and we start over fresh. Dr. Ferber gave me the name of a good therapist, and your place really has a lot of potential."

"That sounds . . . Sigrid, it sounds sort of like, not sort of like, *exactly* like the life we had back in New York. And I was under the impression that that life wasn't working out for either of us."

"Alexander, I'm willing to take my share of the blame for certain shortfalls on my part." Sigrid keeps walking, and I'm starting to wonder if she knows where we're going. "But you need to make some changes too."

"I'm sure I do, Sigrid, but I'm not so sure—"

"And you can start by making them now." She comes to a stop across the street from a picket line of union workers in front of the Roosevelt Hotel, where police are directing traffic but ignoring a line of double-parked black limos that are responsible for the jam. "We're here," Sigrid says in the snaky voice she uses when she knows she has the advantage.

My parents marched with César Chávez, I still can't eat grapes without a twinge of guilt, and I have never, ever crossed a picket line in my life. "I can't, Sigrid."

"This is exactly what I mean, Alexander," she spits. "You never did love me, did you?"

"If we were honest for once, Siggy, we'd agree that feeling

was mutual." Her eyebrows draw together at my very lawyerly answer.

I give her a kiss on the top of the head, and as I'm walking away, I slip the ringing cell phone out of my pocket. "Yeah, hey, Rodney. . . . Tomorrow, nine A.M. See you then."

wednesday . . .

chapter nine
The N-Judah and the J-Church

Evelyn

"Pardon me, ma'am?" I look up at the small, gnomelike woman whose shopping bag is currently lodged in my sternum. Even if I wanted to get up and give her my seat, I couldn't, as I'm practically being impaled by her fresh produce. "Ma'am! Would you like my seat?"

She continues to stare off to the side, ignoring me, even though there's only a mass of jackets, coats, and sweaters, tightly packed like some crazy human quilt, to look at as the N-Judah rattles down the track, past coffee shops, squashed-together homes, and double-parked cars.

"Ma'am?" I try to get her attention one more time before giving up. Assured that I've done my best to do the right thing, I resume knitting (yet another scarf) while trying not to bruise her bok choy and hiding behind my bangs.

The guy in the seat across the aisle rolls his eyes at me over his copy of the *San Francisco Express* when I chance another look at her to make sure there hasn't been a delayed acceptance of my offer. I smile lamely at him and keep knitting, lest I get singled out as the rude knitter who won't give up her seat to an elderly Chinese lady burdened with overflowing pink plastic shopping bags. Now if I was ten months pregnant and knitting, I might be justified in keeping my seat.

I look up again when he leans toward me, folding over the top of his newspaper, so we're only a couple feet apart. I have no choice but to acknowledge him; I can't ignore him without seeming rude. Still, my eyes dart down to his lap to make sure I won't be faced with any unexpected surprise.

"They act," he says just loud enough so the people around us can hear, "like this is the last helicopter out of Saigon."

I open my mouth and then close it like a goldfish that's suddenly found itself in an airless and dry environment. He chuckles and goes back to reading his paper, as if making insensitive racial remarks on a crowded San Francisco light-rail train is normal chitchat. Should I say something? Should I storm off the train (if I could manage to get out) in protest? Alert the driver there is a bigot onboard? Still, I look around before I let myself complete the thought. Would it kill her to step back a few inches? With any luck she'll get off before we descend into the tunnel at Market and Church streets that will take us into downtown. Of course, if she's heading to the Civic Center Farmers' Market, it means at least six more stops of me breathing on her dinner.

I skip a few stitches and unravel methodically, determined not to let this situation get the best of me. Tannin, who I met on my way out the door as she was coming home, offered me a ride, but I turned her down. Evelyn Morgan takes the train to work, just like everyone else at UGotIt.

"I can't do it, baby. It grosses me out," a male voice says directly behind me.

"And you think your cum tastes that great?" a female voice hisses back. "Like butterscotch pudding?"

"This is different, babycakes." He lowers his voice, but since he's less than two feet away from both of my ears, it really doesn't make a difference. "That's blood. *Old blood.* Blood that's been hanging around in there for like a month or whatever."

I feel my face burn red hot, and I duck my head, knitting faster. Even the bok choy lady glances over at the couple, shooting them a dirty look.

"Don't get mad, baby, you know I don't like salty food, and it already tastes a little salty, even when you're not on the rag."

I make a move to stand up, desperate to flee and hail a cab to take me the rest of the way to UGotIt, even though I'll have to crawl over people to get out.

"You are such an asshole!" she yells, and begins to sob, quite loudly. There's movement, and I can feel bodies leaning out of the way to let her out as the train slows down for the next stop.

We all, including myself, turn to look at him, still seated and not making a move to go after her.

"Fuck!" And with that he gets up and off the train.

Bok Choy Lady mumbles to herself as more people cram themselves on the train, but ignores the empty seats.

I shift around and hope the guy next to me doesn't have to get up before I do. There is no way he'll be able to exit the train unless he plans on grabbing the overhead bar and swinging out Tarzan style.

I look over at him, trying to gauge where he's heading by his outfit—jeans, a drab woolly sweater, and a pristine Kangol tweed hat with a sporty off-center orange stripe running across it, and nestled over the top of the hat are an enormous pair of expensive looking earphones—his head bobbing to the music, iPod in hand, his finger constantly spinning and clicking but never losing the beat. He could be either a CEO at a cutting-edge ad agency or a café barista.

I glance over at Mr. Bigot, cringe, and knit faster. He's reading the Events page of the _Express,_ and it's covered with pictures of the "Spectacular Soirée," as the headline reads, I was forced to go to last night under penalty of being exiled from polite society and disinherited by my mother.

I can just make out my arm in one of the pictures. I know it's mine because it shows up as a solid white, oblong shape hovering almost outside the frame as Tannin beams, front and center, her own twiggy arms coquettishly entwined in front of her, drawing attention to the sheerness of her dress, rather than hiding it. Only my sister could turn (my) granny panties into a fashion statement.

So Tannin gets a toothy shot in this morning's *San Francisco Express* along with a mention gushing about her fashion daring (seems wearing a black control-top body shaper under a ten-thousand-dollar white lace dress is all the rage somewhere, or at least it is now), and I got to make nice with eighty-year-old rich, deaf ladies who kept asking me if I knew Evelyn Reed-Sinclair and how much I looked like her, all while I was sucking in my stomach and worrying I smelled, well, less than fresh as a summer's eve.

The train comes to a sudden halt to avoid crashing into a double-parked delivery truck. The Chinese lady yelps and then curses me out in Cantonese when my knitting needle impales her bok choy. I apologize, of course.

"I'm so sorry. Please, take my seat." I half rise, and just as I do the train jerks forward. I plop back into the hard plastic seat with a loud thump.

She ignores me but continues mumbling in my direction. I have no idea what she's saying, but it can't be good. Mr. Bigot makes helicopter noises from behind his paper.

I undo my last row of stitches, even though there's nothing wrong with them, just to have something to do. Resigned to not enjoy myself for the next few minutes, I keep my posture perfect and my face, from what I can see reflected in the window, serene. I could be having tea at the Ritz-Carlton, not traveling to my fake job at a flailing dot-com company on an overstuffed MUNI train with a wallet full of euros I've not yet had time to clean out.

Alexander

I'm in a pissing match with a MUNI light-rail train. Even though I know I'm going to lose, a man has to have his principles, and for me they come in the form of being a disgruntled commuter.

I look at my watch and curl my lip at it, as if it's to blame for my crappy mood and the fact that I'm going to be late on my first day at William, Heller, Lincoln. I could have walked down to Church and Market, and hopped on a random train heading into downtown instead of waiting for the J to show up. But I've already invested too much time, and so I'll wait some more, resolve to not move my ass an inch until it's time to climb on the train.

I thumb through the Wednesday issue of the *San Francisco Express,* where any news nonevent is worthy of being printed as long as it has a good picture, and stop at the Events page.

There's a huge picture of a woman who has an I-don't-give-a-shit smirk on her face wearing a sheer white dress with black underpants, big ones, underneath, but somehow it looks sexy. She's aggressively skinny, with very pale blond hair and sharp but still pretty features and not at all my type.

She looks like she could be Sigrid's sister.

I glance up as someone makes a move to check if the train is coming. Standing on the narrow strip of cement that separates me and about twenty other people from the traffic roaring past us, we all risk our lives, in turn, to walk into the street so we can see around the bend. Even though we all know the J train will get here when it gets here, we can't help thinking this'll make some sort of difference.

The guy shakes his head, and we all go back to waiting after sharing annoyed and sympathetic looks.

"Fuck this!" A guy, young and stressed-out looking, stomps off toward Market Street. "Fuck this late-ass train!"

People around me laugh, some agree, but we stay put. Now that he's gone, he's tipped the balance in the transit cosmos, and the train is sure to appear just as he's walked far enough away so he can't make it back to this stop or up to the next one in time. We all silently thank him for his sacrifice.

I am about to turn to the Sports page, when the train screeches around the corner.

I drop my token in and make my way toward the back of the train, where it's a little less crowded, and give up on reading my paper in favor of keeping my balance while I look out the window.

The commute to my new office takes me past my old high school. The kids at Dolores Park High School are still primarily Latino, African American, Asian, and rowdy, like they were when I went there.

The train slows down to pull into a stop, and I can't help but smile as I see kids doing the same thing I used to do, jumping the fence to ditch school before it even starts, only to find myself frowning when I realize they're going to try to cram themselves on the same train I'm riding.

The driver yells at the kids to move it, and I get a backpack in the kidney from one of them. He doesn't even grunt an apology. The adults cringe away from them, and that only makes them talk louder and take up more space.

Was I ever that young? That obnoxious? Yeah, and more so.

The train slows down as it pulls into the coupling station off Market and Church streets, where a long line of N trains will cut us off on their way into the tunnel and downtown.

Behind me a mother is trying to dig her way off the train with two hands full of shopping bags and a baby in a stroller to contend with. The teenagers, of course, make no move to help her.

Disgusted, I shoulder them out of the way and help her with the stroller. Just before I get back on, I see someone, a woman, through the window of the N train as it gets ready to disappear into the underground tunnels that cut through the heart of the city. She sees me too, I'm almost sure of it. She's beautiful. Dark hair like rich chocolate, pale skin, big blue eyes, and lips like pillows, but what almost floors me are the knitting needles in her hands.

I stare after her, and can't move until the driver yells at me to get back on the train.

Evelyn

"Hey? Lady?"

"I'm so sorry!" I apologize to Mr. iPod when I realize I'm leaning into his lap, my knitting needles dangerously close to the vicinity of his crotch.

I turned away for a second to avoid being blinded by a pointy cucumber as the Chinese lady finally took an empty seat just as a man, tall, in a suit, stepped out of the open door of the waiting J train across from us. I watched him, openmouthed at this point, reach in and carefully swing out a stroller, complete with a toddler in pink, setting it and her carefully on the sidewalk, and then offer a hand to help the child's mother with her shopping bags. And then he looked at me—really looked at me. Or at least I think he did. He was all the things the romance novels I used to read under the covers as a teenager promised: tall, dark, and handsome. What's more, he made my heart stop and start up again in a skittering beat with just one look.

"No worries, man." Mr. iPod gives me a cautious smile, easing his backpack from the floor onto his lap.

"I thought I, um, saw a friend. On the other train," I lie. "But it wasn't him. It was someone else. I mean, it was no one." I take another look, but the windows go dark as we pull into the underground tunnel. "No one I know."

Mr. iPod has lost interest in my babbling and resumes his private concert, putting his sunglasses on for good measure.

"Silly girl."

I whip my head around looking for my mother and I realize it was me who just spoke. Maybe I dismissed the suggestion of going into therapy a bit too hastily.

I put my knitting away, for safety's sake, and yelp in surprise as the phone I found on my desk last night trills. Ted had mentioned something about me having a direct line to him that he expected me to keep open "twenty-four-seven."

"Hello?" I look around, unsure what the etiquette is for taking calls on the train. I suppose, since people seem to be able to discuss finicky palates and bodily fluids, answering a phone call may not be such a huge faux pas.

"Good, you got the phone. A few things. I'm going to be late today, so that means we're working through lunch. Order us sandwiches from that place I like. I'll have the usual, but make sure they toast the bread on one side only. The vending machine people should be stopping by around ten; make sure they stock the machines with the wrappers facing out and all in the same direction. Writing starting from the bottom. What else? Take a look at the website. You have an art and technology background. Take some notes on it. What you like, what you don't. What the experience was for you. And keep a log of who spends how long in your office and what they're doing. Allan's and Jessica's teams need to be in on the meeting. Make sure they're there. I'll be in later."

"Good morning, Ted. Can you repeat the first part, please? Ted?"

He's hung up.

I drop the phone on my lap and root around in my bag for something to write everything down on. I come up with my plane ticket, flip it over, and dig deep for the pen I know is in there somewhere. Instead I come up with the cocktail-straw dog. It's slightly crushed, but everything seems to work fine. The head goes up and down with the slight touch of my finger to the tail. I keep this up until my stop is announced.

chapter ten
Office Life and Life in the Office

Evelyn

I know what I must look like rushing up from the underground metro station, my brightly printed ethnic bag slung over my shoulder, sensible flats, black opaque tights, and matching turtleneck under a tweed jumper, knit scarf around my neck—an escapee from a 1950s Scottish girls' school.

As I step into the lobby of 115 Sansome Street, I turn sideways to avoid being knocked over by a man, even though I have the right-of-way. Predictably, I then find myself holding the door open while three or four other people rush in ahead of me. A therapist I saw for a year when I was fourteen claimed I'd repressed my anger deep down beneath layers of good manners, congenial passivity, and overeating. Of course, I had no choice but to agree with him. When our sessions together had run their course, I let him call them to a halt because I couldn't manage the gall to inform the good doctor I'd stopped listening to him months ago, and since I hadn't lost any weight, Mother agreed that talking therapy wasn't for me.

"You're all very welcome," I mutter at their backsides.

I walk toward the newsstand and browse magazines, pretending to consider *The Economist* before reaching for the last copy of a thick September *Vogue,* only to have a red-tipped, manicured hand swoop in and take it.

"Can I get a pack of cigarettes? Whatever is cheapest? Does anyone have the time? I'm so fucking late, but I'm a temp. What do they expect? You get what you pay for." The Vogue Thief shares a laugh with Hilmi, who keeps one eye out for shoplifters and the other on her cleavage.

I wait for him to realize I'm standing right in front of him, a vague smile on my face, but inside I'm quietly annoyed more at myself than at Hilmi. I've gone out of my way to make myself as inconspicuous as possible. Not an easy feat at five ten, but I've tried very hard, and it's not surprising I'm a tad on the invisible side even when I want to be noticed. If there ever was an occasion where I should demand to be heard and seen, it's now. That *Vogue* was mine.

"Excuse me?" I start after her.

Himli stares after the Vogue Thief as she bounces away without even looking in my direction. I could take this as a sign he trusts me not to shoplift, but even I can't help but look at her retreating figure. She's got a sway to her hips I could never hope to copy. We may have the same general parts, but she wears hers with confidence.

"Ah! Good morning. The hard worker is back for another honest day of labor." The building last night was not as deserted as I had anticipated. Himli had been restocking his newsstand with a fresh crop of magazines. We'd chatted for a bit. He is married with four children in private school, and his mother-in-law lives with them, so their two-bedroom in the Richmond is pretty crowded, and not once did he mention how overdressed I was for after-hours filing. "You could learn a lot from her, Nester."

"Shut up, Himli." Nester is standing behind the security desk glaring at people as they make their way toward the elevators.

"Good morning," I try again. "May I get a pack of gum, mint, please." I smile at Himli, but I'm not showing nearly enough skin to distract him. I, unlike the Vogue Thief, have only my manners to fall back on. I slide a copy of the *S.F. Express* over as casually as possible. "Oh, and this, too."

There's nothing wrong in reading the *S.F. Express,* but it's one of those things that's never talked about. Everyone in Mother's circle uses the Events page as a barometer of who's in the good graces of the big society god in the sky. From underneath the counter, Himli brings out a copy of *Vogue.* The cover is squashed but smoothed out as best it can be. "On the house."

"I couldn't. Please, let me pay."

"Next time, then," he says with a smile but passes me a free pack of gum all the same.

With my faith in humanity (slightly) restored, I get to the elevator just as the door begins to slide closed. No one sticks out an arm or umbrella to stop it. Sighing, I turn toward the stairwell and start my trek up the five floors to UGotIt.

"Evelyn! I hear you got your arm on the Events page!" James is, as usual, far away from the reception desk he's supposed to be manning. He pats the space next to him on the couch, where he's flipping through a magazine and sipping a gargantuan smoothie. "What are you doing taking the stairs? Even I don't take the stairs, and I tell everyone I'm a compulsive exerciser."

"I just felt like it." James is of the opinion, the very vocal opinion, that I'm too nice. He's waged a one-man campaign to "bitchify" me, as he puts it, and so far has been unsuccessful in the effort. I sit down next to him but keep my purse on my lap so he knows I'm not settling in for a chat. "What's your day looking like?"

"Horrible. Ted is on one of his stupid rampages. 'Roid rage or whatever it is yuppie fucks like him are afflicted with these days. He should just come out of the closet already." James, like any self-respecting homosexual, thinks everyone is gay. Except me. As he says, "Evelyn, honey, those hips of yours were made for birthing babies, and for that you need a dick attached to someone whose blood is as blue as yours is." He's a romantic, an elitist, and the best type of friend a girl could ever ask for. "What Ted needs is a Xanax drip inserted up his ass."

James ignores the ringing phone on his desk and instead takes the *Express* out of my hands.

"I think he's under a lot of stress." I sit and watch James flip straight to the horoscopes.

"I guess you would know," he says, trying to pretend he doesn't care if I don't take the bait.

Of course I do. "What does that mean?"

"Total bullshit, but people—and by people I mean that twat Jessica—are saying that you're Ted's girlfriend."

I gasp. "Half the time he forgets I'm in the room with him." The last thing I need is for any more attention to come my way. Especially this kind, from anyone here at UGotIt.

"Don't worry, I sort of let it slip that you prefer tacos over sausage."

"Thank you, James, I knew I could count on you." I pat him on the knee and then stand up. "I guess I should get to my desk."

"If you must." He shrugs and takes a long pull on his smoothie. "Happy birthday, by the way."

"Thanks." I lean in for a quick kiss on each cheek. "Please don't mention it to anyone." The phone rings again and again. I take a deep breath and say, "You going to get that?"

James sighs and trudges over to the ringing phone. "If I must. . . . Good morning, you go tit dot cum . . ."

Alexander

I ride the escalator up to Sansome Street, keeping to the right so people in a hurry can squeeze by on the left. I swing my beat-up handmade leather satchel to my back so it doesn't bang into anyone. I picked it up the summer between high school and college when me and my dad traveled through Mexico by bus, bike, and on foot. We visited the town my grandparents came from all those years ago, reunited with distant cousins, and I translated for my dad, who despite all his work with the Latino community and best efforts to make up for his parents' decision he only learn English, has never been able to pick up anything resembling passable Spanish.

I run my hand down the leather strap, grateful I left this bag behind when I moved to New York, thinking I wouldn't need it. After having left Sigrid again, this time on a street corner, I fully expect to get a box containing the shredded remains of all my possessions.

Rodney Heller carries a sweet Louis Vuitton briefcase—way too obvious in my book. Pete totes his life around in a JanSport backpack that he can carry three different ways and that has a compartment for everything. Women have told me they can't trust a man who owns better bag than they do and would never consider a guy who carries a backpack. If there's one thing I've learned about women—they take their accessories seriously.

Not that I'd ever take this piece of cowhide into court. Clients like to see their lawyers looking the part, and a beat-up sentimental leather messenger bag just won't cut it with a client who is suing or being sued.

I hold open the heavy glass door that leads into 114 Sansome for a cute girl who's juggling a large purse, book, and cup of coffee.

"Thanks." She smiles but doesn't stop to wait for me. We've

both played the game, but I'm not in the mood to make the next move. Instead of picking up my pace to catch up with her at the elevator, I hang back and let her go up without me. I've led enough women on for a twenty-four-hour period. I don't want to get myself into another situation where someone screams I'm an asshole as I walk away from them.

I step into the next elevator, keeping my eyes on my shoelaces, not looking up until the doors slide open onto the minimalist reception area of Williams, Heller, Lincoln.

"Good morning, Mr. Velazquez," Wallace, the single-moniker, ice-cold receptionist–office manager, says without turning around, making me wonder if she has eyes in the back of her head or has hacked into the building's security cameras.

"Hi, uh . . . I'll be in, I guess it's my office." I'm careful not to make eye contact lest I turn to stone or say something stupid. "If you need me for anything."

"Very well, Mr. Velazquez."

Not to make assumptions, but I have the feeling Wallace is the kind of woman who doesn't need a man for anything.

In my new office, I settle into my new Aeron chair and am firing up my equally new laptop when Pete walks in looking like he slept in his suit.

"The chair you're sitting on? At least two K. And they're ordering more for the interns. Interns!" Pete says as he ambles toward the windows and adjusts the shades. Pete is a worrier by nature, and nothing worries him more than business as usual.

"Morning, Pete. Bright and chipper this morning."

"We're burning through money like it was a pack of Zig-Zags and smoking it as fast as we can before Mom and Dad come home from dinner."

"Pete, presentation is key to—"

"Yeah, yeah, spare me. Just because you scored that suit on sale at Macy's doesn't mean you have to drink the Kool-Aid, Alexander." Pete looks tired, and I know why. It's too early to ask him about it or even how he's doing today.

"You should think about upgrading your wardrobe."

"Why bother? We're glorified ambulance chasers, Alexander. Nice suits won't do anything to change that." Pete gets up and nervously paces back and forth. "I think I'll take up smoking. You wanna join me?"

"Hmm, lung cancer before ten A.M. Tempting, but I can't. A new client's coming in, and Rodney wants me at the table for the meet and greet. And since I'm the new guy here, I want to make a good impression."

"It's always the pretty boys who get the up-front-and-center treatment. All right, I know where I'm not wanted. I'll crawl back into my hole now and do what passes for practicing law at this place. Come by when it's feeding time." Pete shuffles out with his shoulders hunched and his chin into his chest.

I sit at my desk doing a search to see if Freud had anything to say about knitting needles and women until it's time to hit the bathroom to brush my teeth, comb my hair, and make sure my shoes are shined for Rodney's big client.

Evelyn

Instead of feeling isolated in the game room, I find it's rather freeing not to have to smell other people's reheated food or force myself not to listen to their phone arguments with their boyfriends or landlords. I've also realized that, if I close the door, people will not come in to complain about Ted. They send e-mail instead.

On the wall opposite, above the big-screen TV, I've tacked up a Modigliani portrait of his much abused lover, Jean Hébuterne, which for whatever reasons is an image that always inspires me. Laurent found my affinity for Modigliani's painting style *"une contradiction charmante,"* and said he hoped as I gained confidence I would broaden my techniques and discover my own style. Now, thinking about it, I realize his comment was the French equivalent of "silly girl."

I pour myself a cup and sip my tea, picking the stray bits of leaves off my tongue while listening to my voice mail (more messages from Ted) and then Ted's voice mail (he also leaves himself messages), which I transcribe for him.

I set the little cocktail-straw dog on top of the computer monitor. Then move it onto the desk before putting it back in my bag, feeling silly for hanging on to cleverly twisted cocktail straws.

I wonder what James would say if I could bring myself to tell him about what happened on the train. Not that anything happened. For all I know the man didn't even see me. He just happened to look up in my direction and I assumed he was looking at me. And what if he *did* look at me? What does it mean? Nothing, because what are the chances that I'll ever see him again? And it wouldn't matter. I just got out of a relationship—not got out, fled is more like it.

But still.

He was good looking, very good looking. But that's not what made my heart flip-flop in my chest. Something about him was different from all the pretty boys I grew up with. He seemed like a man who'd take the garbage out in a rainstorm without being asked or would pull over and help a person change a tire just because it's the right thing to do. How do I know this? I don't, of course, but what he did this morning, helping the mother with her stroller, was just so . . . chivalrous.

Chivalrous? Did I just think of that word in relation to a modern-day man? I've been keeping too much company with the Brontë sisters and my good friend Jane Austen while drinking tea out of delicate vintage porcelain cups alone in my sunny flat. But he did see me. I'm sure of it and that I am a silly girl.

Alexander

Sigrid was right and wrong. I do know what real love is, even if I've never been in love. At twenty-three my dad was working his way through San Francisco State University as a busboy, landscaper, housepainter, you name it, when he met my mom. She had been her high school's valedictorian, but my grandparents pressured her to stay close to home. So instead of Princeton, or even Stanford, she found herself at the local state college ready to make the best of it. During an early-morning economics class, she watched my dad doze off and couldn't help but nudge him awake. When he opened his eyes, his first words to her were "Marry me." She answered, "I will, but I want to graduate from law school first."

And that's just what happened, sort of.

She got accepted to law school, she got pregnant, and they married, in that order. My dad dropped out of college and worked, watched my sister, Nayelli, while my mom studied. By the time my mom took the bar, she was seven months pregnant with me. My dad says falling asleep in that economics class was one of the best decisions he never made in his life.

Nayelli would ask them to tell this story again and again when we were kids, even though she was still the kind of little girl who set her Barbies on fire.

When we were teenagers and she was sitting out yet another high school dance while I was trying to figure out how I was going to escort the two different girls I'd asked, my sister told me she wouldn't be satisfied with anything less than what our parents have, true love at first sight. To me it looked like what they got out of the deal was not enough money, having kids at the wrong time and too close together (Mrs. Ryan next door called us Irish twins), and doing things the hard way. Where was the fun in that?

"There's no such thing as love at first sight, Nayelli," I, age sixteen, declared.

"You'll wind up bitter and alone, Alexander," she predicted.

To which I answered, "You mean, just like you?"

Years later, Nayelli met Lloyd, and it was, as she always knew it would be, love at first sight. That it happened over a cadaver during their second year of medical school only makes the story better. They stayed together through the ups and downs of interning in different cities and the other rigors of becoming doctors, and soon Nayelli, with a little help from her doctor husband, will be declared the winner of the race to produce the first grandchild.

And I am alone but not bitter. Maybe a little bitter, but bitter in the Hermès tie my ex-ex-girlfriend brought with her all the way from New York, which I expect she is now on her way back to.

I wash my hands, drying them just enough so I can pat down my hair—a habit from when my mom would comb my hair.

I know I'm not a bad looking guy, more than one woman has called me the Mexican JFK Jr. There are worse men to be compared to, looks-wise, I guess, even if he is dead. Anyway, women have a thing for JFK Jr., and the lawyer part doesn't hurt either, but it makes me wonder what they see in me.

I'm no poet or philosopher, or even that considerate. Sigrid could attest to that. Sometimes I forget important dates, like anniversaries and birthdays, but I always pick up the check and would never force a woman to go to a movie she wouldn't see on her own. I'd like to think I have a bright future if I manage not to fuck it up this time. I know how to dress and am straight, but shouldn't women want more? Shouldn't they expect more from me besides a steady income and looking good with my shirt off? Shouldn't there be some deeper connection, something that can't be explained by biology, hormones, and the shortage of single heterosexual men in San Francisco and Manhattan? Shouldn't there be something that brings two people together for no other reason than that they belong together? Shouldn't I get to fall in love at first sight? Shouldn't I have made a run for the train she was on instead of just standing there?

I frown at myself in the mirror and try to get my head back into the game.

Evelyn

I look up from the monitor where, per Ted's request, I'm going through clip art images seeking an image of an attractive male or female who personifies the typical UGotIt.com user but who won't alienate actual UGotIt users, either male or female, who might be considered unattractive when I sense someone is trying to get my attention.

There, standing at the door, my door, is Jessica.

"Sorry?" I ask, trying to focus my eyes on an actual living person, who looks more like a jumble of pixels. I blink rapidly, attempting to normalize my pupils and jog my brain into reality.

"The meeting? It's starting. Ted's wondering where you are." She leans into my office, checking it out. "Nice view."

"Thank you, um, thanks. I'm on my way." I stand up, catching my foot on my knitting bag (okay, I knit and drink tea but am, fortunately, deathly allergic to cats), and promptly slosh the rest of my tea onto the dull industrial carpet. "Crap!"

I grab a fistful of tissues and start dabbing at it before I feel a hand on my arm. James's dark purple platform rave boots come into focus. "Don't worry about it."

"I can't just leave it, James." It wouldn't be polite, and if there is one thing I have a firm grasp on, it is my manners.

James hands me more Kleenex but doesn't stoop down to help. "Tea is the least of your carpet's worries."

"I can't just leave it," I say again. When it's as dry as it is going to get, I take James's hand, stand up, and smooth out my skirt. "I'm going to be late."

"I said, 'Tea is the least of your carpet's worries,'" James repeats a little louder.

"Maybe, but—"

"Oh, for fuck's sake, Evelyn, I'm trying to tell you some juicy office gossip." James takes me by the shoulders and gently shakes me.

"I'm sorry. Okay, I'm completely focusing on your gossip." I start walking toward the glassed-in conference room on the other side of the office.

"Reliable sources have told me that a certain someone"—he pauses as we pass the copy room. The office sexpot, Melinda from Marketing, is flirting with some guy from Customer Service— "These sources have told me a certain someone had sex on that very carpet, where the fool's ball table now is."

"No!" I whisper, thoroughly and completely (not) shocked. Melinda from Marketing seems like the kind of woman who reads *Cosmo* and nothing but *Cosmo*.

UGotIt.com may be a struggling Web company, but from what I've heard from James, it's done nothing but rev up employees' sex lives. Everyone seems to have slept, made out, or at least shamelessly flirted with everyone else. James updates a color-coded spreadsheet every afternoon to keep up with it all.

"Who else would be déclassé enough? Except Paul from HR, who masturbates after lunch in the only stall that locks in the men's room." James takes my elbow to get me moving again. "If he files a workers' comp claim for carpal tunnel, I'll personally testify against him. I've recorded it on my phone—just the sounds, nothing visual—so I have proof."

"So who did she . . . do it with?"

I decide to save my own issue with Paul from HR for later. He's been after me to fill out paperwork to make my transfer from temp to UGotIt.com employee official. James has a gnat-size attention span, and if I distract him, I'll never find out who Melinda from Marketing slept with, and for whatever reason it seems like something I should know and a nice distraction from having to face the increasing complexity of working here under dubious pretenses.

"Patience, grasshopper, all will be revealed." James is tasteful enough to wait and even looks behind him to make sure Melinda from Marketing is out of earshot. "You know how she was bitching about being so close to the bathroom?"

"Yeah?" I don't, but if I mention this, it'll set James off on some tangent. "I assume it's a bad place to sit."

"Please, she's a huge bulimic—she's in vomit heaven. She just likes to bitch. Anyway, she didn't get her cubicle moved but now has higher partitions. I guess she was a mediocre lay."

James shrugs, as if this is to be expected for sleeping with someone at work and not doing an entirely satisfactory job of it. I'd at least expect flowers. If not a tin of tea. Imported, not domestic.

"Was the carpet cleaned recently?" I'm sure that carpet absorbed plenty of spilled beer, drool, and flatulence when the tech guys had to pull all-nighters to launch the site. But someone having sex on the carpet in the room where my fussy little china teapot and cup and Modigliani reproduction now live? "If not, do you think it can be—"

"Nice of you to join us, Evelyn." Ted is standing behind me, holding the glass door open. Whatever kept him out of the office this morning has resulted in a sunburn down his nose and across his forehead and the back of his neck.

"Sorry," I apologize, and scamper past him to take the only empty chair. It's positioned behind his, near the window, and I don't have to wonder who it's meant for—me, his right-hand woman.

People asked me to stake out their spots ahead of time, since the closer a person sits to Ted, the better. He's shortsighted, can't handle contacts (I've been on the phone with his eye doctor), but refuses to wear his glasses when he thinks anyone is looking. If you have a point to make, front and center is the place to be or else you don't exist in Ted's world, or at least in his line of vision.

As Ted wears his glasses around me and has positioned me so he doesn't see me, it's pretty clear where I rank in the hierarchy at UGotIt.

I glance back to where James is lurking, just out of Ted's eyesight. He points to Ted, mouths "Him! Him!" and begins to pump his hips while making "I'm coming! I'm coming!" faces. I turn around, toward the window, laughter painfully lodged somewhere between my throat and my belly.

That's when I see him, walking into a conference room in the building across the street. For the second time this Wednesday morning, my heart skips a beat and my breath catches in my throat.

Alexander

"Morning. Alexander Velazquez." I hold out my hand.

"Bryan, B-R-Y-A-N Hearstford, Harvard Law class of 'ninety-five," Bryan says by way of greeting as he gives a firm shake.

"Brian, spelled the non-gay way, Berryman, Harvard Law 'ninety-six." Brian holds out a meaty paw that matches the rest of him. Even the expensive suit he's wearing can't hide the fact that he has no neck.

"Hey. So, Alex, see that chick, the one who works on the seventh floor, yet? It is the seventh, right, Brian?" Bryan asks. "Tits like nobody's business, man."

"Nope. I don't believe I have, Bry." I shouldn't answer, but I know they won't let up until I do, and I'd rather get this over now so we can come to an understanding that I'm not going to play along with their hazing.

"She's smokin' hot, man, I'd do her. Booyah, baby!" Bryan says, watching for my reaction. I don't give him one.

"What's wrong, Alex? Having pecker problems? They got pills for that now, you know." Bryan lets loose with a donkey laugh. Brian, a beat late, joins in.

I drum my fingers on the table and wait for them to notice I'm not playing along.

"You know, Alex? Dick pills!" Bryan says, just in case his first reference was too nuanced for this hour of the morning.

"I know who to ask if I need any." I settle back and look out the window.

"Snap, dawg! Alex totally snapped you, Bryan!" Brian, despite being in his early thirties, talks as if he hangs out at the local 7-Eleven with the rest of his skateboarding buddies.

"I don't—" Bryan's face is beet red, but before he can spit anything out, Rodney comes in, his hand on the elbow of one of the most stunning and, as of late, controversial San Francisco ladies who lunches and marries well for a living.

"Gentlemen." He nods at us to get our shit together, but we're already half rising out of our seats as he pulls out the leather armchair at the head of the table for her. "This is our client—Mrs. Candace Hall. Our new client."

"It's Ms." Her supernaturally plump lips stretch, well, unnaturally around the word, as if it takes extra effort to form the sound correctly. She's smaller in stature than I thought she'd be from the pictures I've seen of her in the *S.F. Express.* Very thin but with what I know are impressive breasts underneath her suit jacket. Her big gray-blue eyes are hidden behind black sunglasses, her skin free from any signs of her actual age, and her ashy blond hair styled into shoulder-length waves. She sort of looks like Sharon Stone, but way more intense, if that's possible.

"Of course. Ms. Hall." Rodney sits down at her left elbow after Brian scrambles out of the way to make room for him. Rodney introduces us in turn, and we shake hands. Her grip is firm, her skin dry and soft. "I'm sure you're all aware of Ms. Hall's recent legal troubles."

We all nod, keeping our faces grave and impassive, as if we don't know the dirty details that have brought her to the conference table. She's what Pete refers to as lawyer chum, and from my reading, there always seems to be blood in the water when Candace Hall is around.

"I'm here with the expectation that the truth will come out about these baseless allegations and to find some justice." Candace dramatically slashes through the empty air in front of her as if she has a knife in her hand. We all instinctively shrink back. "I can't stand by while my name is dragged through the streets!"

"Mud," Bryan says, correcting her. "I think you mean mud. Your name, dragged through the mud."

"Pardon me," says Candace, sounding not at all appreciative of being schooled on clichés.

"And neither will we," Brian croaks out, trying to deflect some of the shrapnel from his frat brother. They're grade-A assholes, but at least they have each other's backs.

"Our number one goal, Ms. Hall, is to win your case, not only in court but in the court of public opinion," Rodney says in his most sincere lawyer voice.

"I should hope so," she says as she digs through her purse. She comes up with a cigarette, holds it out, and waits for someone to light it. "What's happening to me is nothing short of a travesty."

We all nod while waiting for someone to tell Candace Hall she can't smoke in here. But she's Candace Hall and she can very well smoke wherever the hell she wants to. A little thing like a city ordinance isn't going to stop her.

Rodney leans over and gives Candace's arm a reassuring squeeze as he lights her cigarette. "Ms. Hall disputes their claim that they are owed back wages . . ." he begins, pocketing the lighter.

"I treated those people better than I treat some of my own family!" She begins to cry softly, touching a tissue to her nose. Bryan pours her a glass of water and pushes it toward her with a cautious finger. Suddenly her voice is icy clear. "Is that bottled water or from the tap?"

"Sorry?" Bryan looks flustered.

"We have it delivered, Ms. Hall." Rodney gives Bryan a hard look. Brian looks relieved that Bryan beat him to the punch and settles back. "Bryan will find out from where. . . . Right now, Bryan."

"Excuse me." Bryan gets up, smoothing his tie, and hotfoots it out the door. I can't help but smirk.

"In the future, if it wouldn't be too much trouble, I'd like bottled water. Chilled in the bottle, not in a pitcher, but served in a pitcher." She takes a sip of the water, frowns, and sets it away from herself as if she found something nasty in it. "And no ice, unless the cubes are made from the same bottled water."

Brian furiously scribbles down notes and looks up, his Mont Blanc at the ready for more instructions.

"Ms. Hall, you can expect nothing but a hundred and fifty percent from us here at Williams, Heller, Lincoln . . ." Rodney begins his spiel, emphasizing how aggressive we are, and by the look on Ms. Hall's face, she does aggressive.

I stare above the remaining Brian's head, tuning them all out. Like Pete says, I'm just here to make Rodney look good, and when the time comes, he'll serve me up and hope I'm to Ms. Hall's liking. I shift around, look out the window, and almost jump out of my chair when I see the woman from this morning in the building across the street.

Evelyn

I glance away from the window and spare Ted a moment of my attention. He's still droning on, enjoying the sound of his own voice. I nod along in sync with everyone else, even though I'm pretty sure Ted doesn't have eyes in the back of his head. He might be short-sighted, but he can sense a lack of focus on him from a mile away.

"This is a team effort, people." Ted's voice booms across the room, startling me. "Evelyn will be the de facto point person on this, along with Allan, our tech ninja. And Jessica. You guys will coordinate with Evelyn. She's the official interdepartmental liaison. Assume what she says comes directly from me."

"So we don't have to talk to you directly, but go to Evelyn instead?" asks one of the tech guys, looking awake for the first time during the meeting.

"Exactly. Evelyn is my filter. She's got some notes for you on issues with the site, so we'll start there. Let's make it happen, people, and happen fast."

And as if Ted had sounded a starting bell, people spring up from their seats and rush back to their desks to make whatever happen, and happen now. I sit there stunned, having absolutely no idea what I've been named a co–de facto point person of.

Within seconds everyone is gone, leaving me alone with Jessica and Allan. He's tall, thin, dressed in mismatched shades of black, and with hair dyed so black, it's blue. Allan looks over at me and smiles. "Guess we're going to be spending a lotta time together, ladies."

Jessica sits at the table, her arms folded across her chest. She first looks at me, then at Allan, who quickly loses his crooked smile. "So are we going to get something done or just sit here pulling each other's puds until we can leave for the day?"

I may never have worked in an office before, but what I need to do is clear as day to me. I pull out my pen and notebook, smile, and say, "I'm taking lunch orders. What would you guys like from the sandwich place?"

Alexander

Rodney drones on, his practiced monologue smooth, reassuring. Just what a client wants in a lawyer who charges $750 an hour to state the obvious: You're fucked, legally, but there are ways to make it less painful and maybe save face.

". . . the plaintiffs, sympathetic as they might be in the particular social and political climate of San Francisco, are still not infallible. Our goal will be to prove that their lawsuit is nothing but an obscene money grab perpetrated on a vulnerable pillar of the community so soon after the death of her esteemed husband . . ."

Ms. Hall—Candace—is crying quietly, but no tears are coming from behind her sunglasses. I feel her looking at me looking at her and give her what I hope is a reassuring smile before turning my attention to the sheaf of papers detailing the lowlights of the case against her.

I glance toward the window again. She's standing up, and my eyes track her as she goes to sit by a blurry figure in black. She's elegant, even from here it's obvious. Perfect posture, and her skin almost glows, no chronic tanning addiction. In fact, she shouldn't be sitting in the sun—even the watery kind that passes for late summer sun in San Francisco. I tilt my head slightly to the right so I can get a better look and swear for a moment our eyes meet.

I look away, like I've been caught with my hand in the cookie jar, and feel Candace staring at me again. I have no choice but to look over at her. This time she holds my gaze until I shift around in my seat. Only then does she crack a small smile.

Candace has expensive skin, pulled tight but not too tight. From the freckles on her cleavage, I can tell she's been on more than a few sun-drenched vacations before 100+ sunblock was de rigueur. Her skin has that permanently tanned, slightly dehydrated look, kind of like baked chicken skin. I'm sure Candace rubs expensive lotions into it, but the damage is done, no matter how supple it feels after she works the cream in. I fake-cough into my fist, uncomfortable with my unlawyerly train of thoughts.

"I'd like to hear your thoughts on this matter," Candace says in a sharp, clear tone, cutting through Rodney's oration on how kick-ass the firm is.

"Ms. Hall, let me—" Rodney is stopped short with a wave of her hand. It's sporting a hunk of a diamond that probably cost as much as the monthly rent of the offices, which, according to Pete, is a lot. Rodney's eyes trail after it like a cat watching a ball of yarn.

"Not you, Heller." She doesn't even glance in his direction, or take her eyes off mine. "Your thoughtful colleague next to you."

"Alexander Velazquez." Rodney scoots his seat back a bit so she can see me better. "One of our best and brightest, Ms. Hall."

Bryan and Brian swap a frown, realizing they'll be playing backup.

"Thanks" is all I can think to say.

Candace smiles at me, her face not moving in the usual places. My return smile feels just as forced. She's caught me off guard, and she knows it.

"Mr. Velazquez, what are your thoughts on my little predicament?" She leans into the table slightly, causing her long string of pearls to clink against the surface like very expensive school yard marbles.

"It's not so little. Is it?" I automatically slip into flirting mode.

"No, it's not." She lets out a burst of harsh laughter; everyone else hurries to join in a few seconds after Rodney, to give him time to posture without any competition from his employees. After a moment she stops cold. "Heller, I think I'd be a little more comfortable discussing the finer details of my case over an early lunch."

"I'll have my car pulled around." Rodney pitches his keys at Brian. "And we can all—"

"That won't be necessary. I don't want to keep you all from your work. I expect you to win me this case, Heller." She stands up, so we all do the same. "And quickly."

"Don't worry, Ms. Hall. We'll work around the clock and won't rest until you are satisfied," Rodney says, trying to seem like he's in charge. "We'll meet here and pound the hell out of this case right after lunch."

Brian goes red faced to keep from laughing at Rodney's unfortunate choice of words.

"My car is waiting outside. Do you like One Market, Alexander?" Candace doesn't wait. She gets up and strides out the door perfectly balanced on her fuck-me pumps. "Becky. Becky!"

chapter twelve
Going Through the Motions

Alexander

A nervous-looking woman in an ill-fitting business suit, surrounded by enough tote bags to be on a long weekend, jumps up from a chair someone has set near the conference room door for her.

"Any calls, Becky?" Candace snaps. Without stopping or turning around, she continues down the hall, all of us falling in line behind her like hapless ducklings.

"Yes, Ms. Hall." This from the skinny girl, who I assume is Becky or at least answers to that name. She quickens her step and holds out a stack of slips of paper. Candace leafs through them while walking and hands them back without comment.

"Your dress will be ready for Friday." Becky, juggling two cell phones, a BlackBerry, and a large leather day planner, walks backward so she can address her boss. I wonder if this particular skill was in the job description. "Sissy Ross has called three—"

"Becky. Call ahead and tell them to expect us for lunch a little early. Make sure we don't sit by a window." Candace snakes her arm through mine. "I want your undivided attention, Alexander."

"You got that, Ms. Hall," Rodney calls from behind us, "from all of us here at Williams, Heller, Lincoln."

"What time is it?" Candace asks, ignoring him.

From behind me I can hear three French cuffs snap back to reveal Rolexes, with Rodney's being the most impressive. Candace currently has a firm hold on the arm with my Rolex, purchased with my porn lawyer money, so I can't do the honors of telling her it's way too early to be this high maintenance.

"Ten to noon," Rodney answers.

"Becky. Make sure there is no bread on the table. If I see bread on the table, I'll be very unhappy."

"Yes, Ms. Hall," Becky says, putting the phone to her ear even though it'll cut out once we get in the elevator.

"I should stay behind, Ms. Hall." I may as well be asking a caged lion to consider not chewing on a steak. "Get up to speed with your case."

"We'll hold down the fort here, Alex." Rodney claps me on the shoulder and then whispers into my ear, "Make sure she's happy, Alexander, and I'll make sure you're happy. Understand?"

"Yeah, and how do you expect me to do that?" I ask out of the side of my mouth.

Instead of giving me an answer, Rodney gives me a little push into the elevator. As the door closes on all three of them, Rodney, Bryan, and Brian give me a thumbs-up.

"Now, Alexander, we need to come up with a game plan. I'm not merely fighting this battle in court." Candace pauses, tilting her head in my direction, indicating it's my turn to speak.

I nod my head gravely—classic lawyer-caught-with-his-pants-down move. When in doubt, nod with a slight frown. It always buys a couple of seconds of time. "No, you're not. You're also fighting a public relations war."

Fighting and losing, I want to add, but don't. We're in a small space, and I doubt I'd make it to the ground floor in one piece if she turned on me.

"Exactly! I need to make the people see me. The real Candace Hall. Not some spoiled, rich widow. My husband did a lot for this city, gave lots of money away. Of course, now that he's gone, things will have to change, but I'm still a very charitable person." She hands her large bag to Becky without taking her eyes off me. "I want—" She stops. The elevator doors slide open to reveal a poor UPS sap. "If you wouldn't mind waiting for the next one."

Becky, without prompting, pushes the DOOR CLOSE button.

"I want to make sure people see this _thing_ for what it is. These people are trying to extort money from me! I'm being taken advantage of because of who I am. Who my dead husband was. These people have no shame."

Another grave nod from me. No frown, though. I don't want to overdo it. Whatever I may feel about Candace Hall privately—a hot, older, rich woman with too much time and money on her hands—she's still a client. And Rodney has made it clear that her happiness is my number one priority and the key to me keeping my cushy office and leapfrogging ahead of Bryan and Brian.

"Good. I knew from the moment we met that we understood each other." Candace smiles, threads her arm in mine again, and leads me out through the lobby to her double-parked Town Car.

Becky takes the front seat, and I go around to the traffic side and open my own door. Before I get in, I look up at the building where I saw her. She's not in the window. For some reason, I'm stupidly disappointed. It's not as if I was going to wave off Candace, cross the street, and track her down. I make eye contact with the driver, who is now waiting for me to take my place next to his boss, and smile at him. He doesn't smile back . . . or even blink.

Candace arranges herself on the leather seat, her long, tanned legs crossed, knees pointed in my direction, and reaches for the leather day planner Becky is contorted around in the front seat holding out to her, along with a phone. Ignoring all of us, Candace quickly makes a series of chatty phone calls during the short ride to the restaurant.

"Pierre! Darling, you must come to my house. Tell that wicked witch of a boss of yours I can't get my color done in the salon. I simply don't have the time, and I'm being hounded by the press. They'd just love to get a picture of me walking into the salon when I'm supposed to be grieving. . . . Wonderful. . . . I'll see you at nine. Tonight. Until then, doll. Kisses.

"Reed, it's Candace Hall. How are you doing, darling? I'm going to have to ask you for a teeny tiny favor. . . . Could you, doll? I just can't shop with all the tourists gawking at me. I'm buying a Chanel suit, not a fleece sweatshirt with a cable car on it, after all. . . . Yes, black, or do you think I could get away with something gray or navy? You're right. It might be too soon. Let's stick with black, Reed. Just send over a selection. Usual size. Wonderful. . . . Kisses."

Before I have a chance to comment on the weather, Candace is on to another phone call. I stare out the window, the driver drives, and Becky furiously makes notes into another planner.

In front of One Market Street, I reach for the door handle as soon as we come to a stop, but the driver beats me to it and opens my door before he darts to Candace's side. Candace waits until I make my way around and then emerges, long legs first, tucks her hand into the crook of my arm, adjusts her sunglasses, and makes her entrance.

Becky stays in the car with the driver.

It's barely noon, but the dining room at One Market is already buzzing and full of the financial types Candace's dead husband used to call friends, or at least golfing buddies. Not only did she lay claim to his vast real estate fortune, his Pacific Heights mansion, the Stinson Beach retreat, an Aspen lodge, and a Palm Beach villa but she also sits at his old table at One Market at least three times a week and holds court with a rotating cast of sports stars, literary figures, and notable local politicos (all men) who have made it their job to keep her spirits up during this trying time. Or so I've read in the *Express* Events page, which traffics in this kind of story.

"Bob! You old goat! Tell that wife of yours she owes me a phone call." Candace waggles her fingers, calling out here and there, with me bringing up the rear, nodding to acknowledge the curious looks of everyone left in her wake.

We stop near what I assume is her table. The frazzled-looking hostess holds out a seat for Candace, but she's ignored. The both of us are forced to remain standing with our hands on the seat backs as Candace turns a full circuit around the restaurant. I smile at the hostess and she smiles back, and I'm about to apologize when Candace appears and glides into her seat.

"Thank you, dear. Have the waiter send over a large bottle of Pellegrino, and make sure the glasses are chilled, lime not lemon, and please no bread basket. Maybe a small dish of those olives I had last time. Better not, unless they're pitted."

While she's making her demands to the hostess, who'll only have to relay them to the waiter, I take a seat, put my napkin on my lap, waiting for my menu. On the table between us, her phone begins to ring. Candace ignores it, instead focusing her attention on the table next to us.

"Paxton! You old dog. We have to go out for a round of golf. As soon as I'm ready, of course. I insist. And bring that daughter of yours. She should go pro, really. An amazing talent, and such a looker."

"Ms. Hall?" I'm the one suffering the dirty looks from everyone else; Candace is completely oblivious of her bleating phone. "Ms. Hall?"

"Victor, you sneak, where have you been?" She hauls him down for an air kiss.

"Ms. Hall." A little louder, firmer. She's annoying me, and for a moment I slip and let it show.

"Yes, Alexander?" she asks, suddenly very alert.

"Your phone?"

"Oh, that." She snatches it up with a smooth flick of her wrist, her eyes on mine. "Can't talk now, call back later." She shuts it off, shoves it into her purse, and finally takes the menu the hostess has been holding out this entire time. "There. Now, Alexander, tell me all about yourself. And don't leave anything out."

"Excuse me?" I flash back to another New York girlfriend who basically said the same thing. I thought she was joking, but when I started seeing the same sedan parked outside my shitty studio apartment, I knew she wasn't. And what's more fucked up, it's not the reason we broke up. She ended up cheating on me.

"Don't be modest, Alexander. I'm sure your story is absolutely fascinating. Start with your family," Candace says in her husky voice, and instantly it feels like it's just the two of us. She is an attractive woman, a little on the harsh side, but I can see why the late Mr. Hall married her without a prenup.

"My mother is a lawyer, my dad works in the community, and my sister is a doctor." I decide to skip the specifics.

"Fascinating." She smiles, as if I'm just confirming facts for her. "Tell me honestly, Alexander, what do you think about my case?"

"It's been hard to ignore the coverage." This has to be the mildest statement ever uttered by a person who read the latest while eating his breakfast of Golden Grahams this morning.

"Lies. All of it." She flicks her hand, the enormous wedding ring she still wears shooting sparks. "I am thinking of suing the papers *and* the local stations. Radio and TV."

"That'll make Rodney happy," I say before I can stop myself.

Candace gives me a look of stunned silence and then bursts out laughing. "I knew there was a reason I liked you, Alexander. You have balls, and I need someone with balls to tell my side of the story. I want you to do it."

"I'm a lawyer, Ms. Hall," I say, relieved that she didn't take offense at my off-the-cuff remark about my boss. "We can work with your public relations agency, of course—"

"Alexander, you're just too perfect. That little rodent Rodney was right. You *are* the man to take my message to the people. Zachary!" She gets up to make her way to another table. "You old toad!"

"Thanks." I signal to the waiter to pour the water. "And can you bring some bread?"

Evelyn

"I cannot believe you're turning me and my secondhand smoke down to, like, do actual work." James leans a hip on a bare corner of my desk. "Get with the program, sister. This whole place is a day-care center for overpaid suburban brats. Come watch me smoke, and then we'll sneak off to the mall for some food court grub. You know you want to."

"As tempting as lung cancer sounds, I'll have to pass. If you haven't heard, the site is undergoing a redesign. And since the art director and the technology director can't be in the same room together and Ted doesn't want to deal with either of them, I have to function as Switzerland and make it happen." I keep my eyes on my monitor, watching as my in-box fills up with e-mails from Ted, Allan, and Jessica. "Can you tell me which sandwich place is the place where Ted gets his usual and what that usual might be?"

"Don't pay any attention to Ted, he's full of shit. Jessica is just pissed off that he slept with Melinda from Marketing and gave you this 'office.' And Allan was conceived on a radioactive Pong console and is part computer, so you're on your own there." James picks up my teapot and carefully wipes it free from nonexistent dust. After arranging it just so, he continues, "What's there to redesign anyway? We just launched a new version of the site, and it looks great."

"I'm not sure," I say slowly.

I've gone through the report I slapped together for Ted about my impressions of the site, and from what I can see, all he's done is add a cover sheet with his name on it. The site is easy to navigate, attractive to look at, and aside from conflicting ideas about its purpose, everything is fine with the design as it is. I'm not sure Ted actually read my report before having me print out the cover sheet.

"It's the business model that needs revamping, not the site." James tosses this off while inspecting his nails. I stare at him, surprised at his insight. "What? What did I say?" he asks.

"Nothing." I ignore the lump in my stomach and continue to plow through Ted's and Allan's brainstorms and Jessica's increasingly hostile one-sentence responses to them. "I'm going to be pretty busy. Ted is hot and bothered for the mock-up."

James walks to the door, sensing I won't be giving in to his charms. "It's your birthday. We get our birthdays off around here. You shouldn't even be here. For that and other reasons."

"I don't want to lose my job." I shrug and go back to scrolling. "And yes, I know how insane that sounds."

Maybe I should have a meeting with Paul from HR and sort this all out. I'm sure, if I explain it the right way, it'll make sense and won't be a big deal.

"I'm not going to give you a hard time about that. I think it's super fucking funny. But"—James heaves a huge sigh that belongs on-screen in a silent movie—"you have to get over this issue."

"What issue?" I play dumb, but we both know what he's talking about.

"The issue! What do people call it? Oh, yeah! Guilt. Face it, Evelyn, you are a very rich girl who's slumming it. Let it go, lady." James makes wide, sweeping motions with his arms, as if shooing my angst out the window. "Just look at me! I have no problem with being the best friend of someone who happens to be filthy rich and deranged enough to want to pretend to work a regular job and pretend she has to worry about buying her six-hundred-dollar Prada flats on her pretend salary. Like Kirsten Dunst in that boring movie where she gathers eggs from the henhouse after the maids clean off all the chicken poop. Just like that. Nice shoes by the way."

"They were four hundred dollars, and I got them on sale." In Milan. "I'm not rich, my parents are." I can feel the color rise in my cheeks as the words work their way out of my mouth.

"Cry me a river, Evelyn Morgan Reed-Sinclair and the other four names you have I can never remember. Get off the cross, lady. I feel your pain. Me love you long time." James sniffs at me dismissively. "How horrible—your parents are rich. How dare they? The monsters."

"I want to make it on my own, James." I look him straight in the eye to let him know I'm not kidding or making excuses for my wealth. "It's important I do. And I'll sort out the details just as soon as I figure out where to order sandwiches from."

James blows me a kiss. "You make me realize how good it is to be lazy, shallow, and not possess an ounce of ambition. Like that lazy slut Tannin. Ask yourself: what would your sister do?"

"Tannin? She'd take a nap and then she'd go shopping," I answer without thinking. "Don't tell her I said that."

Tannin is my frame of reference for the jet-set, society-gossip, heiress life I could be living. And as tempting as a life full of shopping, elective surgery, and rehab for various ill-defined addictions (like shopping and cosmetic surgery) sounds, it's just not for me. At least not now, and most likely ever, much to the disappointment of James, who craves that kind of lifestyle and has promised to be my number one enabler when I finally do come to my senses.

"See? A nap," he says with a slight sneer, even though, given the opportunity, he'd do the same thing. "And the world would be a better place if she realized napping was her only skill in life."

I drop my head into my hands when I open up another e-mail full of Ted's MBA speak. "Maybe I should resign?"

"You can't!" James gasps loudly.

"Why not?" I look up, startled. Melinda from Marketing pauses on her way to yet another unnecessary trip to the copy machine to see what's going on in my office. I wave her on with a smile. "Why"—I lower my voice—"can't I resign?"

"First of all, you don't really work here, and second, you can't leave me here by myself." He gives me a quick hug, dashes to the door, pulling his cigarettes out of his man purse, and calls out in the hallway for all to hear, "This place is horrible and I'd die without you."

"That's so sweet of you, James," I say with forced mock sincerity. Sarcasm isn't one of my strong points.

"That was pretty good. Oh, by the way, love, Ted wants to see you for a meeting in his office. I'll e-mail you the sandwich info."

James wiggles his fingers at me with an evil smile and calls out over his shoulder as he leaves, "Enjoy!"

I sit at my desk and wait for James's e-mail. What choice do I have? This is my job, after all.

Alexander

"Where have you been?" Pete asks, his arms crossed over his chest and looking smug. His shirt is untucked, and his beer belly precedes him into my office.

"You know where I've been. Half of the financial community of San Francisco knows where I've been." I put my phone down and turn away from my computer. E-mails from Candace via Becky are already pouring in. "If there's a call for 'Ms. Hall's new lawyer,' that's me. She's not a very discreet type of gal."

Candace seemed to know everyone at One Market, or at least every man, and whether he was married, separated, divorced, or on the verge of any of the above, but she stopped short of detailing their stock portfolios and cholesterol counts. She was so busy talking about other people, she only picked at the plate of food in front of her. Since I, obviously, wasn't expected to speak, I ate my lunch and most of hers. She didn't even notice.

When I got back, Rodney pulled me into his office and grilled me on every detail, including what we ordered and how much she drank.

"She's going to be a handful, and it looks like Rodney expects those hands to be yours." Pete wanders over to my couch and flops down. "I've been practicing that line since you guys left."

"It truly was a Cary Grant moment, Pete. Thank you for having it at my expense."

He's about to say something when my phone beeps and Wallace's voice emerges from it. "Mr. Velazquez, you have a delivery coming your way. Thank you."

"Man, that chick gives me the creeps." Pete shudders after she clicks off. "She makes my balls curdle, and not in a good way."

"Thanks for the visual, boss."

"Mr. Velazquez?" A guy in a messenger company T-shirt knocks on the door as best he can with the two boxes in his hands.

"That's me. Just set them down on the floor by the couch. Thanks." I've learned not to jump up and help out. It just makes everyone feel uncomfortable. They don't try to do my job; I don't try to do theirs.

I get up and toe one of the boxes. They're packed solid with legal goodness, I'm sure. "I thought Brian and Bryan were backing me up on this?"

"Those two frat boys only have each other's backs, if you know what I mean. What the fuck?" Pete yelps when a parade of guys carrying box after box make their way into my office and neatly stack about fifteen more on top of the two the first guy brought. "No way, Alex."

"We'll bring up the last batch in a couple of minutes," the clipboard guy says, and holds out the board for me to sign.

"Okay. This is my cue to get the hell out of here." Pete gives me a sympathetic thump on the back and leaves as fast as his Looney Tunes sock–clad feet will carry him.

"Pete," I call out after him, scrawling away my name (life? soul?) on the delivery sheet. "Don't leave me here, buddy!"

"Nice office," the guy says, looking around. "Good view. Ever see anything interesting? I once got an eyeful of a couple of girls—"

"How many boxes is it?" I start checking the docket names; sure enough, they all read "Candace Hall" followed by a series of crossed-out former attorney names.

"Lemme see." He flips through sheet after sheet on his clipboard. "Says here . . . twenty-three." He's already backing out the door. "Good luck."

"Thanks."

I look out the window for a few minutes, pretending I'm somewhere else.

Evelyn

I was raised on opera instead of MTV, tours of museums instead of theme park excursions, and long visits with elderly relatives who couldn't tell me from a Tiffany lampshade. I can do monotony, boredom, and never let on how much I'd much rather be somewhere else.

I had thought all these formative experiences would never come in handy in the real world, but I was wrong. Ted is able to take mind-numbing minutiae to a whole other level. One tangent leads to another until even he doesn't know what he's supposed to be talking about.

"So are we all on the same page?" Ted pauses midstep.

He's been pacing back and forth for the last hour and a half, while Allan has been staring off into space and I have been sporadically taking notes and trying to make sense of what he expects from us. Our lunch meeting got pushed back and back again, so when we finally congregated in Ted's office, it was well after four.

"All clear here, boss." Allan half rises out of his seat. He wants out of here, desperately—fifteen minutes ago he passed me a note that said he had to pee. He bugs his eyes at me. With his all-black clothes and hair and very pale skin, I'd never noticed what a lovely shade of blue they are. Radioactive blue, as James might put it.

"I think so," I say carefully, flipping through my notes, which went from sentences to a series of sketches and doodles, illustrating what Ted was orating about.

Jessica merely rolls her eyes and picks at the tuna sandwich I fetched from Celebrity Sub across the street. It's known as the Bisset, for Jacqueline Bisset, the hearty pieces of homemade white bread standing in for the wet T-shirt she wore in the movie *The Deep*. Allan changed his order three times before finally settling on a Gérard Depardieu, fried eggs and prosciutto on a buttered and toasted brioche with a side of grape jelly. Ted's was a special order: sourdough bread, toasted on one side, deli mustard, ketchup, bologna, American cheese, and iceberg lettuce with a snack-size bag of Fritos crushed between the cheese and bologna. Which I had to do myself since Celebrity Sub proved to be accommodating only to a degree.

I haven't had a chance to eat my own, a plain turkey on wheat, since every time I make a move to put down my pen, Ted stops talking and waits for me.

"Let me reiterate," he begins. "Our numbers are good. Solid, but not great. We want great. To make them phenomenal, we need the site to sing. The focus group said it was serviceable. Toilets are serviceable, guys. UGotIt's site cannot be in the same league as a crapper. We want funky yet functional. A mock-up that'll dazzle as we go in for our next round of funding."

"Dazzle?" I can't help but repeating. Ice skaters dazzle, diamonds dazzle, too-white teeth dazzle. But a website?

"Don't forget the funky functional part," Jessica sneers.

Allan adds through a yawn, "I can handle the technical part. My team is all over this, twenty-four/seven."

"We just won a design award from CNET and got an honorable mention at the Webbies," Jessica says, tossing her sandwich into the trash can.

"We gotta strike while the iron's hot, Jessica. Only losers stand still. People want something new, something cutting edge." Ted makes a fist and lightly pounds it to his chest with each sentence. "Our goal is to be the destination portal of destination portals. Right, Evelyn?"

"Yes." I smile and hope it looks convincing. I was under the impression UGotIt.com was a content site. Yesterday, Ted had me compose and send an e-mail for him announcing the creation of an editorial team to be staffed with a dozen writers to generate in-house content. Each employee who referred a qualified candidate would get a bonus of five hundred dollars if that person was hired. So far I've received fifty e-mails suggesting friends and family members for the position, and Ted has made it my job to sift through the candidates and whittle it down to a more manageable number before he has to deal with the actual interview process.

"Totally," Allan says through another yawn, looking down at his watch.

"Okay, guys. You're my copilots on this effort. It's mission critical. Anything you need—food, cots—you name it, you got it. Just send your requests to Evelyn. We need to make this happen in three weeks."

"Three weeks!" both Allan and Jessica burst out in unison.

"Even if this is just a mock-up, we need at least double that time." Jessica's face is pale. "Unless we work twenty-four hours a day, and as I recall, only Allan has made that pledge." She turns to me. "You wrote that down, right, what Allan said about working twenty-four/seven?"

I nod.

"I work best under the gun, and guys, this isn't a gun. It's a cannon, a big one . . ." Ted trails off as his computer pings with a reminder. "I have a thing. I expect a status report in my in-box by the end of the day."

I sit down at my desk and stare out the window, realizing I left my sandwich in Ted's office. After a few moments of listening to my stomach rumble, I sigh and contemplate the energy it'll take to fix myself a cup of tea.

"Holy crap!" I yelp, startled by the sudden ring of my new cell phone. I dig it out of my knitting bag, knocking my head on the underside of the table for good measure. "Hello?"

"I'm here at Needless Markup." Tannin's singsong voice fills my ear. "Would I be a complete twat if I showed up to your very proper birthday dinner wearing a gold lamé D and G? Strapless with a slit up to my throat."

"No, go right ahead," I say as I scroll through résumés. "Mother will love it."

She'll be scandalized, and it's exactly what Tannin wants. Mother pretends to disapprove of Tannin's lackadaisical attitude toward social graces, but I know she hopes some of Tannin's elitism will rub off on me—minus the party girl tendencies. In the end, we all know, Tannin will make a fine marriage. It's inevitable. And as hard as she tries to pretend she doesn't care, she has her sights set on the second coming of JFK Jr., but Presbyterian and with a modest Napa winery on the side. When she meets him, the poor guy isn't going to know what hit him.

"I had everything waxed in your honor," Tannin continues. "Maybe I'll get lucky with one of the old fogies Mother always has at these things."

"If anyone could get lucky at one of our mother's carefully orchestrated dinner parties, it'd be you."

"I'll make sure to bring rubbers and some Bengay with me," Tannin says loudly. I guess she wants to shock the Neiman Marcus personal shopper she has trailing after her. She covers the mouthpiece, and I hear some muffled conversation. "I gotta go deal with the shoe issue. I got you something, so don't worry about wearing your sack. Laters!"

I hang up and resume looking out the window.

"Evelyn?" A voice behind me calls.

"Yes!" I spring up as if I'm on wires. "Hi! Again!"

"James asked me to tell you that your father is downstairs." Jessica looks around, stopping to take in the Modigliani. "He also said to tell you he'll see you there," she adds, not even bothering to hide how suspicious she finds the whole thing. "Hot date tonight?"

"With my father and James?" Okay, I am acting funny, but she's being rude now. I don't know her well enough to know if she's joking or just being a bitch. "We're all meeting for dinner. At my parents'. Because it's my birthday. For dinner. Nothing hot about that, I can assure you . . . uh . . . Ha ha!"

"Happy birthday!" Jessica takes a step out and then stops. "Hey, I thought we got our birthdays off."

"We do, but since I just started . . ." She looks at me like I'm just the crazy teapot lady who's going to try to bring her dozen cats into the office and claim they're service animals. "I guess I should go tell Ted I'm leaving early today."

Alexander

It's what I've always wanted—a big case with a big-name client. Rodney knows I'm hungry, and he can read clients like a cheap paperback book. He knew Candace would like me because I'm young, attractive, educated, and Latino. What more could she want in a lawyer?

I sit down at my desk and drop my head into my hands with the beginnings of a headache. I pop a few aspirin and open the next box of files with no expectation but to find more of the same.

"Yup, it's time." Pete does a modified cannonball onto my couch without so much as a "Hello. Can I give you a hand there, my drowning friend?"

"Time for what?" I flip through endless piles of paper, not wanting to look up to face the other piles I still need to get through.

Candace is nothing if not thorough in her litigation. Lawsuits, counterlawsuits, and endless depositions. The widow Hall likes to sue the way some people like to go to the bathroom, with great regularity.

"Beer." Pete reaches over and plucks a file out of an open box. I knew he wouldn't be able to resist a juicy case. "It is time for beer."

"You talked me into it."

Outside we jaywalk in front of a shiny double-parked Town Car that's idling in front of her building.

"Good evening," Pete says to the driver, who's standing at the ready by the back passenger door. "So?"

"So what?" I say, playing dumb, looking over my shoulder when I hear the Town Car door slam behind us. I look up at the building, counting five floors to where I know her office is.

"Are you going to tell me about your long lunch with Candace

Hall?" Pete asks, giving me a slight nudge in the ribs. "For a woman her age, you have to admit, she's hot."

"She's not my type." I stop at the corner, waiting for the light to turn green, stepping back on the curb to let the Town Car make the turn in front of us.

"Which part?" Pete dips his head and tries to look into the window to see who is being driven around. "The rich part, the good-looking part, or the eligible part?"

"The terminal bitch part."

Pete looks at me for a second and then doubles over in wheezy laughter. It's the first time I've heard him laugh since I came home.

chapter thirteen
Relative Dangers

Evelyn

As I settle into the backseat of my father's Town Car, I have a flashback of being picked up from my much hated ballet lessons by a chauffeured Mercedes as a kid. It wasn't until I was well into my teens that I realized this was not a usual way for a person to get around. When I insisted I take the bus to lessons, my mother wouldn't hear of it. She relented after I said I'd only go by car if she drove me, and we both agreed the ballet studio, two bus lines away, was too far for me to go on my own.

Tannin was disappointed after finding out the line stopped at the local public high school and she could have widened her flirting universe.

"Hello, Daddy." I give him a quick peck on his cheek and try to compose myself, but I'm a jumble of nervous energy. I had to dash from the lobby to the car as fast as possible in the hope no one from UGotIt would see me climbing into a chauffeured car. "Thank you for picking me up."

"It's the least I can do for my best girl on her birthday." My father, in his three-piece banker suit and businessman-style haircut he's had since he was a teenager (tapered on the back and sides, longer on top, and parted to the left, but now white), looks exactly like the type of person who would refer to a—as of today—twenty-nine-year-old woman as his best girl. "Ike. Let's take the long way home so we can enjoy the view on Embarcadero."

My parents made a sizable donation to revitalize the bay-front street now lined with palm trees, benches, and sculptures, and for the restoration of historic streetcars that travel to and from Fisherman's Wharf. My mother reasoned that, since it was the view outside his office window, it should be a nice one. My father's office is on the thirty-fifth floor of a building he owns, and as far as I know, he never takes time to enjoy the view while working.

After a few moments of silence, my father clears his throat and says, "Evelyn, is that what you're planning on wearing tonight?"

"Don't worry, Daddy, Tannin is bringing me something." I pat his knee the way my mother does when she indulges him.

"Your mother just wants to make sure you have a special time tonight." My father has been making excuses for my mother since she refused to remove her high heels to spare the decking on Aristotle Onassis's "piddly boat."

"Tell me about it." I roll my eyes like a petulant teenager.

Never once did I ever think of saying, "Sorry, Ma, but for this birthday I think I'll just wear jeans and a sweatshirt and maybe order in pizza and drink beer with my friends." For my mother, a birthday, anniversary, or holiday is an opportunity to do what she does best: hostess. She's famous (and infamous) for her dinners and get-togethers. Something as minor as it being my birthday is not going to get in the way of her celebrating it in at fashion she deems appropriate. That she's had merely three days to plan it only adds to the challenge for her.

"How was your day at work, Evelyn?" When in doubt, my father likes to talk shop. My mother talks about the new curtains or problems with the florist. I don't think they actually hear each other.

"Interesting. A lot more complicated than I thought it would be." I sneak a look at my father, not sure how he'll take my next realization. "But I think it might be made more complicated by the people who are running it."

"Evelyn, what have I always told you?" My father answers his own question without even pausing to let me pretend to think about it. "The only people who go into business are those who were too dumb to become doctors or lawyers."

"But, Daddy, aren't you a businessman?" I ask innocently, knowing the joke by heart.

"Yes, but what I really want to do is dance on Broadway." He gives me a rare half smile, his eyes crinkling up at the corners so his bushy brows obscure his clear blue irises.

"You and me both, Daddy. You and me both." I smile back at him, settle in, and enjoy the sights that cost my family millions of dollars and no one will ever know about because, of course, they made their donation anonymously.

Alexander

Kozmos is predictably full of painfully self-aware, edgy hipsters, ambitious financial types, and a smattering of hardened dot-com survivors, but I can tell right away why Pete (the antithesis of anything hip or edgy) wants to try it out. Not for the Asian fusion bar food, exotic mixed drinks, and rampant pickup scene—Pete is here for the pristine pool tables and Pabst on tap. Pete is just a simple midwestern guy at heart, and to him Pabst on tap isn't ironic, it's just Pabst on tap.

"What about that one?" He tips his glass toward a pretty blonde sitting with a group of friends, all women and all pretending they aren't watching us watching them.

"Nah." I refuse to drink Pete's beloved Pabst and am enjoying a Bohemia—my father's favorite and mine too since he let me have my first sip of it at age twelve.

"What's wrong with her?" Pete puts down his beer and picks up the cue stick, lining up his shot. A natural-born pool shark, Pete paid for his books and beer through college and law school with his skills at the table. He looks like the last person who can hustle a game. "She's cute."

"Nothing is wrong with her. She's not my type."

Pete neatly pockets his desired shot and steps away and back to his beer. I concentrate on the pool table, imagining what I want to do on it, and it's not the cute blonde. I bungle my turn and gesture for Pete to get on with the slaughter.

"They're all your type, Alexander. Something must be wrong with her since you haven't gone over to get her phone number." Pete stays firmly seated on the barstool. He'd never think of approaching a beautiful woman, or even an okay-looking one, to ask what her sign is. It's just not his style.

How he ended up married to Melissa, a former professional cheerleader with an eBay addiction and the morals of a lemur in heat, I'll never know. He's never given me a believable story on how they met, and I know all too well why they're not together anymore.

"Have another on me." Pete waves back to my green-felted humiliation.

"You're a true pool table Samaritan, Pete. Fucking Gandhi." I miss my shot and hand over the cue stick. "Hey, you know that building right across from us?"

Pete knows everything about anything going on around work since he's friendly with security guards. The guards fill him in on all the gossip, and I'm hoping he's just as clued in about what is going on across the street. Namely flower deliveries to the fifth floor to a beautiful, tall woman with hair like rich chocolate who has been on my mind since I saw her this morning. I may not know her name, but I'm definitely sure she's not the kind of woman who is impressed by a dozen red roses.

"What about it?" Pete expertly sinks two balls and blocks my only viable shot.

"I saw . . . There was a woman. I saw her this morning on the train, the N, and later in the building across from us. She's cute—not cute. Beautiful." I stop stammering and take the cue stick. "She knits."

"Interesting." Pete looks at me closely, nodding. "Hey, Alexander, have I ever told you I minored in psychology in college?"

"Several times." I take my shot, pathetically moving things around so it'll take Pete a few minutes longer to beat me. "What's your diagnosis, Dr. Freud?"

"It's all part of your pattern of behavior. The pursuit of the unattainable." Pete holds out his hand to stop me from wasting my breath. "Hear me out. How many girlfriends have you had since I met you? Don't bother. I've kept count. An average of one every three-point-five months, and every single one of them a lovely young woman in her own way."

"What? Are you keeping some sort of spreadsheet on my dating habits?" I don't mention how close I came to making the mistake of fully committing to Sigrid. Pete doesn't need to know—plus, he never really liked her. When I asked what he thought of her, he said, "Her hair looks very blond, and she has nice teeth."

"Yes." Pete points at me accusingly and continues, "I'm not saying all were marriage material, but you found something wrong with each and every one."

"I didn't. Things just haven't worked out. That's normal. It's called dating."

Pete, as far as I know, has slept with only three women in his entire life: his prom date, a girl he saw through most of college before she joined the Peace Corps (at least that's the story she stuck to), and Melissa.

"Remember Michelle?" Pete asks in a rather accusatory tone.

"Which one?" I've dated more than my share of Michelles. And Jennifers. But only one Sigrid, and that was enough.

"First year of law school. Cute as a button—" Only Pete could get away with calling a grown woman, a future lawyer, cute as a button.

"That must have been the problem. I don't usually go for cute. I usually go for exotic, cruel, and unstable."

Pete ignores me. "You broke up with her because she wouldn't eat sushi. You broke up with one, Diane, because she read her horoscope."

"So? I admit, those are pretty lame reasons for breaking up with a girl. But I've been dumped by women my fair share of times, too. I'm sure their reasons, if I bothered to remember them, would be just as lame."

Pete paces back and forth, surveying the pool table. "This knitting thing is new. I'll have to look it up on the Internet."

"Are you trying to tell me something, buddy?"

I sit down with my back to the girls. I don't feel like flirting or making small talk, and I can feel their pull from here, even though I'm not interested. If I give in, which would be easy to do, I'd end up going home with one of them, maybe the blonde, and repeating the process Pete is currently finding fault with.

Pete clears his throat and stand up straight, momentarily losing the ever-present slump to his shoulders. "Just give it a chance, Alexander, before you make up your mind."

"It?"

I know what Pete means by "it," and I've done a pretty good job of avoiding the real it for whatever reason. Up until now, this morning, I had no idea what the real it might be.

"Love. It might be under your nose or at that table not ten feet from you. You never know." Pete clears his throat. This is why he stays out of the courtroom; he's a brilliant strategist, but he lets his emotions get the better of him, and lawyers can't afford to be emotional at the wrong time.

"Anyone ever tell you you're a hopeless romantic, Pete?" I throw an arm around him and signal the waitress for another round of beers. It's going to be a long night.

"My wife," Pete says, "just before she left me."

Evelyn

In nothing but my sensible cotton underpants and bra, I stand in the middle of my mother's pale gray and cream dressing room and wait for Tannin to appear with my birthday dress.

"My God! Evelyn, darling, what are you wearing?" My mother, followed by Ying, her personal everything from seamstress to vitamin wrangler, stops short at the sight of me. Ying has a Neiman's garment bag draped over her arm.

"Underwear?"

I look down at myself, catching sight of my body from all angles in the three-sided mirror in the corner. Hey, I'm no Kate Moss but no cow either. My legs are strong, my butt rounded and firm, my shoulders have a hint of muscle, and even though my belly is not concave, I think I'd look pretty darn good in a bikini. Maybe I'd get second looks on Saint-Tropez or in the Hamptons, but I'd never parade around in two pieces of Lycra anyway. Not with my complexion.

"You can't possibly wear those things under your dress, Evelyn. You'll have lumps."

Mother, already dressed and in her usual three-inch Dior heels and black check evening suit, strides over to a bank of cabinets, barely making an indentation in the thick carpet. She pulls out a handful of flesh-colored foundation garments from one of the drawers.

I stare at the body shaper—a girdle sewed on to bike shorts, matching bra with at least an inch of foam padding where my nipples might sit if hiked into the correct spot—and take a step back. There doesn't even appear to be a slit in the crotch of the pants for bathroom breaks, and the foam nipple barrier pads stand at attention in the otherwise shapeless bra. "I didn't know there was a fetish theme for the party, Mother."

"Silly girl, just put them on. I don't need you to make a fuss. I'm running late and need to finalize the seating arrangements. No matter what I say, Sissy will insist on arriving early to help me when all she wants to do is make sure her husband is seated as far away from her as possible."

"I think I'll look fine without these, Mother," I say, pushing the high-tech and unyielding fabric back into her hands. It's my birthday. Is it too much to ask not to be trussed like sausage in too tight casing for one night? "And why do you have this kind of stuff in here anyway?"

"A lady is always prepared, Evelyn." My mother sits at her dressing table to pat her hair into shape even though I haven't seen it move from its current style since 1997.

"Fine. I can see I'm outnumbered here." I take the body shaper and bra and step behind the screen.

I manage not to break much of a sweat while encasing myself in a girdle that comes up right under my bra band. The matching bra with wide straps, the kind I've only seen in reprints of 1950s and 1960s lingerie ads, completes the ensemble. If she tries to force a pair of support hose on me, I'm walking out right now.

"Is this underwear or birth control?" I peek out from behind the screen.

"Such drama, Evelyn," my mother sighs as she sifts through her jewelry drawer. "I'd expect it from Tannin, but not you."

Ying steps in and discreetly helps me into the dark teal, flared-bottom skirt, and I pull on the matching bateau-neck, long-sleeved, fitted sweater. I can tell immediately that she bought the size based on me wearing foundation garments. Ying fusses with nonexistent stray threads and shrugs. Traitor Tannin. Good thing I didn't step on a scale in front of my sister, or I'm sure that information would have found itself into my mother's journal, where she notes divorces, affairs, whose offspring is in rehab, birthdays, et cetera.

Once I'm dressed, Ying hands me a pair of black d'orsay Ferragamos with modest two-inch heels. My feet are a reliable size nine and a half, and there's nothing my mother can do about that. Then Ying sends me out for inspection.

"A little plain," says the woman who had not a hair out of place when she gave birth to me. "But with the right jewelry, it'll brighten you up. You do look so trim, and I expect you're still losing . . ." She trails off, and I force myself not to encourage her to pick up her train of thought. A trick James taught me in the art of proactive passive-aggressiveness. "Evelyn?"

"I've been at this weight for a couple of months now, Mother."

I'm sorry to disappoint the woman who is of the opinion I need to wear a girdle to my own birthday party. "I think this is where my body wants to be."

Considering I'm off my diet consisting entirely of mineral water, French cigarettes, and self-pity, I doubt I'll be dipping anywhere near the negative digit that makes up Mother's and Tannin's clothes size. My mother is petite and birdlike, same as my sister. I'm decidedly not. I have a body, even after losing all the weight, that's meant to be paired with a lacrosse stick, while Mother wears cashmere sweaters in all but the warmest of weather, summer trips to Palm Springs included.

"Evelyn, I'm wondering, if you're not too busy with this new job of yours, if you could attend an event in my place this Friday?" Mother asks.

My answer is no, but I can't be that blunt. "I'd love to, Mother, but I have plans with a few friends from Pearson. They want to catch up with me and hear all about Paris. Maybe Tannin could go instead?"

"Never mind. Your father and I will just have to make our excuses. I'll be downstairs with Cook. Come down when you're finished getting ready." She clears her throat and stands up. She doesn't like to be reminded of unpleasantries, especially those involving a broken heart and weight gain.

Once Mother and Ying are gone, I plop down, the seat still warm where my mother's (I look around before I think it) bony ass was perched on the tufted silk cushion. I ignore the jewelry, a long-strand pearl and diamond necklace, matching earrings the size of half dollars, and cuff bracelet she's set out for me. I am a plain person; even Tannin accepts that. My makeup, which I threw into a Ziploc bag this morning as I rushed out for work, is carefully laid out waiting for me to paint my face, something that I'm quite adept at after years of painting lessons. I pull my hair back into a loose chignon, and when I'm satisfied it will pass my mother's muster, I pick up a makeup brush and get to work.

Alexander

As I line up my shot, I catch the eye of the blonde perched on one of the barstools opposite us. I could go through all the motions in my sleep—a few times I have. All I have to do is wander over, feed her some line, and we'll wind up at either her place or mine. After sex, she'll start talking about herself, asking questions about me. After making some small talk about getting together again for a real date and exchanging business cards, we'll part ways and think of each other only when we have that particular itch and there isn't anyone handy around to scratch it.

"Take the shot, Don Juan," Pete says through a mouthful of overpriced bar food. "And leave the ladies' panties dry for once."

"I object to your bigoted as well as pathetically dated racial slur and blatantly sexist comment, my good man Pete."

I look up at the group of women and regret it. The blonde might as well be waving her panties at me. I take my shot, botching it, but I just want to get out of her line of vision. She's had enough of being coy. She wants to get laid, and she wants me to do the honors.

"And I object to your ability to seduce women by merely blinking." Pete circles the table, looking for the best angle to end my misery in the most humiliating fashion. "Eight ball, right corner pocket."

I watch as he neatly sends the ball spinning, once again beating me.

"It's truly sickening," Pete says and swallows the rest of his food.

"Okay, it's time to call it a night," I say, holding my hands up in defeat. "I'm just getting drunker and poorer, and you're getting better and better."

"I may not have your looks, my friend, but in the end nature has a way of keeping the world in balance." Pete racks the balls for the next players.

"Hey." One of the women from the group wanders over, a little unsteady on her high heels.

"Hi." I stand behind Pete, even though it's clear she's addressing only me.

"My girlfriends and I were wondering if you were a model or a lawyer." She giggles. Her friends catcall and urge her on. "My vote is a lawyer. Who looks like a model."

"He is," I say, pushing Pete forward.

"What?" She looks from me to Pete.

"Both!" I hold Pete's arm up, prize-fighter style.

"Oh." She looks back at her friends, shrugging. "Okay."

"Ouch," Pete says, rubbing the patchy stubble on his chin. "I think I've just been rejected without even first being considered. That's a new low for me."

"There's always tomorrow night, my man. Don't stop believing," I sing off key and shoot the girls a dirty look. Why do they have to be such bitches? "Pete, *you are* a great guy. She could do a lot worse. Like me, for instance."

"Eh, who needs them?" Pete pops another fried cheese ball into his mouth.

I sit at our table and glance at my phone. It's blinking with voice mails and text messages. I scroll through quickly, feeling my buzz disappear. "Fuck. My parents are looking for me and so is Candace."

"Candace?" Pete asks, wiggling his eyebrows like some silent movie pervert. "Is she requesting your attention for a midnight strategy meeting?"

"Shut up, Pete."

"So who do you respond to first? The client or the people who gave you life, shelter, and impossibly good looks?"

I look at Pete helplessly. "Do I really have a choice?"

He nudges the last of the beer toward me. "Drink up, mate. You're going to need all the help you can get."

Evelyn

"You look beautiful," my father says from the doorway, where he's standing. "May I come in?"

"Of course, Daddy. I'm all done here."

I carefully put the lid on my custom-blended lipstick. I've mixed three colors to get the perfect shade of red, and I wear it only in the evening. Yes, my mother has an opinion on women who wear bright lipstick during the day, and it's not good.

He holds out a hand to help me up. "I have something to show you."

I follow my father into the sitting room that separates his bedroom from my mother's dressing room, which is next to her bedroom. The three solid walnut doors that separate them are usually kept closed.

But who am I to criticize their sleeping arrangements? My last relationship was with a married man, and the one before that with a guy who flossed his teeth before and after sex.

I perch myself on one of the tightly upholstered side chairs that flank the marble fireplace, and my father sits on the other. He's wearing a fresh dark navy suit, white monogrammed shirt, and Windsor-knotted tie. A creamy silk pocket square is precisely tucked into his breast pocket. He was very amused when I let him know that they were finally back in style.

"You're looking dapper tonight, Daddy." I pat smooth my skirt over my thighs, happy I didn't fight my mother about wearing a girdle. This party is for them, not me, after all, and the outfit looks wonderful.

"The least I can do for my best girl." He twiddles his thumbs. "What's that I see there?"

My father looks pleased with himself, and I can't help but play along. I turn my head toward where he's looking. "Where?"

"Could it be a gift for the birthday girl?" He gets up and carries a box over to me. "Now this is only half of it. I couldn't manage to wrap the rest."

"Daddy, it's not a pony, is it?" I pause as I untie the thick gros-grain ribbon that is carefully affixed into a bow around the cream-colored box.

"No, no." He sits down and then stands up again, putting his hands in his trouser pockets and rocking back and forth on his heels. "Did you really want a pony?"

"Daddy, what girl doesn't?"

I open the box. Inside, tucked in a cushion of tissue paper, is an inlaid wood and mother-of-pearl box holding an array of fine paintbrushes. My throat closes, and I feel tears well up in my eyes. Not from the residual hurt of what happened in Paris but from the realization that it doesn't hurt to hold the paintbrushes in my hand.

"Now if you don't like it, just let me know. I'll write you a check," my father says in one quick rush. "Your mother mentioned that you had to leave all your supplies in Paris, and I thought this might tide you over until your aunt Jane can ship them back."

I stand up and give him a kiss on the top of his head. "I couldn't have asked for anything more perfect, Daddy. Really."

"Well, that's good to hear." He clears his throat. "We better get downstairs or your mother will disinvite us from her next dinner party for being tardy. May I have the pleasure of escorting the guest of honor?"

I entwine my arm in his. "I'd be delighted if you would, kind sir."

Alexander

I straighten my tie before ringing the doorbell. Candace lives in a tasteful Pacific Heights mansion—the kind of house I used to fantasize about living in when I was a kid and didn't realize people like me don't live in houses like this. Not unless we sell a lot of drugs or sneakers. Or build a reputation as an ace lawyer who can handle the kinds of problems people behind the doors of mansions up and down the block have.

I look at my watch—it's almost 8:30. If I'm lucky, I'll get out of here quickly so I can take a cab down to the Mission and make amends with my mother and father, who no doubt have gotten wind of who my newest client is. Impatient, I ring the bell again, and it echoes through the house. A few seconds later I hear the muffled footsteps of someone coming to answer the door.

"*Buenas noches. ¿La Señora Hall está en casa?*" I say in my most polite Spanish to the older Latina in a maid's uniform who answers the door.

"Good evening, Mr. Velazquez," she replies in clipped English, a faint South American accent coloring her words.

I give her a moment to enjoy the feeling of making me feel like a jackass. "I'm here to see Ms. Hall. I'm her lawyer."

"Yes." She steps off to the side to let me slip in past her.

I stand there, feet firmly planted on the marble floor, while she presses a security code into the panel by the door, shielding it as best as she can with her body. When she's done, she sniffs and looks me over before she says, "This way, please, Mr. Velazquez."

I'm forced to walk a step or two behind her as she leads me to what may be either a sitting room or a living room (something tells me this place has at least two of each). The slow pace gives me plenty of time to admire Candace's art collection. I don't know much about art, but even I can tell she has some pretty impressive stuff on her walls.

"Would you like something to drink?" the maid asks or, more like, orders.

I pause in the middle of sitting down on a cream-colored sofa my *abuelita* would have kept under a double layer of plastic. "Water, please. Thank you."

"Ms. Candace will be here shortly. Please wait," she says stiffly and retreats, shutting me inside the room.

I lean my satchel on the side of the couch, then move it to the floor by my feet before setting it right in front of me on the coffee table next to a perfectly arranged plate of cheese, crackers, and grapes, so Candace knows I'm on the clock. As Rodney said to me this afternoon on my way to take a leak, "You start billing her before the phone even rings, you get me?"

I wait, and then I wait some more. I'm about to get up and poke my head into the hallway when I hear the sharp clicking of very high heels outside. I quickly settle back down, throwing an arm over the couch, and pretend to be looking through this month's *Architectural Digest* for the first time.

"I know I ordered it in black, but I won't be needing it in black. I want it in the cream." Candace sweeps in, midconversation, her cell held a few inches from her ear like it's a corner pay phone. "I don't care what time it is in New York. . . . I'll expect a call from Vera, personally, to explain why this can't happen."

She snaps her phone closed and then turns on the wattage. "Alexander! So glad you could make it."

I'm stuck, half in, half out of my seat waiting for her to sit down, and when it looks like she's going to stand there so I can admire her looking dangerously sexy in a dark pencil skirt (I've always been a sucker for those), white silk blouse, and heels, I stand straight up and offer her my hand to shake.

"Ms. Hall."

"Candace." She ignores my hand and plants an air kiss on either cheek, her hands squeezing my biceps. "Working out, I see."

She sits down, crosses those long legs, and then looks up at me. I sit down opposite her and wait for her to tell me why I'm here. It's been less than five hours since I saw her last, and I can't imagine she's managed to find someone else to sue in that short time, but I'm ready to be wrong.

When she doesn't say anything, I reach into my bag for a list of questions I have about her case. "If you could just—"

She waves her hands at me; even at this hour she has the doorknob-size diamond on her finger. "Let's not, Alexander."

"It's why I'm here, Candace." I keep the question out of my voice like an Amazon explorer keeps blood out of a piranha-infested river.

"Alexander, you do own a decent tux, don't you?" she asks.

"A tux?"

Candace ignores me and takes a drink and a folded piece of paper from a tray offered by the maid, who has crept in like a cat when I wasn't looking. "Thank you, Raymunda."

Candace studies the piece of paper, her eyes narrowing as they go down what looks like a list of names. With a grimace, she crumples up the sheet and tosses it on the table next to my satchel.

"I'm a very rich woman," she says, more to herself than to me. "You'd think with all the money I could continue to give to their charities, causes, and endowments, I'd be included on the guest list to a simple fucking dinner party for Lila's fat daughter. If Lila and the rest of them think I'm going to just ignore this snub, they're in for a big surprise."

I say nothing because I get the feeling I'm here in the capacity of a spectator, not a participant, in Candace's one-woman drama. I accept my glass of water from the silent Raymunda and wait.

"She may not want my company at her precious daughter's dinner party, but she certainly counts on my money." Her cell phone rings. "This better be about my dress arriving tomorrow or you'll have some more lawyer work in the morning, Alexander. . . . Yes. First flight in the morning? Wonderful, Vera. I knew you would come through for me. You're a dear."

She snaps the phone closed and tosses it onto the couch next to me. We stare at each other for a few seconds before I fold and break the silence by saying the most lame sentence ever uttered by man. "So you made clothes for dogs? You must love animals." I grab a handful of grapes and shove them into my mouth to stem the flow.

Candace gives me a long, humorless smile before answering. "Actually, Alexander, I can't stand the little fuckers."

Evelyn

After cocktails and small talk where I give polite but evasive answers about how I enjoyed Paris, my mother clears her throat.

"I know we are all engrossed in conversation, but Cook will be angry with me if we ruin the delicious food she's prepared for Evelyn's birthday dinner." She smiles and then turns and makes her way into the formal dining room. We, and twenty guests, Tannin and James being the only two I was allowed to invite, follow and take our preassigned seats. Who I'm sandwiched between makes it obvious my mother is of the mind that this will be a working dinner for me.

Harold Ernest Montgomery (IV or is it VI?), recently divorced banker, avid yachts man, and trophy wife/girlfriend collector, is seated to my right.

"I'm done with coked-up models and unstable actresses," Hank, as I've always called him, says as we are served the soup course. "I want someone who has her own money, life, and none of that hiring a surrogate to carry my sons. At least not for the first one."

"I'm afraid," I say with all the sincerity I can muster over a bowl of crab and roasted pepper soup, "that wouldn't be me, Hank. I'm a big believer in outsourcing such menial tasks to those who have the time and inclination."

Hank gives me a funny look and turns his attention to the woman on his right, Celine Masters. She's an editor of a popular quirky local arts and culture blog, and just the type of person my mother likes to have at these kinds of dinners. But, from the twist of Mother's mouth, I can tell she's peeved that Celine's cleavage is competing with me for Hank's attention.

I turn to my left, where Whit ("Whitless to my friends and enemies") Felix Neilson, pharmaceutical heir and perpetual fuckup extraordinaire, sits. Whit was Tannin's escort for Le Bal Crillon des Débutantes, when she was presented to international society in Paris. I went along to support her and was trussed up in a couture gown and miserable. Tannin, of course, had a great time and wound up hooking up with some minor Russian prince while I had to entertain Whit.

"So, Whit, how is Los Angeles?" I ask him. "I hear you're in the movie business now."

"Yeah, movies. Mostly straight-to-DVD stuff, but I've got big plans." Whit throws an arm over the back of my chair.

I doubt he remembers he vomited on the hem of my Christian Dior gown and then asked me to blow him before passing out. Mother must be desperate to marry me off to have him at her table for my official birthday dinner.

"Hey, Tannin, how'd you like to star in my next movie?" he asked.

"I don't know, Whit. Does it involve double penetration?" Tannin shoots back at him.

Whit looks at Tannin, and she tosses her long blond hair back. They'll be going home together, and I won't hear from Tannin until she breaks up with him or he falls asleep on top of her. But I'm sure they'll have plenty of fun while it lasts, and at least some of Mother's machinations won't go to waste.

"Is she kidding?" Celine asks Hank, who's trying to look down the front of her dress.

"Of course she is. So tell us more about this blog of yours," Hank says. "I would blog, but my lawyers would have a heart attack."

"Speaking of lawyers and heart attacks," Sissy interrupts. "Have you heard the latest?"

"Latest?" Mother expertly feigns ignorance. Her circle lives, breathes, and trades in gossip. I'm sure my mother not only knows what Sissy is talking about but probably told the person who then shared this tidbit with Sissy.

"About Candace?" Sissy tries to raise her surgically raised brow and succeeds only in looking slightly more mummified. "She's on to another firm."

My mother looks mildly sympathetic, disapproving, and bored at the same time. "It's such a shame. She must have so much on her plate right now, what with her legal entanglements and fighting to keep Redford's chair on the board."

I chew and watch them, trying to understand what it is that keeps them friends. It's pretty clear they can't stand each other. They didn't speak for two solid years over a disagreement involving perennial plantings for the San Francisco Botanical Society Ball in 1986, but when Sissy nearly died after a face-lift, my mother rushed to her bedside and made her public amends by hosting a dinner in her honor after Sissy got out of the hospital.

"Yes, I spoke to her this afternoon, and she sent her regards to our lovely Evelyn." Sissy turns to me, sensing that my mother won't be dishing about the latest topic of scandalized conversation at this particular dinner table.

"I suppose you'll have to send a note, Evelyn." Mother sighs, twisting the diamond pendant dangling from the end of her necklace.

"Pardon me," I say, surprised. I've met only Candace Hall a handful of times and always found her confidence and focus a little scary.

"Evelyn, darling, Candace wishes you a very happy birthday and is so sorry she couldn't make it to the dinner party." Sissy watches Mother's face for a reaction out of the corners of her recently redone eyes.

"Perhaps next year," I say, as insincere as Sissy. Whatever feud she's trying to fan between Mother and Candace Hall is none of my business.

"I hear that, uh . . ." Celine falters slightly as all eyes turn to her. She's expected to sing for her supper and as of yet hasn't delivered. "I hear that she's rethinking how, uh, she allocates her funding portfolio."

Everyone stares at Celine, and Mother lets her stew before coming to her rescue.

"I'm sure Mrs. Hall is rethinking a lot of things right now," Mother says. She gestures to Cook, who gestures to the servers, who start clearing away the soup course. "Whit, please tell me that you aren't perpetuating any of those god-awful reality shows."

I hide a smile behind my napkin and avoid looking over at Celine Masters, who is all ears and wide eyes. I have a feeling her blog will be a little less highbrow tomorrow.

Alexander

An hour later I take another cab to my parents' house and have the driver let me out a block away. My dad drove a cab for years to help put my mom through law school, and with my luck the cabbie would know my dad and get invited in and be one more witness to him not welcoming home his prodigal son.

I let myself in, not bothering to knock, and call into the hall- way, "Anyone home?"

"Alexander." My mother rushes out from the living room. She's wearing a silk robe I gave her last Mother's Day over her pajamas. I kiss her, and she takes my arm to lead me toward the couch.

"What is this, Son?" My father, still dressed in khakis and a random union T-shirt, waves a fax in my face.

"Sergio." My mother sighs as she settles down next to me, keeping a hold on my hand.

"What's what?" And just like that I fall back into my teenage habit of playing dumb in the face of parental disapproval.

"Don't you 'what's what' me, Itzlacoliuhque." My father shoves the paper at me, calling me by my rarely used (except by him) legal first name.

Unable to figure out how to pronounce it (its-lah-kol-e-KWA-ke), teachers and friends called me Izzy for short until I got wise and demanded everyone use my middle name. The first of the many disappointments I was to deal out to my father. But can you blame me?

Itzlacoliuhque.

Try saying that when you're missing your front teeth and a bully is punching you in the stomach. But that's what you get for being born to hard-core Chicano parents whose own parents refused to teach them Spanish because they thought it would give them a leg up in life. Instead, my parents embraced everything about the culture (even the names), and though their Spanish is rudimentary at best, they made sure Nayelli and I grew up bilingual.

I skim the text of the story that will be running in tomorrow's *S.F. Express,* no doubt leaked early to my dad by one of his union buddies at the printing plant.

The headline reads SOCIAL JUSTICE: HALL MOVES ON TO HOT FIRM. It's nothing but the usual scuttlebutt that passes for journalism at the *Express*—short on facts but heavy with breathless speculation about the "dark and dapper mystery lawyer" Candace had a "cozy and canoodling lunch" with.

"What is this *chingadera*, Son?" My father crosses his arms over his chest and waits. His conversational Spanish might be limited, but despite my grandparents' best efforts, he picked up every imaginable cussword from south of the border and the neighboring *barrios*.

"How can you be so sure it's talking about me?" I shrug and hand my mom the fax. She sets it aside, facedown, on the coffee table.

"He's being a smart-ass!" My father throws his hands up in despair. He is nothing if not theatrical. "Go get me my belt, *mujer*."

"Get your own belt, Sergio." My mother rubs her eyes. "Alexander. We just want to hear your side of the story."

My father grunts but doesn't make a move to speak or get his belt.

"She's a client." Not a girlfriend, lover, or paramour, three words I caught in the story. "And no, we weren't 'canoodling' at One Market. It was a business lunch. My boss made me go."

"Tell your boss you won't work on her case! Tell them you quit," my dad shouts, but he knows he can't make me do anything.

We've both learned this the hard way. Even when it's in my best interest, the more he says I can't or shouldn't, the more I want to do whatever it is he's taken a stand against.

"This woman took advantage of her employees," my dad almost shouts. "She kept the union out of her sweatshop and cheated them out of fair wages and basic workers' rights."

"The employees voted not to unionize, Dad," I say, echoing one of the main talking points from Rodney's memo.

"Bah! Intimidation!"

"Sergio," my mother says in her familiar calming voice, "the vote was fair."

I turn to my mother, the lawyer, the pragmatic one, the only person who will be able to understand that sometimes practicing law is not a pretty thing. "She's just a client, Mom. She invited me out to lunch. I couldn't say no without being rude."

"For this he goes to six years of college?" My father addresses my mother. "Talk some sense into your *hijo*, Carina."

She's silent for a moment, gathering her thoughts. My father and I wait, not making eye contact.

"He took an oath, Sergio. Alexander is doing what he thinks is right." But before I can feel a little less guilty about the whole thing, she turns to me. "Is that correct, Alexander? You are not compromising your beliefs or principles by representing this client?"

Like any good lawyer and son with lots of experience in bullshitting his way out of a tight spot, I hedge. "I just got the case today. I haven't had a chance to digest all the details."

My mother pats her hands on her thighs, signaling the end of the conversation, and stands up. "That'll have to be good enough for all of us for now. Who's hungry? Your sister dropped off *pan dulce* from the bakery near the hospital this afternoon."

My dad follows her, ignoring me. "This is all because we let him change his name. That was where we went wrong."

"Alexander was your father's name, Sergio." My mother's tired voice drifts back from the hallway.

I sit for a moment, and when I think it's safe—my dad is no longer yelling about Aztec pride—join them in the kitchen for a piece of bread and a mug of grainy Mexican hot chocolate.

chapter fourteen
Compromising Positions

Evelyn

James leans into my doorjamb, smelling slightly of his usual late morning American Spirit cigarette. "Anyone give you anything you can actually use? Besides yours truly, of course."

I look up from my screen, grateful for a reason to take a break. Even though I got to work early—the security guy had to key open the elevator for me—I'm still struggling to make a dent in my day's to-do list per Ted, Jessica, and Allan, who now seem to be under the impression that I'm also here to function as their assistant.

"Let's see, besides your most appreciated heart-embossed, seven-inch glass dildo," I say in a lowered voice, "I got the usual assortment of hideous accessories, thoughtless tchotchkes, and discreet offers to set me up with a friend of a cousin, et cetera. You were there, remember?"

"I was drunk on fine wine and frivolous conversation, my dear. I can't be expected to remember the details."

Sometimes I think James and I were switched at birth. He seems more at home around my family than I do. I envy him for how easy it is for him to fit in, until I remember how he doesn't fit in with his own family.

Up until he told his parents he was gay, James had the kind of life I'd always fantasized about—a regular house with two normal parents (his dad was a plumber, his mom worked at the library), an older brother (now a dentist), a younger sister (now a mom and PTA dynamo), and a succession of golden retrievers, all named

Giggles. He played baseball, went to family reunions held at theme parks, and picked names out of a hat at Christmastime for Secret Santa.

James hasn't spoken to his own parents for about a dozen years, since they literally left him high and dry. He's always been sketchy about the specifics, but from what I've gathered, a category four tornado was bearing down on the only home he'd ever known, and thinking they were all going to die, James fessed up about his sexuality. He found himself on the street with a duffel bag, a bologna sandwich, his aunt's address in San Francisco, and instructions never to darken their doorway again. He was fifteen.

Given all this, James is remarkably good-natured about his family. He sends his parents cards for any and every occasion— some of which he's made up, like Accept Your Son Is Gay and Get Over It Day. I don't think his parents have responded to any of his attempts to reach out to them, but it hasn't stopped James. He still loves them and puts their narrow-mindedness down to being born and bred in Kansas.

"Are you coming with me to do the returns?" I ask him. He is, after all, the person who initiated this after-birthday ritual when he saw all the tasteful but useless stuff I was left with from my last ten birthdays, since my mother's friends decided I was the right age for grown-up gifts.

Most are decorative but useless, except James's romantic dildo (which he knows I can't and wouldn't ever return to Good Vibrations, another San Francisco shopping institution) and Tannin's big box of designer workout gear and brochure for a yoga retreat in Mexico she's threatening to take me to this winter. My sister never works out (she's a big believer in passive exercise through colonics), but in her mind it would be worth going through the motions just to be able to wear the adorable (her word) yoga wear. "Plus," she added, "the retreat is near Cabo, and we can sneak out and party until we puke up our livers."

Everything else, though, is going back. I know I should feel bad, but I don't. I have no use for another handcrafted glass paperweight or red leather hatbox. And it's expected of me to return the gifts. It's why the givers' assistants discreetly tucked in the gift receipts with the cards. I get to unload some expensive crap I don't need and know what to gush about in the thank-you card. Everyone is happy, except Gump's, but since it's where I buy my mother her gifts, it all evens out in the end.

"Of course I'm coming!" James exclaims. "I live for this kind of shit. I mean, it's not like they can be rude to us. It's Gump's!"

I glance out the window. I've been so busy I'd forgotten all about him. Or at least convinced myself he hasn't been on my mind. I dreamed about him last night. He was shrouded in mist while I tried to reach him on a windswept moor, my long skirt sodden and slowing me down, always leaving him just out of reach. And yes, I just reread *Jane Eyre* for the millionth time.

"What are you looking at?" James asks through a huge yawn as he curls up on the sleek ivory leather Barcelona chair my mother had delivered this morning because I made the mistake of mentioning that beanbags were also the guest chairs in my office. It's the real deal, not from the pages of the Design Within Reach catalog, because as she said on her way to a fitting at Chanel, "I just can't abide by reproductions, Evelyn, and neither should you."

"Evelyn? What are you looking at?" James asks again, sounding more awake.

"Sorry?" I whip my eyes away from the window, thereby making myself look even guiltier than merely daydreaming. "Pardon me?"

"What is it?" James cranes his neck and scans my limited vista.

"I'm not looking at anyone," I answer too quickly.

"Anyone? It's a person? Now you have to tell me," James says, suddenly fully awake. He gets up to go to the window and then halts midstep. "Nerd alert!"

"What?" Confused, I watch James flee my office.

Allan appears, holding a Big Gulp in each hand. "We should interface off-site."

"Interface?" I stare at him blankly as he takes a long sip from the soda in his right hand. "Oh! You mean talk about the redesign. Of course. I'll e-mail Jessica."

"Don't bother, she's busy. You. Me. Lunch." He's dressed in his usual mismatched shades of black, with what I notice are brand-new green Chucks already customized with black Sharpie lettering. No doubt something arcane written in HTML code.

"Lunch?" I look up from his feet, confused but cognizant of where this conversation is going and that there's nothing I can do to stop it. "Just us?"

"Dinner?" He takes a sip from the drink in his left hand.

"Lunch is fine." Salvage what I can is my motto for the day. "I have to, uh, donate plasma after work."

"Whatever. My treat." He takes a small sip from each drink, mixing them in his mouth the way people savor good red wine.

"I . . ." I shake my head a little too vigorously. One of my earrings gets caught in my hair, leaving me with my head crooked at an odd angle. Allan doesn't seem to notice. "It's okay, Allan. Really—"

"Don't worry. I'll expense it." Allan turns away from me, talking as he leaves. "I'll see you down in the lobby after the meeting."

"Allan!" Ted calls out, almost running into him as he makes his way into my office. "My main man! My technical ninja! My—"

"Yeah, bye," Allan mumbles and continues his coordinated sip, step walk back to his office.

"Evelyn." Ted puts his UCLA mug on my desk and takes a seat, running his hands over the leather of my Barcelona chair.

"Yes? Ted?" I'm going to have to take that thing home before it's fondled into half its value.

"Evelyn, Evelyn, Evelyn." He drums his fingers on his belly and stares up at the ceiling.

"Ted, Ted, Ted?"

"You're one spunky gal." He laughs, using two terms I haven't heard since my ninety-seven-year-old grandmother passed away a few years ago.

"Thank you." Always graciously accept a compliment, no matter how archaic and creepy. That way it's easier to move along and end a conversation with minimal weirdness. "Is there something you needed from me?"

"There's this thing on Friday night." Ted stands with his back to me, hands clasped behind him, looking out the window.

I scan through his appointment calendar. "Do you need me to put together some press kits?"

"It'll give us a chance to get to know each other a little better." Ted rocks back and forth on his heels in time with each word.

"Is this something work related?" I ask.

Ted smiles at me, without the apparent need to elaborate or acknowledge the fact I've asked him a direct question.

"We'll talk off-line later." Ted, hands still clasped behind his back like some tweedy English professor in a company-logo polo shirt, glides out of my office.

"Isn't this off-line?" I call after him, completely bewildered. "You forgot your mug. Ted?"

Within seconds, James reappears at my door. "What's up his butt?"

"Something about something he wants to talk to me about tomorrow night."

"Did he just ask you out? On a date?" James sits down, kicking off his shoes to reveal Oscar the Grouch socks before tucking his legs under him. "With him?"

"I don't think so!" My hands fly to my face. "I don't know. Maybe!" My e-mail pings with a message from Ted. "How did he send that so fast?"

James lunges over me to open it, reading rapidly as I bite my knuckle to keep from screaming.

"Da, da, da, networking event . . . drinks . . . da, da, da . . . ballet benefit . . . UGotIt is a donor. . . . Put a face to the name. . . . Will pick you up at your place, da, da, da. . . . Wear a nice dress."

For a second neither of us says anything.

"You're going out on a date with your boss!" James bounces up and down like some well-dressed chimpanzee. "And he's telling you what to wear!"

I drop my head into my hands as a message appointment for lunch with Allan pings into my in-box. "Oh, God."

"God can't help you now." James rubs my neck and shoulders. "Never mind all that. What are you going to wear? You don't want to show too much tit or thigh and give Ted ideas on your big date. He might try to slip you more than the tongue when he gives you a good night kiss."

"Kill me now, James," I moan.

"Knowing Ted, he won't take death as a reason for you not going out with him." James pats the top of my head gently.

I sigh. I stare blankly out the window. Even the sight of him walking into his office doesn't make my day any brighter. "As they say, *viennes m'enculer.*"

James asks, "Hey, don't you have to referee a meeting between Jessica and Allan in the conference room?"

"I believe I do." I allow myself one minute to relax before I get back to work.

Alexander

I walk straight into my office, ignoring Wallace's arched eyebrow at the hour I've shown up. I don't need her attitude when I know I'll be buried under the mass of e-mails, phone messages, and other related Candace crap even though that's what I've been dealing with since dawn. I'll have to work double time to slog through it all and deal with the actual case she'd retained me to represent her in.

I toss my stuff on the couch and automatically look through my window.

I pick up the cold cup of coffee and start to walk it back into the kitchen when I almost crash into the same delivery guy from yesterday. "No. No more."

"She's a regular, what can I say?" He thrusts the clipboard at me and motions for his guy to add a few more boxes to the stack I've pushed against the wall, obscuring the Rodney-provided modern art prints.

Pete wanders in, hands in pockets, and whistles as he surveys what has to be on the brink of a fire hazard at this point. "Your girlfriend is a mite bit litigious, amigo."

"She's not my girlfriend." I roll my head back and forth, cracking the tension out of my neck.

Along with being the lead attorney on her case, I am expected to coordinate with Candace's New York–based PR firm. From what I've gathered, Candace is not content with seeing her name in the local papers; she wants to conquer the New York tabloids as well. I spent hours on the phone with them while they brainstormed positive spin on this whole thing. I would have hung up, only Rodney, who was also in on the conference call, kept interrupting so he could offer me up to contribute the circle jerk. Though she was officially represented by her assistant, Becky, I would bet my right nut Candace was listening in on the whole thing.

"And she documents thoroughly," Pete continues.

"Are you here to help or gloat?" I snap.

I'm in a crappy mood from too little sleep and too much guilt. I even got into a pointless shouting match with a MUNI driver who stopped midtrack so he could jump out and take a long smoke. The rest of my day doesn't look to be shaping up any better. I sit back on the couch, leaning my head on the backrest, eyes staring up blankly at the ceiling.

"A little of both, but I can see you're not in the mood for either." Pete holds his hands up and backs out of the door. "Later, dude."

"Another fax for you, Mr. Velazquez," Wallace says, appearing out of thin air. She's in her usual black skirt, matching black top, and red lipstick and nails.

"Thanks." I take it and cover my face with it. Making out what it reads without bothering to hold it a healthy distance away from my eyes.

Becky has faxed over a revised list of New York people her boss feels I need to contact to familiarize myself with her situation. She wants character witnesses from outside the city, since she feels certain people in her circle are biased against her.

I crumple up the paper and shoot it toward the trash can, missing by a few feet. Cussing under my breath, I open one of the new boxes. A note scribbled on her personal stationery reads, "You're the best! XOXO, Candace."

"Alex. Good, you got the files." Rodney pokes his head in, his hair perfectly gelled and no sign that he's losing sleep over this case. "Priority one is still the lawsuit, but these will look good on your billing sheet."

I stare at his hand, waggling the hang-loose gesture in my direction until he gets the idea I'm not at all happy with having to take on Candace's other lawsuits. When he's gone, I go back to skimming dockets.

"Fuck me."

The woman is suing everyone from her "landscape artist and plant visionary" to her manicurists, several of them. It's official. I'm now Ms. Hall's legal whipping boy. XOXO.

"Mr. Velazquez." Wallace's voice cuts in from my desk phone.

I plod over, throw myself in my chair, and pick up the handset. "Yeah?"

"You have a call, Mr. Velazquez." Her voice is free from any nuance of human emotion. She might as well be a recording.

"Thanks, Wallace. If you could just take a message—"

"She's quite insistent, Mr. Velazquez." Her voice cracks ever so slightly. Wallace pauses to compose herself before she trusts herself to speak again. "It's Ms. Hall."

With my free hand I rub the spot on my forehead where my brain is trying to pound through. "But tell me how you really feel, Wallace."

Wallace is silent, and I am humbled.

"Put her through, and thanks, Wallace. For everything."

"Of course." Wallace clicks off.

"Alexander?" Candace's voice comes through with an echo from her end of the phone. She has me on speaker, or else she's doing that thing where she holds her cell half a foot away from her face.

"Hello, Candace," I say, cutting out the usual "call me Candace" dance that is more like foreplay than anything. I look at my watch. It's a quarter past noon, and I still haven't had a cup of coffee or any real food since last night at my parents'. I was stuck in my food-free flat all morning and sincerely considered eating toothpaste.

"Two issues. But the most pressing one is you need to be here tomorrow. I'll have my driver pick you up at your office."

I say nothing, absorbing the fact that I've slipped another notch from pretty boy counselor to legal whipping boy and am now firmly entering man-whore territory.

"Are you there?" Her voice leaves a metallic taste in my mouth but makes me sit up straighter.

"Sorry. Yeah. I don't see any—" To make myself feel less dirty, I scan through my calendar, checking for a deposition date (she'll only do them at home) or some other legal obligation, but I find nothing.

"I went for a narrow lapel. You can carry it off with your height. I have a good eye for this kind of thing, but my husband's tailor will take care of any minor fixes. Thank God I still have him on retainer. This is my official coming out of mourning event, and I want to make sure you look perfect, Alexander."

I'm about to ask her straight up what the hell she's talking about when Wallace runway stomps into my office, leading in a small, nervous-looking Asian man with a tape measure around his neck. He's holding up a suit bag with some difficulty to keep it from touching the ground. I watch as he opens it and pulls out an Armani tuxedo. He stands at the ready with tailor's chalk and pins.

"You have a guest, Mr. Velazquez," Wallace announces, giving me a steely glare, and retreats.

"Don't do the bow tie thing." Candace sighs in my ear. "It's so old. Wear that tie you had on at our first meeting. The Hermès. Bill me for the dry cleaning."

"I—" The line light blinks off, and I'm left holding a dead phone. "Well, fuck you very much."

"You ready now?" asks Candace Hall's dead husband's former tailor who is on retainer. Thank God.

"Am I ever!" He doesn't share my forced enthusiasm. "Sorry."

About half an hour later, I shrug back into my own suit jacket after seeing the tailor out to the reception area and go find Pete. From my office, I can hear my phone ringing. Seconds later, my cell phone chirps in my pocket. I shut it off even though I'm sure Wallace will shoot me dagger eyes for all the trips she'll have to make from the fax machine to my office.

"Alex!" Bryan and Brian wave me over. I shrug them off, not wanting to join in as they check out a paralegal who is making a show of pulling files from the lower cabinet drawers.

"What are you? Gay?" Bryan asks, watching Brian, almost as if daring him not to play along.

Brian hesitates. He's the toady in the relationship, but he's a lawyer with a clear understanding of California harassment laws. For a moment the battle between barrister and frat boy plays across his face before he gives in.

"Yeah!" he crows. "What are you? Gay? Not that there's anything wrong with that."

"You are so fucking lame, Brian," Bryan says, sounding betrayed.

I ignore them and make my way to Pete's office. He's been stuck way in the back, near the file and storage rooms. His office doesn't even have a window, which he claims to prefer, saying it helps him focus. What it really does is keep him off Rodney's and Brian's and Bryan's radar.

I walk in just as Pete is about to take a bite out of what looks to be a peanut butter and jelly sandwich.

"Don't eat that!" I yelp. No one over twelve should have to eat PB & J for lunch unless hungover. "You're one of the top legal minds in San Francisco, my brother. It's time you started eating like one."

"Huh?" Pete looks up from where he's buried behind legal briefs, holding the sandwich close to his mouth.

"We're going out to lunch. A big fucking long one. And, yeah, we're billing Candace for it."

Evelyn

I stare up at the Celebrity Sub menu, pretending I have no idea what I'm going to order. If I look hard enough, maybe I'll find some clue that will tell me how I've found myself here. Not helping is how close Allan is standing next to me. James has promised to come rescue me in half an hour so we can do the Gump's returns, but I'm not sure I'll be able to make it that long.

First thing Allan said to me after I rushed down to the lobby—
even if I didn't want to have lunch with him, it still didn't mean I
could be late—was "Just a warning. I'm planning on having onions.
Lots of onions."

"So," Allan says. He's wearing his sunglasses even though we're
inside and it's overcast outside.

"So?" I answer him and then go back to reading the menu.

"Why don't you get what you got yesterday? The turkey on
wheat?" Allan asks, as if it's the most normal thing in the world for
him to know what my preferred sandwich order is.

"I was thinking of trying something new." I have no choice
but to make eye contact, briefly, as we move up steadily in line. My
usual sandwich order has turned out to be fat-free roasted turkey (if
there is such a thing) with sliced cucumbers and sprouts on organic
cracked wheat bread. No dressing or cheese but plenty of water to
wash it down.

"How can you eat something like that?" Allan says as he digs
through his pockets and comes up with nothing but lint, which he
flicks off his fingers onto the floor. "What's wrong with mustard or
mayo? Do you get it because you think you need to lose weight or
something?"

"I can help who's next," the cashier calls in our direction.

"I . . . I'll pay." What else can I say?

"You've come a long way, baby." Allan steps up to the counter
and leans his hip onto it. "I'll have the Brando, extra white onions.
Raw, not grilled. Sliced, not diced. Extra-large half Wild Cherry
Pepsi, half unsweetened iced tea. No ice. She'll have the Aniston
and a large bottle of water."

When he's done ordering for the both of us, he steps aside
to let me pay. Mutely I hand over a twenty-dollar bill, having rel-

egated anything with identifying information on it to a separate wallet.

"You snag us a table and I'll wait here for the food," he offers, chewing on a straw.

I scramble away and find a table by the window facing the street. I reach down and realize I didn't bring my knitting. "I can do this," I whisper to myself. If anything, I'm sure James will find some humor in it.

A few minutes later Allan appears with lunch carefully balanced on a plastic tray. He sits down, scooting his chair a little closer to mine.

"So tell me all about you," he says as he liberally salts and peppers his sandwich.

"Pardon me?" I halt the progress of my sandwich from the table to my mouth.

"This project is going to mean a lot of late nights." Allan takes a huge bite of his Brando, any and all forms of deli meat, four different types of glistening condiments, including those extra raw white onions with a layer of potato salad in between everything on an onion roll. He maneuvers the food into his left cheek before he continues. I can already smell those onions. "Late, late nights. For you and me."

"It's part of the job," I say, and take a quick, tiny bite of my sandwich.

"Yeah, sure." He gestures with his monstrous meat-filled lunch so that I rear back to avoid flying edible shrapnel. "Don't get me wrong. I'm not complaining."

"I suppose." I happen to know, via James, that Allan earns $160,000 and he lives in his parents' in-law apartment. "It'll be over soon, and then we can get back to working normal hours."

I want to add, "And to our separate lives and sides of the office." Of course I don't, and even if I did, I doubt Allan would take offense to it.

"How's your end coming along?" He takes a huge sip of his drink.

"It's going well." I glance down at my sandwich, my stomach growling, and look out the window so I don't have to watch him swish the liquid around in his mouth. And then suddenly all my breath whooshes out of my body.

"Are you okay?" Allan asks, edging his chair back as if he expects me to vomit or pass out. "Are you choking on your dry sandwich?"

"I'm fine," I gasp, not taking my eyes off the other side of the street, where he's waiting to cross, aiming straight for the front door of Celebrity Sub, which is only a few feet away from where I'm sitting with Allan. And then it gets worse. Allan starts to rub my back.

Alexander

Pete keeps up a steady chatter about arcane tariff law and how we might be able to contort it in Candace's favor when I finally notice where he's leading us to.

"Hey, hold up." I pause outside the doors of Celebrity Sub, stepping off to the side so we don't block foot traffic. "Why here, Pete?"

"It's tasty, fast, and cheap. What more can you want in a mid-day meal?"

"I'm hoping that's also not your criteria for women," I say as I take a step forward to open the door and realize Pete isn't moving. "Pete?"

"Melissa," Pete says.

I look around. It's not hard to find her, with her fiery red hair. Pete always said he hoped their future daughters would inherit it, but not the boys. As he put it, "A redheaded boy is just asking to be beat up in the school yard."

She, Melissa, is making out with a guy (and not the one she left Pete for) as they stand by the door of a double-parked cab.

"Oh, man. Pete, come on." I tug at his arm, but he's rooted to the spot.

"Right on the street. Where everyone can see them." Pete's shoulders slump forward, and his chin sinks into his chest. We all know, even Pete does, his ex-wife was a third-rate skank, but the woman he loved, loves, nonetheless.

"Buddy." I pull him into my arms, turning him so he can't see his ex-wife, my hand on the back of his neck, and tuck his head into my shoulder. I feel his arms go around my middle. I look up to check if they're gone when I see her sitting at a table inside the sub shop with some guy who is rubbing her back.

I feel as if I've been sucker-punched. It only gets worse when she glances up at me and her eyes go wide and her cheeks flush pink, like I've caught her doing something naughty.

"Let's go, Pete."

I throw my arm around him and lead him away from Celebrity Sub and the sight of some guy's hand on her. His hand on her. Her. My her.

Why do I even care? I don't know her name. I've never met her. All I know about her is that she likes to knit, works in the building across from mine, and makes me want to rip that skinny guy's legs off for even sitting next to her. Where does he get off putting his hand on her? Why did she let him?

Because she's with him and he's with her, that's why. Did I expect her to be waiting around for me, knitting scarves until I came around and noticed her? If the train hadn't been late, none of this would even matter. She'd just be another beautiful woman having a sandwich with her boyfriend and wouldn't even be bothered to look in my direction. And if we did happen to look at each other, it'd just be the normal checking each other out, nothing special, nothing like what I felt like on Wednesday morning. Nothing like what I'm feeling now.

"I'm fucking nuts," I mutter under my breath, maneuvering Pete through the lunchtime crowds that clog the sidewalks.

"What?" asks Pete, emerging from his stupor. "Who's nuts?"

"Nothing, buddy."

Of course she has a boyfriend. Maybe she's even married. To him. That guy. I keep walking and look straight head and make sure Pete doesn't look back either.

Evelyn

"What are you looking at?" Allan asks, still rubbing my back.

"No one!" I shrink away from his touch, hoping he gets the hint. When he doesn't, I shrug off his hand, which is now stroking my shoulder. "I'll be right back."

I get up and step outside to stare off in the direction he walked with his friend. Before they turn the corner, I see he still has his arm around his *friend,* almost cupping the back of his head, like one does a baby or a lover. Allan taps on the glass to get my attention, and I have no choice but to go back inside and join him.

"See someone from work?" Allan asks, trying to be too casual. "Was it Ted?"

"No. I just. I just needed some air," I lie, rewinding what I just saw in my mind. And what I saw looked a lot like two men hugging tenderly.

It's not like I haven't seen that and more. James once talked me into going out to a club and I found myself at an all-guy S & M leather party in my cashmere sweater and tasteful jewelry.

"If you had them put some mayo on that thing, it would go down easier." Allan seems to be fixated on my sandwich. "Mayo is like lubricant."

"Yes." I wrap it up and shove it away from me. I feel sad. Sad and stupid for even caring about a stupid guy I am aware of only because my stupid boss made me come in to my stupid fake job on my stupid birthday.

"Anyway, as I was saying. Coding is an art. At least I like to think of it as one. You know how a sculptor uses clay or stone? I take binary numbers and turn them into code and make things happen. When you think of it, it's really powerful. So in a way, we're not too different."

My eyes glaze over, my mind spins round and round, but I make sure to nod every so often as Allan drones on.

"Hi!" James nosily pulls up a chair and props his elbows on the table. "Don't you two look cozy? Mind if I join you?"

"Please," I gasp and then try to play it off as a sneeze.

"Sure," Allan mumbles and begins to attack what's left of his Brando.

chapter fifteen
The Right Kind of Wrong

Evelyn

I trail after a saleslady at Gump's in her staid black skirt suit carefully accessorized with a spidery red stone pin on the lapel. I discreetly, if that's possible, chew a piece of sugarless gum, trying to get the dry taste of sandwich and realization out of my mouth. Next to me, James keeps up a running commentary about the wonderful impracticality of selected items.

"This is exactly what your flat needs, Evelyn," he says, picking up a carefully aged tin planter box that's stuffed with silk geraniums. "Who doesn't need fake flowers for a little splash of color that never dies or needs watering?"

When he gets zero reaction from me, James does an impromptu tap dance and ends it on bended knee with jazz hands. I lean over, help him up, and give him a kiss on the cheek. He's been trying to cheer me up since I got back from my Allan lunch, even after I made it clear I wasn't going to share the reason for my glum mood.

"Not even a smile?" he asks.

"Maybe later."

The saleslady pauses on her way to the register, where she's lugging a shopping bag full of returns. "We'd be happy to give you store credit, Miss Sinclair, and you can look around while I ring you up. We have some lovely new Limoges boxes I know your mother would love."

"Thank you," I say in a noncommittal voice as I pretend to

inspect a hand-carved teak wall medallion. "But I really don't have time to shop today. Maybe next time?"

"Of course," she says brightly.

We both know I have no plans to buy anything today. Maybe once I've accumulated enough credit for a hand-knotted Tibetan rug, but for now I intend to walk out empty-handed.

"I'll take a turn around," I can't help adding. She smiles at me and walks over to the counter to begin the process.

"Oh, look, just what I've always wanted: a metal bird sculpture and at the bargain price of only fourteen hundred for the small one! Who needs to pay rent when this could sit on my toilet tank and poke me in the head when I fall asleep on the john?"

"We should get back to work," I say to James, glancing at my watch. It's already closing in on 2:00 P.M., and I know I'm bound to find a small mountain of e-mail to sort through.

"Why bother?" James asks with great indifference that can only come from knowing his job is in no danger of disappearing anytime soon.

"Because that's what we get paid for?" I suggest. "To show up, sit at our desks, and do work."

"We get paid whether we're there or not. Except for you." James frowns. "I left the new intern manning reception—see what a fancy degree from Yale will get you? And I told Ted you had an emergency appointment with your gynecologist to get fitted for a new diaphragm."

"James. You didn't." But I know he might have or at least told him something equally embarrassing and untrue.

"When's the last time you had sex, anyway?" James asks, changing the subject to his second favorite thing to talk about in the world—the first being him.

"That's really beside the point, James." I quickly make my way to a bright display of vases and pick one up. "This vase looks like a candy-colored polyp."

"My God! It should be illegal to make things that ugly." James is momentarily distracted.

"Oh, I'm so sorry!" I say when I notice the saleswoman standing next to me with a gift card.

"Here is your gift card, Miss Sinclair. And we hope to see you soon," she continues, tactfully ignoring our churlish behavior.

"I think I'll put it toward the one of the metal herons there," I say, pointing to the bronze bird sculptures, and hand her back the gift card.

"Are you serious?" James asks in mock surprise.

"Don't say no, James. It's just what your bathroom needs. It's what every bathroom needs."

Alexander

I tuck my wallet back into my pocket, making sure to set aside the receipt for billing. Pete is slumped in a lobby chair at the Four Seasons in post–big lunch stupor.

"I need to run a quick errand," I say as I give his foot a nudge to get him moving.

I'm in no mood to get back to work. The whole time I was trying to enjoy my twenty-dollar salad, twenty-eight-dollar hamburger, and nine-dollar scoop of vanilla bean ice cream at the hotel's restaurant, my cell phone was buzzing angrily in my pocket. I finally had to ask the waiter, who got a big fat tip, to stow it somewhere far away while we ate. I would have turned it off, but if asked by Rodney and Candace, who were taking turns calling me, I could honestly say I couldn't hear it ring inside the restaurant.

"What for?" Pete looks slightly fuzzy around the edges, having enjoyed a couple of artisan beers with his Kobe flat-iron steak. He skipped dessert, claiming he was trying to lose a few pounds, and had a couple more beers instead, reasoning that liquid calories are easier to burn off than the chocolate cake kind.

"I need to get my sister something." We walk outside, dodging the usual mix of locals and tourists who crowd Market Street. I make eye contact with a good-looking woman but steer my gaze away as politely as possible. "For Nayelli, not the baby. Her birthday is coming up."

The one problem is Nayelli has refused to find out the sex of the baby, so everyone is stuck buying gender-neutral stuff or gift cards.

"What are you going to get her?" Pete asks, trying to rub some of the drunk out of his face.

"I have no idea." It can't be anything raunchy, like the blow-up sailor sex doll I got her last year. She's going to be someone's mother in a few weeks, and I think I'm more freaked out about the idea than she is. "Something for a mom, I guess."

Pete looks over at me. "You ever think you'll have a kid?"

"Are you asking if I live in fear of getting served with paternity papers at the office by some one-night stand whose name I can't remember? Every day, my friend, every day." I smooth down my tie after a gust of wind blows it over my shoulder.

"No, I'm serious," Pete says with a catch in his voice.

Pete had his whole life planned out. He and Melissa would wait two years and then get going on producing the four, minimum, kids Pete wanted. They'd live in the Oakland Hills, he'd open a small law practice to serve the community, and she'd be the office manager. They'd send their kids to the local public schools, where they'd be active in the PTA, and maybe someday, Pete would run for a city office where he could make a difference. In the meantime, he'd set a good example for his kids and be a loving husband to his wife.

I'd never tell Pete the woman he thought was the love of his life is a slut and he's better off without her. Pete's my friend and a man. He doesn't need to hear that from me. It's my job to make sure the beer is cold and he gets home safe.

"As you pointed out the other night, I haven't met anyone who can stand me for longer than six months, Pete." I clap him on the back to lighten the mood. "But when it happens, I'll let you know."

"So it hasn't happened yet?" Pete asks.

"What hasn't?" Rule number one for a lawyer, play dumb when the truth may be involved and employ diversionary tactics. "So what should I get my overachieving sister?"

"Not perfume. That's creepy coming from a brother. Underwear too, even if you're giving it as a joke." Pete has obviously given this issue some thought.

"I want to get her something pretty useless so she knows it's from me."

"I know just the place." Pete jaywalks across Market and heads up toward the more quiet streets, away from the tourists and the cable car turnaround. "When we got married, we got a bunch of useless stuff from this one store. . . ."

Pete stops in front of Gump's, and I scan the window displays. This is a store my sister would never set foot in. "Looks about right. Let's do it."

I wander around, not sure what would be more useless as a gift. A set of mother-of-pearl coasters that would look just right in my loft or a heart-shaped Limoges box. Maybe I'll be a total dick and give her a gift card so she has to come here herself.

"I'm too drunk to be in here, dude. This place is freaking me out," Pete says, making a visible effort to keep his arms close to his sides so he doesn't knock into anything. "Let's get out of here."

I take one more look around and spot the perfect gift. A saleswoman behind the counter is carrying it to a table.

"I think I've found it," I say, pointing it out.

"That?" Pete asks. "What is it?"

"I don't know, but it's perfect. She's a doctor, and it looks sort of anatomical. Excuse me, ma'am?" I walk over to the woman holding the brightly colored vase; I think it's a vase, or at least could be used as one. "Can I buy that? It's a gift for my sister."

"Of course, sir." She turns back toward the counter, me right on her heels. "Would you like a gift receipt?"

"Nah, thanks." This is one present Nayelli will have a pain in the ass time trying to return. "I'm sure you hear this all the time, but doesn't that thing remind you of a twisted intestine or something?"

"A polyp," she offers.

"Yeah! A polyp," I agree, thinking of all the medical textbooks Nayelli would leave open on the dining room table when she knew I'd be around.

"You're not the first one to mention that today."

Evelyn

"So, how was your rendezvous with Allan? *Très* dorky?" James asks, shielding his eyes against the weak summer sun with sunglasses. "You forgot to give me the details after I rescued you."

"It was fine," I say, not feeling the need to point out it was more a case of him forgetting to ask instead of me neglecting to share the details. I'm still freaked out by the whole thing—Allan rubbing my back, seeing him with another man, him seeing Allan rubbing my back. The images loop endlessly in my mind like some bad B movie.

"So who are you going to bag next in the office?" James asks as he struggles with the box containing his new toilet heron on our way back to work. We're taking the long way there so we can lose ourselves in the crowds of tourists who congregate at the cable car turnaround. "I've got twenty dollars on Paul from HR."

"We could have had it delivered, James." I step aside for a group of German-speaking tourists, complete with too-short shorts, socks with sandals, and San Francisco pullover fleeces.

"No, I'm going to set it on my desk, so I can admire it and tell everyone how much it cost." James grunts as he tries to find a comfortable way to carry the box.

"Just don't . . ." I just spent almost seventeen hundred dollars on what essentially is a gag gift, and I know if people found out, they would look at me differently. For now I'm content being the sad single girl. Being the rich crazy girl is a whole other thing.

"Okay, undercover heiress, I won't mention it came from you. I'll just let everyone assume I blow older men during my lunch break for trinkets and baubles." James struts along like he's holding a scepter instead of a box and gives up when a sharp corner of the box pokes him in the upper thigh. He stops midstride to rub the spot with a curse. "Ted's been asking about Tannin, by the way."

"He has?" I pull James off to the side. "What's he asking?"

"How well you know her. How I know her."

"What did you tell him?" I grab the top of James's arm and squeeze.

"Jesus, Evelyn! You're scaring me. It's no big deal. He's been sniffing around, and he's done a few searches on his computer. I told him we were all just friends. That's about it."

I drop my hand and start walking again, only to double back to where James is still standing. I'm not surprised James knows what's on Ted's computer. He knows everything that's going on in the office. This is why I'm a little put out he hadn't warned me about Ted earlier.

"I'm sorry I didn't tell you. I knew you'd freak out."

"I'm not freaking out. Okay, maybe just a little."

We start walking again.

"Listen, Evelyn. Even if he does find out you're Evelyn Morgan Reed-Sinclair, what can he do? He can't fire you since you don't officially work for him." James halts at a corner, puts the box down, and faces me. "And it's not like I'd let you marry him after he tries to sweep you off your feet tomorrow night."

"Yes, there's always that danger." I sigh, watching the light turn from red to green. "God knows, my mother is willing to consider any and all options nowadays."

"I'd marry you, but I'm saving myself for Mr. Right, who by the way I was planning on meeting at your wedding."

I look over at James and realize he just might be waiting for Mr. Right. And considering that he actually goes out on dates and tries to meet people, he might just meet him and live happily ever after in domestic partner bliss while I'm no closer to anything resembling a real relationship. If anything, my new activity of fantasizing about a stranger probably is lessening my chances of me getting my romantic life in order, or at least resuscitating it from the brink of comfortable spinsterhood.

"Evelyn?" James waves a hand in front of my face. "You're

doing that staring off into space thing again. Stop it, it freaks me out."

"The last thing I'd want to do is come between you and your happiness, James, but I really don't see a wedding in my future. Sorry." I lean in and give him a quick hug. "Maybe Tannin will come through with an opportunity for you to meet your dream man at one of her weddings. She has at least three different wedding dresses picked out, and she's determined to wear each one of them."

Tannin, even with her impossible standards, endless issues with food, her weight, and high-level partying, is still more likely to end up walking down the aisle than I am.

"You might be right. I should be nicer to that twat," James says, nodding his head. "You should just go ahead and have a baby, then. Stop fucking around and get pregnant."

"First I'd have to have some"—I pause until we pass a mother and her toddler—"sex."

"Not necessarily."

"Let's not start that again, James." In the past, he has suggested I find a boyfriend by wearing tight T-shirts that read RICH AND EASY or hiring a plane to fly my phone number over San Francisco during Fleet Week. "Call me old-fashioned, but I'd like a man involved, one I preferably know and somewhat like."

"Pah! That's just crazy talk." James stops to light a cigarette. "Nowadays you can have a whole relationship with a guy, at least his sperm, and never even meet him."

I watch my best friend through a cloud of smoke. "You don't know the half of it, James."

Alexander

"Mr. Velazquez. Mr. McCray."

"Wallace," we both mumble as Pete and I are forced to take the walk of shame past her and head to our respective offices with our heads down.

A stack of faxes from Candace via Becky is neatly set in the middle of my desk along with a piping hot cup of black coffee.

Pete wanders in, holding his own cup of coffee. "See what I told you? She's always watching, man."

Before I can answer, Wallace appears at his elbow, causing him to let out a yelp.

"Mr. Velazquez. You have a visitor." Wallace sounds as if she's stepped out of some 1940s noir movie.

"Thanks." I stand up, expecting it to be another delivery of boxes. Instead my mom walks in, wearing the boxy business-woman's suit she puts on only when she has to go to court. "Mom!"

"Alexander." She pauses to give Pete a hug and kiss. "Wow, fancy office. Pete, Sergio expects you on Saturday, so bring your cleats. And don't let him bully you into playing goalie. If you don't want to, just tell me and I'll have a word with him. We're hoping to see Melissa. We've missed her these last few times."

"Sure thing." Pete stares into his cup of coffee. He's asked me not to share the news of Melissa walking out on him yet. "I'll have to check with, uh . . . I better get back to work."

"Wow, this is some office, Alexander," Mom says as she settles down onto one of the sleek leather and chrome visitor's chair in front of my desk after taking a look at all the file boxes with Candace's name and court numbers on them. "Very you."

"Thanks. I think." I wipe my hands on my pants, feeling like she's just walked into my room at home and it's littered with dirty socks and girlie magazines. "So, Mom. What's up?"

"Cut the crap, honey. What happened with you and Sigrid?" She tilts her head to the side so a strand of her graying brown hair coils onto her shoulder. "And what's going on with the Wish 'n' Wash?"

"Yeah, Sigrid. The Wish 'n' Wash. Where to start?" I ask, stalling for time. At least she doesn't want to talk about me compromising my ideals by working here at Williams, Heller, Lincoln and representing Candace Hall.

"You can start by being honest, Alexander." My mother sits back.

"Fine, Sigrid and I are over, Mom. And it didn't end well. As for the Laundromat, it's closed for renovations."

"See? Was that so hard, honey?" She stands up, looking at her watch. "I have to meet the workers from the Roosevelt. The police issued a few too many citations, and we're going to see about getting them excused. I'll see you tomorrow, honey."

"Aren't you going to ask me about . . ." I gesture around me.

"Oh, that." She kisses the top of my head. "Like I told your father, Alexander, that's for you to figure out."

I stare after her for a few minutes before getting up, drawing the blinds, and shutting the door.

Evelyn

I sit in Ted's office shutting down his computer. Before he left for the day, he asked me to search his name and all variations (Ted Port, Theodor S. Port, Theodor Scott Port, TS Port) and print out anything that popped up, but to his personal printer since, as he said, "I don't want to tie up the network."

I run my finger down the to-do list Ted left me to make sure I haven't missed a step. Place printouts into a folder. Check. Put the folder in an envelope. Check. Seal the envelope. Check. Lock envelope in the file cabinet (where Ted keeps an assortment of golf tees, a little black book held together with a rubber band, and a shaving kit). Check. Retape the key to the back of Ted's framed UCLA Anderson School of Management diploma, which is hung at the height to be best seen from a seated position across from Ted's desk. Check.

I look at my watch. It's a quarter to seven, and the office is deserted. James left promptly at six with his heron and Tannin to kick off Friday a day early at some dance club. I turn out the lights, nod to the cleaning crew in the reception area, take the elevator downstairs, and head to Grant Avenue, right at the gates of China-town. I need to take care of a few errands for this whatever it might be tomorrow night thing with Ted.

I take a deep breath and walk into Fancy Lady Pamper Nails and Wax. I stand off to the side while the mostly Vietnamese women crouch at the feet or over the hands of the predominately white fancy-lady clientele who want their pamper(ing) fast and cheap. I start to back out, and suddenly I feel all eyes on me.

"Come sit! A little wait for mani-pedi," the woman closest to me says and points behind me. "Magazines."

"Oh, okay . . ." I approach her, sending an apologetic look to the woman whose calluses she's pumicing. I lower my voice and stoop over. "How long is the wait for a . . . wax? Bikini wax?"

The woman, behind her paper mask, looks me up and down, and then calls out something in Vietnamese. A voice from the back answers, and she looks up at me and says, "She ready now. You go to back."

I walk the gauntlet, part the beaded curtain that separates the main part of the salon from the waxing part. A woman who only comes up to the undersides of my boobs is standing in a room, snapping on latex gloves.

"Everything off?" She gestures to the paper-covered table. "Take panties off. Put your things here."

"Okay. But if we could"—there's no *we* in this. She's the one with the hot wax on the end of a tongue depressor—"leave a little something, that would be great."

"Heart shape, light bold, ten dollars extra."

"How about a triangle?" I slip off my tights and underwear and lay down on the table, staring up at the yellowed drop-down ceiling panels.

"Eh," she says, not impressed with my choice of pubic hair motifs. She lifts my skirt. *"Ai-ya!"*

"It's been a while." I feel myself blushing. Everywhere.

For the next twenty minutes I experience more introspection than a year doing self-portraits in Paris. My legs are lifted, spread, and at one point, I find myself on my hands and knees while she's wearing a headlamp.

"Okay. All clean!" she finally announces and shoves a hand mirror at me.

"Thank you, but I think I'll pass." I get up from the table. "But if I could get your card?" I figure I know her and she knows me, and I never, ever want to have to go through this again with someone else.

I tip generously and, like a sleepwalker, wander into the Banana Republic on the corner, tell the clerk I'm looking for a nice dress that isn't too dressy, but dressy enough. She leads me into the dressing room and hands me a purple silk dress with a cinched waist. It's a size ten and it fits, but I'm too out of it to even enjoy the moment.

chapter sixteen
Spying and Lying

Evelyn

My Friday starts off with another crowded train ride (I've learned to pack an iPod along with my knitting) followed by a trek up five flights of stairs and too many e-mails from Ted, Allan, but curiously none from Jessica.

I'm holding a mug of tea (because sometimes a cup won't do it) staring slack jawed at my computer monitor when James saunters in wearing what I assume is his version of Friday casual: skinny black jeans that effectively render him unable to be a sperm donor to any lesbian couple who may ask for a bit of his DNA and my favorite purple suede platform boots, topped off with a Yohji Yamamoto black and gray swirl pattern crewneck sweater he found at the Haight Street Goodwill for seven dollars.

"You're a woman on the verge of either a grand sexual awakening or a prolonged sojourn to some third world country to find yourself." James takes my mug from me and sniffs its contents. "Not tipping a bit of whiskey to dull the pain, are we?"

"Have you been reading the short stories on Nerve.com again, James?"

"Your attempt at a cutting barb is duly noted and ignored." James flicks his fingers at me. "I'm off to make an appearance at the reception desk in my seven-dollar Yohji Yamamoto sweater."

Every ticking second brings me closer to my "date" with Ted. And just as I did in Paris, I allow my work to distract me from the reality of my situation so I can pretend there is nothing for me to worry about.

"Working hard?" Ted glides into my office a few hours later. "About tonight . . ."

"You can't make it?" I ask a little too quickly, but Ted is oblivious to my desperate attempt to find some way out of this, whatever this might be.

"I'll swing around to your place at six to pick you up."

"Thank you." I was hoping to meet him there and . . . then what?

Ted checks his watch, making sure I get a good look at it. A Rolex. Yawn. "Why don't you cut out a bit early so you can take care of things?"

"Things?" I look at my own watch, a vintage Timex. It's barely three.

Ted gives me a long, hard survey from top to toe. His mouth is screwing up in the way it does when he's just not happy with something, like the order in which his sandwich has been constructed (the problem easily remedied by me flipping it over) or that a candy bar in the vending machine is, God forbid, upside down (again, a simple matter of me buying the upside-down bar so that the next correctly facing one can take its place).

"Take a cab home and expense it."

"Ted? About tonight, I just want to make sure this is . . . I mean, that this, what we are going to do—not that we're going to do anything—"

"I got this for you." He places a small white box on my desk and, without another word, leaves my office.

I wait a few moments before opening it—it's full of my new business cards, "Evelyn Morgan, Senior Executive Assistant." I slump at my desk with my head in my hands. I automatically pick up the phone when it rings, punctual even in the depths of anxiety and misery. "Evelyn Morgan, Senior Executive Assistant and Interdepartmental Liaison."

"Good morning!" Tannin trills into my ear. "You got a promotion! A long one."

"It's almost three, Tannin."

"Is it? Oh, my God! I'm so sorry! I was out last night with Whit, and we ran into some male model, or at least he said he was a model. We all ended up at a dance club in San Jose. Don't ask me how it happned."

"I won't." I wait for my sister to tell me why she's really calling.

"Anyway, I'm such a wreck. We stopped at a Taco Bell and I Hoovered up half the menu." Ever since Tannin broke up with some English guy a few years ago, she's peppered her sentences with words like *singleton* when describing my status, *bump* when talking about someone's pregnant belly, *bum* for butt, and *Hoovering* for bingeing, or in her case, eating a normal meal. "And Whit, that man whore, has talked me into a weekend in La-La Land. Will you cover for me? Tell everyone I'm on my deathbed with menstrual cramps, and unless they come bearing gifts of powerful painkillers, I am not to be bothered."

"I don't know, Tannin." I'm not a good liar, current circumstances notwithstanding.

"I'm so so so so sorry. I know you hate lying for me, Evelyn. But just this once?" She's using her singsong, babyish voice, knowing I'll agree to pardon her just to get her to stop. "I promise! Never, ever again."

"Of course, Tannin." I send off an e-mail to Jessica asking

her something banal, since I don't want to go around to her desk. It would look like I was checking up on her. "Hey, uh, Tannin. Mother is sitting out this thing tonight, right? The ballet thing?"

"Because of that twat Candace Hall." We both wait for Tannin to work through a huge yawn. "Mother says, and I'm sure Sissy will pass it on, that Candace is trying to buy respectability. Even with all that money her dead hubby left her, you're either part of that club or you're not, and Mother has decided that she's not," Tannin says, parroting with complete acceptance what our mother has decreed in the matter of Candace Hall.

"I'm so bloated," Tannin continues. "Beyond bloated, you wouldn't believe it. I don't think I could ever eat again. Don't you hate that feeling?"

"Yes." I clear my throat, ready to cut my sister off, knowing she can spend hours on the phone talking about nothing. Instead, Tannin beats me to it, as usual, two steps ahead in the game.

"Oh, that's my massage therapist at the door. I'll call you later!"

I hang up and briefly debate the merits of joining Tannin in her life of shopping, partying, and having someone come to my home to knead out the stress that such a life brings with it.

Instead, I make the senior executive assistant decision to go look out the window and see him standing in front of his, looking straight in my direction.

I hit the floor.

"What are you doing?" James asks. He hurries into my office, closing the door behind him to preserve what's left of my dignity. Dear James, dear dear James.

"Nothing." I stand up quickly, feeling dizzy. "I'm just . . . Nothing. So how is life these days?"

"You're about as subtle as a sailor on shore leave, Evelyn." James peers out the window, and I have to keep myself from tackling him to the ground.

I edge back toward my desk, hoping he'll follow me. "I was just taking in the view."

"Is someone boning it up in another office?" James asks excitedly, scanning windows. "Where? It's like free porn! I can write it up for a story on Nerve.com."

"No one is doing any boning. See that guy . . . man?" I stand off to the side and gesture to his window.

"Which window?" James asks, joining me so we're both crammed into the small blind spot between the windows.

"Five floors up from the street, middle window. Do you see him? Tall. Dark hair."

"Oh, yummy," James breathes. "You lucky bitch. Your own office and a view."

"He is cute, isn't he?" I ask. James has very good aesthetics, shallow and otherwise, and prides himself on being blunt. He will tell me the truth.

"Puppies are cute, babies in magazines are cute. This man-god is gorgeous. And well hung, I bet." James smacks his lips, and I punch him. "Ouch! Please, Evelyn, you know you've thought about it."

"And he's gay?" I add a little hopefully, ignoring James's last (accurate) comment.

"Gay?" James cranes his neck, bumping his forehead against the glass, and then takes off at a sprint out my office door. "Be right back!" he calls over his shoulder.

"Wait! Forget it!" I stop at the doorway and smile like a fool at Jessica's team of designers, who are huddled over the color printer, no doubt talking about me and my weird ways. "Hi. It's all, uh, really coming together."

I back into my office, resuming my post between the two windows, taking quick peeks when I think he isn't looking.

"You're such an amateur, Evelyn." James comes in, a little breathless, holding a pair of promotional opera glasses. They're cheap plastic things, but right now I'd give my left arm for a look through them. I grab at them, but James bats my hand away. "Let's see . . . from the cut of his suit . . . Hugo Boss maybe . . . Good haircut . . . Not a hair product abuser. Don't you just hate it when guys have that crunchy hair? That's a good sign. No wedding ring." James gives me a thumbs-up and goes back to his observation. "No visible tattoos or piercings . . . Well."

He hands me the binoculars, looking very serious. I look through them. They're blurry and weak but work well enough. I zero in on his desk, making out a baseball displayed in a small glass case. He likes baseball. That's better than a monster truck fan. Also on his desk is a coffee cup, but besides the piles of papers, I can't make out much more.

"Well?" I ask James after my eyes start stinging with the effort of trying to compensate for the toy binoculars.

"I can most assuredly proclaim him disgustingly heterosexual," James says with mock sadness. "Positively and painfully so."

"How can you be sure?"

Flashes of him hugging his friend race across my mind. I hand James the binoculars and rub my hands together like I do when I'm nervous or about to start a painting.

"The walk, the way he dresses—nice, yeah, but he's dressing for himself, not other men or even women. He's a sports fan, hardcore but tasteful about it. No fitness magazines on his desk, and he just oozes breeder." James tickles my ribs until I smack his hand away. "Congratulations, Evelyn, you may have finally fallen in love with someone you might actually have a chance at a happy future with."

"I don't even know him," I say, trying to seem casual about it even though all I want to do is jump up and down and giggle with joy. "How could I possibly be in love with him?"

James doesn't bother with humoring me. "Now all you have to do is introduce yourself." He knocks on the window even though there's no chance of him hearing and then waves his arms, something he will notice. "Yoo-hoo! Over here!"

"No!" I lunge at him and wrestle him to the floor, pinning his torso between my thighs. "Stop laughing. That's not funny. Promise me you'll never, ever do it again! Promise me!"

"Your. Thighs. Are. Amazingly. Strong." James gasps as he makes a head motion between a nod and a shake, red faced with laughter. I squeeze my knees into his sides, which only makes him grunt and laugh at the same time.

"Am I interrupting something?" Ted asks, standing at my door. He has the biggest and best office, but what good is it if he's never in there?

"Ted!" Surprised, I loosen my hold on James.

James wiggles out from under me and stands up. "As a matter of fact, you are. I'll be at my desk. Flossing."

I arrange myself as demurely as I can and ask from the floor, "Is there something you wanted, Ted?"

Ted extends a hand to help me up, and I have no choice but to take it. As I'm rising, I step on the hem of my skirt and stumble into him. His arms (surprisingly muscled) go around me to keep me from falling. For a moment we're frozen in an awkward embrace and, not knowing where to look, I turn my head toward the window. I can see him, looking in this direction. For a moment our eyes lock, my heartbeat kicks up a notch and then plummets. He looks from me to Ted, and then his eyes narrow.

Ted clears his throat to get my attention. "Evelyn—"

"I'm just shutting down now." I break away from Ted before he can say anything. At my desk I cram some random papers and my stapler into my bag and back away toward the door, right into Allan. "No! I mean, hello. Allan. I'll see you . . . I'll see you later. Not you, Allan. I mean . . . Sorry. Good night!" I rush toward the front of the office, pausing at James's desk. "Meet me at my place in an hour. I'm going to need plenty of help getting things together."

James stands up. He's already wearing his jacket, his murse (man purse) slung around him with the latest issue of *Paper* magazine, a pack of American Spirits, and hand sanitizer, along with the Prada wallet I gave him for his last birthday stuffed inside.

"Ted told me I should come along to help you out." He entwines his arm in mine and leads me to the elevator bank.

"I bought a dress at Banana Republic. And it's completely appropriate."

"Uh-huh," James says, nodding slowly with a concerned expression on his face. "We can borrow some jewelry from Tannin and forget you ever let the words 'I bought a dress from Banana Republic' come from your patrician lips. Let's go."

"Does he really think I'm that clueless?" I ask James, hoping for a different answer than the one I know I'm about to get.

James starts from the bottom up, taking in my favorite pair of brown calf-length leather boots I had custom made in Prague, my charcoal gray shift dress with a long-sleeved white cotton shirt underneath, and ending at my hair, which I've pulled into a ponytail with bangs now just a centimeter or three too long to be considered chic.

"So does he?" I ask, feeling the weight of James's fashion assessment.

"Yes."

Alexander

I blink a couple of times, trying to process what I just saw happen. What it looked like, no matter which way my mind tries to spin it, was her in the arms of another guy. Then we were looking at each other, I'm sure of it, then the other guy, the one from lunch, comes into her office and she's gone like a shot, leaving both guys standing there looking as dumb as I feel.

"What the fuck . . ." I scan the windows, trying to see if she'll pop up somewhere else. Maybe there's another guy at the office she has a thing with.

"Hey, buddy." Pete wanders in, his head buried in a case file. "I've been going over . . . What the fuck are you doing?"

"Nothing." I casually as possible hop off my leather couch and make my way to my desk, hands shoved deep in my pockets.

"Nothing my ass." Pete goes over to the window. "Is this about that girl, woman, whatever at the sandwich place from yesterday?"

"You saw her?" I ask, relieved.

"I saw your face, Alexander. I didn't get a good look at her, but I'm sure she's beautiful. With you they're always beautiful." Pete stands up on my couch to peer out the window and looks down. "Is she walking down the street? Maybe she works around here."

"She works in that office right there." I stand next to him and point to her window. "The one with the big-screen TV."

"You sure it's her? The one from yesterday?" Pete asks. I nod. "Wasn't she with . . . some geeky looking guy?"

"How did you see this? I thought you were too busy having an emotional breakdown."

"Did I ever tell you I once considered joining the FBI? Taught myself all sorts of surveillance tricks before I realized I wasn't going to be able to hack the training. Plus, the no drinking beer or anything was a huge deterrent. I love my country, but I have to admit it wouldn't be worth defending if I couldn't end the day with a cold Pabst." Pete continues to stare in the direction of her office. "I'm always watching, always aware. It's what makes me a good lawyer."

"And a scary potential boyfriend. Just what any girl would love in a man."

"Hold on." Pete sprints out of my office.

I keep my eyes on the window, noticing details for the first time, when he walks back in and stands behind me. "I don't see her, Pete. I think she's gone."

"Are you eyeballing a hot piece of ass?" It's Rodney who is putting his Prada lace-ups on my couch.

"Hey, Rodney." I step down and hope Rodney does the same. Instead he sits on the couch back, his feet on the seat. "What's up?"

"I hear you're seeing our star client tonight." Rodney works his cuff link. It's his tell. He fiddles with it when he's trying hard not to be obvious about something, like asking me if I'll be a good lawyer and play nice with Candace.

"Yeah." I don't need to elaborate. If Rodney wants details, he'll have to nut up and come right out and ask.

"If this goes our way, and it will, it would do a lot for your standing here at the firm, Alex." Rodney looks me straight in the eye, almost daring me to look away.

We both stare at each other, knowing that "if it goes _our_ way" means I'll leapfrog ahead of Bryan and Brian and be made partner a lot sooner. If it doesn't go _my_ way, I'll be looking for a new firm to hang my shingle.

"That's good to know, Rodney."

"I got them— Hey, Rodney . . ." Pete casually tries to play off having an enormous pair of binoculars in his hands as completely normal. "I can come back."

"We're done here, Petey," Rodney says, ignoring Pete's wince at the sound of the hated nickname. "Have fun tonight, Alex. I'll expect a status report before Monday."

We stand there a minute, trying to regain our equilibrium.

"Call me fucking Petey," Pete mumbles under his breath. "I graduated from law with honors, for shit's sake."

"I don't even want know why you have those in your office," I say to Pete as I watch him adjust various knobs before training the binoculars on her office window.

"I went a little crazy during the separation. . . . Anyway . . . it looks like her office is in the game room. . . . Paintings of sad look-ing women over the TV. Desk is very neat, there's only one photo-graph. In a Tiffany frame on the desk," Pete says, pointing as if I can see it as clearly as he can.

"How the hell do you know what kind of frame it is? You're starting to scare me, Pete," I say, trying to make a joke, but I'm drinking in every detail.

He shrugs and goes back to his surveillance. "Melissa's parents got one for us for our wedding photo. They engraved it so I can't return it. But it's waiting for a Pete and Melissa on eBay right this minute. It's not of a boyfriend. She's single."

"How can you tell?" I reach for the binoculars, but Pete shifts his body away.

"If she had a boyfriend or whatever, she'd have his picture stuck to her monitor. At least one. Girls do things like that." Pete shrugs and goes back to his inspection. "I can maybe make the name of the company on the far wall there . . ."

"What for?" I ask, panicking slightly.

"So you can call her and introduce yourself," Pete says, giving me a look.

"Yeah, because that wouldn't freak her out at all." I lean my head against the window and stare at nothing, feeling very low all of a sudden. "I'll just call up the front desk and ask for the woman who I've fallen in love with even though I don't know her name and haven't even met her but have been spying on her with a pair of weapon-grade binoculars. I'll introduce myself as her stalker and then ask her out for a cup of coffee."

"You love her." Pete nods as if confirming something he already knew.

"It's just a figure of speech, my rotund friend." I look away, embarrassed at being caught admitting something that could quite possibly be true. Insane, but true.

"Have I ever told you I minored—"

"Yeah, yeah." I wave him off and slump on the couch. "I don't love her. I don't even know her. How could I be in love with someone I don't know?"

"Exactly! And, what's more, you don't want to know her. Right now she's perfect. That's the way you want to keep it, and the only way you can keep things, her, perfect is if you don't meet her." Pete pauses to take a breath and then continues, his cheeks getting a little red like they do when he's arguing a legal point he's passionate about. "And when you think about it, maybe it's better you don't ever meet her. She'll just end up breaking your heart, or worse, disappointing you with her very human flaws, like leaving her used tea bags in the sink or keeping too neat a house. Or running off with your golfing buddy."

"Pete, and I say this with the love for a brother I never had until I met you, life has made you bitter." I pull him down so he's sitting on the other side of the couch. We both put our feet up on the coffee table. "We need to find you a good woman."

"What for? I just got my satellite TV set up." He picks lint off his company-logo fleece vest. Pete is the only person I've ever seen wear it. "More sports and porno than I know what to do with. Life couldn't be better for me."

"Sounds like you're set, my friend," I say, relieved we've stopped talking about me. "What more could a man possibly want?"

"Love, for one thing, Alexander. Admit it. You've fallen in love with a woman you refuse to let yourself meet." Pete turns so that he faces me. "But I'm not surprised you're not gung ho to take a chance right now. Your family is feeling betrayed by your professional choices. Your client and her legal issues are taking over your life. Sigrid? I could go on."

"Thanks, Pete, but don't. It hurts too much already." I rub my eyes with the heels of my hands.

Pete gets up to inspect the tux, tie, and shirt hanging at the ready on the door hook; the tailor personally delivered them this morning. "I'll make you a deal."

"Which is?" I look up. When Pete offers to make a deal, I know to take it. He puts a lot of thought into what he says.

"You really ask yourself why staying on this case is important to you, and I'll pitch in to help you put together a settlement offer for your girlfriend."

"She's not my girlfriend. And from what I can see, she owes these people a lot of money and a big apology. And knowing her, as *little* as I do"—I stress the last bit for emphasis—"and the official word coming down from our boss, Rodney, they aren't going to get either. She won't settle, but she should."

"Maybe you should ask to be taken off the case?" Pete asks, but he knows I won't.

"Rodney is no fool. He knows I'm ambitious and eager to prove myself. I'm locked in."

"You ever ask yourself why?" Pete takes up the binoculars and starts scanning outside again. He's uncomfortable, but I get the feeling he's wanted to talk to me about this for a while.

"Could it be the way I look in a suit?" I laugh, but it's more like a painful groan. Even I can't fool myself into thinking Rodney put me on this case because he thinks I'm the best lawyer to handle it.

"Admit it, Alexander, they're trying to fight fire with fire. In putting a minority face on the defense, they're trying to diffuse the fact that this woman ran a sweatshop that employed—and I use that term loosely—only minorities and royally shafted them."

"No one said capitalism is illegal." A lame, pat answer, and another example of how I try to avoid the consequences of my choices and behavior—even to someone who totally accepts me for who I am.

"How about immoral?" he asks from behind the binoculars.

Pete rarely takes a black-and-white stance on anything but his devotion to his beloved Wisconsin Badgers and the superiority of Pabst draft beer. He is a lawyer after all and has always concentrated on how the law can benefit the client. Pete questioning the morality of my working on Candace's case is a little unnerving. He wants me to look deep within myself, something I've avoided for most of my life.

"You've been talking to my dad, haven't you?" I take the binoculars from him and stare into her office, trying to glean something more about her from the contents. "Because that's great. At least he's talking to one of us."

Pete shoves his hands into the pockets of his faded Dockers—his usual choice for pants on Fridays. "Your dad is a good guy, Alexander. A little intense, maybe, but he's not half as bad as you make him out to be sometimes."

"Thank you, Oprah." I clap him on the shoulder, steering him toward the door at the same time. "I'm going to ask you something, and you don't have to say yes or no. Just nod if I'm right. Pete, are you in therapy?"

"Fuck off, Alexander." Pete blushes, confirming without actually coming right out and admitting it. "I like using the law to win, but we should ask ourselves, is it really worth the price?"

"You better not let Rodney or Bryan and Brian hear you talking like this." I make sure my wallet is in my pocket so I can head down to the barbershop for a pre–escorting Candace to an event shave. "We're lawyers, Pete. We always want to win."

chapter seventeen

Evelyn

"Now we can start on your hair and makeup." James rubs his hands together. He stands behind me and twists my hair into a bun, then lets it down. "We don't want to make you look too fussy. After all, you don't want to scare off any eligible millionaires with grandma hair."

"No, we wouldn't want that," I agree.

He smoothes my slightly too long bangs off to the side, pinning them back so they blend into the rest of my hair, then neatly parts my hair off to the same side, bringing the back up and under so it looks like I've cut about six inches off of it. I hold up a handful of bobby pins for him as he gets to work making sure it stays there. He drapes a towel over my shoulders and gives the whole thing a finishing spray for hold and shine.

"Perfect! Even if a piece here or there falls down, it'll look like you had a torrid make-out session. Very Belle de Jour after she'd been working in the whorehouse awhile. I don't care what anyone says, French prostitutes are stylish, and I'll stand by that until my dying day." James pats the air above my hair as if testing an invisible bubble around me. "Then your Prince Charming will sweep you out there for a night of thorough boning that will give you that glow. God, I miss that glow."

"Oh, I'm sure that'll happen. I'm on a date with my boss, why shouldn't my love life finally fall into place tonight?"

"Evelyn! You never know. There you'll be, waltzing around the dance floor in the clutches of the evil Ted, and suddenly—you'll see him and he'll draw you in with his devastatingly irresistible smile," says James, fussing with the tiny pots and jars on my dressing table. James is a big fan of bodice rippers; even though I've tried to steer him to Austen and the Brontë sisters, he says he can't do without the sex and the happy ending. "Your tits look amazing, by the way. Like ripe melons."

"Thanks, I think."

I hold still as he starts my makeup and look at my watch, a slim gold Rolex I got for my high school graduation. A classic. At least this is what my mother said after she saw my face when I realized I wasn't getting one of those Return to Tiffany bracelets that were all the rage with the girls in my class.

"We only have forty minutes, James. Something tells me he'll be here right on time or really late."

"Sssst! Barbie doesn't talk."

James, fortunately, works quickly with a sure hand and complete confidence in the colors he's reaching for even though a tiny mew of protest escapes my lips every so often. He's cleaned up my eyebrows so they frame everything, made my lashes look almost false by winging out the liner just slightly past my natural lid, added just a slight touch of color on my cheeks and a wash of gloss on my lips. I don't even recognize myself. I look . . . sexy.

I don't do sexy. I do prim, proper, and respectable.

"It's all about the eyes, Evelyn," James says, turning my face this way and that to inspect his handiwork. "If we did your usual evening red lip, you'd look like a whore. Or a clown. But we have to make up for that dress you're wearing."

"What's wrong with it?" I ask, looking down at myself. It fits, is flattering, and yes, normally I'd dress up more for a benefit dinner, but I'm not going, Evelyn Morgan is.

"So how are you going to keep your mother's friends from outing you to Ted?" James asks, fussing over me. "You got lucky with your mom sitting this thing out, but someone is bound to recognize you."

"My plan is to hide out in the bathroom for as long as possible, keep my parents out of the conversation, and leave very early with a migraine."

"Sounds like me on a first date." James nods. "It just might work."

"Why am I even bothering?" I drop my head into my hands, careful not to smudge my makeup or touch my hair.

"Because you're too polite." James starts putting things away. He's spending the night, and he likes his environment tidy.

"Am I?" I ask while staring at myself in the mirror. "I'm not."

"Which one of us is getting ready for a date with her boss?" James walks over to the bed with an armful of padded hangers and lovingly begins to hang things up. "Not me, so it must be"—he looks around theatrically—"you."

"He didn't give me a chance to say no." But even if he had, we all know I wouldn't have had the nerve to say it. My heart kick-starts in my chest, my throat goes dry. No amount of makeup, hair, and fashion can distract me from what is about to happen. "Oh, my God. I'm going out on a real date with my fake boss."

Alexander

I sit back as Candace's driver eases the car into late-afternoon downtown traffic. He arrived early, and since I was looking out the window and spotted him, I decided I may as well get my butt down there instead of letting him hold up traffic by double-parking.

"Can we make a quick stop?" I ask him, leaning forward even

though it's whisper quiet in here. Gotta love those Germans and their Mercedes engineering—I can even hear the driver grinding his teeth in frustration.

"Ms. Hall is expecting you to arrive—"

"We'll be there in plenty of time." I give him directions to my sister's work and sit back. It's not on the way, but I'm no one's lapdog, even if I am being driven to take Candace out on a date wearing the clothes she's picked out for me.

It takes a little longer than I thought, but we finally pull into the roundabout in front of San Francisco General Hospital. I get out, walking quickly through the beat-up-looking sliding glass doors, and head into the emergency room. Patients and hospital workers look at me funny as I wait my turn to talk to the admit nurse.

"Hi. I need to speak to Dr. Velazquez."

"Is this an emergency?" She eyes me up and down like she expects me to pull out a boom box, start gyrating, and produce a bunch of Happy Birthday balloons out of my ass.

"Does an ongoing moral and identity crisis count as an emergency?" I get nothing back, not even a smile. "I don't think it's technically an emergency, but it is sort of urgent. I should be at my obscenely rich and seductive client's house in fifteen minutes to escort her to a fancy benefit as her arm candy, but instead I'm holding her driver hostage outside since he can't show up without me or she'll kill him while I stand here talking to you wishing I had appendicitis."

"Alexander? What the fuck is up with the monkey suit?"

My sister, Nayelli, very pregnant and wearing scrubs under her open white doctor's coat, waddles over to the desk. Our mom has been asking Nayelli to take it easy and cut back her shifts at the hospital, but my sister, being my sister, has ignored her. Now, after seeing how pregnant she is, I can't help but agree that maybe Nayelli should kick back and watch daytime TV at home instead of dealing with gunshot victims, bad-trippin' wannabe hippies, and the general stream of misery that comes through the doors of San Francisco General.

"It's okay, Loren, he's my brother," Nayelli says to the nurse.

I reach out automatically and take her elbow, only to have her ram that same elbow into my ribs. My sister, the most antidelicate girl I've ever known, is in a delicate condition but still a bitch.

"Is your brother single?" the nurse asks, licking her lips.

"Yeah, he is, but you're not. Me and my swollen feet will be in the lounge." Nayelli avoids making eye contact with the people sitting on the hard plastic chairs. "I bet we're a sight—a whale in blue pajamas and the Mexican 007."

She swipes her keycard to get into the lounge, and we sit down on the sad, worn-looking couch by the wall farthest from a sleeping intern who is contorted in an armchair. Nayelli kicks off her leather doctor clogs with a sigh. She's wearing rainbow-striped socks, which do nothing for her feet.

"You going to show face tomorrow at the house, or are you banished forever?" She plops her foot into my lap, and I have no choice but to rub it.

"Shouldn't your husband be doing this?" I ask as I start kneading.

"He's just getting out of surgery." She leans back, closing her eyes and resting her hands high on her belly. I can't help but smile. "Oh, don't look at me that way. There's nothing glorious or romantic about it. If you ever talk some chick into having your baby, she'll wipe the stupid smile off your face with the back of her swollen hand, little brother. Being pregnant sucks monkey ass. I swear, I feel like I'm wearing panty hose with a bowling ball in the crotch."

"You would be a vision of motherhood, Nayelli, if you just didn't have that problem with speaking."

"Did I say you could stop rubbing. So what's up with the tux?" She gives me a once-over and sniffs when she can't find anything to make fun of besides the way I'm dressed. "You going to the prom?"

"I have to escort a client to an event that starts"—I check my watch—"in a little under half an hour."

"Which client?" When I don't answer, she sticks a rainbow foot in my face. "Which client?"

"Candace Hall," I mutter to her toes. "She's making me go with her to some fancy benefit dinner."

"You're kidding me!" Nayelli yanks her feet out of my lap and sits up as straight as my future niece or nephew will let her. "You're going out on a date with sweatshop owner?"

"Alleged sweatshop owner." I don't look at her when I say it.

"Man! Dad must be pissed, and I bet Mom is doing that understanding thing she does when she knows she's right and everyone else is wrong." Nayelli lets loose with a hysterical giggle. "This is too good to be fucking true!"

"I'm glad one of us is enjoying it." I drop my head into my hands, resting my elbows on my knees. "What do I do, Nayelli?"

She gives me a few soft pats on the back, which end with a pretty firm punch on my upper arm. "Lawyers sometimes escort their clients to events. Like Anna Nicole and her lawyer. He also wound up falsely claiming paternity of her baby and marrying her and then . . . she died."

"Thanks for that most enlightening and unhelpful example." I reach for her feet again, figuring it'll be safer to lull her into relaxation so she can't hit me anymore. "I don't want to be her escort, just her lawyer, and maybe not even that."

"Look at it this way—at least you haven't hooked up with some toothless old hag with a hairy upper lip and saggy boobs." For emphasis, Nayelli pulls her lips across her teeth and places her hands low like she's trying to hold up hanging knockers.

"I haven't 'hooked up' with anyone." I try to make my voice sound genuinely offended.

"Tell that to our parents when they have to hear about it from their friends. Just because they're all socialists doesn't mean they don't gossip."

"Fuck" is all I can say.

"Don't even think of doing that," Nayelli says, wagging a finger at me. "Looks like it's all you on this one, Alexander."

"That's what I'm afraid of." I look at my watch. "I should get going. I'm already late."

"Typical. You're late for some hot date and running out on a reality check at the same time." Nayelli's cell phone rings, and Lloyd's picture pops up on the screen. "So we'll see you tomorrow?"

"I can't hide forever." I give her a kiss on the top of her head and walk toward the door.

I look back to give her a wave and hear her say, "Lloyd, we are *so* going over to my parents' tomorrow."

Evelyn

Whereas my flat is done in a careful mix of Danish Modern and American mid-century pieces, Tannin's place is an expanded version of the frilly and very feminine bedroom she had as a girl. Each room is decorated with maximum amounts of gilt, silks, and filigree, and makes it very clear that this is the home of a single woman and any man should enter at his own risk.

"Where is Tannin anyway?" James calls from her walk-in closet, formerly the pantry, but since my sister prefers size zero to food, it made sense to convert the space to one she'd actually use.

"She's hanging out with Whit." I wander around her apartment, adjusting frames and fluffing voluminous tablecloths and window hangings. "In L.A. She'll be back soon. She hates L.A. And she hates Whit, she's just forgotten she does. But we're supposed to say she's home with bad cramps if anyone asks."

"That man whore"—James emerges with a handful of jewelry—"is not worth the fifty-dollar pomade he puts in his hair. He's perfect for Tannin."

"That looks like a lot of stuff," I say, warily eyeing the strands of gold chains, big beads, and hat he's holding. "I'm not entirely sure about the *chapeau.*"

"Oh, that's for me," James says, carefully setting down the snow-white Balenciaga mod riding hat Tannin had me overnight from Paris when she couldn't find it in San Francisco. "The rest is for you. We have to do something to distract from the dress you're wearing."

"Fair enough."

I stand still as he fastens a chunky three-strand rock-crystal necklace, whose mix of colors plays off the purple shade of my dress, then adds a few strands of gold chains that end in a deliberate cluster of charms and pendants just below the undersides of my breasts. To finish things off, James doubles up the baroque South Sea pearl necklace Tannin was bequeathed by Grandmother Helen around my wrist so the aggie-size, organically shaped, luminescent orbs almost obscure my watch.

"There." He stands back to survey his handiwork. "All it takes is a few hundred thousand dollars' worth of jewelry, a great rack, and perfect makeup, and anyone can make an off-the-rack mass-retail frock look fucking fabulous."

"Thank you, James." I give him a light kiss on the cheek and then start back up to my place to wait for my boss.

Alexander

Thanks to some *Ronin*-style driving on part of the chauffeur, we arrive at Candace's door a little after six. He doesn't bother to hop out to open my door, and I take this as a hint that I'm on my own if Candace chooses to be pissed off at my tardiness. I don't blame him, and I realize I don't even know his name.

He must think I'm such an asshole. Hey, even I think I'm an asshole, but there's no point in going back, apologizing, and introducing myself. I'd just confirm his assessment of me.

I trudge up the stairs, ring the bell, adjust my tie, and wait for the door to open, this time fully prepared to address Raymunda in English and nothing but English. Instead the intercom off to my left squawks to life, issuing Candace's smoky voice.

"Alexander? Be a dear and let yourself in. I'll just be a minute or two." She clicks off and the door clicks open. Taking one more look behind me and at freedom, I step inside, shutting the door behind me.

"Hello?" My voice would echo, but plush rugs have been laid out over the previously bare marble floor. No one appears, so I make my way to the living room and am relieved to see that a tray of fruit, cheese, and crackers is laid out for me. At least I hope it's for me.

I take a seat and lean forward to reach for a grape when my

phone rings. Guiltily, I snatch my hand away from the food and fumble with my cell.

"Hello. This is Alexander."

"It's me." Nayelli sounds out of breath.

"Are you okay?" I stand up with a rush of adrenaline while my brain starts to run through all sorts of worst-case pregnant-lady scenarios based on my compulsive late-night watching of *ER* reruns. "Nayelli?"

"Why does everyone keep asking me that?" She sounds annoyed but still out of breath, like she's panting. "I'm pregnant, a pregnant doctor, and I'm taking the stairs instead of waiting for the elevator to go one floor up. Big deal. Anyway, I wanted to give you a heads-up about tonight."

"Yeah?" I pour myself a glass of water and nix the idea of eating anything. According to the itinerary Becky sent me, cocktail hour is from six to seven, and the sit-down dinner starts right after that. I'll save my appetite for dinner. I hate to admit it, but I'm pretty excited to be going to this benefit dinner, even under the almost sleazy circumstances. "What about tonight?"

"Dad's going to be there." I can hear Nayelli practically holding her breath, waiting for my reaction to this little piece of news. "Alexander?"

"I'm here." I look around for something stronger than water, like pure grain alcohol. "Shitting a brick."

Of course my father is going to be there, with his bullhorn and one of his union T-shirts. Some dads never miss a baseball game or soccer match; my father attends rallies for fun.

"Alexander?" Candace is standing in the doorway wearing a silky robe that gapes in all the right places.

"I'll call you back. Take it easy, Nayelli." Feeling like I'm an unwitting actor in some sort of warped sex-play fantasy, I stand up. "Candace."

"I'm running a little late." She gestures to her cleavage. "I'd like to talk a bit about strategy. Kill two birds with one stone, so to speak."

I gulp. "Big birds."

"Come upstairs and keep me company while I throw something on, Alexander."

Without waiting for me to agree or to see if I'm man enough to follow, she heads upstairs.

"Fuck." I wait long enough for her to make it to the top landing so I won't have to watch her ass as she climb the stairs.

The hallway carpeting up here is even more plush than the rugs downstairs. More paintings are on the walls and, as with the downstairs, I notice there aren't any personal photos here either. I guess Candace isn't big on sentimentality or being reminded of her past.

There are at least half a dozen closed doors on either side of me, but there's no question where I'm supposed to head. At the end of the hall, a door is ajar. Soft golden light and sexy Euro music spills out like in some bad soft-core porn movie. At least I'm dressed for the part.

At the threshold I stop, pushing the door open wider with my hand. "Candace?"

"In here." Her drowsy voice comes from somewhere deeper inside.

"Ah"—I look at my watch, not registering the time, and scan the bedroom from the safety of the doorway—"we should get going."

"Listen to you." She laughs, as if I've just said something very suave and witty. "So professional and uptight. Relax, Alexander. Didn't anyone ever tell you things will hurt a lot less if you just let them happen?"

"I just thought we had to be there at a specific time." I step in, standing off to the side of the dressing room where she's moving around.

"My dead, rich husband was a major donor, and he left everything to me. If they want to make sure they see a penny of my money, they'll hold off on the important stuff," she says, and I hear hangers being pushed down a rod and drawers opening and closing. "Don't worry, Alexander, you're not missing anything. Right now they're just jerking each other off and analyzing the bad facelifts in the room."

"Okay."

Candace has the world by the nuts, and she's not afraid to give them a firm squeeze when she needs to. She comes out. Still wearing the robe, now fully open, but at least she has underwear on under it, including garters and stockings.

There go my nuts.

"I'm going to need a little help . . . in here." She inclines her head, one of her big diamond earrings dipping onto her almost bare shoulder.

I take a step back. "I'll go call Raymunda." Candace shakes her head at me. I take another step back. "Becky?"

"It's just us here." She walks back into the other room, calling over her shoulder, "Don't worry, I won't bite."

I take my time getting there. When I do, she's standing facing the mirror, her eyes on mine, her dress unzipped so I can see her naked back and the top curve of her ass under her flesh-colored thong. I take three long strides forward, zip up the creamy silk in one motion, causing her to let out a yelp, and turn around and walk out and back downstairs to wait by the door.

Evelyn

I stand at my front door, the only thing between me going out on a date with Ted. Just outside, he leans on the buzzer again.

"Help me, James," I hiss at him. He waves me off and ducks into the hall closet, where he can see everything but can hide from Ted.

"Evelyn? Ted here." To emphasize the point, he knocks, then rings the bell again.

I take a step back from the door, seriously considering the option of joining James in the closet, but take a deep breath and open the door.

"Hi, Ted."

"We'd better get going. We're late."

He's late, I was ready on time, but that's beside the point.

"Let me get my purse." I turn toward the closet, where James's arm is sticking out holding the gold clutch. I stick my head inside. "I can't do this! It's wrong on so many levels."

"You okay in there?" Ted asks. I look back at him, and he's scoping out my place, no doubt feeling like he's discovering clues to the real me.

"Just a second." I duck into the closet, wedging a little more of my body inside. "I can't, James!"

"You can do it! It'll be fun. Like the kind of horrible fun junior high was." James gives me a firm push, and I stumble out, just as he slams the door.

"Did you paint this?" Ted asks. He's standing in front of the canvas I started last night after being unable to sleep. "Is that the building across from UGotIt? It looks like the window outside your office."

"It's just a hobby." I take a tentative step forward and then feel James give me a mighty push on the rump so I stumble. "I quit smoking and I, uh, need to keep my hands busy."

"Tobacco companies have the ultimate business model. A never-ending stream of new customers to replace the ones they lose," Ted says to my antique Danish sideboard, having moved on to perusing the rest of my belongings. "Ready?"

"Ready!" James answers for me in a muffled high falsetto from the closet.

I smile at Ted and rush out into the hallway, stepping aside so I can lock the door. Before I can reach for my key, a series of clicks issues from the other side. Locked out of my own home, I lead the way down the stairs and onto the street, careful to stay a step or two ahead of my boss and my date for the evening.

Ted walks over to the driver's side of his double-parked car, then stops as if something just occurred to him. "You're not one of those women who need doors opened for them, right?" he asks, a little unsure. "Women's lib, feminism, and all that jazz?"

"Me? No." I look up at my front window, where James has his faced pressed to the glass, looking both horrified and amused. "I've never been much of a jazz fan, Ted."

"Right, so hop in."

I take a deep breath and slide into the seat.

Ted waits until I'm settled, then turns up the volume on the radio so I and everyone within a twenty-five-foot perimeter of his car's speakers can enjoy Bon Jovi's "Wanted Dead or Alive." He guns the motor and takes off down the street. I feel like I'm back in 1986, when Winthrop Huffington picked me up for a movie date and had the driver circle the block twice so we could all enjoy the whole song. The driver came in with us so we could get into *Fatal Attraction,* and after buying the three tickets and escorting us in, he went back out to wait in the car.

At the time, it really didn't seem absurd. Unlike this, which seems not only absurd but very wrong.

We don't say much on the ride over, and we say even less when Ted circles around looking for a free parking spot, eventually wedging his babied BMW into an impossibly tight spot blocks away from City Hall.

"I don't know why people bitch about there not being any parking in the city. It's there if you look for it," he says as we start the trek back toward the limousines and valet stand, where everyone else is being dropped off.

"Right," I snap, momentarily losing my composure, "who doesn't like walking six blocks through one of the most dangerous neighborhoods in the city?"

"Don't worry. I have Mace in my pocket." Ted reaches into his trouser pocket, comes up empty, and then looks panicked. "I forgot it in the car."

"Let's just go," I say.

I walk a little behind Ted since he's not taking into account that I'm wearing heels and maybe not really in a rush to get to where we're going.

But we get there. Men in tuxes and ladies in gowns make a measured ascent up the red-carpeted stairs as local and society photographers take pictures. They're not the only ones here to watch the spectacle. Police have set up those metal barriers to pen in a group of protesters who are chanting and waving signs.

Suddenly finding a burst of energy, I start quickly up the steps, only to have Ted take hold of my upper arm and force me to pose for the photographers, like a hunter showing off a ten-point buck. Bursts of lights blind me as I grit my teeth and try to make my face as placid as possible.

"Did you bring any business cards?" Ted asks out of the side of his mouth, still smiling for the photographers, who have no idea who he is and know me only through my mother.

"Business cards?" I ask, trying not to move my mouth too much, knowing a bad picture is worse than no picture at all in my mother's mind.

"Never mind, I did." He pats his breast pocket and finally starts up the stairs. "You see anyone you know?"

I exchange stiff nods and half smiles with a few people who look like well-preserved, diamond-laden cadavers. Exactly the types of people you'd expect to see at one of these events. "No."

At the top of the stairs, Ted stands aside so I can step through the doors before him, finally realizing that good manners are good manners, feminism or not.

"An investor is an investor," he says with naked excitement in his voice as he hands our tickets over to one of the costumed attendants.

I stop short, causing Ted to execute a clumsy box step to avoid crashing into me. "You want me to ask people for money?"

Even with the din of people talking and a quartet playing off to the side, my words seem to echo around the marble rotunda. A few more stiff nods and smiles are exchanged before people go back to sipping their drinks and inspecting the canapé trays held aloft by waiters.

Ted shuffles me off to the side and gives me what I suppose he considers a very grave look. To make it worse, he takes my hands in his, giving them a slight squeeze with every word. "Evelyn, I didn't want to say anything, but funding is drying up."

I nod, unsure how he wants me respond. Should I offer to share my office, bring my own hot water from home for my tea? I'm already working for free, so I'm not sure how much more cost-effective I can make myself. I ease my hands out of his, and when he keeps staring at me, I say, "I see."

Ted pulls out a sheet of paper with a series of names printed on both sides. "I figure since you are friends with Tannin Sinclair—"

"I can't. I can't do that," I blurt out, again raising my voice. "You can't honestly expect me to do something like that."

Waiters meander through the crowd carrying trays of drinks and food, but what I really want is a cream pie to push into Ted's face. He invited me to accompany him, when all he ever had in mind was to use me as a fund-raising tool. Why am I so surprised? This is Ted. The man who has me send out e-mails reminding everyone that working at UGotIt.com isn't just a job, it's a lifestyle.

"Forget I mentioned it." Ted tucks his list away. "Let's just have a good time tonight. Friends?"

"Of course," I say, mustering up every ounce of decorum I can manage. I smile at Ted, ready to go through the motions, prepared to engage in the niceties of behaving in polite society. "Friends."

"I'll meet you back here right before they seat us for dinner." Ted turns on his heel and leaves me standing there as he sets off after some big-money game.

I make my way through the crowd, stopping to chat and accepting the occasional compliment on Mother's tireless efforts to support the arts and to receive messages that people wish she were here to enjoy the night. I say nothing, not wanting to add to my mother's absence by making excuses for her and possibly tripping up her story. They know she's not here because Candace Hall is supposed to come, and they're disappointed not to have ringside seats to the first official confrontation.

Finally I make it to the bar. I slip a dollar into the tip jar and keep my eyes firmly off in middle distance. "Can I get a glass of wine, please? White."

The bartender sets a glass in front of me and then moves off to the other side of the bar, where someone is snapping his fingers to get his attention.

Before I have a chance to start drowning myself in white wine, my eye is caught by an elderly couple. I put the glass down, prepare to make nice and then start on getting plastered.

"Good evening," I say, not betraying how much I'd rather be doing something else very far away from here.

"Evelyn?" the white-haired lady exclaims to the man beside her. "It is! I told you it was little Evelyn Sinclair."

"Hello. How are you?" I look around to see if Ted is in the vicinity. I don't know who they are, but most likely I've been to parties at their house, gone to school with their grandnieces, or met them at the last event I had to attend. "It's so nice to see you again."

"Oh, just fine, dear. Such a pity your mother is under the weather tonight. She always does such fine work for the ballet." The woman does all the talking. Her husband, a hearing aid in each ear, rocks back and forth on his heels slightly and smiles benignly. "Are you here with a lucky young man?"

"I . . . well. No. Not really. What I mean is I am here with . . . Oh, look, there's . . . I'll make sure to pass your kind words on to my mother!" I grab hold of my glass and ease myself away from the bar.

"Good night, dear. Tell your mother we said hello," she calls after me. I turn back to give one final wave and catch her whispering into her husband's ear.

"What! Speak up!" he barks, cupping his hand to his fuzzy ear.

"I said," she repeats, raising her voice loud enough so it carries over the din, "it's a shame about Lila's daughter. Do you think she's one of those lesbians?"

"Lebanese?" he asks. "She's not Lebanese."

I could say something. Hell, I *should* say something, but I decide against it. Instead I duck into the bathroom to the left of the bar. Maybe I can hide out in one of the stalls until this is over. And people wonder why I like to stay home.

Alexander

I wait another ten minutes for Candace to come downstairs. When she does, it's without a word or a glance in my direction. She walks past me, opens the front door, and heads right into the car, looking like a pissed-off Grace Kelly, complete with shawl draped around her shoulders and secured on one side by a tarantula-size diamond brooch.

I shut the front door behind me and my phone rings. "Alexander here."

"Alex." It's Rodney, and he sounds agitated. I get into the car beside Candace, and as soon as I close the door, the driver takes off at a good clip.

"What's up, Rodney?" I ask, hazarding a look in my client's direction.

Candace stares out the window, so all I can see is the back of her head, clearly still pissed off at me. But there's not much either of us can say. I can't apologize for not wanting to give her services above and beyond my legal skills and she can't bring it up without acknowledging I turned her down.

At least that's one thing I can be proud of.

"You need to get your affairs in order. Right now," Rodney yelps into the phone.

"What do you mean?" I look over at Candace, trying to figure out if she got on the phone to Rodney to complain about me not wanting to bang her.

"Your father," Rodney spits into my ear, "is currently on the radio disparaging your client, Alex."

"Is he?" I want to add I'm not surprised but doubt Rodney would find that cute.

"He is leading a protest at the event you are supposed to be at. And he's doing it right now."

"What do you want me to do, Rodney?" I ask.

"Deal with it." In the background, I hear Bryan and Brian cheering. While I get to go to a ballet benefit in a tux, Rodney took the boys out to a baseball game to be enjoyed in a private box. "And make sure you don't upset Candace. I don't need any more faxes from her tonight."

Rodney clicks off.

When we pull into the Civic Center, I tap the driver on the shoulder. "Could you let me off at the corner and then circle the block? Candace, there might be some protesters. I'm going to see what I can do. I'll meet you at the curb."

Candace pulls out a compact and checks her makeup. "Fine."

I hop out and walk quickly toward the group of protesters

behind the portable metal barricades the police have set up to keep them off the red-carpeted steps leading into City Hall.

It doesn't take me long to find my dad. He's standing on top of a stepladder, his chipped yellow bullhorn in one hand, jabbing a picket sign into the air with the other.

"What do we want?" he calls out.

"Justice!" the crowd of about fifty or so answers it back.

"Candace Hall! Pay your workers!" My father's amplified voice booms over them. The crowd cheers, bangs pots, and blows whistles. My father waves them down to a dull roar before he continues. "Do the right thing, Candace Hall! Treat your employees like human beings!"

I tug at my dad's pant leg, and he looks down at me. He hands his sign and bullhorn to someone else in a union T-shirt and hops off the stepladder. Nayelli and I take turns giving him one every other Father's Day. He manages to lose them on a regular basis, when protests are broken up and he has to leave his ladder on the street as he's being hauled away in the back of the police car. Plus, our dad is just not a sweater-vest kind of guy, and we'd rather give him something he can actually appreciate and use.

"Alexander." He gives me a stiff hug, but a hug nonetheless. "You look good, *hijo*. You should stop by the house and show your mother."

"I'll try to, Dad."

We watch the protesters on his side of the barricade and the rich people on my side for a few seconds.

"I guess I'd be wasting my time by asking you to . . ." I begin. To what? Stop? Put aside what he believes in to make my job easier? Not be himself? "Never mind, Dad. I'm going to escort my client inside because that's what I want to do. I want to see what's on the other side of those doors. And I'll deal with what that means tomorrow."

I give my dad another hug and step away as Candace's car pulls up to the curb.

"Son," he calls after me, "I hope you find what you're looking for in there because you sure haven't found it out here in the real world."

I nod at my father; he takes his place back on the stepladder. I wait for the driver to open the car door for Candace.

Evelyn

I peek into my handbag to see what time it is on my cell phone. In about ten minutes the lights will flicker and people will begin to make their way upstairs for the sit-down dinner portion of this endless night's activities.

I hid out in the bathroom as long as I could, spent twenty minutes listening to Fiona Hughes Parker go on about the powers of feng shui, and then floated around making the small talk that is expected of me while sidestepping Ted as much as possible. I excuse myself from the periphery of yet another pointless conversation and make my way over to my date, having decided my migraine is now unbearable and I will have to take a cab home.

"Ted?" I smile at the arty-looking couple he's talking to, having timed my interruption for when he's with people I don't know and assume my parents don't either. He's wearing a shrunken blue and black checked suit, and she's dressed in what could only be termed thrift store couture, complete with a spangled bag missing a few spangles.

Ted's hand rests lightly on my waist, making my skin tingle, and not in a good way. "This is my assistant, Evelyn—"

"Pleased to meet you," I say, not giving them a chance to actually introduce themselves. "Ted, could I speak to you for a moment?"

"Sure."

"I have a migraine. I need to go home." My pulse picks up a notch as I catch sight of Sissy with her husband lumbering behind her heading in our direction. "Now."

"Now?" Ted asks in a decidedly unsympathetic manner.

"Don't worry, I'll"—I take a step to the right so I can hide behind a large portrait of my mother—"take a cab home. Not a problem."

"I'm going out for a smoke, I'll walk out with you," Mr. Shrunken Suit offers. I smile at him with no choice but to accept his escort. "I'm going nuts in here."

"Are you sure, Evelyn?" Ted is already looking over his shoulder for fresh prey. "I'm sure someone can get you an aspirin."

"Completely sure, Ted." I glance at Mr. Shrunken Suit, who is shifting from foot to foot, his cigarette and lighter already in hand. "You have fun and I'll see you on Monday."

"Yeah, about that. I'm making Allan and Jessica and their teams work through the weekend, and I need you there for crisis management."

"Is there a crisis to manage?" I ask, despite wanting to get the hell out of here. "I'm sure Allan and Jessica don't need me—"

"Evelyn?" I hear Sissy ask over the din.

"Fine. I'll be there, but I have to go to, uh, church on Saturday morning, so I'll be in after noon." I ease even farther into the long shadow cast by Mother's John Singer Sargent–inspired portrait. "I'm feeling quite ill now, Ted."

"No worries. I gave them both your cell, and they can call you with any issues."

"Crazy night, huh?" Mr. Shrunken Suit asks as we start our charge for the door.

All I can do is nod and avoid eye contact.

Alexander

Candace poses for the photographers, ignoring the shouts of the protesters, who are chanting, "Hey, hey, lady, you've got to pay!" and holding signs with her picture under the words THE SWEAT-SHOP QUEEN.

I stand off to the side in a small sliver of no-man's-land between them.

"Hey, hey, Candace! Who makes your clothes?" my father shouts into the bullhorn as a news cameraman focuses first on her, then on the protesters like it's some sort of class-based tennis match and he doesn't want to miss a volley.

A TV reporter with hurricane-proof hair waves his microphone, trying to get Candace's attention. "Ms. Hall! Channel Seven News, Wyatt Fellows. Ms. Hall!"

Candace grabs hold of my arm and leads me toward the reporter and his cameraman, dragging me out of the shadows and straight into the media glare. For some reason, I thought my first time would be a lot more romantic.

"I think I'll just hang back—" I start before the look on her face tells me I won't be doing any such thing.

"Wyatt, darling!" Candace holds out her right hand, and the reporter gives it a couple of weak pumps.

"You look gorgeous, as always," Wyatt says, positioning the

microphone between them. "And let me just express condolences from everyone at Channel Seven Eyewitness News on your husband's untimely passing."

"Thank you for your kind words." Candace looks down as if she's touched by what he said and uses the moment to nudge the microphone lower so it doesn't block her face. She turns slightly so she's facing the camera in a flattering three-quarter profile. "Thank you, Wyatt. It's been a while since I had a reason as good as this one to dress up and spend a night on the town. I think my husband would be proud to see me here, continuing his long relationship with the San Francisco Ballet and the vital work the auxiliary does to keep the arts alive and well in our beautiful city."

"What about these protesters? Are they putting a damper on your official coming out of mourning?" Wyatt gestures toward them, and they ratchet up the noise, my father now hopping up and down on the stepladder in time with their chants.

Candace gives a hollow laugh, shrugging her bare shoulders. "This is San Francisco. One of the wonderful things about this city is how diverse and vocal people are."

This is almost verbatim from the talking points the New York PR people came up with, and it's delivered with such sincerity that I can't help but do a double take.

"Do you think you'll win the case?" Wyatt flips through his scribbled reporter's notebook with one hand looking for information that will (he hopes) lead to a sound bite that will sum up what he wants his viewers to think about Candace Hall.

"The truth will come out, Wyatt. For now, on advice of my very able attorney"—she gives my arm a squeeze—"I'll have to leave that particular topic of conversation alone until I have my day in court."

"Are you looking forward to tonight's festivities?" Wyatt switches over to fluff, realizing Candace isn't going to screw the legal pooch in front of his microphone by saying anything disparaging about the people suing her.

"My wonderful husband"—she touches a hand to her chest—"was an enthusiastic supporter of the arts in the city. I can't wait to see what the auxiliary has planned for us tonight. I'm sure they won't disappoint. Not with Lila Reed Sinclair as chairwoman."

"And what about the tensions between you and the committee?" Wyatt doesn't pause for Candace to answer. "Rumors that you and Lila Sinclair have had a falling-out over how the committee is composed and it's the reason she's not here tonight?"

She gives him a tight and cold smile. "These events are always a wonderful way for supporters of the arts to come together and celebrate the arts. And in the end, that's why we're here, to celebrate the arts in San Francisco."

"What about their refusal to let you on the committee despite the very sizable donations you and your estranged husband made before his death?" Wyatt plunges on. He might as well. From the look on Candace's face, he's just burned whatever bridge she'd let him on. "Is it true that it was Lila Sinclair's direct intervention that kept you off the committee?"

Candace tips her head in a way that reminds me of a lioness just before she pounces on her prey. "Mere gossip, Wyatt. I'm sure your viewers expect much more from such an established journalist as yourself." She reaches out, gives him a sharp pat on the arm, and takes a step away, signaling that the interview is over. "I'm looking forward to tonight, and I'm sure, if my husband were still here with us, he would be too."

Candace stalks up the steps, the sharp tips of her high heels digging into the thin red carpet. I look back at my father, who's put down his bullhorn, and shrug. He motions for me to get going after her.

When I catch up to her, she hisses out of the side of her mouth, "I want him fired! How dare he talk to me like that? Does he fucking know who I am? I know people who can have him off the air before he has time to trowel on another coat of makeup. I want him destroyed. I don't care how you do it, but do it. Do you understand me?"

I nod slowly, a little scared to make any sudden movements. Candace composes her face and glides in, her hand on my arm. She waits a few seconds for people to notice she's arrived, then shrugs out of her silk wrap and hands it to me.

She smiles, showing a lot of teeth along with an almost indecent expanse of cleavage. "Why don't you go find us a drink, Alex? Fiona! You look gorgeous."

"I have an idea. Why don't I get us something to drink?" I ask no one. "You know? A drink is exactly what I need. A drink, a spine, and a fucking clue."

I make my way through the crowd, pretending I'm not impressed at what I'm seeing. These people are rich, the kind of rich where they don't talk about money rich. The smell of wealth and privilege hangs in the air like a haze of smog over the East Bay.

I lean up against the bar, feeling guilty over the rush I'm getting because of where I am instead of being outside with my dad, who actually has ideals, beliefs, and standards that can't be so easily bought.

"Two glasses of wine."

"Young man?" An older guy with a hearing aid in each ear waves me over.

"Yes, sir?" The bartender slides over two glasses of white and then moves on to help someone else. I pick them up and turn my attention back to the old man.

"My wife needs her wrap checked." He thrusts something furry into my direction.

"Excuse me?" I look from the fur to their faces.

"The wrap." He thrusts it at me. "It needs to be checked."

I continue to stare at them both, equally embarrassed and pissed off. "You want me to check your wife's wrap?"

"Offer him a tip," the wife says, loudly, into his ear.

"That won't be necessary." I put down the glasses, take the wrap, and give them a little bow for good measure. I turn on my heel and stride toward the trash can by the ladies' room. I turn back to them, give another little bow, and then drop it in the can before I go back to the bar and pick up the glasses of wine. "You two have a good night."

I find Candace, who is talking loudly in the middle of the room. She takes the glass without looking at me. "And I said to Lexie, Fiona has the corner on—"

"Candace?"

I'm leaving. I'm ripping off my tie, giving my jacket to the first homeless guy I see, rolling up my sleeves, and taking my place next to my dad behind the police barricade. What did I expect? For these people to accept me as one of them, to see that I belong here as much as they do? To them I'm just another brown-faced waiter, Armani tux or no Armani tux.

"Oh, there you are." Candace snakes her arm through mine. "Fiona, have you met my new lawyer?"

"Pleased to meet you." I give her hand a quick shake and then turn to Candace. "Candace, I'm—"

"No, I haven't." This Fiona woman looks me up and down like I'm a slab of fat-free beef jerky. "Well played, Candace."

"Thank you, Fiona. The fact that this is such ugly business doesn't mean it all has to be so unattractive." Candace laughs, pleased with her friend's reaction to me.

"Listen to me!" I jerk my arm away from her and open my mouth to lay it all out for Candace when I see her heading toward the door.

"Alexander," Candace hisses at me through her teeth, "what is wrong with you?"

"I'll get us something to drink." I grab her glass and zigzag my way through the crowd, stopping to hand the glasses to the old couple who asked me to check their dead fox or whatever kind of animal pelt it was.

I push through the front doors, the sounds of the last few protesters dying away, and watch as she talks to a guy in a checked Thom Browne suit who is holding his hand out to hail a cab.

"Hey!" Not the smoothest line, but she turns toward me, searching for who called out. I lift my hand to wave at her, only to find it in Candace's viselike grip.

"Alexander," she spits. "It's time to come back inside now."

I look back toward where she is, and for a moment our eyes lock, and then the man shuts the cab door.

I shake my hand loose from Candace's and make my way down the steps to where the guy is smoking. "Do you know her? Her name?"

"Nah, just met her. Sorry."

"Thanks, man." I stare after the cab as it disappears into traffic.

Evelyn

"Someone you know?" the cabdriver asks.

"In a way." I try to shake out of my head the image of him standing with Candace Hall, holding hands. "But no. I have no idea who he is."

"Where to?" the driver asks, leaning on his horn to get a few people carrying signs out of the way.

"The In-N-Out on Fisherman's Wharf." I'm in the mood for a burger, fries, and a milk shake. A big fat one.

Evelyn

"Good morning!" James hops onto my bed, forcibly scooting me over to make room for his skinny body, clad, of all things, in flannel Groucho Marx duck print pajamas. "What's for breakfast?"

"You're already eating. In my bed," I say, gesturing to the tin of imported butter cookies he's balancing on his impossibly flat belly.

"This isn't at all nutritious. I'll get scurvy or something," James says through a mouthful of cookie. I listen to him crunch for a few minutes before reaching for one. He bats my hand away. "Uh-uh. No cookie for you until you give me a graphic, detailed, and omission-free recounting of your date with Ted."

"What's to tell? It was a disaster." I sigh. "From start to finish. And it wasn't a date."

"But you looked great, at least, thanks to me," James says brightly.

I roll over onto my back and stare up at the ceiling. So his name is Alexander Velazquez, son of a lawyer and community activist, graduate of Berkeley, and, if the stories are right, more than just Candace Hall's lawyer.

"So? Did he put the moves on you?" James asks, offering me a cookie.

"Not on me, but just about everyone else had their ears violated by him." I take a bite, then toss the cookie aside, feeling grossed out. "Last night was purely a networking opportunity for

Ted. He wanted me to trade on 'my friend' Tannin Reed-Sinclair's good name."

"Eh"—James shrugs—"I figured as much."

"Thanks for clueing me in." I get out of bed, determined to shake all of this off. I get down on the floor and do some push-ups, straight-leg style, just to make up for last night and the bite of cookie this morning. The old me would drown herself in comfort food, or paint, but now I can't do either of those things.

James retrieves the cookie and pops it into his mouth as he watches me. "So his interest in you was purely business? He didn't try to feel you up? Not even a little, or try to play off a boob grab as an accident?"

"Not once." I switch over to sit-ups, inhaling deeply each time I come up. I huff through three sets of fifty, amazed at how strong I've gotten in the past few months.

"Stop eating those," I snap. Not that I'm jealous James can shovel down food, the worst kind, and never seem to gain a pound, but, okay, I am. "We're due at my parents' for brunch and tennis in an hour."

"We are?" James says in a falsely surprised tone.

Mother enjoys his off-color humor, and he's Daddy's preferred tennis partner. Daddy swears he'll bring James around to croquet, but James always says, if he wanted to bang balls, he'd go out to Club Eros on a Thursday night, when the place is overflowing with just as smooth balls.

"Damn me. Why must I be a poor person with a rich person's appetite?" James gets out of bed, leaving the open cookie tin on the coverlet.

"Are you saying the only reason you hang out with me is because I'm rich?"

"No. That's why I hang out with Tannin. I hang out with you because you're you, and if Ted is too stupid to not give your melons a squeeze, I'll do it for him."

"You always know exactly what to say, James." I sneak another cookie, this one tasting too good for my thighs. Candace is thin, thin, thin. Like I'd have to have my entire stomach removed, not just reduced by 30 percent. I chew quickly.

"You don't know how good you have it," James says, watching me delicately wipe the crumbs from my cleavage.

"Please, if you were me, not you, you'd be in some sham of a marriage to an anorexic former debutante, trolling gay bars at night. Is that how you'd want to live?"

"Better an anorexic than a fat girl." James reaches over and pinches my hip. "But I'd make an exception for you."

"I'm not fat!" I slap his hand away and hop up. "Am I?"

"Not yet," he says, prying the cookies away from me.

Alexander

I'm rounding the corner on foot, having taken the long way here, when Lloyd and Nayelli pull up to my parents' house in their new family-friendly red Subaru Outback. My dad has blocked off the space for them so Nayelli doesn't have to troop up from some distant parking spot to the house. I watch as Lloyd jumps out and rushes over to my sister's side to open her door.

"I can still operate simple machinery, Lloyd," she says in an annoyed tone. Even though I saw her less than twenty-four hours ago, she looks noticeably more pregnant and equally miserable. "Is it like ten thousand fucking degrees here or what?"

"Nayelli," Lloyd says in a gentle warning tone. He's full of theories, backed up by plenty of websites and wordy medical journals, on the supersensitive hearing of babies while in utero. I think he's latched on to the idea only because he's hoping it'll get my sister to curb her cussing.

"Don't just stand there looking gorgeous and dumb, Alexander, help Lloyd." Nayelli turns her back on us and starts her careful ascent of the steps to the open front door of our parents' house.

"Alexander! Morning!" Lloyd moves slowly and deliberately. Even out of his doctor's scrubs and white coat, he looks reassuringly clinical. With his neatly combed light brown hair, blue eyes, and easygoing personality, he seems the most unlikely person to have wound up with my sister, who is a force of nature.

"Looks like Nayelli's bright and sunny as usual." I hold out my hands so Lloyd can place a couple of carefully wrapped dishes on them.

"The baby was moving around a lot last night." Lloyd stops what he's doing to gaze up at my sister, who pauses at the top of the stairs to catch her breath. When she notices us looking at her, she gives us both the finger before going inside. "She's just a bit cranky today."

"Yeah, uh, Lloyd, I think there's another word for what she is every day."

Inside, the place is packed with friends, family, and neighbors. My parents do this once a month, inviting everyone from my mom's clients to hotel workers my dad is trying to unionize for a day of eating, drinking, and playing soccer in the backyard. Developers have been bugging my parents to sell so they can build million-dollar live-work lofts on the land.

I'm kissed by aunts who are waving around their knitting needles, slapped on the back by uncles who already are cracking open bottles of Corona, and get more than a few knowing looks as I make my way into the kitchen, where my mother presides over what she calls "the command center." Here she can monitor what people are eating, doing, and more important, drinking. My mother is the family lawyer, but she'll charge out the nose for a DUI defense, family or not.

My dad is at the stove, poaching an enormous blue-speckled pot of ribs for barbecuing later on.

"Hey." I hesitate at the doorway, especially when all conversation ceases as soon as I make my appearance. "Okay, then. That wasn't totally weird."

I glance over at my dad, who just grunts and turns up the volume on the radio, where he's listening to Pacifica as usual. The Saturday issue of the *S.F. Express* is open to the Society pages next to him. And there I am, looking like some sort of Mexican Ken doll Secret Service agent, one hand out to ward off photographers, the other on Candace's elbow as she gives a well-practiced smile.

I set the dishes down on the table where my mother and Nayelli are shucking corn, handing the corn silk and leaves to my cousins, who'll twist them into little dolls that they'll get to chuck into the barbecue later on. Savages.

"Let me try that again." I clear my throat. "*Hola, familia.* How are you all this fine Saturday morning?"

"Come give your mother a kiss." My mom tilts her cheek up for me, her hands still busy with the corn. "I was telling Nayelli she should take it easy. Doesn't she look tired, Alexander? Your dad thinks you look tired, Nayelli."

This is my mother's way of getting us on the same team, by double-teaming Nayelli.

"I agree with Dad." I send Nayelli an apologetic shrug. She

sticks her tongue out at me since her fingers are otherwise occupied. "Nayelli should take it easy for the sake of your future grandchild and my niece or nephew."

My dad turns up the volume. Lloyd comes in struggling with a kid on his back and one on each leg, carrying the last of the food Nayelli cooked up. My sister has started baking desserts in bulk. I read somewhere, or most likely Lloyd told me, that when a woman gets close to giving birth, she'll become weirdly domestic, cleaning tile grout with a toothbrush or, in my sister's case, making three different types of bread pudding.

"*Oye,*" Nayelli barks at the kids, "my husband is not a jungle gym. Go bother your own parents."

"It's okay, honey." Lloyd struggles over to the table, puts the dishes on a bare spot, and sends each kid off with a pat on the head. "I'm just glad they like me even though they know what I do for a living."

The man was a born pediatrician, but Lloyd had to take it one step further and become a pediatric surgeon. And when they asked, he told them, in graphic detail, how he spends his days cutting open kids just like them and then sewing them back together. He said this in such a matter-of-fact manner that he actually looked devastated when a few of the kids burst into tears and ran away from him in horror.

"Lloyd, *hijo.*" My father claps Lloyd on the back and gives him a one-arm man embrace. "You ready to play some *fútbol?*"

"I got my cleats in the car." Lloyd drapes his arm around my dad, towering over him by a good half foot. Then, noticing the tension in the room when I narrow my eyes at him and my mother grimaces, he beats a hasty retreat. "I think I'll go get them."

"That's a good idea, Lloyd," Nayelli says, shaking her head at him. "And tell everyone else out there"—she raises her voice—"that there won't be any show today, so they can just go back to their drinking and knitting!"

My dad turns back to his ribs and says, "*Itzlacoliuhque,* we need to talk."

"I know we do, Dad." I sigh and take a seat at the table.

While he's finishing up, I pick up the *S.F. Express* to gauge the damage.

Evelyn

My parents host a weekly Saturday brunch and tennis game, and invites are as coveted as an invitation to the mayor's for an official dinner. The formal dining table is laid out with the best china and antique linens, the staff is instructed to remain unobtrusive but attentive, and my mother works with her chef to make sure only the freshest and best foods grace her table.

Besides my father, myself, Tannin, and James, everyone has to vie for an invitation. And vie they do. People used to call me up and not so subtly try to maneuver themselves into a space at the table by becoming instant friends or allies. Even when I was away at Brown, I still had to deal with someone's mother or nephew hitting me up for an introduction. It all stopped when I left for Paris. There I could pretend I was just another expat art student. No one knew who I was, and for a while I made a small name for myself based on my talent as a painter.

Mother carefully balances the exact mix of politicos, those in the world of business (from finance to technology), and handpicked names from the art world and old as well as some new money. It's not just brunch but an institution. My parents, or rather my mother, signaled her preference as to who should be the next mayor of San Francisco by having her favored candidate and his wife over for brunch before his opponent and his wife; the opponent went on to lose gracefully and is now an occasional brunch invitee in his new line of work, as the president of one of my mother's pet nonprofits.

It's amazing the power a plate of poached eggs with asparagus and prosciutto can have in this city when it's served on Reed-Sinclair china.

I've packed my tennis whites in a gym bag even though I have no intention of playing; Mother would be very upset if I at least don't make the appearance of wanting to participate. James, by contrast, is resplendent in very short white shorts, a polo T, and a terry-cloth headband.

Guests must arrive by noon. My mother doesn't tolerate tardiness, not from me or from a U.S. congresswoman. James and I join the orderly conga line of vaguely familiar faces as we troop up the stairs, already exchanging empty pleasantries and air kisses but not dawdling. The real action happens inside, and that's where everyone wants to be.

I just want a cup of coffee, a whole-wheat bagel, and an early edition of *The New York Times.* But that's not going to happen here or today.

My mother likes to start with coffee or tea in the sitting room; then we move to the formal dining room, where we fill our plates buffet style, my mother's one concession to informality, and take our assigned seats.

"So your young man, Evelyn?" Mother says to me after she's done her first circuit around the room greeting guests. "I hear he's quite a talker."

"He's just someone I work with, Mother." I won't admit I

thought it was a date. That would be too humiliating, and my mother would never forgive me for being so naïve. James, kindly, keeps his opinion on my whatever last night to himself.

"I wish you would have told me you were going, Evelyn. I could have had you sit at our table. Sissy mentioned you were wearing a very interesting dress." I'm sure Mother has been filled in about all the particulars, including what I was wearing, by her dear friend Sissy, whom I snubbed.

"I had to leave early. Cramps. I'll apologize to Sissy for not having a chance to say hello last night."

"Sissy said he, this Ted, mentioned something about funding shortfalls." If there's one topic of conversation that is never welcome around my mother, it is anything that has to do with money.

I stand there mortified for Ted. It's obvious there are some things he didn't learn at MBA school. "All companies could use funding? Like ours might? Right, James?".

"What? Oh, yeah. Money." James slaps his palm to his forehead. "Who doesn't need it? Especially when you're a schmuck like Ted."

"Schmuck?" my mother asks, looking amused.

"They don't see eye to eye on some things," I explain, hoping to head off James's saying something wildly inappropriate, which will delight my mother no end.

"That guy doesn't know his butthole from a portal. Pardon my French, Mrs. Sinclair," James says.

"Speaking of which. I have a commitment and will have to leave early. I'm sorry, Mother."

"Work," James adds.

"Working on the weekend, Evelyn?" She sniffs disdainfully.

"Exactly how I feel, Mrs. Sinclair."

"We have a deadline to meet." I promised myself I would not try to justify having to leave early. If I offer too many excuses, Mother will just find a way to pick them apart and I'll end up spending the night in my old room.

"If you must." She sighs and squares her shoulders to start her second circuit around the room, arm in arm with James. "Have Ike drive you. I don't like the idea of you jumping on the bus so close to where everyone can see you."

"I wouldn't dream of it, Mother." I look around me and spot Sissy Ross and her red-nosed husband by the Renoir my father gave my mother as an engagement present. I make my way over to her. If anyone knows what's really going on with Candace Hall, it'll be Sissy.

"Evelyn! Darling, you looked simply delicious last night." Sissy presses her cheek to mine as we carefully hold our cups of tea away from each other. "That was a divine dress you wore. Oh, to have your figure! But I never was athletic like you girls are nowadays. With your biceps and stomach exercises."

"Thank you," I say as demurely as possible.

"I do hope you are on game today, Sissy," her husband says as he takes his leave from us, most likely to have his coffee spiked with my father's private-reserve whiskey. "I have fifty dollars on our match against James and Gerald, and I'm not in the mood to be on the losing end."

"Of course, dear." Sissy gives him a sandpaper dry kiss and then turns her attention back to me. She sighs dramatically. "Men and their pride. It's just a silly game of tennis between friends, but you'd think there was more than pocket change to lose. I envy you, Evelyn. Now is the time to be young and alone. No worries about cranky husbands who are more like overgrown children."

"I suppose being single does have its benefits. I hardly have time between getting together with friends and work to worry about anything," I answer, as if her husband hadn't completely ignored me and she hasn't implied that I have little or no reason to live because I'm not as unhappily married as she is. "I hope you enjoyed yourself last night."

"I did, I did. Your mother, as always, puts us all to shame. You must tell me all her secrets." Sissy leans in, laying a spidery hand on my arm. "And don't think I didn't notice your new young man. Do tell, Evelyn! Your mother has been as silent as the grave about it all."

"He's not my young man." I make sure to smile as I say it, as if we're sharing a private moment. "Just a friend."

"How modern of you." Sissy nods. She knows if Ted was anyone of consequence he'd be here with me. And he's not, and it doesn't take much for her to put two and two together and surmise I'm still just a one.

"Sissy?" I know my mother's friend is a vicious gossip, so my asking about Candace may become a topic of gossip itself if I'm not careful. "May I ask you something about Candace Hall?"

"What would you like to know?" Sissy maneuvers us over to an empty love seat off to the side of the room, where we'll have more privacy.

"Oh, nothing really. It's so sad about her husband. His passing and such." Tannin had chattered on about the dirty details of the whole affair, but I'd largely tuned her out.

"Yes, tragic, but not a surprise. Redford was, as they used to say in my time, randy as a goat." Sissy laughs. "But with a wife like Candace Hall, I'm not surprised it's all gotten so . . . messy. And it would have gotten a lot more messy if he hadn't done the smart thing and passed on when he did."

I nod my head. By *messy* she means public. Her own husband has a second family up in Napa Valley, complete with two kids under ten, a dog, and a Volvo station wagon for his weekend wife. Sissy tolerates it as long as he is discreet, while he is happy to go along with the arrangement since a divorce would cost him half of everything and a wife who's willing to put up with him.

"He was rich, yes, but he had the manners and couth of a common farm animal," Sissy continues after casting an eye around to make sure no one is eavesdropping. "Not that his shiny penny of a wife let it stop her. Candace is determined to sit at all the right tables in this city, and now that he's gone, any modicum of respectability that woman had is gone with him."

"That's unfortunate."

"Most of this happened while you were in Paris . . ." Sissy lets the word hang as if she expects me to share the whole story of what happened. "So I'm not surprised you're not in the know. Plus, with your lifestyle change . . ."

"Yes," I say vaguely and take a sip of my tea. Sissy hasn't gotten it all out, and I know I can just sit and wait and she'll continue on until she's satisfied I've been brought completely up to speed.

"But now with that lawsuit." Sissy closes her eyes as if she can't bear the horror of it. "There are ways to treat the help. You don't let them walk all over you, but you are fair or you have someone else handle that side of your affairs. Candace's fault, and I've told her this myself, is that she likes to get too involved with the people she has working for her. I remember when she first married Redford and the things some people said about her. 'A man-eater,' they called her, 'blatant social climber,' and then, when they got to know her better, 'alluring but untrustworthy.' Candace came into this whole thing with the cards stacked against her. And this legal mess she's gotten herself into is not helping her case one bit."

I nod and don't say anything, so I can almost feel a little less dirty about gossiping.

"And now she's cavorting around town with her hunky lawyer!" Sissy signals a server to take away her now cold tea and waves him off when he offers her a fresh cup.

"Really?" I say as I hand over my still full cup.

"How can you blame her? He's gorgeous. And Latin! You know what they say about Latin lovers. Candace is a free spirit, and she'll rattle cages wherever she goes. Plus, she has all that money Redford left her. We can't write her off just yet."

Sissy segues into the rest of the day's gossip, including trying to pump me for details on what's up with Tannin. (She canceled at the last minute for today, claiming "female issues." My mother merely shrugged and said, "Tannin better get herself a good husband quick before her theatrics leave her no choice but to move to Los Angeles." I didn't think it appropriate to enlighten my mother with the detail that Tannin is in Los Angeles with Whit.)

After we're ushered into the dining room, I can barely pick at my plate, and when it comes time for me to make my excuse to leave, Mother takes me at my word that I'm just not feeling up to tennis and lets me go with minimal guilt. I climb into my parents' car feeling listless and blue.

"Where to Miss Sinclair?" Ike asks as soon as he settles himself behind the wheel.

I look at my watch; it's 1:30. I have at least a full day's worth of work to slog through, but right now my responsibilities to UGotIt are the last thing on my mind.

"I think home, Ike." What I need is a long bubble bath and a good cry. Then I'll be ready to face my computer.

Alexander

I make sure to keep my dirty cleats on the runner Mom puts down between the back door and the bathroom.

"So what's the big emergency? I was doing pretty good—even your dad was impressed enough not to bench me." Pete walks in wearing a ratty T-shirt and basketball shorts. He has dirt smudges on his face and arms, and the flushed look of someone who's had too much sun. "I think he actually almost congratulated me on a save I made."

"Really?" I ask, not wanting to shoot him down. I love Pete, but he's a lousy soccer player.

"I was sucking big time. But my new strategy is to not drink any beer. Everyone else gets toasted and it ups my game exponentially."

"Did you bring them?" I ask, waving to Dad, who is gesturing me to get back into the game.

"Maybe." Pete gives me a suspicious look. "What do you want them for?"

"Pigeon watching. It's my new hobby."

Pete knows why I want to borrow his binoculars. "I could understand you looking in her bedroom while she changed or something. But spying on a woman while she's working. Alexander, my brother, even you have to admit that's kind of sick."

"I'm not spying. I'm just maybe interested in her in a slightly creepy and unhealthy way," I say.

"So talk to her," Pete says. "You do it all the time with other women."

"Exactly. I don't need another failed relationship. Things are fine the way they are. Honestly, this is my most healthy relation-ship to date."

"So you are going to call her, right? That's the whole point of this thing?" Pete asks.

"Yeah, and say what?" I sit down. "Hi, pretty lady. I've been watching you and think I love you."

"Love. There's that word again." Before I can protest, Pete con-tinues. "You can have these. I don't need them anymore." He hands me the binoculars. "It's obvious you need therapy and a restraining order."

"What are you doing in here?" Nayelli, belly first, makes her way down the hallway toward the bathroom. "Dad's looking for you two."

"Hey." Pete tries to pull his stomach in to give Nayelli more room to pass. "Your dad has made me goalie again. I think he hates me."

"It's because you cover a lot of the goal by just standing there." Nayelli has her knitting bag in her hand, and I'm guessing she's come looking for me before she settles down to watch the men play soccer and come close to heatstroke.

"Thanks, I think," Pete says.

Nayelli gives him a look. "Pete, you need to find yourself a woman with a firm hand."

My phone beeps to life with an e-mail. A Candace issue, via Rodney. "It looks like I'm going to have to go into the office to do a little cleanup from last night and prep for the hearing on Mon-day."

"Sure, sure, you big chicken. You're in here hiding from Dad, who is ready to whup your ass," Nayelli says through a huge yawn. "He's all geared up to rip you a new one during the . . . the . . ."

"Soccer game," I finish for her.

"Yeah, whatever." Nayelli waves me off and picks through her knitting bag, then stops looking at it as if she's surprised she's holding it.

"Maybe you should go take a nap?" Pete suggests, taking his life in his hands.

"Maybe," Nayelli responds, sounding uncharacteristically listless.

"Are you okay? Should I go get Lloyd?" I ask. It's still about three weeks till her due date, but I'm not used to seeing my sister this vulnerable.

"What I need is a margarita with salt on the rim and a big plate of *chicharrón.*" She puts her hand on her belly and grimaces.

"That sounds good," Pete says. "What is it?"

"You don't want to know," my sister and I answer at the same time.

"Fuck, I have to pee again." She waddles into the bathroom and slams the door.

"I'll make you a deal," Pete says as we start back outside. "If you help me out on defense so I don't make a bigger fool of myself, I'll help you out with your fake girlfriend."

"Which one?" I ask with a snort.

Pete claps me on the back. "Both of them."

Alexander

Even though there's no chance she'll be in her office on a Saturday afternoon, I've closed the blinds to mine in the hope it'll help me concentrate on the real reason I'm supposed to be here. On Monday I'll be standing in front of Judge Ramona Rizzoli and asking her, with a straight face, to dismiss the entire class-action suit against Candace and, per her e-mail, requesting that her legal fees incurred by the case be paid by the prosecution.

I set the binoculars on the coffee table, feeling stupid. Pete's right. The only thing that's keeping me from introducing myself to her is me. Not the guys I've seen her with. It's all me. I glance over at my desk, with its pile of paperwork, unread depositions, and my billing sheet.

A case like this could make my name and be my entrée into the world I've only read about. I've already gotten a taste of it, and I liked it, more than I thought I would, even if it's left a bitter after-taste in my mouth. But that's the price of selling out—sometimes people will assume you're just another brown-faced waiter in a very nice suit.

On Monday, I'll stand in front of Judge Rizzoli, plead Candace's case, make nice for the media, and become a brand-name lawyer. The kind of lawyer CNN calls when they need a telegenic talking head with credentials after some airhead socialite is arrested for being coked up to the gills and driving the wrong way on the freeway or some faithful wife goes berserk and shoots her millionaire husband of twenty years after finding out he has a family on the side.

I'd field calls from *Vanity Fair* and producers of ABC's *The Bachelor* on the same day, my law school would use me as a recruitment tool. I'd be on my way to becoming a marquee name who can finesse clients and situations and look good doing it regardless of my skills as a lawyer. Rodney knows this, and this is why he put me at the table when he'd finally talked Candace into going with the firm. He knows I'm hungry for more than practicing law, and I can't pretend to him, Pete, my family, or myself that I didn't let him lead me by the nose to exactly where I've always wanted to be.

Evelyn

I take the train into work from my flat, enjoying the spaciousness that comes with the weekend's lack of commuters. I sign in with the security guard, noticing that it's just past three and my fingers are still slightly pruned from my marathon soak in the tub.

Feeling bad about my burger and fries binge last night, plus the waffle I had at brunch, I take the stairs up to UGotIt, making sure to pump my arms before I realize there are security cameras on each landing. Mortified, I sprint up the rest of the stairs, and when I get to the UGotIt door, I'm huffing slightly and thankful no one is around to see what a dork I am.

I pause at James's desk where he's left out a copy of *Guns & Ammo* with bright yellow stickies affixed to most of the pages. Shaking my head and trying not to laugh, I unlock the sliding office door that closes off the reception area from the rest of the office when no one is here and take a deep breath. Even though the air is still and slightly stuffy, it feels nice to have the place all to myself. No smells of burnt coffee, bad aftershave, or reheating leftovers. Just the faint traces of the cleaning supplies the maintenance staff uses, and blessedly Ted-free.

I wander around the perimeter of the office, pausing by Melinda from Marketing's desk. She has pictures ripped out from fashion magazines, old birthday cards, and notes pinned to the walls of her cubicle. On the tabletop is an open makeup case full of glittery eye shadows, lip glosses, and nail polish.

I sit down at her desk and try to imagine what it's like to be her. A woman like Melinda from Marketing wouldn't let a little something like shyness and the fact that he might be involved with a woman like Candace Hall stop her from introducing herself to Alexander Velazquez. Or feel pathetic about snooping from a safe distance into his, I hope, empty office.

Channeling Melinda from Marketing, I walk quickly into my office, grabbing the cheap plastic opera glasses James conveniently left on my desk, and lean forward into the window, only to see his blinds are down.

"Perfect!"

"What's perfect?" a voice asks from behind me.

"Shit!" I bang my head against the window latch and drop the binoculars. I spin around, and there's Allan, resplendent in his usual outfit of mismatched, faded black separates. "Hasn't anyone ever told you not to sneak up on people?"

"I didn't sneak. You were busy spying," Allan correctly points out. He's holding an enormous soft drink and sack of food from the Taco Bell around the corner.

"I wasn't spying. I was just . . ." I step forward and crunch the toy binoculars under my foot but keep walking as if nothing happened. "Anyway, what are you doing here?"

"Same thing you're supposed to be doing." He takes a sip of

his drink and grimaces. "Ugh, too much Cherry Coke. You don't happen to have any iced tea in your office?"

We look around at my office, a minishrine to all things tea, for a moment.

"So what are you doing here besides spying on the building next door?" Allan asks as suavely as possible.

"I'm working." I sit at my desk and pretend to be busy shuffling around stray sheets of paper. As nonchalantly as possible, I turn on my computer, since if I had been working, it would already be running. "Well, I don't want to keep you, Allan."

"You're not." He settles down into the sleek Barcelona chair, balancing his bag of food on his lap and sitting on my favorite cashmere sweater. The smell of refried beans and greasy meat fills my office. "This chair is really comfortable. IKEA?"

"Sort of." I try not to be offended for Ludwig Mies van der Rohe, whom I'm sure could never have imagined such a thing as IKEA when he designed the original chair way back in 1929 for the king and queen of Spain. "Is there something you want to talk about?" I ask, swallowing the rush of saliva in my mouth.

"Yeah," Allan says around a mouthful of cheesy taco, "when did you start dating the boss?"

"I'm not dating Ted," I snap at him, feeling a hot flush start somewhere at my toes and work its way up to my cheeks. "I meant if you have something to ask about the redesign."

"Yeah, well, that's not going anywhere either." After a second or two, Allan laughs at his own inadvertent joke.

"What do you mean?"

"I mean"—he wipes his mouth with the back of his hand—"maybe Ted isn't God's gift to the Internet like he tries to make himself out to be. Or to women."

"Allan—" I might as well make it perfectly clear that I'm not involved with Ted. I gather my saying outright that we're not dating isn't going to cut it with Allan. Maybe I should rephrase it in HTML code?

"Meaning," Allan continues, "maybe this whole redesign is just his way of making sure he has a reason to be here. Meaning, maybe I heard that the board isn't too pleased with where he's taking the company. Meaning, Ted is on his way out unless the board is really, really happy with what we have to show them."

"Who did you hear this from?"

"People talk," Allan says and rips open a sauce packet, squirting the entire thing on another taco.

"Then that's just what it is. Talk," I snap.

According to James, people around here spend about 75 percent of their time online shopping, IMing, gossiping, and taking smoke and coffee breaks. Another 20 percent is spent in meetings, and the last 5 percent figuring out how much their next paycheck will be.

"Don't shoot the messenger." Allan shrugs, neatly fits the entire taco into his mouth, and takes a long pull on his drink to wash it down. "Just thought you should know."

"Thanks for the info, but I have enough on my mind."

"Yeah, I'm sure you do." He gathers up his trash. "So about you and Ted. What's up with that?"

"I'm not sure I know what you're talking about, Allan." I don't dare blink as I say it, not sure how I should handle this type of situation. If Allan thinks there's something between me and Ted, so will other people around the office, and the last thing I need is that kind of gossip following me around.

"Whatever." He gets up and closes the door behind him. "Oh,

yeah, Jessica was in here clearing out her desk. She quit and is suing Ted for sexual harassment."

I rub the sore spot on my head and get down to work. After a few minutes I get up and draw my own office blinds, effectively sealing myself off from the outside world.

Alexander

"Ready for the head cheese?" Pete asks. I nod, and he picks up my phone. "Hi, Wallace, can you track Rodney down for us? . . . Thanks. He's on his way."

I straighten my tie and make sure I look every inch the lawyer. Nerves get the best of me, and I start to fold Post-it notes into butterflies, frogs, and crickets.

"Do you think they'll go for it?" Pete shadowboxes to work out some of the nervous tension we've been operating under since last night.

"Who knows?" I shrug.

We've put together a solid if boring offer. Candace doesn't have to admit any wrongdoing, just pay the back wages while dropping her countersuit for damages. We have to convince Rodney to let us present it to Candace, and if she goes for it, I can retain some sort of integrity as the son of a labor activist and make a name for myself as a hotshot lawyer who can finesse a difficult client. If she doesn't go for it, in less than twenty-four hours we'll be in court, where I'll have to take a stand against what my parents believe in and let the world know that I'm a gun for hire in a passable suit.

"You guys work your magic?" Rodney ambles in, resplendent in his Sunday best: khaki shorts, polo shirt, and golf shoes. He flips through the pages and hands them back to Pete, looking impressed.

"This is good work. Good solid work, boys. If I didn't know better as a Harvard man, I might have to admit they might be teaching something like real law at Berkeley."

Rodney picks up one of my origami butterflies. "You think she'll bite, Alex?"

"She definitely bites." Pete chuckles. "Sorry."

"Financially, she can afford to drag this out in court, but socially, it'd do her more damage than she can afford." I boil it down to the bare essence of the matter. "If she doesn't bite, we show up at the courthouse tomorrow to plead her case to a judge who is pro-labor in a city that is pro-labor."

"A rich blond bitch, stripper mistress, dead husband, fashion, society, money, alleged sweatshop owner . . . What's not to love? Did I tell you who I had lunch with today? A producer from Court TV. This would be great exposure for the firm and you, Alex."

"Exposure is right," I say, trying to play it cool. As well as money, some degree of fame, and job security.

Rodney sits at my desk, dials, and tosses the phone in my direction. He rubs his hands together. "Magic time, Alex."

And just like that, I know Rodney is positive she won't bite.

"Hi, Becky. It's Alexander. . . . Do you think we could get Candace in here for a quick meeting? . . . Three-thirty? That works for us here. . . . Okay, see you then. Thanks, Becky."

"Make sure Wallace has the conference room ready." Rodney stands up, looks at his watch, and then walks out.

"Well, this should be fun." Pete starts shadowboxing again, and I wish I could join him, but I have a feeling I'll be breaking a sweat soon enough.

Evelyn

"James, have you heard anything about the board being unhappy with Ted?" I line up my Scrabble tiles, nudging them into place with my knitting needle.

"Who told you that?" he asks after taking a bite of his peanut butter and jelly on thick white bread, the Rockwell, that he had delivered from Celebrity Sub. "Is *flummox* really a word?"

"It means to confuse." I shake the crumbs from my Jennifer Aniston off my latest knitting project, a poncho. Yes, a poncho, but I've promised myself and James I'll wear it only at home. "Allan mentioned something about Ted and the board."

"I did maybe, by innocent mistake, overhear Ted arguing with one of the board members about something or other when I *accidentally* patched my phone into their call last week." James lays down an *A* and an *E* on either side of my *X* from *flummox* and greedily tallies his points. "But you know how these guys are. It's like belching contests at the frat house. They just like to blow smoke up each other's butts."

I put down tiles to spell out *compunction* and then hold up my poncho to check my progress, ignoring James's grimace. "Do you think I'm wasting my time with this redesign?"

"Evelyn, you know I think you are wasting your time, period. You had something going with your art. I've seen what you can do, and it goes beyond making animated GIFs or scanning business cards." James tries to peer over at my tiles, and I jab my needle at him.

"Is that a sex term?" James asks, eyeing the tiles I've just put down. He flips through the Scrabble dictionary. "'Compunction. Uneasy because of guilt.' Yeah, sounds like a word you'd know, Evelyn."

"What should I do?" I ask him from behind the safety of knitted silk mohair yarn. "Quit my fake job, which I've just received another promotion at, and do the starving artist thing?"

"You're rich, Evelyn. You wouldn't starve," James says with more than a hint of disgust in his voice. "Anyway, I have an idea that will solve most of both our problems. You and me, we can get married, have a lavish wedding, and live a couple of years off the profits from returning all those gifts. We'll each get our sausage on the side, and when the time comes—and let's face it, it's coming soon, lady—I'll hand over a turkey baster full of my love and affection for you, and we will make a mini James or Evelyn, who will start therapy the minute after your C-section."

"As tempting as this all sounds, James, I think I'll hold out for a little romance." I pat his hand to show that on some level I'm touched by his offer.

"Spying on some guy through your window at work, that's real romantic." James lays down four tiles to spell *dirt*.

"Don't knock it until you try it. It's the ultimate in relationships. Considering my rather limited, and unsuccessful, track record with men and romance, I've halfway convinced myself that I am, finally, in a healthy relationship."

"Do tell how this can be possible." He sweeps the tiles off the board and into the bag, signaling the end of the game and my lunch break. "Evelyn."

I shake my head. I was listening to myself, and there's only so much I can blame on lack of sleep. After I called Ted and told him Jessica had quit, but not about the possible lawsuit, he immediately bumped me up to interim art director as well as allowing me to retain the title (and duties) of his executive assistant. Since then I have been tweaking pixels, layouts, and color schemes.

"Ted is coming in for a meeting in a couple of hours," I say, thinking out loud. He hasn't shown up but had me call in the entire art department to give them the news that I was now their boss. They took it surprisingly well.

"Are you ever going to actually introduce yourself to him?" James asks, not unreasonably, "and, I don't know, find out what kind of music he sings to in the shower?"

"Are you crazy?" I say through a hysterical giggle. As soon as it starts, I force myself to stop, knowing I'm about two seconds away from really losing it.

"One of us is," says James. "You have a meeting in Ted's office in ten minutes."

I stick my tongue out at his retreating back and return to smoothing pixels and tweaking images as if my life depended on it. The other stuff, like the sorry state of my love life, will have to wait until after the board meeting, when things make more sense.

Evelyn

I skid to a stop outside the door of Ted's office, where members of the redesign team are crowded inside, all looking disgruntled at having to be here on a Sunday afternoon. "Sorry. I went outside for some air and the door to the stairwell locked. I had wait for a security guard to let me out."

"Why didn't you just take the elevator?" one of the geeks from Allan's code posse asks.

"Elevator?" I widen my eyes at him like the thought never occurred to me.

"Shut the door. Let's get this meeting started," Ted says, not looking like his usual MBA self. There are dark circles under his eyes, and his shirt doesn't look as pressed as usual.

Allan motions me over to the empty chair next to him, right off to the side of Ted's desk. I carefully pick my way across the empty bits of floor so I don't trample on anyone's fingers and gather my poncho around me so the tassels don't swish into people's faces. I glance at him to mouth a quick thanks; he gives me a hard stare.

Gesturing toward Ted, he whispers with a smirk, "Your boyfriend isn't looking too hot. You think he's stressed out about something?"

"How should I know, Allan?" I snap.

Ted adjusts the connections between his laptop and the projector, bringing up an image of the site on the wall above my and Allan's heads. Someone flips the switch, and the only light in the room is from the fruit of all our labors and what's peeking through the window blinds. Even though I've had less than twenty-four hours to pick up where Jessica left off, from the looks of her work sometime on Wednesday, I think I've done a pretty decent job.

"We've all had time to take a look at the dummy site. Right?"

People offer their tepid agreement, unsure if they should hate it or love it. They'll wait for Ted to tell them what to think. I should feel betrayed, I suppose, but art school taught me to take a step away from my own work. Even though a website isn't a painting, I've still poured a good amount of my heart and soul into it and want it to be the best it can possibly be. "Allan assures me the bugs the QA team found are being worked on. Right?"

"As we speak," Allan says, as if truer words have never been spoken. The entire tech team is currently crammed into Ted's office; nothing is getting done until we all get out of here and go back to work.

"QA team?" I ask. I wasn't aware there was a quality assurance team. Ted had me click through the entire site, looking for bad links and missing graphics, send them to a central e-mail address, and then parcel out the errors to the appropriate departments.

"I gave Allan the okay to conscript the editorial department. This redesign is mission critical." Ted nods, we all nod. Pleased to see that we are going along with what he's saying, Ted uses his ever-present laser pointer to call attention to specific parts of the design. "I'd like to give a shout-out to the design department for delivering a pretty solid effort."

I sit back and let out a sigh. He doesn't hate it. Now comes the long slog to clean it up and make it perfect, or as close to perfect as I can, until a real art director is hired or promoted from within the group, to make it in less than two weeks. Still, I start to get excited. I think we can actually do it. Maybe Allan and James are wrong. Ted's MBA-speak might actually mean something real. The evidence of our collective efforts on the wall above my head is proof of that.

"But we've got a problem," Ted says, shutting off the projector and plunging us into semidarkness.

"We do?" I blurt out, my stomach and jaw dropping at the same time.

"It's the board. They want something with a little more grab." Ted hands me a a thick packet of handouts to pass around.

There are printouts of the screenshots of the site, with notes (all in Ted's handwriting) scribbled in the margins. He's even included shots of totally unrelated sites for "inspiration." I flip through the sheets, silently, growing more alarmed with each page.

I speak without looking up, trying to keep my voice calm. "I'm not sure it's possible, Ted."

Allan backs me up to a point. "From a technological perspective, we could do it, but it would be overkill. We'd need at least six months to implement and test all the new code."

"Yeah, I thought we wanted to keep it simple. Not clutter the page with bells and whistles," someone adds from the far corner.

"The board wants bells and whistles," Ted says, as if he's Moses coming down from the mountain.

"Do they?" I ask and look directly at Ted as I do.

"What?" Ted says, first looking at the other side of the room, as if he can't believe it's me who spoke.

"I mean"—I sit up a little straighter—"maybe it's just a case of walking them through the site, giving them an idea of what they can expect if we stay the course, they would—"

"This was discussed at an off-site, Evelyn." Ted's temples start to go noticeably red; a vein pulses in his throat. "I speak with full authority from the—"

"I'm sure you do, but it would be, uh, helpful to have some insight into what the board thinks. Firsthand," I say in a rush, not wanting to lose my nerve in the face of Ted's growing displeasure with me.

"You don't need insight," he spits out, unplugging the projector and shoving the cords at me. "What you need to focus on is making the changes that will make the board happy. Understand?"

People shift around uncomfortably, giving me furtive glances to see if I'll back down or stand up to the boss.

"Understand?" Ted asks, louder this time.

"Oh, I understand," I say as mildly as possible, as if I'm coddling a temperamental child. "You've made yourself pretty clear, Ted. I think we can all agree on that."

Ted looks pissed, but I feel good. I may have backed off and let him win this pissing match, but it's not a clean win, and right now that makes me feel pretty good about myself.

"That's what I want to hear." Ted makes eye contact with each of us, making us squirm in turn. When it's my turn, I openly glare at him and feel a slight thrill when he looks away first. "I expect the top-priority changes to be made in time for the board meeting."

"But . . . but isn't that tomorrow?" Allan asks, actually gasping with surprise at Ted's words.

"Tomorrow." Ted turns to face the windows, hands clasped behind him, ruining the effect by forgetting the blinds are still closed.

Voices rise as everyone starts talking at once. Ted's phone rings and he doesn't hesitate to answer it, effectively dismissing us from his presence. We get up and walk out, breaking into little groups to bitch about what just happened.

"Evelyn! You should say something!" one of the women from the art department pleads with me, taking my hands in hers. "He'll listen to you."

"I did say something, and he didn't." I don't have any sway over Ted, no matter what they might think. What just happened in there should prove that.

"I was totally going to back you up in there, but I figured it would be easier for Ted to take coming from you," Allan says, shifting from foot to foot like a puppy that has just made a mess on the rug and wants to be forgiven for it.

I purse my lips the way I've seen my mother do so many times when something or someone falls far short of her expectations. "Don't worry about it, Allan."

"It's what the board wants," says Allan, falling into line just like that, "and Ted is the boss."

"Yeah, but for how long?" I ask myself more than anyone else.

Alexander

We sit around the conference table, me, Pete, Rodney, and Bryan and Brian, waiting for Candace to show up from wherever it is she spends her Sunday afternoons.

Pete taps out a tune with his pen on the tabletop, unable to contain his jitters.

"She'll be here any second," I say, feeling for whatever reason that I have to make excuses for her keeping us waiting.

"I don't care, I bill by the millisecond," says Bryan. Brian laughs like a good toady should and even offers up a hand for an awkward high five that Bryan ignores.

Just then the door opens and Candace sweeps in, wearing a fur coat, sunglasses, and a scarf wrapped around her head. Becky brings up the rear and takes a seat off in the corner, handling the usual array of phones and notebooks. Candace stands at the head of the table, making no apologies or even acknowledging we're in the room, and waits for someone to pull out her chair. I reluctantly get up and do it for her.

"Well, gentlemen, I trust everyone is ready for court tomorrow." She shrugs off the coat, draping it on the chairback like it was a sweatshirt, and crosses her legs.

"Candace," I start. I figure my best bet is to be as direct as possible.

"Yes?" A raised eyebrow appears above one of the sunglasses lenses.

"We've gone through all the depositions, work logs, you name it"—I slide a point-by-point breakdown of the pros and cons in front of her—"and it's our opinion that it wouldn't be prudent to try and pursue this in court."

She skims the paper and lets it drop from her fingers as if it's something distasteful. "Well."

"A settlement would—" Rodney begins, but she cuts him off.

"I won't settle," she states from behind her sunglasses. "I gave those people jobs, good jobs. It was the fucking union that incited them. They caused all this mess. If anything, I should be suing those union agitators."

"You *are* suing them," Pete says, and then tries to disappear back into the woodwork when Candace fixes her gaze on him.

"Speaking in purely financial terms"—I strive for a tone that is between firm and understanding—"it would cost you less to settle than to go to court."

"Are you saying I would lose?" Candace asks, her voice dripping with contempt. "Because I'm not paying you people to lose."

"Then there is the cost to your standing in the community," I say, hoping to play into the one area of her life where she really has the most to lose. Candace has plenty of money, more than enough to settle with her workers a thousand times over, but all of that cash won't buy her way back into the social circle that's ready to see her to the edge of the village and close its gates on her.

"I won't be blackmailed by a bunch of people who can't even speak English." Candace inspects her nails as she says it.

"Pardon me?" A hot jolt of anger rushes through me. "What did you say?"

"Ms. Hall, I'm sure—" Rodney steps in after getting a good look at my face.

"No. We go to trial, or I take my case, and my money, somewhere else!" Candace gets up and walks out the door.

Becky stands. She dips her head, keeping her eyes on the floor, and snatches up Candace's fur coat before taking off after her boss.

We sit there for a few minutes, even Bryan and Brian dumbstruck by what just happened.

"You heard her, boys," Rodney says as he rubs his hands over his face. "This is going all the way."

"You up for this, Alex?" Pete asks me as we gather our papers and coffee cups.

I stare out the window at the closed blinds of her office. "I'm a lawyer, Pete. As much as I hate to admit it right now, it's what I am."

Evelyn

"Hey." James drags himself into my office and melts into a puddle on the floor beside my desk. It's already after six. "I came to rescue you. I have Tannin's car."

"Hi." I spare him a look and keep typing.

"Cute shoes," he says from the vicinity of my ankles.

"Thanks." I smile. I look down at them, barely remembering that I put them on this morning especially because they make me feel cheerful.

"So I'm guessing you're sticking around here for a little longer?" James asks, drumming his fingers lightly on the underside of my desk.

"I'm going to be here for hours. Hours upon hours. Hours, James," I say in a singsong voice.

"But why?" He knows why, but he wouldn't be James if he didn't ask.

"I'm glad you asked, James." I type an updated to-do list for my team, my fingers flying over the keyboard. "I have a whole speech prepared. You ready for it?" I look down, he nods. I clear my throat and begin. "I've decided to be a team player on this one. That's why I'm here, right? To work on a team, to be a cog in an organization where I have to pull my own weight and do what's expected of me regardless of my fancy education or privileged upbringing. I'm a worker bee, what I've always thought I wanted to be. And I'm going to try to make as many of the changes Ted wants as humanly can be made because it's my job."

"But they suck." He sounds drowsy. "And you don't really work here."

"They do suck." I keep typing, updating tasks, signing off on changes, devoid of emotion and attachment to what I'm actually doing. "And the other thing is beside the point."

Allan comes in and stands right in front of my desk so his crotch is directly in my sight line. "Evelyn, you got a minute?"

"Sure." I rip my eyes upward and keep them trained on Allan's forehead.

"I went over this with my team, and there is no way we can handle the load." His dark hair is sticking up in peaks, as if he's been tugging at it. "It'll mean spending a buttload more on servers. Hundreds of thousands of dollars."

"I can tell you right now, Allan, we don't have the money for that," James says from the floor. Allan looks around startled, unaware that I had company when he and his crotch walked in.

"But it's what the board wants." I hazard a look at my monitor, but his package pulls my eyes as if it is one impressively sized magnet. "You said so yourself, Allan."

"Someone has to talk to them." Allan shrugs as if what he says and what he thinks are two different things and I'm expected to know the difference and care about it.

"Tell them what, Allan?" I know I'm drawing this out by playing dumb, but it's the most fun I've had all day. Frustration and stress have made me cruel. "Do you want me to march in there tomorrow and tell Ted off in front of the board? I'm just his assistant and the interim art director."

"He listens to you," Allan says with a slight whine.

"Yeah!" James scrambles up to his knees.

"Do you want me to tell him that he's running us into the ground? That we're wasting time and resources on a redesign that's unnecessary?" I continue, pounding the tabletop with each word. Allan takes a step back, looking scared and half in love with me at the same time. "And that we, the loyal employees of UGotIt.com, are not going to stand by and let him destroy what could be a truly great company for the sake of his ego!"

"Yeah!" James hops up. "Evelyn, you're totally going to have your very own Norma Rae moment! Union! Union! Union! Please tell me you're going to wear a bandanna tomorrow. The vintage Pucci that twat Tannin gave you for Christmas would be perfect!"

"But I can't. We'll make the changes, or as many as we can"—I pat James on the arm to force him to break eye contact with a now visibly sweating Allan—"but I'll insist that we be allowed to address the board directly."

"Hold on there," Allan says, trying to take control of the situation.

I ignore Allan, which really is not such a hard thing to do, his surprisingly plump crotch notwithstanding.

"We will, me and you, Allan, explain to the board why the current design with just some minor tweaks is better than what they think they want or have been talked into by Ted. If we do it ourselves instead of filtering it through Ted, we can make them understand why—"

"Ted is a dipshit who is in way over his head," James finishes for me.

"Thank you, James." I smile up at him for having the guts to say what's on everyone's mind.

"Just like that? We're going to bust in on the meeting and set them all straight and maybe get Ted fired?" Allan asks, as if he can't believe my naïveté and his involvement in what looks to be a suicide mission.

"Yes, Allan, just like that. Except getting Ted fired, that's up to the board." I have no designs on his job, even though that's what people are going to think. "And as his executive assistant, it is my duty to keep Ted cognizant of what's going on in the office. Especially this office."

"I have to get back to work." Allan scurries out.

"Evelyn"—James half strangles me with his hug—"you were such a bitch—a scary bitch! I'm so proud of you."

"I learned from the best, James."

I won't even try to deny I enjoyed it, a lot. Now all I have to do is stand up to Ted and the board, and make them see why they should believe a twenty-nine-year-old society princess with limited real-world workplace experience.

"And what's up with Allan?" James wanders over to the window and peeks out between the slats. "Is he half donkey or what?"

Alexander

I lean back in my office chair, trying to rub the headache out of my temples while Pete paces back and forth, paging through thick law books and pausing every so often to make notes. Wallace glides in and sets a fax in front of me.

"What now?" Pete asks, shivering slightly as he watches Wallace glide back out without a word.

"Looks like Candace is nixing Rodney's suggestion of arriving at the courthouse with us." I begin to fold the fax into a rose, figuring something pretty should come of this impending shitstorm. "Her publicist says she'll look guilty if she shows up with her small army of lawyers. So we're meeting her there."

Catching movement out of the corner of my eye, I glance toward her office, Evelyn's office, and see the blinds twitch but remain closed. I look away and put the finishing creases on the paper rose, rolling the stem, and set it with other fax roses, one short of a dozen.

Wallace walks in with another fax. Even on a Sunday her suit is as black as night and her lipstick is perfect. I glance through the fax and start folding.

"What now? She change her mind about which side of the

street she wants you guys to park on?" Pete asks, watching me. I've tried to teach him the finer points of origami, but he claims his hands are better suited to chain-saw sculpture.

"She wants us all to wear charcoal-colored suits and solid colored ties." I gather the roses, wrapping the stems together with a rubber band so they form a paper bouquet.

"You're a fucking lawyer, not a Ken doll, Alexander." Pete's face goes red. Rodney has already told him he'll be staying in the office, holding down the fort. "She acts like this is some sort of movie or something. She's being fucking sued. She's going to lose. Everyone knows that. Who cares what color suit you wear?"

"Pete, this is no longer about the law—it's a media event." I let out a breath, trying to keep my voice even for his sake. "It doesn't matter if she wins or loses, my job is to make sure she doesn't embarrass herself," I continue after a few minutes of silence. "I'm nothing more than an overeducated babysitter at this point."

"And you're okay with that?" Pete drops a ten-pound law book on my desk with a thump.

"It's what I signed up for the moment I sat at that conference table and let Rodney pimp me out." I stand and look out the window. "I'm a mediocre lawyer, amigo, who looks good in a suit."

"That's harsh," Pete says, but he doesn't bother to try to contradict me.

"Ain't it, though." I stare at her window, wondering what kind of flower she smells like.

"I'll order us a pizza," Pete says after a few minutes.

I grin at him, knowing this is his way of saying he's still my friend. I don't deserve him.

monday . . .

chapter twenty-two

Coming and Going

Evelyn

"Oh, my God, there you are," James says from behind the reception desk, where he's signing for a delivery of flower arrangements. "I went to look for you under your desk and I couldn't find you!"

"I went home for a shower and to change before the board meeting."

"So that's water dripping from the tip of your ponytail, not sweat?" James asks, pointing to the wet spot creeping down my shirt.

I have to think for a minute. Exhaustion has made my brain sluggish. "It's water. From my shower. I didn't have time to blow-dry my hair, and now my bangs will dry funny."

"That's not the only thing that looks funny. Is that your version of a power suit?" James asks, checking my outfit with a critical eye.

I'm wearing a black pencil skirt, topped with a matching cropped blazer from Banana Republic and jewel-tone silk-blend camisole, along with a pair of sensible black pointy-toe pumps from Nine West. All purchased last night right before closing time when I realized I couldn't storm a board meeting in my usual meek separates and sensible flats.

"What's wrong with what I'm wearing? It's a normal working type of outfit. Right?" I tug at the blazer. It's a little snug around the bust unless I'm ramrod straight, which I always am. "Melinda from Marketing was wearing almost the exact same thing on Friday. . . . Is that weird? For me to go out and buy something so similar?"

"It is"—James frowns at me—"and on you it just looks so wrong."

I give him the finger as another delivery guy steps up to the desk holding a couple of paper bags.

"I'm just here with the bagels and coffee you guys ordered," he says, looking offended.

"I'm so sorry! That was for him, not you," I yelp and cover my mouth with my hand.

"Ignore her," James says to the delivery guy, "she's experiencing a visit from Aunt Flo."

"Huh?" he asks, blankly.

"Is Allan in?" I ask after the bagel guy leaves.

"Yeah, and he looks like he slept under his desk. He was main-lining caffeine in the men's room a little earlier, but I haven't seen him since."

"It was a pretty rough night."

The real work didn't start until Ted finally left and we began to upload the new tweaked site to the test server. Then "the code hit the fan," as Allan so succinctly put it. I sent my people home when it was obvious there was nothing they could do, and I was here until 5:30, working with Allan to iron out any last-minute bugs. When I left, he was walking into walls and I was speaking in tongues.

"What about Ted?"

"Our hero Ted is across the street getting a shave at the bar-ber's so he looks extra pretty for the board. I'm under orders to call him the minute you get here, but I think he can wait until you get settled in." James sets out a bowl of Hershey's Kisses, stacking them into a perfect foil-wrapped, chocolate-scented pyramid. The Kisses are to come out only when important people and potential recruits are expected at the office, per Ted's directive which, as his executive assistant, I was asked to pass along to James.

"Thanks. I think I need a minute before I talk to Ted. I'd at least like to deal with him with dry hair." I take a deep breath and start toward my office, but I can't help but stop and do a double take. "What are you wearing, James?"

He stands up and models his outfit, a too bright, too tight shirt, snug leather pants, and chunky platform boots. "You like? I wore it especially for the board members."

I stare at him, transfixed. With less than two hours of sleep, I'm feeling a tad out of it. James takes me by the shoulders and guides me to my office chair, where I slump in a decidedly unlady-like manner.

"I'll get you a big, fat cup of tea," he says as he crosses my legs for me. "You just sit and collect your thoughts. I'll let you know when the meeting starts."

All I can do is nod, desperate not to fall asleep, as James drops my finished poncho on my shoulders and tiptoes out, closing the door behind him.

I set my head on my desk and stare out the window. He, Alexander Velazquez, age thirty-one, single (but might be dating Candace Hall), lawyer, son to local activists, and the man I've been fantasizing about and sort of spying on, is wearing a nice suit today and a reddish tie. I watch as he rushes out of the office, talking into his cell phone. Curious, I go to the window just in time to see him sprint across the street and disappear into my building. I lunge for my desk to call James when there's a sharp knock on my door and it's pushed open and he steps in.

"Hi. *Casablanca* is one of my favorite movies." It's all I can think to say. He smiles at me. I smile at him. He opens his mouth to speak, and James's voice comes out of his mouth. "Evelyn? Wake up. Evelyn!"

I open my eyes and feel a puddle of drool under my cheek. "Oh, it's you. Leave me alone."

"It's time for the meeting." He's overcaffeinated and flutters around me, trying to set my hair straight, tossing my poncho into the recycling bin. "They're attacking the bagels as we speak."

"The meeting? The meeting!" I jump up, wipe my face with a fistful of tissues, and gather my notes in a messy pile. I feel James right behind me, smoothing out the creases in my clothes.

"Wait!" James hisses at I reach for the doorknob to the closed conference room door. He licks the tip of his finger and wipes away what I'm sure are raccoonlike smudges of mascara from under my eyes.

"Good?" I ask as I desperately try to get my notes in order. "Where's Allan?"

"Go get 'em, Evelyn!" James opens the door and gives me a shove on the rump without answering my question.

Alexander

Like an athlete before a big game, I visualize how I want my court appearance to play out. And since I do my best mental work on my back, I lie down on the couch, stretching my legs out. If I weren't at work and going on a few hours of sleep, I'd actually feel pretty damn good about what I managed to accomplish with Pete's help in the last sixteen hours.

We haven't been able to turn Candace into the misunderstood, victimized, and unappreciated woman she thinks she is, but we can convince a judge and the press she's almost human. Through the night, Becky fed us a steady stream of heartwarming stories about Candace's good works (she gives money away like there's no tomorrow, or at least used to when her husband was alive) and carefully selected secrets about Candace's past (she worked at a nursing home during college) that will do a lot to soften her image. Candace also sent over a thick file on all the plaintiffs. She had a private investigator check, and there are some unflattering revelations about the people suing her, like arrests for drunk driving and various dubious workers' comp claims.

But right now, none of that matters. We'll win or lose this case the minute we walk up those courthouse steps. I focus on the feeling of being in control, prepared and calm, walking next to Candace and not letting her walk me. Cops, the media, protesters on either side of us, but they fade into the background. Then I see him. My father on his stepladder (it's my turn to get him a new one), looking at me with the same eyes that stare back at me every morning when I'm brushing my teeth.

"Fuck!" Nerves get the best of me and I stand up, pacing back and forth in front of the window while pretending I'm not looking for her.

She's sitting at her desk but looking over at me, not even pretending she isn't. I wave to her, and she waves back. Feeling like I'm floating out of my body, I reach for the window and push it open. She gets up and does the same. Below us traffic noise wafts up.

"I love you," I say in a loud, clear voice that starts from somewhere around the bottom of my feet.

"I love you too, buddy."

"What?" My eyes fly open at the sound of Pete's voice.

"Good morning. You look like shit, my brother." He closes the door and steps in. I sent him home about 3:00 A.M., when he started babbling about the differences between leprechauns and trolls, but he still looks as if he slept in his office like I did.

"I don't doubt it." I sit up on the couch. My hair is a mess, and I can feel a couple days' worth of stubble on my face.

"And it smells in here."

"So? You're the one who wanted to get falafels delivered for dinner, remember?" I get up to check my suit for the hundredth time. I'll put it on after I get a shave and trim at the barber's.

"Just reminds me of my apartment. Becky dropped this off for you." Pete tosses me an orange shopping bag. I bat it away to keep it from beaning me. It hits the floor with a thunk, and a box spills out. "It's fancy schmancy. Louis Viewshun . . ."

"It's Louis Vuitton," I say, pronouncing it the French way and feeling like a total dick.

"Louie, Louis, whatever," Pete says, waving his middle finger at me.

I pull out a briefcase and hold it up by the handle. "Fuck me."

Pete takes it and digs around looking for a price tag. "You are so going to have to put out for such a fine piece of leather like this, my friend."

I grab it and set it on the coffee table, where we just stare at it for a few minutes. "What time is it?"

"Don't worry, you've got"—he shoves his floppy cuff aside to look at his Fossil watch—"forty-five minutes."

"Fuck. Fuck. Fuck." I shove my feet into my sneakers, not bothering to lace them up, and start for the door. If I'm lucky, I can get there and back with some time to give myself a hooker shower at one of the sinks in the men's room. "What am I doing, Pete?"

"I don't know, but I hope one of those things is brushing your teeth."

chapter twenty-three

Alexander

I sit beside Rodney with Bryan and Brian in the backseat of Rodney's Mercedes. Like the rest of them, I don't have my seat belt on. None of us wants to risk the extra creases in our suits. I still smell like shaving cream and made good use of the hand dryer to almost dry off from my impromptu sink bath in the men's room.

None of us bother with small talk, preferring to use these last few minutes of quiet to get our heads into the game. Bryan and Brian are here just for show, and Rodney wouldn't let a chance to get his face on the local news pass him, but we all know I'm the main attraction.

We pull into the underground parking lot and take the elevator up to street level, walking the couple of blocks to the courthouse. When we get there, it's just as I expected—a crush of reporters and chanting protesters being halfheartedly corralled by half a dozen uniformed cops. We stay at the fringes, blending in with the rest of the lawyers and city workers who are milling around waiting for the show to start.

"Where is she?" Bryan asks, nervously scanning the crowd. "Did she get here before us?"

"Not here yet. There'd be a clusterfuck of media hags with her at the center of it," Brian says as he straightens his tie and clears his throat at the same time. "Looks like they're all waiting around just like we are."

"How about your dad, Alex?" Rodney asks. "He making an appearance?"

"I don't know, Rodney." I look him straight in the eye as I say it, my face reflected back to me in his sunglasses. "He might be in Salinas with the strawberry pickers for all I know. My dad works with a lot of people."

Even if he's not on the sidewalk in front of the courthouse, that doesn't mean he isn't orchestrating the whole thing via cell phone from the Burger King on the corner.

"Maybe we caught a break on that," Rodney says. "Last thing we want is some wannabe Woodward and Bernstein putting the two of you together."

"Maybe." I shrug. I'm not going to justify what my father does to someone like Rodney, who'd take his own mother to court for having him via C-section and depriving him of the experience of a natural birth.

Just then the crowd hushes as a shiny black limousine pulls up to the curb and parks right smack in the middle of a red zone.

"Fuck!" Rodney swears. "Don't tell me she came in a limo with a chauffeur!"

I lunge forward and get to the door before the driver can make his way to it, averting the first crisis of the day. The last thing we need is a picture of Candace being helped out of her stretch limo by a driver in uniform and cap. I yank the door open, reach in, and take her by the elbow as reporters swarm us, sticking microphones in our faces and shouting questions that mix in with the protesters' chants and whistles.

"Ms. Hall, what do you have to say—" a reporter shouts over the din. Bryan and Brian step in and block him.

"Who are you wearing, Candace?" a female voice shouts over

the clicks of the cameras from somewhere behind my left shoulder.

"Chanel," she calls out with a slight smile until I tighten my hand on her arm and she looks down.

"Are your shoes Chanel, too? Do you plan on wearing Chanel throughout the trial, Ms. Hall?" the voice calls out again. More insistent now that she knows she has an in with Candace.

I don't need to look back to see whose voice it is, to know she's working with the red-faced photographer who's wearing an *S.F. Express* press badge over his washed-out Giants T-shirt. He has his massive camera trained on Candace's high heels at the moment. My client, who is being sued for not paying wages to people who barely have high school diplomas, obliges by pausing for a moment and positioning her feet so he gets a good shot. I give her a little yank, and she starts walking again, after a slight stumble.

"She's wearing head-to-toe Chanel," one of the TV reporters yells over at his producer, a harried-looking woman in a white T-shirt and army pants holding steady the legs of a cameraman who is standing on top of a fire hydrant. She gives him a thumbs-up. They've already found the angle for the story.

"Candace! Candace! Is that the same kind of purse Martha Stewart took to her trial?" another reporter calls out. All eyes and lenses zoom in on Candace's impressive leather handbag. "Did you pay for it yourself, or is it a gift from the designer?"

"What do you say about the stories that claim you don't even like dogs?" someone else yells.

"No comment." I push forward, but not too hard, and trying to block Candace with my shoulders in a way I hope doesn't make her (and me) look guilty.

"Mr. Velazquez, how do you answer critics, even your own

father, who is a union organizer, that say you are representing—"
Another reporter, his voice dripping with disdain, tries to get things
back to the reason we're here. He must be from one of the alterna-
tive weeklies.

"I'm not on trial here," I say with my eyes forward as I keep
moving. "No one is. This is just a preliminary hearing."

"What Mr. Velazquez means to say is that we fully expect Ms.
Hall to be cleared of these blatantly opportunistic claims," Rodney
chimes in from somewhere behind us, a slight edge in his voice.

We make our way into the vestibule, where guards are standing at the doors to stem the stampede of microphones and cameras. We're quickly ushered through the security check and into an
elevator. Besides us, the clerk assigned to us, and a couple of cops,
there's an intimidated-looking couple crammed in there.

"Where's Becky?" I yelp, startling everyone. My head is filled
with visions of her being pulled under by a swell of ravenous reporters who want the inside scoop.

"She'll be fine, Alexander." Candace stares straight ahead,
at my side, her sunglasses still on. "Remember, I'm the one you
should be worried about. Not my assistant."

"You have had her sign a nondisclosure, right?" asks Brian.
Then he turns to me, gearing himself up for some lawyerly grand-
standing. "Alex, please tell me you've had the assistant sign an
NDA?"

"I always advise my clients to draw up a nondisclosure for
staff," Bryan adds. "It's the only way you can make sure they don't
talk."

"And if they do, you sue the fuck out of them." Brian nods.

"Becky would never talk," Candace says in an airy tone that
sounds just this side of forced, "if she knows what's good for her."

"This isn't the time to discuss it." Rodney inclines his head toward the couple, who are watching us with wide eyes and open ears.

"We're just looking for the county clerk's office," the man says apologetically, his arm going around the woman's waist.

"We're getting married today," the woman adds, moving in closer to him and holding up a small bouquet of flowers as proof.

"Congratulations!" I reach over to shake their hands, unable to help myself. "That's really great, but I think you need to go across the street. This is the place where you go if you're doing the other thing. Getting unmarried."

"I told you!" she says to him with an affectionate nudge. "He never listens to me!"

The elevator pings open, and they step aside so we can file out. I stand there grinning stupidly at them, enjoying how in love they are at this moment.

"Are you coming, Alexander?" Candace asks in a tone that effectively sucks the happy out of the elevator.

As we make our way down the hall, people instinctively press closer to the walls to avoid the four lawyers in gradient shades of gray and a woman in a five-thousand-dollar suit she'll wear only once. I don't even want to guess what her purse cost, but know I won't have to since I'm sure her outfit will be broken down piece to price in the next edition of the *S.F. Express.*

One of the guards holds open the door, and we make our way to a heavy oak table in front.

Candace sits in the middle, bookended by me and Rodney. Bryan and Brian have been relegated to the first row of chairs behind the defense table. Rodney says he doesn't want Candace to look "lawyered up," so we're keeping the table as clutter free as possible. Not a bad strategy for a woman who is known as a chronic law firm hopper.

"Is it possible to get a more comfortable chair?" she asks in my direction without turning to face me.

"No!" all four of us suits say at once. The last thing we want is to ask for special treatment.

"I suppose this will have to do," she says with an exasperated sigh. "I don't expect it will take very long."

Candace ignores the other side of the room, where the people who are suing her are sitting behind their own lawyers. Reporters and other spectators start to fill the rest of the seats. Becky rushes in, making her way to the front, and waits for Candace to acknowledge her. Candace spares Becky a glance and then waves her away. I smile as I watch her take a seat next to Bryan and Brian, then move down a couple of chairs when she thinks better of it.

"What do I need to know about this judge?" Candace asks, eyes still forward, but at least she's taken off her sunglasses.

"Fair, tough. It's all in the fax I sent last night." I reach into my bag for a copy of the memo and realize I forgot to switch from my leather satchel to the briefcase Candace sent over this morning. I nudge it under the table, surprised no one has noticed I'm not in full uniform.

"Something Becky neglected to share with me," Candace says with a sour twist to her mouth.

"But I did . . ." Becky trails off, and all her boss has to do is raise an eyebrow at her.

"Working-class background. A minus for us"—Rodney jumps in to fill the awkward silence—"but she is married to a business owner."

"Why haven't I heard of her?" Candace waves Becky over

and whispers something into her ear. With a bowed head, Becky quickly leaves the courtroom, dialing her cell phone as she goes. "She must be on some committee or board? What's her favorite cause? I can make a very generous donation and have Becky messenger it over."

"Pretty low profile," Rodney answers. "She doesn't socialize in any of the usual circles."

The bailiff clears his throat. "All rise. The Honorable Judge Ramona Rizzoli presiding."

We stand up, Candace waiting a beat or two before she lifts her ass off the chair. The judge makes her way to the bench, settles her glasses on her nose. She sits; we sit and wait. She opens her mouth to speak.

"I don't care if the queen of England is in there," my father's voice rings out, loud and clear from the back of the courtroom, "this is a court of law, not some fancy country club."

My head, along with everyone else's, swivels back to where my father is being restrained by two cops. Pete squeezes his way through and skids to a stop a few feet short of the defense table. He's pale and sweaty, as if he's run all the way here from the office. I start to get up, only to feel Candace dig her nails into my arm to keep me at her side.

"Yes?" Judge Rizzoli asks Pete, who's waiting to be acknowledged by her.

"Pardon me, Your Honor. I need to speak to Mr. Velazquez." Pete bobs his head at Judge Rizzoli and points at me. When she nods, Pete shuffles over and squats down next to me. "It's Nayelli. The baby. They can't find a heartbeat. Everyone is going to the hospital, Saint Francis."

Evelyn

Silicon Valley types sit around the UGotIt conference table wearing almost identical khaki pants and a rainbow of button-down shirts with the sleeves rolled up, fiddling with every imaginable piece of techno gadget currently on the market. I'm the only woman in the room and way overdressed in my two-hundred-dollar Banana Republic and Nine West pumps ensemble. Plus, I'm taking notes, or pretending to at least, with a pen on paper.

Ted—khaki pants, blue and lavender check pattern shirt—is standing at the front of the room giving the PowerPoint presentation of his life, judging from the sweat stains creeping from under his arms.

After James shoved me into the room, where I obviously had not been expected, Ted took me aside while everyone was chomping on bagels and sipping coffee to tell me in no uncertain terms that I was on my own.

"We're not just B2B or B2G. UGotIt's aim is to go B2A," Ted intones. I concentrate hard, knowing he's speaking some form of English, but am unable to decipher much meaning out of what he's saying. "We're going wide with cobranding and doing more targeted outreach to bring eyeballs to the site."

Khaki Pants Light Sage Shirt leans toward Khaki Pants French Blue Shirt and whispers, "Can you believe he gets paid for this shit?"

They both look over at me and smirk. All I can do is give a little shrug and zoom my eyes back onto the doodles on the paper in front of me. So this is what an MBA does to a person—he (or she) finds ways to say nothing for a solid forty minutes while those who speak the same language seem to agree, all the time sharpening their knives underneath the table.

"That's why we're taking a build-it-and-they-will-come approach going forward in this next round of site developments. We want to make UGotIt a destination site for all the alpha pups in the industry." Ted raises his voice, and it cracks slightly. He's losing them, and he knows it. "So now, our art director would like to walk you through some of the changes on the site that will implement these new objectives. Evelyn?"

I take a deep breath, my hands sweaty, and walk to the front of the room, where one of the tech minions has set up a laptop. Allan has called in sick with strep throat, strep throat he developed sometime between 4:00 A.M. and the meeting.

"Good morning, everyone." The men shift around in their seats, waiting. "I guess I should just cut right to the chase. As you know, the site has recently undergone some changes."

Ted leans forward and clears his throat, ready to spring into action and contradict me. "We've amped up the look and feel to maximize the user experience. We're about ninety-five percent a go and should be able to have everything live within the next two weeks."

"Actually"—I send Ted a quick apologetic look and start passing out a sheet detailing the changes we've managed to make per his wish list—"we've found that changes on the test site have overloaded the servers. But since Allan, our technical director, is out sick, I can't really speak to that. My job is to speak to how the site looks and why it looks the way it does."

I'm not nervous anymore, and they look like they're actually listening to what I have to say. I've always hated public speaking, but for the first time in my life I feel a surge of power at commanding the attention of a roomful of people.

"We've put together a little comparison of both sites." I click the remote, and the site—both as is and as Ted wants it—pops up on the screen behind me. "The image on the left incorporates the changes we were asked to make and on the right is the site that's live and which we are improving on daily without any major redesigning or reorganization."

Khaki Pants Chocolate Brown Shirt uses his laser pointer on the image of the changes Ted asked us to make. "The site on the left looks garish and cluttered."

"It's awful," another adds. "And will take forever to load."

"If we made the suggested changes point by point, it's what we would end up with," I say and avoid looking at Ted.

"Who said to make any changes?" the first guy asks.

"These are just proposed site tweaks," Ted says quickly. "Evelyn is not, as she said, a technical person. She's also just stepping in for the art director, who left the company. She really doesn't have the familiarity with the site she should have before making this type of presentation. I'm sure she didn't know that most of these features aren't feasible."

"I was under the impression," I say in a clear, firm voice, not bothering to decipher what Ted has just tried to imply, "that the board had requested a complete overhaul of the site. And these changes are the ones you wanted made."

"What Evelyn means to say is that—" Ted begins when there is a firm knock on the door and James steps in. "We're in the middle of a—"

"Sorry, but Evelyn is needed on the phone." He looks stressed out, something I've never seen him look like before.

"Take a message," Ted snaps, wiping away the beads of sweat on his forehead.

"I'll be right back," I say, seeing the look on James's face. "If you would excuse me." I make my way out of the conference room and find my best friend slumped against a wall. "What's wrong?"

"Oh, Evelyn." He looks up at me with tears welling in his eyes. "It's your mother. She's in the hospital. Saint Francis. She's had a heart attack."

James leads me by the hand to the reception desk and sets me down in his chair. He picks up the phone and speaks into it before handing it to me. "Mr. Sinclair? She's right here. Here you go, Evelyn. It's your dad."

"Daddy?" I feel numb, as if my whole body has been shot full of Novocain.

"Evelyn." My father's voice is short, almost gruff. "Your mother has been admitted to Saint Francis. I've sent Ike to pick you up. He should be downstairs in five minutes."

"Yes, Daddy." I hang up the phone and stare at it as if it will explain how my mother could have had a heart attack.

"I'm coming with you," James says, grabbing his bag and sweater. He takes my hand and helps me up. "Let's get your stuff."

We start back to my office, walking quickly, ignoring the stares and whispers emanating from the cubicles.

Ted strides over to us, looking harried and drenched in flop sweat. "Evelyn, we can't keep the board waiting. They have questions."

"Questions?" James sprints past us and into my office as I try to process what Ted is saying to me. "I can't stay. I have to go. It's an emergency."

I start again toward my office to get my purse, only to realize James is back and already holding my stuff out for me. "Thank you," I say automatically. I pivot on my heel, forcing Ted to walk in a circle to keep up with me.

"You need to answer a few questions. You can go after we're done."

"No, I have to go." I sling my bag over my shoulder, hitting him in the side. I don't apologize.

"Evelyn." Ted maneuvers himself in front of me, blocking my way, and leans in close, almost as if he were going to kiss me. "I don't have to tell you how important this is for the company. For your job."

"For fuck's sake, you ass," James yells, pulling me away, "her mother's had a heart attack."

"I'm sorry, of course." Ted snaps his fingers. "I'll call your cell and we'll patch you in on speakerphone from the hospital. No problem. Someone from Allan's department can set it up."

"Ted, I'm going to the hospital to be with my family." I jab at the down button for the elevator. The doors ping open, and we step inside. "And no, I won't be available on my cell."

"Yeah, and order your own friggin' sandwiches!" James adds right before the doors close.

Alexander

"Is there a problem, Mr. Velazquez?" Judge Rizzoli asks.

"Pardon me, Your Honor, but there is a family emergency for Mr. Velazquez," Pete answers for me from where he's still squatting.

"Judge, may we have a moment, please?" Rodney asks, standing up.

"Very well. Court will adjourn for ten minutes." Judge Rizzoli leans over to speak to the bailiff. Immediately people begin talking.

Candace, looking predictably annoyed, hisses at me, "You're on my clock, gentlemen. I don't think I need to remind you of that."

"I have to go." I reach under the table for my satchel and make to stand up, my only thought getting the hell out of here and to the hospital as fast as I can. "Now."

"What?" Candace digs her polished fingernails into my arm and yanks me down. "You're not going anywhere!" she shrieks.

"Is there a problem, Mr. Velazquez?" Judge Rizzoli asks. The courtroom has gone dead silent, and all eyes are on us.

I shake loose from Candace's surprisingly strong grip and stand up. "May I approach the bench, Your Honor?"

"Please," she says, surveying the defense table from over her glasses.

"This is not going to happen, Heller," Candace yells. Rodney hands Candace off to Brian and Bryan, who descend upon her to try to keep her quiet.

We, along with the plaintiffs' lawyers, approach the bench.

"I'm going to have to excuse myself." I sling my bag over my shoulder.

"Why?" she asks in an unfazed manner that makes her indecipherable as a judge.

"I need to go to the hospital, Your Honor. My sister . . ." I gesture to the back of the courtroom, where my father (who's had more than his share of time in front of Judge Rizzoli) is being held back by two guards.

"Very well, Mr. Velazquez. It's understandable. I'm sure your colleagues can handle your client. Correct?" she asks Rodney. "You can control your client, Mr. Heller?"

"Of course, Your Honor." He sounds doubtful.

"Ms. McIntyre and Mr. Chang, are you okay with Mr. Velazquez excusing himself from today's proceedings?"

"Not a problem for us, Your Honor," they answer simultaneously. I won't even pretend to be flattered that they might be relieved not to have to duel me in court.

"Very well. I'll leave it to you, Mr. Velazquez, to tell your client you'll be absent for the day's proceedings." Judge Rizzoli scribbles a series of notes and looks up as I take a step away from the bench. "My thoughts are with your sister, Mr. Velazquez. Say hello to your parents for me."

"Thank you, Your Honor." I head back toward the table. "Candace. I have to go. Rodney is going to step in for me. And Bryan and Brian are here to back him up."

"Where do you think you're going?" Candace demands. "*You're* my lawyer, Alexander. I'm paying *you* to take care of this for me. I don't need Huey and Louie here fucking this up for me, Alexander."

"My sister is in labor." I look her right in the eye as I say it. "I'm going to be with my family at the hospital."

"Excuse me?" she scoffs. "And how is this my problem?"

"She's having a baby," Pete offers up.

"Can't that wait?" she asks me, ignoring Pete.

"No, Candace, I'm afraid it can't." I turn my back on her and start out of the courtroom, reaching my dad, who takes one look at me before he gives me a quick, strong hug.

"Alexander! Where is he going? Your Honor, I object!" Candace's voice carries into the hallway.

"Go ahead and object all you want, Ms. Hall." Judge Rizzoli bangs the gavel. "Are we ready to start now? Good."

chapter twenty-four
The Heart of the Matter

Evelyn

I sit in a plastic chair chewing what's left of my fingernails and wait. A small army of doctors, interns, and nurses are in the room behind me, along with my father. Sissy has taken the seat next to me and is dabbing at her eyes, giving me watery smiles when I make the mistake of looking up from the same spot on the floor I've been staring at since I got here three hours ago.

My cell rings, and I step away to answer it. "Hello."

"I'm at SFO. I'm taking a cab," Tannin says in a breathless rush.

"She's stabilized, last I heard." I don't have much news to offer her, but I'm hoping this will at least make her feel better. "Is Whit with you?"

"Whit? That coked-up fuck? Doubt we'll be seeing him until he needs to hit up his mommy and daddy for more movie money."

"Oh, so you guys aren't—"

"Never again, and I made sure there wasn't any film in the camera, so no one has to worry about anything."

"Tannin, I'm going to go sit down now." I click the phone closed and sit back down next to Sissy, who begins talking at once.

"I told her it was too cold for a game of tennis. A shock to the system after being inside. But you know your mother, Evelyn. She's always doing three things at once." She sniffs wetly into a crumpled tissue. James hands her a fresh one from the box a nurse gave him earlier. "I knew something was wrong when she dropped her phone."

Ike walks by, pausing in front of me on his hundredth trip up and down the corridor. "Can I get anyone anything? Coffee?"

"No, thanks, Ike. I think we're fine." I smile up at him.

"Just say the word and I'll take care of it." He walks on, jangling his keys in his pocket as he goes.

"I hope you don't blame me, Evelyn," Sissy continues as soon as he's a few paces away. "Your mother has always been as healthy as a horse. If I'd had any idea this would happen, I would—"

"Of course not, Sissy. I'm glad you were with her." I reach over and give her arm a few short and what I hope are reassuring pats, just wanting her to leave me alone so I can resume staring at the scuffed linoleum in relative peace. I don't feel like playing the accommodating hostess right now.

"Thank God Dr. Gregory decided to stay home instead of jetting off to Bermuda." Sissy keeps talking, something she does when nervous, drunk, sober, or bored. She worries the large diamond ring on her finger, twisting it this way and that. "He's the best, Evelyn. He'll make sure our Lila is back on her feet in no time. As good as new, if not better."

I nod at the floor and find another nail to chew to keep myself from adding that it was a killer hurricane that derailed Dr. Gregory's usual end of summer vacation plans, not something more altruistic on his part.

The door opens, and a stream of people in white coats and clogs file out, careful not to make eye contact with any of us. We stand up and watch them, looking for someone who can answer our questions.

Finally, my father emerges, looking his age for the first time in his life. He reaches out and hugs me, hard.

"Is she . . ." My voice catches and I can't speak anymore.

"She's stabilized," Dr. Gregory, the chief of cardiac surgery and an old family friend, says as he makes a series of notes on a clipboard before handing it over to a nurse, "but we're going to give that ticker of hers a little help with a pacemaker."

My father sags against me. James takes him by the elbow and guides him into the chair I'd been sitting in. "Thank you, James. The doctor says you can go see her now, Evelyn."

"Just don't get her too excited or let her near the phone. The lady needs her rest." Dr. Gregory claps my father on the shoulder and strides off.

I walk carefully into my mother's room, trying to keep the heels of my shoes from clicking on the floor. The steady beep of the heart monitor fills the room like the sound of a ticking clock.

A nurse is taking her pulse. She looks up at me and smiles. "You must be Evelyn. Your mother has been asking for you. Lila . . . Lila, your daughter is here." The nurse gathers her things and heads for the door. "Don't get her too excited. We need to keep your mom nice and relaxed. Doctor's orders."

"I will, thank you." I pull up a chair by the bed and sit down. "Hi, Mom? Are you comfortable? Can I get you anything?"

"Evelyn . . ." My mother's lips are dry and colorless. She turns her head toward me but keeps her eyes closed and lets out a long sigh.

"Yes, Mom?" I reach for her hand, cool and delicate and free from jewelry or her ever-present phone for once.

"Have I ever told you"—her chest jerks slightly with her

labored breath—"told you how proud I am of you, my beautiful daughter?"

"No, Mom, I don't think you ever have." I'm too stunned by her words to not be honest in my answer.

"Your poor father. I've given him a scare, haven't I?"

"All of us, Mom." I squeeze her hand. "We would be lost without you."

"Evelyn, would you do something for me?"

"Yes, anything." I feel tears starting to trickle down my cheeks.

"I need you to . . ." She swallows loudly.

I pour her a glass of water and help her drink it, the weight of her head resting in my palm. She sighs again, a little more comfortable now, and settles back onto her pillow.

"Yes, Mom?" I'm standing up now, hovering over her. "You need me to what?"

"Make an appointment to get those bangs of yours trimmed." She opens her eyes and looks at me. "Just because you have a job doesn't mean you can neglect your personal appearance, Evelyn."

Dr. Gregory wanders in, humming under his breath. "How is my patient doing?"

I look up at him from where my mother has settled down to sleep. I can't help but smile when I say, "I think she's going to be fine."

Alexander

I check my watch. It's been twenty minutes since I last hit the nurses up for information and was told to sit and wait. There's a lot of activity down the hall through the double doors, so I figure something is going on with either my sister or the woman who was wheeled in a little while ago swearing at the top of her lungs about ripping her boyfriend's dick off.

I get up to approach one of the younger nurses and try my luck again. "Hi, my sister—"

"As soon as the doctor has any information, she'll come right out and tell you," she says, but at least it's with a smile.

"Right. Thanks." I go sit back down, ignoring my buzzing phone, and flip through a three-year-old *People* magazine for about the hundredth time.

"Alexander!" My mother rushes out of the maternity ward. She's wearing one of those blue surgical doctor shirts and booties over her shoes. Fortunately, all free from any sign of blood. I think I would have passed out on the spot if she had any of my sister's blood on her.

"Mom!" I yell, startling Pete out of his light doze beside me. I jump up, run to her, and we crash into each other, hugging. "Is she okay?"

"The doctor is in with her and Lloyd." Her face is flushed and breathless. "Where is your dad?"

"In the chapel," I say to my mother's retreating figure. She's taken off before I even finished speaking. "Wait! Did she have a boy or a girl?"

"Do you want me to go after her?" Pete asks as he shifts from foot to foot.

"Ah, the Velazquez family!" Nayelli's doctor walks up to us with a big smile on her face. "Both mother and baby are doing fine. The baby's on a heart monitor, just as a precaution, but everything looks fine."

"Can we go see her?" I ask, grabbing hold of Pete.

"Of course." She hands over a clipboard to the nurse. "Just make sure to wash your hands before you hold the baby, and don't tell her she looks beautiful. Your sister has a very astute bullshit detector."

We walk toward Nayelli's room, Pete lagging a bit behind.

"Maybe I should wait outside?" he asks, nervously keeping his eyes straight ahead as we pass the room with the cursing soon-to-be mom. I reach back and take him by the arm.

I knock on the door and poke my head in. "Hello? Is it safe to come in?"

"Alexander! Pete!" Lloyd straightens from where he's leaning over Nayelli. "Come meet my daughter, the future Dr. Velazquez-Connors."

"You're naming your kid Doctor?" Pete asks, his eyes wide as he tries to look anywhere but at my sister, who has a small bundle of life against her enormous and bare breast.

"No, Pete. We're still deciding." Nayelli laughs, sounding and looking exhausted. "So what do you think? Pretty ugly, huh?"

"All babies are beautiful," Lloyd says, sounding hurt. "Ours especially so."

I stare at her, the both of them, speechless. Then overhead we hear, "Alexander Velazquez, please report to the nurses' station. You have a phone call. Alexander Velazquez. Please report to the nurses' station."

"Sorry," I say, feeling my face grow hot with embarrassment and anger. "Just ignore that."

"I hope we aren't keeping you from something, little brother," Nayelli says, handing the baby to me.

"Shouldn't you save your strength and sarcasm, big sister?" I look down at my niece, my heart full and close to bursting. I let the tears stream down my cheeks, careful to keep them from splashing on her little face.

"Flowers!" Pete bursts out, startling us. "I forgot to get flowers."

"Lloyd, honey, can you go find my mom and dad?" Nayelli asks after Pete rushes from the room. "And maybe get me some juice. But not orange, apple, or grape."

"Sure, sure. Anything." He places a soft kiss on his daughter's forehead and his wife's dry and pale lips. I get a bear hug and a watery smile before he sets off on his juice quest.

"How is your client doing?" Nayelli asks, closing her eyes.

"I don't know"—I shrug—"I turned off my phone."

"I'm going to guess she wasn't too happy with your family emergency getting in the way of her trial." Nayelli opens her eyes and looks over at me, worried. "But you know what Dad would say: 'Sometimes family has to come before career, Son.' So if she chews you out, tell her your dad will write you a note."

"Trust me, she's the last person I'd put before my family." I hazard to give my sister a quick pat on the arm and then put my hand back to hold my niece, who seems to weigh close to nothing. "My dog, even, would come first, and I don't have a dog."

We stare at the baby for a minute, and she starts to fuss, her eyes still firmly shut, tiny hands curled into fists.

"I think I did the wrong thing, getting involved with this case."

"Professionally or personally?" Nayelli asks, holding her arms out for her daughter. Reluctantly, I hand her back over, knowing I can't provide her with what she wants. Only her mother, my sister, can.

"Both and then some. I tried to fool myself that I could be objective and put the case before my own beliefs, and then I realized, I don't have any beliefs." I laugh drily, feeling bad for bringing such negativity into the room with me.

"But you did your best, right?" Nayelli asks as she puts the baby on her other breast. "And that's what counts. That's what Mom and Dad have always wanted from us."

I look out the window to give them both some privacy. "How about being proud of what you do?"

"I can't tell you how to feel, Alexander, but I can say this woman couldn't have asked for a better lawyer, no matter what color your skin is." Her voice is strong and sure. "This is all just a small part of life, Alexander."

"It's easy for you to say, you've just given birth to a new life, Nayelli." My lame attempt at a joke sounds hollow even to my own ears.

"Alexander, you need to get your head out of your butt and realize that we love you no matter how much you insist on screwing up." She shifts around in the bed to look more imposing, but she just looks like a new mother who is nursing her baby. "We're your family. You're stuck with us. All of us. Now are you going to shape up and fly right and be a good example for your niece?"

"You don't think it's too late for me to make something respectable out of myself?" I ask the window.

"No, not too late for you, little brother, but my juice is late. Where the fu——" She stops, clears her throat, and looks down at my niece. "Where the heck is that husband of mine?"

chapter twenty-five
Really and Truly

Alexander

I head back to the office once I'm sure everything is okay at the hospital and Nayelli has kicked me out, saying, "I need to bond with my kid and husband now. Go get your own family, Alexander."

I flip through the stack of messages Wallace silently handed to me on my way in, crumpling one after another. I shut the door, take off my jacket and tie, and stare out the window. Her office is empty. I pick up the briefcase, weighing it in my hands, seeing how it fits. It doesn't. It feels good, expensive, but all wrong.

The door bursts open. Candace stands in the threshold with Rodney and Bryan and Brian right on her heels.

"Candace," I say, feeling perfectly calm and detached.

"So good of you to show up, Alexander." She stalks in and stands very close to me. "After that little stunt you pulled this morning, we had to ask for a continuance. Which is going to cost me more money."

"I'm sure Rodney with Bryan and Brian's help was perfectly capable of handling your case, Candace." I gesture to the guys who are huddled just outside the door, looking completely whipped.

"I didn't hire Rodney and a couple of frat boys," she spits. "I paid for you!"

"I'm not for sale, Candace." I hand her the briefcase. "Despite what you may have heard or been led to believe. Consider this my resignation from the case and the firm."

"I don't have time for your games, Alexander! I can—"

I hold up my hand to stop her and say very clearly into her face, "I quit. I'm done. I'm not interested in any of it."

"Woo-hoo!" Pete whoops from somewhere in the office.

"You what!" Rodney splutters, finally coming alive. "He what?"

"You can't quit on me!" Candace hisses at Rodney, who shrinks away from her. "Can he, Heller? I won't have it! I'll sue you! I'll have your license! I'll make life a living hell for you."

"Be my guest, Candace. But just to let you know, I'll be represented by my mom, and she's one lady who doesn't take shit from anybody."

I take her by the arm, lead her out of my office, and slam the door in her face.

Evelyn

"Good, you're back. Company meeting in five minutes," Ted says when he sees me stagger into the reception area with James.

"Ted? Can I talk to you for a minute?" I ask him, giving James a look to let him know I'm okay.

"Make it quick." Ted looks down at his BlackBerry, typing furiously. "I'm meeting some of the board members for drinks at the Four Seasons at six-thirty. The board was impressed by the implemented changes but wants to scale back on any radical redesigns. Good work, by the way."

I take a deep breath, "Ted, I think—"

"Listen, Evelyn, I didn't want it to be this way, but the company is going through changes—" Ted stops beside the glass wall that separates the reception area from the main office floor.

"Yes, isn't that what the whole redesign was about?" I interrupt him. He won't look at me. I reach out and grab the BlackBerry from his hand. "Wasn't it, Ted?"

He looks startled. He pulls me off to the side, leaning in close and lowering his voice. "Since you're interim senior management, I guess I can tell you. We're going to be laying off some people today." Ted eases his BlackBerry out of my hand. "And it looks like you'll be losing four people in your department. We're going to outsource the work to India, with you taking care of things on this end."

"What the hell?" I yelp. People turn to look at us. "There are only five people in *my* department right now. And outsource what? When did this happen?"

"Keep your voice down! Things are tight, and we've had to reallocate resources and funds." Ted shrugs his shoulders. He's put on a fresh shirt, but I can already see wet circles under the arms. "There's nothing I can do about it."

"So *my* whole department has been reallocated out of a job?" I ask, not bothering to lower my voice to spare Ted the embarrassment.

"This is business, Evelyn. This is the real world, and people lose their jobs in the real world." Ted puts his fingers in his mouth and lets out a sharp whistle. He picks up the handset on James's desk and speaks into it, his voice echoing above. "Let's get this meeting started, people!"

"No." It comes from somewhere deep inside me.

"Sorry?" Teds says, turning away from where a crowd is forming in front of us in a messy half circle.

"No!" Blood pounds through my veins. "This isn't how it's going to be, Ted."

"This isn't the time or place for this conversation, Evelyn," Ted hisses at me, trying to stare me down.

"You want to strip down this company, even though you're already acting like this is a sweatshop, dangling worthless stock options in front of them, running this place like it was your own personal website," I say in a rush. "Well, now you can take all the credit and do all the work. It's all yours, Ted."

"Let's talk about this in my office." He reaches out to grab my arm, but I jerk away.

"Save it. I quit."

"No, you don't." He blanches, still speaking into the intercom. "You can't. I'll fire you first."

"You can't!" James explodes. "She doesn't even work here! She never was the temp. I forgot to call the temp agency, and she's just been showing up and working here for no other reason than she has nothing better to do."

"Thank you, James," I say.

"James"—Ted's face goes pale—"call the police."

I close my eyes for a moment and say very clearly, my voice carrying to every corner of the office, "Ted, you truly are an idiot."

A cheer erupts from everyone watching us.

"Meeting over, Ted?" James asks, taking the handset out of his white-knuckled death grip.

I stride toward my office, the crowd parts, and a few people pat me on the back. I grin stupidly. It truly is my own Norma Rae moment. I just wish I was wearing my own clothes.

Alexander

"Buy you a beer later?" Pete sits on my couch, now his, as if he's trying it out for the first time.

"Tell you what, stop by the Wish 'n' Wash and help me move broken washers and dryers and I'll give you beer," I say, watching him.

"You bet," he says. He clears his throat, wiping at the sudden tears in his eyes. "Alexander, I'm proud of you."

"I know you are, buddy." I give him a halfhearted noogie, smoothing his hair into place when I'm done and topping my work off with a quick kiss. "And you want to know something, *amigo*? I don't think I've ever felt this way in my life. You walking me out?"

"I think I'll just stay here and enjoy my new office," he says, his voice thick, his hands covering his face.

"Hey, I'd do the same, Pete. This office changed my life, man."

I slip the coaster of the knitting hands I had framed into my satchel, take one more look out the window at her empty office, and pick up the box of my stuff. As I pass the conference room, I can hear Candace yelling at Rodney, Bryan, and Brian behind the closed door.

I awkwardly shake some hands, hug more than a few paralegals before I get to the reception area. Wallace sits behind her desk looking as placid and icy as ever.

"I'm leaving now, Wallace," I say. "It's too late to declare your love for me or beg me to stay, I'm going."

She looks up at me and smiles. She has the bouquet of paper roses I made her on her desk. "Have a nice day, Alexander."

I press the down button and, instead of waiting, walk to my left and take the stairs.

Evelyn

"You okay, James?" I ask as I try to cram one more thing into the bulging canvas bag emblazoned with the UGotIt.com logo James has given me. I pick up the cocktail-straw dog and place it into my suit pocket, not wanting it to get crushed in the jumble of things in my bag.

"I'm just so happy," James says from where he's carefully wrapping my teacups and putting in tissue paper. "I mean, not happy that you don't have a job, even though you don't need one, but happy that Ted finally got a little of what he deserves."

My phone rings, and I answer it on speakerphone. "Hello?"

"Evelyn?"

"Hi, Allan. I guess you heard." I look over at James, wondering if my eyebrows are as high as his.

"Yeah. I heard." He clears his throat. "And I guess since we don't work together anymore, it's okay if we go out now."

"Um, I don't think my shrink would recommend it," I say with a completely straight face as James hits the floor in silent paroxysms of laughter. "Too many bad memories, you know?"

"Yeah, sure," Allan says quickly. "You want to make a clean break. I can understand that. It's cool. Catch you later."

I look down at James, and we laugh until tears run down our faces.

"Are you going to walk me out?" I say, using the hem of my blouse to wipe my face.

"No," James answers stiffly.

"No?" I shift the bag into a more comfortable position on my shoulder.

"Because I'd leave right behind you, and I've got to make some copies of my résumé, call my ex-ex-ex in France, and send myself office supplies by FedEx," he explains.

"A person has to have his priorities." I nod.

"But I'll join you soon." James throws an arm out, gesturing to the world outside my ex-office window. "Out there. Someday we'll be together. Again."

I stare outside, looking for him. He's not there. And what would it matter if he was? After a few minutes I say, "Maybe the fellow who sells pretzels on the corner will have to step away for a smoke and ask me to watch his cart and I'll start yet another new phase in my life."

"Very likely to happen," James says through a sudden rush of tears. We kiss and hug hard.

A few people stop me to say good-bye, but I walk out to wait for the elevator alone. I press the button and wait.

There's no way in hell I'm taking the stairs on my last day here.

Alexander

So here's the part where I cross the street, ignoring screeching tires and car horns. Then I'll open the lobby door, head straight to the elevator, which will be waiting, and press the button for the fifth floor. When the doors slide open, I'll walk in and . . . then what? I'll smile at her and hope for the best.

Evelyn

In the lobby I take a moment to listen for signs that Ted has called the police. Not hearing sirens or seeing a waiting cruiser parked outside, I figure it's safe for me to leave. I push open the door, walk down the few steps to the sidewalk.

Alexander

I see her standing there across the street and feel my heart jump up into my throat. And, just like that, I know why my dad worked three jobs to help my mother achieve her dreams, why my mom never fails to bail him out of jail, no matter what time of night it is, and why my sister will never curse in front of her daughter and gazes at Lloyd the way she does when she thinks no one is looking. I finally know why. Now all I have to do is ask her her name and the rest we can figure out together.

Evelyn

For the first time in my life, I don't look behind me to double check I'm not presuming to be the focus of someone's attention. He is smiling at me. Not at Tannin or Mother, not because of my weighty last names. Alexander Velazquez, son of community activists, lawyer and the only man who has ever made my heart skip a beat, is smiling only for me. I've never been surer of anything in my life. The rest we'll figure out together.

More Than This

After living in Paris for a year, Evelyn Reed-Sinclair returns home to San Francisco nursing a broken heart. An heiress to a coffee and tea empire, she has no desire to participate in the high-society, party-hopping lifestyle in which her younger sister revels. And when a mix-up leads to a job at a struggling dot com company, Evelyn keeps mum about her true identity and joins the nine-to-five workforce.

Meanwhile, Alexander Velasquez, an ambitious lawyer from a working-class San Francisco neighborhood, signs on with a posh law firm. His defense of a rich, conniving widow (who has designs on more than his legal skills) brings him into conflict with his labor activist father and ultimately leads him to question his professional path.

As Evelyn and Alexander endeavor to sort out their lives, they become attracted to each other . . . from a distance. A series of near meetings and missed connections—and occasionally peeping into each other's offices with binoculars—brings them ever closer, but neither one is willing to take the next step.

Told in alternating narratives from Evelyn and Alexander's points of view, *More Than This* is a wise and witty story that asks: Can two people who have never exchanged even a single word fall in love?

For Discusson

1. *More Than This* opens with Evelyn and Alexander each ending a romantic relationship. What is your initial impression of both characters? Why is each one compelled to return home to San Francisco after their breakups?

2. What are your thoughts on the novel's structure—the alternating narratives told from Evelyn and Alexander's perspectives—as well as the fact that the two main characters are romantically linked and yet never meet?

3. Discuss the overall theme of secrecy in the novel. Evelyn kept her identity a secret in Paris, posing as a struggling art student, and she keeps quiet about who she really is while working at UGotIt.com. Why does Evelyn hide behind different personas? What did she achieve by moving to Paris, which she described as an attempt "to try to escape" (page 16) herself?

4. "It makes me wonder what [women] see in me," Alexander muses. "I'm no poet or philosopher or even that considerate" (page 132). What makes Alexander so attractive to the opposite sex? Is it merely his looks? In contrast to Alexander, who is described as looking like a Mexican JFK, Jr., Evelyn has struggled with her appearance. Discuss Evelyn's self-image. In what ways did her life change after she lost a significant amount of weight?

5. What motivates Evelyn to work at UGotIt.com? If, as she told James, she wants to "make it on my own" (page 153), why is she working for no pay?

6. Alexander and Evelyn have each built up an image of the other based on chance encounters, fleeting looks, press accounts, and a few instances of spying through office windows. How accurate are their assessments of each other? Is it possible to fall in love with someone with whom you've never exchanged a word? Could a relationship between the two of them work? Why or why not? Why do

both Evelyn and Alexander refer to their preoccupation with each other as a "healthy relationship"? Why is neither one willing to make the first move and orchestrate a meeting?

7. Evelyn and Tannin are opposites in looks and personality. How does each one view their upbringing and lifestyle? Why does Evelyn struggle with what Tannin accepts?

8. Discuss Alexander's relationship with his family and in particular with his father. "Even when it's in my best interest, the more he says I can't or shouldn't, the more I want to do whatever it is he's taken a stand against," Alexander says (page 187). Is he really as different from his father as he thinks he is? How so?

9. Alexander knows that by leaving the courtroom in the middle of Candace's hearing he'll likely be forfeiting his job at Williams, Heller, Lincoln. Why does he decide to walk out anyway?

10. How does the book's title apply to the characters in the story? What "more than this" is each one searching for, and do they find it?

11. Discuss the novel's ending. What do you imagine the future holds for Evelyn and Alexander—personally, professionally, and romantically?

A Conversation with Margo Candela

Why did you choose San Francisco as the setting for *More Than This*? Do you have connections to the City by the Bay?

I moved up to San Francisco for college and ended up staying a decade. It's a wonderful city—very diverse, great food, beautiful weather and scenery—everything you'd want in a place to live. But for me it was a love affair that had run its course and it was time to come home to Los Angeles to be closer to family and start a new phase in my life. I go up to visit friends every chance I get and I fall in love all over again and realize, even with all its flaws, San Francisco is one of the most romantic cities in the world. And since *More Than This* is my version of a love story, I knew this is where it had to take place.

What appealed to you about creating such an interesting structure for a novel—one where the two main characters become romantically entwined and yet never exchange a word?

If you ask people, many of them will have a memory about that one person they shared something with, a look or even a hello and they just knew something was there but for whatever reason let the opportunity pass. There's always that feeling of what if . . . and what ifs are the most interesting concepts to explore as a writer.

In your previous two novels the heroines were Latina. In *More Than This*, why did you decide to have Alexander as the main character with a Mexican-American heritage? Was it challenging to write from a male perspective?

It wasn't hard for me to write Alexander because, even though his equipment is different from that of my previous Latina characters, he still comes from the same cultural background. I write about people who are enmeshed with their families. Still, I have to be conscious that I am writing in a male character's voice and men are different and that's what made it fun to do. I look forward to doing a whole book in a first-person male perspective in the future.

Why did you choose to end the novel where you did? At any time did you consider ending with Alexander and Evelyn speaking to each other?

More Than This started out as a screenplay, and the ending I had written for it was much more conventional. When I adapted it for the book, I played with different endings—having them meet a year later, having them just stand across the street from each other—but I think the one I chose is a good compromise. I'll leave it to the reader to figure out who takes that first step to cross the street— if either does.

What does the cast of secondary characters—including Tannin, James, and Nayelli—add to the story?

Every story needs characters who'll say or do what the main character can't, just like in real life. It's all about finding the right balance of salty and sweet. It's what I look for in friends, and it just makes life—and books—more interesting.

How important is humor in this book and in your writing in general?

I'll confess, I don't think *More Than This* is funny-funny or, rather, as funny as my stuff usually can be. It's a love story, not necessarily a comedic one, but it does have light and absurd moments which I look forward to experiencing in my own life. I figure a person should laugh out loud at least once or twice a day. There's nothing I like to do more than fall over laughing. It's such a joy to be around people who can make you laugh. And since I spend a lot time on my own writing, it falls to me to be my own entertainment.

How does *More Than This* differ from your previous books? What similarities are there?

The alternating two-person perspective, sometimes occurring simultaneously, was as fancy as I've gotten with my writing. At first I tried to keep it at a one-two rhythm—Evelyn sees Alexander, then Alexander picks it up from there. As I went on, I let myself loosen it up a bit and didn't worry about being exactly chronological. *More Than This* is still a book about flawed people making hasty decisions and trying to make things right, and that's a common theme in all my books. People who let themselves make mistakes are much more interesting to me than someone who tries to be perfect all the time.

Evelyn is an avid knitter, and Alexander is drawn to women who knit. Is knitting one of your hobbies? What do you think Freud would say about women and knitting needles, as Alexander wonders?

I can't knit. For whatever reason, it never clicked with me, though I'd love to be able to. It's one of those skills I ascribe to characters because I would like to have it. Freud said a lot of things about just about everything, and I'm sure women and knitting needles would be vaguely disturbing but probably accurate where Alexander is concerned.

Are you, like Evelyn, a fan of Jane Austen and the Brontë sisters' novels? What other classic writers do you count among your favorites?

I admire Austen and the Brontës because they lived when women writers were not the norm and they still went for it. I also am infatuated by the whole idea of someone like Evelyn trying to lose herself in books that are about romantic love tinged with tragedy and that deal with social constraints. It was very in keeping with her character to have her be an Austen and Brontë fan and a little funny since she herself is almost living a Austen heroine–like life. My all-time favorite writer is much more contemporary, Anne Tyler. She's the bee's knees as far as I'm concerned.

More Than This is your third novel, and you're currently at work on another. As you write more and more books, how do you come up with new plot ideas?

I have a trove of ideas just waiting to brought to life. I want to write young adult novels, and I have a very speedy romantic thriller that I've been itching to do. I love movies like *Two Moon Junction* and *Fire with Fire* and macho movies like *The Peacemaker* and *Ronin,* and I have this one idea that combines the two. Maybe someday, but it'll be under a pen name since it's such a huge departure from my current work. I'd like the flexibility to write as a completely different person. And in the end, that's what I love about my job.

Enhance Your Book Club

1. In a nod to Alexander's heritage, dine at a Mexican restaurant for your book club discussion of *More Than This* or serve a meal similar to the one his family enjoys in the novel—chili con carne, home-made flour tortillas, rice and beans. Recipes for Mexican cuisine are available at www.allrecipes.com and www.recipezaar.com.

2. Brew up some tea, Evelyn's drink of choice, and serve it in style in a china teapot and cups. One hundred and fifty varieties of loose tea can be found at www.theteatable.com.

3. Have each member bring a gift-wrapped copy of a novel by Jane Austen or the Brontë sisters, Evelyn's favorite writers. Take turns picking from the wrapped copies, and everyone will leave with a surprise classic to read.